Date: 06/14/12

FIC MISSALL
Missall, John,
Hollow victory : a novel of
the Second Seminole War /

D0888106

Hollow Victory

A Novel of the Second Seminole War

By

John and Mary Lou Missall

Hollow Victory
A Novel of the Second Seminole War

Cover design by Jackson Walker Studio
Cover painting: "Here we make our stand" by Jackson Walker © 2010.

ISBN 10: 1-886104-45-X
ISBN 13: 978-1-886104-45-7

The Florida Historical Society Press
435 Brevard Avenue
Cocoa, FL 32922
www.myfloridahistory.org/fhspress

P•R•E•S•S

Authors' Notes

In writing this book, we have taken a personal passion, the history of the Seminole Wars, and have let our imaginations have some fun with it. We've always loved reading historical fiction, but we've also been wary of it, both as writers and as readers. In a genre such as science fiction or fantasy, everyone knows that reality can safely be ignored. Even the immutable laws of Nature can be changed. We all know that according to Einstein's equations, nothing can travel faster than the speed of light. That certainly hasn't stopped many a science fiction writer from zipping us across several thousand light-years of space in a matter of hours. And while no one has ever satisfactorily explained how lightning bolts can shoot from a wizard's fingertips, no one seems to mind, either.

Historical fiction is another matter. The author has to decide where the line between fact and fiction will be drawn. If the author's creation is compelling and none of the facts are easily disputed, the reader may say, "That's the way it must have been." We can never really know at what point the creator's views replace historical facts. Indeed, there is nothing more suspect than a motion picture that claims to be "based on" or "inspired by" a true story. The closer a story claims to be to the truth, the less faith we should have in it.

While we may have used the basic events and major players of the Second Seminole War as a framework, we would never contend that this is precisely what happened and that these are accurate representations of historic characters. The war provides a time, a place, and a situation. We supply characters who must deal with that situation, and in the process we hope to provide the reader with an insight into the difficult decisions people were often forced to make and the consequences they had to live with. When necessary, we invent details, move characters and events around, and do whatever else we feel is required to tell what is hopefully an entertaining, enlightening, and thought-provoking story. When we were writing our history book, *The Seminole Wars: America's Longest Indian Conflict*, it was our job to present the facts. In this instance, as novelists, it is our job to tell a good tale. Please do not confuse the two.

The reader should also be aware that all characters are fictional, even if they represent historic figures. The characters' personalities in this story are certainly not meant to be historically accurate, and no attempt was made to make them so. If some particular fictional character's personality comes off as less-than-flattering, that is absolutely no reflection on the corresponding historic character's personality. Obviously, we've never met these people, so we have no way of knowing how they truly felt. To present a balanced story, we needed inept leaders and evil people on both sides. To have done otherwise would have served to de-humanize one side or the other, something that has been done all too often in real life. In the end, history will never adequately record the contents of a person's mind or heart, and as historians we should be careful not to put our own thoughts or feelings into someone else's life, no matter how long ago they've passed from this Earth. That belongs to the realm of fiction.

One of the most annoying things about having to write a story that deals with so many ethnic groups is the matter of having to use dialects and accents. When we speak to a person, their mannerisms of speech can tell us quite a bit about their background. Unfortunately, those mannerisms often tend to be stereotypical and sometimes insulting. As an example, Native Americans do not always speak in the third person, and they know perfectly well how to use contractions. Such inaccuracies are the commonly accepted literary norms for conveying Indian speech, and if you try to eliminate this convention, the characters tend to lose their identity as Indians. The same thing happens with blacks from ante-bellum time period. As awkward as dialects and accents may be, they help the reader visualize the characters. In the end, it is not how a person speaks, but what he or she says. If the words convey intelligence, the character will be seen as intelligent.

A note about names used in this book: Generally, the closer a character is to an actual person, the closer the spelling will be. The principal generals and politicians are filling their historical positions and are therefore given their actual names. Other military names were chosen rather arbitrarily. Those familiar with the Seminole Wars will see names that are close to or suggestive of actual participants.

Indian names tend to be less accurate. In truth, many names are actually honorific titles (Micco, Tustenuggee, Hadjo, Fixico, Emathla) accompanied by a given name. The spelling of Indian names is even more hap-hazard. These were a people who did not possess a written language, which means that all written names were nothing more than phonetic assumptions by whites. The classic example is Osceola, which is a corruption of his Indian name, Asi-Yahola. Then again, depending on the accent of whoever was speaking the name, it could just as easily have been Asi-Yoholo. As will be readily apparent to any Seminole who reads this book, we are obviously not expert in either of the Seminole tongues.

For those of you who do not keep a copy of *The Complete Works of Shakespeare* close at hand, we offer the following guide to what MacDuff was thinking:

"What! all my pretty chickens and their dam / At one fell swoop?" *MacBeth*, IV:iii.

"Then should the war-like Harry, like himself, / Assume the port of Mars." *Henry V*, I:i.

"Cowards die many times before their deaths, / The valiant never taste of death but once." *Julius Caesar*, II:ii.

"Tell the Constable we are but warriors for the working-day." *Henry V*, IV:iii.

"We few, we happy few, we band of brothers." *Henry V*, IV:iii.

"Our doubts are traitors, / And make us lose the good we oft might win / By fearing to attempt." *Measure for Measure*, I:v.

"O, she doth teach the torches to burn bright! / It seems she hangs upon the cheek of night / Like a rich jewel in an Ethiop's ear; / Beauty too rich for use, for earth too dear!" *Romeo and Juliet*, I:v.

"For, as thou urgest justice, be assur'd Thou shalt have justice, more than thou desir'st." *The Merchant of Venice*, IV:i.

"Though this be madness, yet there is method in 't." *Hamlet*, II:ii

"Oft expectation fails, and most oft there where most it promises; and oft it hits where hope is coldest, and despair most fits." *All's Well That Ends Well*, II:i

Finally, we would like to thank our families for their continued support and encouragement, along with our many friends in the Seminole Wars community. Special thanks go to Jackson Walker for the wonderful cover art, Willie Johns for help with Seminole customs and language, and to the Florida Historical Society for taking an interest in our work.

June 15, 1835
St. Augustine
E. Florida Territory

To:
Mrs. David Kilgour
Cincinnati, Ohio

My Dear Sister:

Please forgive the brevity, for I write in haste. Having arrived but this afternoon, I find that I must depart at first light in the morning.

How I came to be at this place is a tale unto itself. Upon graduation from the Military Academy, I received orders to report for immediate duty in the Florida Territory. The voyage from New York to Charleston was pleasant enough, the Lord providing moderate breezes and agreeable weather for better than a week. The remainder of the voyage proved much more tedious. After waiting three days in Charleston, I caught what appeared to be a swift schooner bound for Savannah. Unfortunately, when we were no more than two hours clear of Ft. Moultrie the winds died completely, leaving us adrift and flowing northward with a steady current measuring some few knots. Having nothing better to occupy their time, the crew, captain included, broke open the barrel of grog and spent a good many hours in a drunken state. In this condition we stayed for four days, passing well north of Charleston. When at last the breezes resumed, they did so with uncommon fury from the south, accompanied by torrents of rain. Yet instead of putting on shortened sail and proceeding in a prudent manner, the captain set every sheet he had and turned the bow close to the wind, moving us forward at a frightful pace. Every other wave seemed to crash over the bow and sweep clear the deck. Anything not securely fastened became airborne. Fearful for the safety of the other passengers, I expressed my concerns to the captain, who laughed mightily and said "This, lad, is *sailing!"*

After thanking the Almighty for a safe arrival in Savannah, I looked about for a ship to convey me further south. Wishing to experience no more "sailing," I next booked passage on a steam packet bound for St. Augustine. Alas, dear Emily, what the lack of wind is to the sailing vessel, the abundance of wind is to the steam-powered vessel. The same south wind that had sped us into Savannah now served to nearly halt our progress entirely. Churn as the paddles might, we could make little or no headway against wind, rain, and current. So slow was our progress that the vessel's supply of firewood ran out, and the crew was forced to throw many of the ship's tables and chairs into the boiler-fire. To say the least, we were much relieved when the ship reached the safety of the St. Johns River, where we could drop anchor in calm waters and arrange for the purchase of fuel. I can say with some certainty that while steam-powered vessels will forever be the queens of our many rivers, they will never replace the sailing vessel in the open ocean.

It must be pointed out that although passage is booked to St. Augustine, the vessel does not in reality take you there. Although the old city guards the finest harbor in East Florida, the bar is considered too treacherous for all but the most shallow draft ships to pass with ease. Due to this fact, vessels bound for St. Augustine navigate up the St. Johns and discharge their cargo and passengers at Picolata, a small depot some fifteen miles west of the city. From there the passenger is left to make his own arrangements for transport to St. Augustine, and let it be known that the local teamsters are well paid for their services!

As to my situation here, I am afraid there is little I can say with certitude. There is some talk of war with the Seminole Indians, and our company is under orders to proceed to Ft. King, deep in the interior, tomorrow morning. Fear not for my safety, dear sister. By all reports, the Seminoles are a ragged batch of savages who will no doubt cower before our grand little army.

My commanding officer, Col. William A. Wooster, 4th Infantry, served with great distinction in the late war with Britain and was, I am pleased to relate, a close acquaintance of our father's at Ft. Eire. I have never been satisfied with the official reports of father's death, and perhaps we shall learn something that is new to our ears. The Col. is an odd sort, a hard man to fathom. Throughout the day's conversation he was not unpleasant to me, but rather abrupt. Indeed, he seems rather short with everyone, barking orders to the household much the same as he would to his men whilst in battle. I hope in time he warms to me, as I am to be his aide and will be spending near all my time in his presence for some months to come.

\As the hour is now late and the candle near burnt, I shall close. The day's events have exhausted my senses more than enough to ensure a sound night's sleep. I shall write to you again after I have become familiar with my fellows and we reach the safety of Ft. King. Give my love to David and the children and to all the unmarried ladies of Cincinnati.

Your most affectionate brother,
Jacob

The afternoon air was thick and hot, with the only possible respite coming from a line of dark clouds gathering offshore. Lieutenant Jacob Sparkes tugged at the collar of his dark blue woolen uniform, wiped the sweat from his brow, and looked about with curious eyes. St. Augustine was a small town, not much more than a mile or two in length and only a few streets in width, dominated by the massive stone fortress of Fort Marion. Most of the buildings looked old, and many had balconies that overhung the street in the fashion of their Spanish builders. The town looked busy, but certainly not prosperous.

Sparkes walked toward Fort Marion along a wide, slightly elevated pathway that led to a wooden drawbridge. Following several yards behind, a young black man, clothed in dirty brown trousers and a shirt that had long since ceased to be white, pushed a battered cart carrying the officer's small wooden trunk and a large canvas bag. Standing near the drawbridge was a sentry dressed in sky blue woolen trousers and a matching waistcoat, his head covered by a tall leather forage cap. By the soldier's side was a well-worn flintlock musket, and twin white leather belts crossed his chest. Suspended from the belt on his left side was a bayonet, while on the right there hung a leather box that contained the powder and shot for his musket. The soldier stiffened and offered a salute as the officer approached. Sparkes made a short inquiry, to which the sentry gave a shorter answer, and then pointed south.

With the porter following dutifully, the young officer turned away from the fort and proceeded toward the promenade that had been constructed behind the city's seawall. There was so much that was new to Sparkes. This was his first trip to the South, and the first time he had been in a frontier town with such a foreign flavor. Less than fifteen years had passed since Florida had been ceded to the United States, and the town still maintained its Spanish essence. He watched as two fishermen unloaded their day's catch, tossing a wide variety of silvery specimens into a large cart perched atop the seawall. *Odd*, he thought, as he caught a few of their words, *that doesn't sound like Spanish. Greek, maybe?* As he continued on he noticed that a number of the town's citizens were out for a mid-day stroll. A distinguished-looking older gentleman dressed in Spanish attire and accompanied by a young dark-haired woman with Mediterranean features approached from the opposite direction. The gentleman nodded and touched his hat in recognition of the officer, who returned the favor. The woman, turning slightly as they passed, smiled invitingly.

As his mind lingered on the image of the woman's smile, Sparkes's gaze fell upon the face of an African standing on a platform in front of a small storefront. The black man's eyes, devoid of emotion, locked onto Sparkes's, who then caught the words of the well-dressed man standing beside the African. "Gentlemen, please! Is this not the finest field hand I have presented to you in many weeks? Surely worth more than the four hundred dollars I've been offered. A good breeder, too. I have it on indisputable authority that he has sired seven young pickaninnies this year alone. Such a purchase is not an expense, it is an investment! Now please! What am I bid?" Sparkes continued on, his mind somewhat troubled by the scene. Not far past the slave auction was a tavern, and in front stood a sailor passing the time with a young woman. Although their conversation was whispered, the subject was apparent. The woman smiled as the sailor placed a gold coin in her hand, then turned and led the man indoors. Sparkes shook his head ever so slightly. *Catholics, slavers, and whores,* he thought. *A Godless place at best.*

As he walked, Sparkes began to notice the sounds and smells of animals. A small pig raced out of an unfenced courtyard, followed by a child in fast pursuit. A mongrel dog sniffed the dirt in front of a bakery, arched its back, and then defecated by the door. Peering over a short wall, Sparkes noticed someone tying a decapitated chicken to a tree limb so the blood might drain from its unstopped neck. Near the end of the street a heated transaction was taking place between a tall Indian and the rotund proprietor of a general store. The Indian rested his foot on a small stack of deerskins as he examined the firing mechanism of a rifle. Even from a distance, Sparkes could see that it was a fine weapon, far superior to the old muskets the army generally used.

Sparkes soon reached the south end of the street and stood before St. Francis Barracks, headquarters for the army in St. Augustine. Motioning for the porter to remain standing with the pushcart, Sparkes approached a passing soldier, exchanged a few words, and was directed to a house behind the barracks. Returning to the porter, Sparkes said a few words, pointed toward the barracks, then handed the man a small coin.

~~~

He was nervous now. Up until this moment, he hadn't really felt like a soldier. Even during the graduation ceremony at West Point, when the commandant had shaken his hand and addressed him as *"Lieutenant* Sparkes," he hadn't felt as if he were truly part of the army. Now, the idea of meeting his first commanding officer and receiving his first assignment seemed to change all that. He would now be a part of it all. He looked skyward and imagined his grandfather looking down on him, a proud smile on the old man's face. Sparkes hoped his father was also looking down, but could not imagine the man's face. He had never seen it.

Removing his leather hat, Sparkes smoothed his sand-colored hair then gripped the cord hanging from a bell by the door. His wrist hesitated, however, as he heard the faint sounds of a heated exchange taking place from within. For a moment he thought of waiting for the conversation to end. Then he heard the echo of his grandfather's voice. *The battle doesn't start until someone pulls the trigger.* Taking a deep breath, he pulled on the cord.

Within a few moments a small black man with sparse gray hair slowly opened the dark wooden door. Casting his eyes downward in a respectful manner, the servant asked, "May I say who be calling, Massa Lieutenant?"

"Lieutenant Sparkes to see Colonel Wooster." The servant stepped back, opening the door farther as he moved, then motioned the young officer inside to a nearby chair.

"I'll inform the colonel of your arrival, Massa Lieutenant." He disappeared quickly around the corner, leaving Sparkes alone.

Gazing around, Sparkes could see that the house was a stout structure with a low ceiling and massive beams to support the upper story. The design of the home seemed rather like that of a fortress. The outer walls were of stone, covered with whitewashed plaster, with few openings to the outside. The living area was contained in the building's periphery, which surrounded a large courtyard. The interior doors were all thrown open, drawing in a refreshing breeze from the courtyard. Sparkes was surprised by how cool the home was.

The lieutenant could overhear the conversation taking place around the corner, in the next room. One of the voices was that of a frustrated Spaniard reacting to some very unwelcome news: "This cannot be, *Señor Colónel*! If you take your soldiers to Fort King, who will be left to defend the city?"

The second voice responded in a strong and measured northeastern accent. "That is what your militia is for, *Don José*."

"Then surely we are doomed!" Don José shouted. "There are not ten serviceable weapons among all my soldiers! Perhaps I should have the men gather stones so that we have something to throw at the savages!"

"And what of the one hundred muskets you received last year?"

Don José almost exploded. "Those were not weapons, they were an insult! Not a one was less than thirty years old, they were rusty and broken, and most every one had parts that were missing. *Dios mio!* They are more dangerous to my men than to any enemy." There was a moment of silence before the Spaniard erupted again. "And how am I supposed to train my militiamen? When has your Congress given me money to pay them? Do you think they will muster for training if I do not pay them? By the Blessed Virgin, your American government is no better than the Spanish! They are all *idiots*!"

Sparkes could only imagine what would happen next. In his mind he saw swords being drawn. He held his breath. Could he, should he, intervene? At long last there was an audible sigh followed by a sympathetic voice. "As understanding of your situation as I may be, *Don José*, I simply do not have the authority to requisition additional muskets. You will have to discuss these matters with General Clinch when he returns. Conditions permitting, that should be within a fortnight. Be assured that when I see him at Fort King I will argue forcefully on your behalf. I can do no more, my friend."

The Spaniard's voice softened. The battle was lost. "As always, *Señor Colónel*, you have been most honest with me. I can ask no more of you. I shall convey my appreciation to *Generalè* Clinch when next I meet him."

Sparkes rose from the chair as he heard heavy footsteps on the wooden floor. From around the corner came a tall man, well formed, his dark hair peppered lightly with gray, dressed in blue military trousers and a white linen shirt. Sparkes also noticed that he walked with a slight limp. Behind him came the Spaniard, a slim, dignified man with sharp features, dressed in a well-tailored suit. As the colonel came to a halt in front of him the young officer saluted and handed forth his orders. "Second Lieutenant Jacob Sparkes reporting as ordered, sir!"

Returning the salute, Colonel Wooster took the folded paper, broke the seal, and looked it over. "About damn time they sent someone," he muttered, looking up at Sparkes. "Well-timed arrival, Lieutenant. We leave for Fort King in the morning." The colonel then introduced his companion. "Lieutenant, this is General Hernandez of the local militia."

Hernandez bowed slightly and offered his hand. "A pleasure, *Señor* Lieutenant." He then smiled at the colonel. "Give my best to *Generalè* Clinch and wish him a safe journey. May our Blessed Lady be with you at all times." He bowed and turned toward the door. "*Buenos dias, mi amigos.*"

Wooster shook his head as the door closed. When Hernandez was out of earshot, the colonel turned to Sparkes. "It is a law of nature, Lieutenant: For every blessing there is a burden. You could not ask for a better militia officer, nor for anyone more damn worrisome. I honestly believe the man cannot last the week without coming over to argue or complain about *something* that I can do absolutely *nothing* about." The colonel's frustration was beginning to show. "Is it *my* fault the militia doesn't have enough weapons? Did *I* write the orders sending us to Fort King? Did *I* get the damn Indians all stirred up?" He huffed slightly then continued. "I am a colonel, damn it, not God. For *that* I would need to be a general, and the army has not yet chosen to grant me that exalted status." He then turned and shouted, "Nettie! Lemonade for the lieutenant! He might die of thirst 'fore long!" Then, as an afterthought, "Coffee!"

The echo of his voice had barely died when a thin, aged black woman entered the room carrying a tray with a glass and a cup on it. Nettie looked at the younger man then imparted what she considered to be some very useful information. "The colonel sho' do like his coffee."

The two men took the refreshments as Colonel Wooster led the way into the parlor. "Your baggage, Lieutenant?"

"I had them taken to the barracks, sir."

"Nero!" The servant who had answered the door hurried into the room. "Fetch the lieutenant's baggage from the barracks. He'll be lodging with us tonight."

"Yes sir, Massa Colonel."

The colonel's voice boomed once more. "Maria!" Sparkes turned at the sound of delicate footsteps almost skipping down the stairway. From the way the colonel had called out, Sparkes expected another servant to appear. Instead, his eyes fell upon a young white girl, barely in her teens, well dressed, her dark hair made up into tight curls that hung to her shoulders. Stopping before the two officers, she curtsied politely then held out her hand to the younger man. The colonel's face softened. "Lieutenant: my daughter Maria." Sparkes bowed his head then kissed the girl's hand lightly. "Maria, this is Mr. Sparkes, our new Second Lieutenant. He'll be staying the night with us."

"A pleasure to meet you, Lieutenant. Welcome to the Florida Territory." She had the soft face of a child and possessed few of her father's features, with the exception of the confident look in her eyes.

The colonel then asked, "Do you write with a clear hand, Lieutenant?"

"Fair, sir."

"Good. You're my new aide. I've had to employ the hospital steward to keep the regiment's papers in order. Only enlisted man around who could write worth a damn." He noticed the quizzical look on the young man's face. Wooster was commander of the Fourth

Infantry Regiment and should have had a staff officer to maintain the regiment's paperwork. "Your arrival was much looked-for, Lieutenant. The regiment is extremely short of officers. By law, each company should have a captain, a first, and a second lieutenant. For the past seven months Company 'B' has existed with naught but a single first lieutenant." As the colonel looked at Sparkes's face, a bittersweet memory came to mind. "Are you perchance some relation to the Sparkes of Rhode Island?"

The lieutenant nodded and smiled proudly. "I believe you may have known my father, sir: Lieutenant Erastus Sparkes of the Thirty-ninth Infantry."

The colonel's recollection was no longer bittersweet. It was painful. Wooster shook his head slowly. Something wasn't right. "Sparkes had no son."

The young officer spoke hesitantly, surprised that Wooster had known his father that well. "None that he knew of, sir. I was conceived just prior to his departure for the Niagara frontier."

Wooster's next statement was a fact, not a question, and seemed almost a lament. "You never knew your father."

"No, sir."

Wooster regained his composure and stood tall. "Then I will tell you this about your father, Lieutenant: He was a good man, a dear friend, and a true hero." He then turned to Maria. "Please entertain the lieutenant while I finish packing my bags. I shan't be long."

"My pleasure, Father." She turned to Sparkes. "Would the lieutenant care for a walk in our garden? The air is much fresher in the courtyard."

Leaving the parlor, they entered a well-tended garden, a mixture of herbs and flowers of different sorts. Sparkes was impressed. Someone had spent considerable time tending to the plantings. The colonel certainly didn't look like the type who would fuss over flowers and small bushes. "This is really quite beautiful."

Maria smiled broadly. "Do you like it? I do spend quite a bit of time out here."

"Your efforts look as if they have been well rewarded, Miss Maria." Sparkes motioned toward a small tree at the center of the courtyard. "A mulberry, I believe."

"The white variety, for silkworm culture. Some believe the production of silk will be the next great industry of Florida. I amuse myself with the little worms. Father said I may keep the tree until it begins to bear fruit. After that it will be most untidy, he says." Maria looked at the man closely. He was too young, too clean, and too proper to have been in the army any length of time. He had no doubt just finished four years at the military academy, where they had taught him little of life in the real army. She had seen dozens of such men; she would see hundreds more.

Yet she instinctively liked the young man. He was very good looking, with light hair and a face that would always look youthful. He was of medium build and wore his uniform very smartly. The smile had been quick to show, and his manner had been sincere. For some reason he just didn't look the sort who would be in the army. "What draws you to the military life, Lieutenant?"

"It has always been a dream of mine. My grandfather fought the entire Revolution, from Bunker Hill to Yorktown, and was an aide to General Washington when the army disbanded at the close of the war. Although he took up the trade of bookbinder and quietly raised a large family, he always spoke warmly of his days in the military. He was especially proud of my father."

Her voice softened slightly. "I am sorry to hear that you never knew your father. Was he slain in the war with Britain?"

"At Fort Erie. From the reports I've read, he died when the wall was breached. Beyond that, I know very little of the circumstances of his passing. Perhaps your father will be able to enlighten me to some degree. I understand he was also there."

She looked away. "It was where he received the wound that nearly cost him his leg. An explosion drove a large piece of wood into his thigh. He was in the hospital for months."

Sparkes could see it was a painful subject for her to think about and decided to change it. "Has your father been stationed long in Florida?"

"For the past four years, since my mother died." Maria plucked a bright yellow flower and twirled the stem between her fingers. "He had hoped to apply for a transfer later this year, but with the threat of war, that may be delayed."

Sparkes was truly surprised. He had assumed General Hernandez had been concerned about some minor troublemakers, not a full-scale war. "A war, Miss Maria? With whom?"

She laughed. "You *are* new to Florida!" She then lowered her voice, as if passing along a well-guarded secret. "All the talk in St. Augustine is about the possibility of an Indian war. The Seminoles have signed a treaty that obligates them to emigrate to the new Indian Territory, but few seem willing to go. Father says that unless the government sends more troops, the Indians will resist. He is afraid that if the army is called upon to use force, the Seminoles will take up arms and fight."

Sparkes relaxed. His training at the Academy had instilled an unshakable sense of pride in the capabilities of the army. "Would be a foolish thing to do! Do these Seminoles not remember the drubbing General Jackson gave them in '18? Do they think they can stand up to him again, now that he is president? I should think we have little to fear from such a ragged band of savages."

Maria knew better. Every experienced officer in Florida believed that if war broke out it would be a difficult and bloody contest. The lieutenant was a nice enough man, but he knew nothing of the realities of war. "Perhaps, Lieutenant, but even in the shortest war there are dangers. It takes but one bullet to bring a man down." She looked straight into Sparkes's eyes. "You do not yet know my father. Should there be a battle, no matter how trivial, he will be at the forefront, leading his men onward. You have seen how Father walks. What would have happened had the wound been in his chest?"

It was a question Sparkes chose not to answer.

~~~

Colonel Wooster looked out of the second story window, down at his daughter and the young lieutenant. *So 'Rastus had a son.* A memory came to mind, a vision filled with the color red. There were Red Coat soldiers charging through a battered wall, a bayonet dripping with blood, and the bright red flame of the cannon fire. Wooster lowered his head, turned away, and began to fold a shirt. He owed that young man something. He just didn't know what it was or how to pay the debt.

~~~

The President of the United States was feeling old. He had fought the English and the Spanish, more Indian tribes than he could name, and had been wounded in more than one duel, but none of his enemies had succeeding in killing Andrew Jackson. Only one adversary remained: time. At the age of 68, the old general knew he could not go on forever. In a way, he was surprised he had lasted as long as he had. He could not remember ever doing anything to protect his health or preserve his life. He winced slightly from the pain in his shoulder, part of the stiffness that would never go away. He had been president for over six years, and the tediousness of the office was beginning to wear on him. Every day brought a flood of petitioners of one sort or another. Abolitionists wanted to free the slaves, while plantation owners wanted to lynch the abolitionists. Northern manufacturers wanted to raise tariffs, while southern consumers wanted to lower them. Unemployed ne'er-do-wells begged for government jobs while those who had the jobs complained of low pay or uncomfortable postings. No one in Congress, either the opposition Whigs or his own Democrats, had any idea what it took to run the country, but all of them were anxious to tell him how to do it.

It was not any easier dealing with foreign nations. Spain was complaining about American aid to rebels in Latin America, while the rebels were complaining about a lack of support from their neighbors to the north. England would not agree to an exact position of the border between Canada and Maine, while France was threatening war if American monetary claims weren't dropped. Let them come! He had smashed the best England could send against him at New Orleans, and he would make quick work of the effeminate French. At times he wondered if he would survive the next two years and live to retire to his beloved estate outside Nashville.

It was a hot day in Washington City with an insufficient breeze. Jackson sat underneath a tree in front of the White House, watching carriages pass down Pennsylvania Avenue, occasionally waving at the passers-by. Closing his eyes, he listened to the chirping of the birds perched in the branches above. He heard footsteps approaching on the gravel behind him, but kept his eyes closed. Perhaps whoever it was would simply go away. The footsteps stopped next to his chair. For some moments there was silence. Finally there was a slight cough. It was Lewis Cass. Jackson opened his eyes and turned to his Secretary of War. "At least you're not the Vice President."

Cass smiled. "I'm sure Mr. Van Buren will be along shortly, General."

"At times I feel as if his whole purpose in life is to bore me to death so that he might attain this dreadful office without having to bother with an election. Are you going to run against him, Cass?"

"I have not made the decision as yet, sir."

"Don't wait too long, or you'll be an old man like me. So what brings you to the White House this fine day?"

Cass hesitated slightly. He knew the subject was a sore point with the president. "Florida, sir. Within the past week I have received letters from Governor Eaton, General Clinch, and Agent Thompson, all requesting that more troops be sent to the territory."

"Four hundred aren't enough? What do they want? The whole damned army? What's the problem this time?"

"The Seminoles still contend that the Treaty of Payne's Landing is not binding upon them. They claim the chiefs who inspected the land in the Indian Territory were coerced and lied to while out there. They claim they still have ten years remaining on the old treaty and are not willing to emigrate."

Jackson flared. "And I, Mr. Cass, am unwilling to discuss the matter any longer. They signed the damn treaty, and they damn well best remove themselves. If they won't do it peaceably, they'll do it at the point of a god-damn bayonet! What good will more troops do? After the whipping we gave them in the last war, I doubt if they can field five-hundred warriors. Tell Clinch I could take fifty women and round up all the warriors in Florida within a month."

Cass squirmed a bit. "Mr. President, even Governor Eaton questions the validity of the treaty."

"Well I don't, damn it, and I'm the only one whose opinion matters! What did Clinch and Thompson have to say?"

"Both feel that if it comes to war, the Indians will scatter and we'll never be able to round them up."

Jackson huffed. "Nonsense. Just capture the women and children. The men will soon follow." The president gave his Secretary of War a serious look. "Mr. Cass, I twisted more than a few arms in order to get the Indian Removal Act pushed through Congress. I have no intention of letting a few ragged Seminoles ruin the whole damn project. They'll be better off in the Indian Territory, whether they know it or not, whether they like it or not. The lands east of the Mississippi are too valuable to let the savages remain. If you make an exception for one tribe, all the rest will expect the same."

Cass pushed his luck. "Then why not give Clinch more men, sir? If we can overawe the savages, they may go peaceably. I'll be the first to say we should show no mercy to the Seminoles, but if war breaks out, many of our own citizens will be in danger."

Jackson shook his head, but did not dismiss the secretary's proposal. Of all the Indians in the nation, he liked the Seminoles the least. In both the Revolution and the War of 1812 they had allied themselves with the British and the Spanish. In addition, they had the temerity to welcome runaway slaves into their villages. That alone made them an enemy to the South. There was a defiant attitude among the Seminoles that conflicted directly with Jackson's own arrogance. After a number of cross-border incidents in 1817, President Monroe had ordered Jackson to invade Florida, destroy their villages in north Florida, and drive them far enough south to eliminate any threat they might pose. Jackson had done as ordered, and had taken control of Spanish West Florida in the process. He thought he had taken care of the Seminole problem. Evidently not. He looked at Cass. "How many men?"

"Well, sir, we don't have that many to spare, but I feel we could move some around at the end of summer. As things begin to cool down in the north, we'll be able to shift a few companies south. We could easily spare another two-hundred men by October or November."

Jackson nodded reluctantly. "Make it a hundred, no more. If it gets that bad, Eaton can call out the militia."

2

15 June 1835
St. Augustine

To:
Genl. Duncan L. Clinch
Commanding, Ft. King

Genl.

By express rider, I send word that in compliance with your order of the 28th ultimo, I proceed, with staff, to Ft. King at dawn tomorrow. As requested, I am accompanied by Co. B, 4th Infty., which will relieve Co. F, 2nd Arty. At present, Co. B is thirty-one strong, with the balance, 8 men, too sick to travel. Should conditions permit, they will rejoin their company when their health is restored. A new 2nd Lt. has arrived this day.

Due to the recent heavy rains, the roads may prove difficult for our wagons to pass, thus delaying our arrival by some few days. We will, where practical, improve the road in order to ease the progress of your return journey to St. Augustine.

Because of the danger and the difficulties of our present situation, I have chosen to leave my daughter and servants in St. Augustine. Knowing the fondness you have for Maria and the love she has for you, I feel secure in knowing that should any emergency arise, you will look to her well-being as you would to one of your own.

Your Most Obedient Srvt.
Wm. A. Wooster
Col. Comdg., 4th Infty.

The sun had yet to rise above Anastasia Island, which lay across the harbor east of St. Augustine. A column of soldiers rested in front of the colonel's residence, some of them chatting quietly, others yawning. The stillness gave way slowly to the sound of horses and wagons approaching along the hard-packed dirt road. As the wagons drew to a halt in front of the colonel's residence, the soldiers began to load baggage on board. Moments later the door of the house opened, and Colonel Wooster, Lieutenant Sparkes, and Maria stepped out. Behind them came Nettie and Nero.

Wooster drained the final drops of coffee from his cup and handed it to Nettie. He then looked down at Maria. It always pained him to leave her beyond the grasp of his protection. This time he was even more apprehensive. The situation with the Seminoles was too unpredictable. It was the great irony of his life: He hated the army for the hundreds of small injustices he had been forced to endure throughout his career, yet he loved the military life. The same organization that was taking him away from Maria had been his greatest comfort when his wife had been taken from him. Other officers had stepped in for him when duty called, while their wives had taken care of Maria whenever he could not. He felt confident that while he was away on duty his daughter would not be alone.

Bending over, Wooster wrapped his arms around Maria and lifted her from the ground. "You be a proper young lady until I send word that it is safe for you to come to Fort King. In the meantime, you listen to Nettie and Nero. If there are any problems, you know to see Major Belmont or Mrs. Belmont." He then turned to Nettie as he lowered his daughter to the ground. "You watch over her, now." No longer was he shouting orders. The look of trust and affection was genuine.

"Like she were my own chile', Massa Colonel."

Wooster then turned to Nero. "And you watch over them both, Nero."

A proud smile came to the old man's gentle face. "Ain't no man fool enough to mess with the women o' this house whiles Nero watches over 'em." They were brave words from a frail old man, yet Wooster knew if Nero had to, he would lay down his life not only for Nettie, but also for Maria.

Rising on her tiptoes, Maria kissed her father on the cheek. She then turned to Sparkes. "A pleasure to have met you, Lieutenant. Do have a safe trip."

The lieutenant bowed his head and tipped his hat slightly. "My pleasure also, Miss Maria. May the Lord watch over you in your father's absence."

~~~

A hundred miles away, deep in the interior of the peninsula, a parley was taking place in a clearing outside the simple wooden palisades of Fort King. Kachi-Hadjo, a prominent young Seminole leader, yawned as he listened to the tall white man lecture the assembled Indians from behind a crude table. To the young chief's ears Indian Agent Wiley Thompson's speech was as predictable as the squawk of a blue jay and much less pleasant to hear.

Behind Thompson stood General Duncan Clinch and a squad of soldiers. Facing those white officials were the two most powerful men in the Seminole Nation. The shorter of the two was Micco Nopy, headman of all the Seminoles and leader of the Alachua band. Next to him was Micco Phillip, head of the Mikasuki band. Behind the two Indian leaders stood a handful of lesser chiefs and a large group of warriors. Among those warriors were a number of black men, dressed in the manner of the Seminoles, with colorful long-shirts and leather leggings. Some of the warriors wore a simple cloth turban, and most had beaded sashes and shot bags. Neither side looked happy.

Thompson, wearing tight brown trousers, an old waistcoat, and a wide-brimmed hat, picked up a piece of paper and waved it in front of the two chiefs. "Three winters have passed since you placed your marks upon this treaty, a treaty that says you will go to your new homes in the west." He stopped, allowing Micco Nopy's trusted slave Abraham time to interpret. "For three years you have failed to prepare your people for the journey they must take. The time has now come.

Like the setting sun, it must happen. You cannot stop it. By the end of the year, six moons from now, you must be aboard the ships and headed for your new homes. If you do not do this, then General Jackson, the Great Father in Washington, will send his soldiers against you." Kachi-Hadjo was mildly surprised: Thompson sounded as if he truly meant it this time. The agent must have gotten a scolding from the Great Father in Washington.

Kachi-Hadjo knew precisely how the two Seminole leaders would react. Micco Nopy was his uncle and had helped raise him. Micco Phillip was his father, who had been married to Micco Nopy's sister. All his life, Kachi-Hadjo had studied how the two men led their people. It wasn't just curiosity; it was an apprenticeship. There was always the chance that he might someday have to take the place of one or perhaps both of them.

Micco Nopy, with perspiration running down his round face, looked worried. No matter what stance he took, it was bound to cost him. Once again, the only thing he could think to do was stall. "We do not like this new land. There are bad Indians all around. They will attack our villages and take our black brothers. We are happy here."

Thompson shook his head. "You should have thought of that before you placed your mark upon this paper."

Micco Nopy squirmed, as he always did when someone mentioned that he had signed the hated treaty. "That is not my mark! I did not touch the pen!"

Exasperated, Thompson turned to the other chief. "Will Micco Phillip act in a manner that befits a great chief? Will he keep his word and take his people to their new homes, or will he face the wrath of the long knives?"

Phillip stood tall and erect, his stature unaffected by his many years. He turned to Abraham and spoke in a confidential manner. "Did I hear the snake-man ask if the Seminole will keep his word? You know my answer to that question. Tell him."

Abraham, a small black man who was much less subservient than he acted, turned hesitantly toward the agent. "Micco Phillip says that the Seminoles gonna honor their word just as soon as the white man honors his." Kachi-Hadjo smiled. The older Phillip got, the less impressed he was by threats.

Thompson clenched his teeth. If there was one thing he could not tolerate, it was an insolent Indian. With a sudden jerk of his arm, he pounded his fist into the table. Micco Nopy jumped. Phillip did not so much as blink. Thompson was turning red. "I will argue no longer! What is your answer? Will you go peaceably or must General Clinch call out his troops?"

As Micco Nopy listened to Abraham's interpretation he looked nervously about, hoping someone would supply him with an answer. Phillip let the tension build for a moment before he responded. Kachi-Hadjo knew his father was enjoying himself. Too old to take to the warpath, Phillip was now a warrior of words. "These are not decisions that can be made in haste. We must meet in council. Tell snake-man he will have our answer in three days." Having said his piece, Phillip turned to leave. The discussion was over. As he had often said, there was more than one way to scalp a white man.

~~~

A small procession marched down St. George Street, through the St. Augustine city gates, past Fort Marion, and then onto the Picolata road. Colonel Wooster led the way with Sparkes riding next to him. Behind them rode Dr. Weightman, a jolly, portly man who served as the regimental surgeon, and Lieutenant Smith, the commander of Company "B." Two wagons followed, and behind them walked a solitary drummer who, when the troops were clear of the town, took off the drum, tossed it in one of the wagons, and picked up a musket. Twenty-eight soldiers in two columns came next, muskets shouldered and packs on their backs.

Once clear of the city, Wooster nodded to Lieutenant Smith, who rode out ahead of the column, taking up a position about twenty yards in advance of the main body. Four soldiers broke ranks, ran up to his position, and fell in behind him. Two others ran ahead and began searching the woods on either side of the column. Wooster turned to Sparkes, giving the young man his first lesson in practical soldiering.

"Always employ an advance guard, even in times of peace, and especially when in Indian territory. If hostilities are possible, also send out flankers. There is nothing an Indian likes better than an ambush, and nothing prevents one better than flankers and an advance guard." The colonel then turned his gaze forward. The lesson was over. There would be no discussion.

They rode on in silence for the remainder of the morning, stopping just long enough to chew through a piece of dried beef and a hard biscuit soaked in water. While resting, Dr. Weightman whispered in Sparkes's ear, "You can tell when the colonel is in a rush: He won't take the time to brew the coffee. He wants the men on board the steamer by nightfall so we can head up river in the morning."

As they rode on, Wooster could sense his new aide beginning to fidget. The colonel wasn't sure what to make of the young man. He was proper in his etiquette, but that was to be expected from someone straight out of the Academy. Sparkes appeared to be very religious, which wasn't a problem in itself, as long as he was willing to accept the decidedly blasphemous nature of most military men. He seemed to be of reasonably strong build, though no one would call the young man "muscular." At least he had shown no negative qualities. Wooster could sense that Sparkes had questions, especially about his father, but the colonel wanted to see how long the young man could go without asking them. Self-discipline was important in an officer.

It was well past noon before Sparkes worked up the courage to attempt some small talk. "Your daughter, sir, is an interesting young lady."

It was time for the colonel to make something perfectly clear. "My daughter is not a subject for discussion, Lieutenant."

The young man was momentarily speechless. "My . . . my apologies, sir. I was just. . ."

". . . just making conversation. I am well aware of that, Lieutenant, but if you feel the need to clutter up the silence of this otherwise dreary day, please confine the conversations to matters of military importance." Behind them, Dr. Weightman smiled. Wooster had always been protective of his daughter, and now that Maria was approaching womanhood, the colonel was even more watchful over her.

Silence once again fell over the officers. Behind them, the soldiers joked among themselves and occasionally broke into song. Sparkes thought they ought to be more disciplined, but the colonel didn't seem to mind, so he said nothing. Storm clouds began to form in the sky overhead, forcing Sparkes to cast a wary eye toward the heavens. Sensing the young man's concern about the weather, Dr. Weightman offered his advice. "Get used to them, my friend. It happens most every afternoon, from now 'til October. Before too long the roads will be impassable and the whole damn Territory will be under water."

From the wagon behind them, the voice of an Englishman gently interrupted. It was Bemrose, the young hospital steward. "Begging your pardon, Doctor, sir . . ." He then pointed to the bayonets pointing skyward from the soldiers' muskets.

Dr. Weightman took the cue. Addressing the sergeant who marched at the front of the column, he asked, "Why do the men have bayonets fixed, Sergeant Bigelow?"

"Lieutenant Smith's orders, sir. I reckon he meant the men to make a charge, just for drill, but I'm supposin' he hasn't found the opportunity as yet."

"Well, I believe Dr. Franklin has already invented the lightning rod, Sergeant, and we do not need to repeat any of his experiments. Kindly remove them."

The sergeant turned his head toward the men. "Bayonets away, lads! There'll be no warriors to run 'em through today, and no Indian maids to run your own points into tonight." Sparkes peered at Bigelow. There was a sly, nearly toothless smile on the tough old sergeant's weathered face. The thought of Indian maids had obviously remained in Bigelow's mind. Sparkes wondered if all the men were so lecherous.

Wooster turned to the surgeon. "A wise thought, Doctor. An equally wise thought by Lieutenant Smith. With an Indian war on the way, the men need to be ready to fix and charge at the first volley."

Sparkes was beginning to feel as if he were in the dark about something important. Maria had mentioned the possibility of trouble with the Seminoles, but the colonel made war sound imminent. "Is there an actual threat of war, sir?"

"A distinct possibility, Lieutenant. The Seminoles refuse to move to their new homelands west of the Mississippi and, quite frankly, we do not have the forces necessary to compel them to."

"But I thought they signed a treaty, sir."

Wooster shook his head. The boy obviously knew nothing of Indian relations. "A farce, Lieutenant, as are nearly all the treaties we sign with the Indians."

Dr. Weightman cleared his throat, smiled as Sparkes turned his direction, and gave forth with an oft-told lecture. "Let me explain the delicate art of treaty negotiations, Lieutenant. The government negotiators, as fine a set of swindlers as the president can find, will promise the redskins everything they want, and, of course, Congress will provide nothing. Then, when the poor savages realize what all they have given away, they will say, with complete justification, that they were tricked or forced into signing, but alas, all their protestations will come to naught. In the meanwhiles, a bunch of miserable, filthy squatters move in to what was once Indian land. Before long, someone gets killed and the army is called in to gather up the blood-thirsty heathens and put them in their place." Weightman smiled, pleased with his recital. "You see, Lieutenant? It's all very simple and effective."

The colonel spat on the ground. "No damn honor in this Indian business, Lieutenant."

Sparkes was intrigued. In all his years at the Academy, no one had ever spoken so bluntly about government policy. "Where does our duty lie in these matters, sir?"

Wooster's eyes narrowed. "Our duty, Lieutenant, is to keep the peace. If that means removing squatters from Indian land, we do it. If it means crushing the red men, we will, whether the treaty was just or not. As men of war, we must never lose sight of the fact that our primary mission is to keep or restore the peace."

"If I may ask, sir, what will happen if it does come to war?"

"Normally, Mr. Sparkes, it is all very routine. We gather an army of overwhelming numbers and force the hostiles to either give up or fight a losing battle. We then exile them onto land the settlers haven't gotten to yet, then repeat the whole damn process in another ten years, when the settlers move deeper into Indian territory."

"And this time, sir?"

"I fear we may find the routine disrupted, Lieutenant. The Seminoles may be less in number than the other tribes of the South, but they are much more defiant. They also have allies. Both the British and the Spanish supply them with weapons from Cuba and the Bahamas. In addition, they have a large number of Negro warriors. Some are their own slaves, some are runaways, but all will fight harder than any Indian. Most of all, they have an ally in this land. Most other Indian tribes are surrounded by white settlement and have no place to hide. The Seminoles have this entire peninsula to seek refuge in. If they take to the bushes, we may never find them."

"Surely there are guides who can lead us to their hiding places and maps to show us the most likely refuges."

Doctor Weightman let out a laugh. Even Wooster smiled, saying, "The only guides are the Indians themselves, who aren't likely to be very reliable, and as far as I am aware, no mapmaker has ever been to the interior of this peninsula. Hell, a half-witted Negro could draw a map in the sand that would be superior to anything the War Department could give us. There are hundreds of lakes and streams in this Territory that no white man has ever seen and countless swamps that only alligators and Seminoles can live in. On top of that there are untold acres of heavily wooded hammocks that can conceal villages and fields that would not be noticeable from a quarter mile away. Believe me, Lieutenant, if the Seminoles flee, it will take the better part of a decade to find them."

Sparkes fell into silence, pondering the situation and his own ignorance. The few reports he had heard of the Seminoles had described them as being a small, destitute band of savages that could pose little threat to an organized military offensive. Could the colonel be mistaken? He doubted it. Everyone else seemed just as concerned. Maria had been worried for her father's safety. Lieutenant Smith had been contemplating a drill. Even the doctor seemed in agreement with the colonel.

Sparkes's thoughts were interrupted by the flash and thunder of a lightning bolt several hundred yards behind. The men began to cover their weapons under their coats and pull their caps a little tighter over their heads. A heavy rain began to pelt them as the men tightened their collars and hunched their shoulders, giving themselves what little protection they could.

Wooster contemplated his new aide. The boy seemed worried about the possibility of an Indian war. Most young officers would be excited, eager for the fight. Was it something to be concerned about? Probably not; the lad's father had been the same way.

Brothers! We have heard the talk of the Agent Thompson, and we must respond like men. We shall not speak with anger like a woman, or with frustration like a child, as did the Agent Thompson. We shall hold council and seek the wisdom of each other and that of Hesaketa-Mese, the Breath Giver. We shall know each other's minds so that we may speak with one voice.

The Agent Thompson says we have put our marks to the paper given to us at Payne's Landing, and that we must honor our words and move to this new land that lies toward the sunset. He says we have sent chiefs to this new land, and they have agreed for us to go there. All this we say is false. We have put our marks to treaties of peace with the white man and we have sent our chiefs to see this new land, but we have not given our word to live there.

The Agent Thompson says we are men with no honor, that we give our word then break it. He says the time for talk is over and that we must gather our women, our old men, and our children and place them on the ships that will take us to this new land. He has spoken to us as if we are children, but we must answer him as men. Let us pass the pipe, search our hearts, and speak what we see as true.

The clearing in the woods was small, barely large enough for the smoldering remains of a campfire and the seven chiefs who sat around it. It was late afternoon and the ground was still damp from a short rain that had recently passed through. About eighty warriors and a few women were gathered in the thin pine forest that surrounded the chiefs. A few of the warriors spoke among themselves softly, but the majority fixed their attention on their leaders. Everyone had heard the threats from Agent Thompson the previous morning. It was now up to the assembled leaders to decide upon a response.

Micco Phillip probed a long twig into the embers of the fire, waiting for the tip to catch fire. When it did, he placed the tip into the bowl of a pipe and drew repeated breaths through the long, ornately carved stem until his mouth filled with smoke. He looked around the campfire at the chiefs who were assembled for the council. They were all good men, each of them strong in their own way. The only chief who was conspicuous in his absence was Micco Nopy, who had sent word that he was ill. Phillip understood: Micco Nopy was a good chief, one who cared for his people. He was, however, a man who could not make up his mind. This was a council that required a firm hand to lead it and a resolute mind to make the final decision. Micco Nopy was a "white chief," a man of peace. Phillip was a "red chief," a man of war.

Phillip blew the smoke slowly from his mouth, letting it drift skyward toward the Breath Giver. Turning to his right he passed the pipe to an old man, thin and wiry and nearly eighty years of age. His name was Abee-Aka, known to the whites as Medicine Man Sam, or, in a rhyme, "Foxy old Sam, The Medicine Man." That the whites knew him at all was surprising. Abee-Aka kept to himself, tending his medicine bundles, casting spells and healing the sick. Among the Mikasukis, he and Phillip were equally revered, one as a political leader, the other as the spiritual leader of the tribe.

After saying a few words over the pipe and drawing a breath through it, Abee-Aka passed it to the next chief, Phillip's son Kachi-Hadjo. The young man took the pipe with almost no thought, drew on it, and then passed it on. Phillip smiled. His son, now in this thirtieth year, was strong in both body and spirit. He was deep in thought and would make no hasty judgment. Most whites referred to Kachi-Hadjo by the name Mad Panther, a rather rough interpretation of his Indian name. More than any other Indian seated at the fire, Kachi-Hadjo understood the white man. He had spent much time in St. Augustine and had learned the white man's tongue. If it came to war, Kachi-Hadjo would be a formidable leader.

Phillip watched as his son handed the pipe to Asi-Yoholo, a small, powerfully built young warrior. Phillip saw the anger in Asi-Yoholo's expression and knew the reasons for it. Asi-Yoholo's mother had been a Creek woman, the daughter of a well-known war leader. His father had been a white trader but had left when war broke out among the different factions of the Creek Nation. When the Americans entered the war, the mother and her young son were driven from Alabama into Florida by General Jackson's army. Years later, Jackson invaded Florida, driving the Seminoles, the Mikasukis, and the Creeks who were living among them deeper into the peninsula. Asi-Yoholo had watched as drunken soldiers beat his mother, violated her, and pierced her heart with a bayonet. He had suffered much at the hands of the white man, and if it came to war, the white man would suffer much at the hands of Asi-Yoholo. Taking a quick, nervous draw on the pipe, he passed it on to the next man.

Chalo Emathla, a thoughtful man of middle years and much revered for his wisdom, accepted the pipe. Phillip remembered when they had fought against the whites almost twenty years earlier. None had been braver or more fearless than Chalo Emathla. But time had softened the man, and Emathla now counseled for peace, rather than war. Still, it was a voice that was needed at times such as these, someone to balance the anger of Asi-Yoholo.

The pipe passed next to Halek Tustenuggee, the principal war leader of Micco Nopy's Alachua band. Phillip looked at the man and saw no emotion in his eyes. Tustenuggee would offer no opinion, only his resolve. If emigration were decided upon, Tustenuggee would gather his belongings and board the ship without complaint. If war were decided upon, Tustenuggee would be the most ruthless, deadly warrior on the field of battle. Large and strong, he was a man to be feared.

The last man in the circle, sitting to Phillip's left, was a black Seminole who went by the name of Gator John. Phillip had known him since he was a child, born among the Indians, the son of a woman who had fled a plantation in Georgia when she had become pregnant. He had grown up an Indian, but was truly a man of two worlds, having lived with other blacks in a separate village near Phillip's. The old chief admired the cool common sense and courage of Gator John, and knew that if it came to war, black man and red man would stand side by side.

As the pipe returned to Phillip's hands, the chief held it aloft for The Breath Giver to see. Setting it down, he drew a deep breath. "Brothers! Let us speak our minds!" There were murmurs from the warriors gathered about them, but everyone knew that Phillip would speak first.

Asi-Yoholo also knew the etiquette, but could not contain himself. "I will say no more to the white man."

Phillip paid no attention to him. "The Agent Thompson says the time for talk has passed and that we must soon abandon our homes and go to the new land in the west. He asks whether we will gather in peace or whether he must bring soldiers against us. How shall we answer him?"

Asi-Yoholo's mind was already decided. "My rifle shall give the Agent Thompson his answer. Did he not bind me in chains and confine me in prison? Such an insult must be avenged."

Gator John gave a short laugh. "You was one foul-mouthed Injen, Asi-Yoholo. What you expect?" Like Kachi-Hadjo, Asi-Yoholo knew the white man's tongue, but was much less proficient in it and had learned most of his words from drunken soldiers.

The young chief stared angrily at the black man. "And what of our hunting party at the Black Swamp? Are we to forget that? Were not our brothers beaten and whipped by the white men? Was not one of our warriors slain?"

Phillip held up a hand. He would not let anger rule the council. "We will soon have satisfaction for the loss of our warrior. I have spoken to Tustenuggee. He is to seek the soldier who carries the mail through our land from the fort at Tampa Bay to the Agency at Fort King and take our revenge upon him. The white men shall see that we are just."

Halek Tustenuggee smiled. He was clearly looking forward to the kill. "His end shall not come swiftly. If The Breath Giver be willing, I will lift this soldier's scalp while yet he breathes. Then we shall see how brave these soldiers are."

Chalo Emathla was worried. "Will the white man not see this as an act of war? Will they not send their soldiers against us?"

Tustenuggee scowled. "Let them! I do not fear the white soldiers. Their scalps shall cover the entrance to my lodge. I have been insulted for the last time by the white man. Have they not abused our women and children? Have they not stolen our cattle and taken our black brothers? Did they not drive us from our homes in the Alachua prairie and Tallahassee hills? Did they not force us to sign a treaty that gave us this land for twenty summers? Only ten summers passed and did they not force us to sign another treaty that calls upon us to give up all our land? Tustenuggee shall talk no more."

Asi-Yoholo looked at Emathla with contempt. "You quake at the thought of the white soldiers. Is this how the great Chalo Emathla shook when he put his mark to the paper that the Agent Thompson says proves we are willing to move to the land in the west?"

"The paper is a lie! We said only that the land was good. We did not bind our people to sell their homes and leave for the west. Only the council can decide such things. The Agent Thompson lied to us."

Asi-Yoholo shook his head in disbelief. "Because you believed his lies must we all now leave our homes? Is this how the mighty Emathla stands up to the white man?"

Emathla's eyes narrowed. "When you were but a child I fought the white man and have never quaked at his feet. But to fight him now would be foolish. He has offered us good land in the west. He has offered to pay us well for the cattle and horses we are to leave behind. He will pay us for the land we leave behind and will give us a large annuity. Make war, and we shall have none of this. We will lose this war you long for. When it is over the white men will gather us like cattle and send us west with nothing. We have placed our marks upon a treaty that provides well for our people. We must accept it."

"Asi-Yoholo will accept none of it! Will you live under the Creeks, as the treaty says we must? I was born a Creek but was driven from my home by those Creeks who were friendly to the whites. Never shall I live with those people." He cast his eyes around. "I do not fear war. The soldiers have rifles; so do we. They have powder and lead; so do we. Do we not have three warriors for every soldier that covers our land? We shall make the soil red with their blood."

Phillip had heard enough of the argument. "Gator John, you smile, as does the she-bear as she watches her cubs fight."

"More like the hawk watchin' the squirrels play. The way I sees it, ain't no white man got to worry so long as the red man fights with himself. Ain't no mo' use to argue. We all knows how we got here. We all knows the white man ain't gonna go away. What we gots to know is if *we* gonna go away."

Phillip nodded. "Do our black brothers stand with us?"

"Who else we gonna stand with? The white man? Ain't no slave chains for this warrior. I was born a Seminole and I'll die one. My momma may have been a slave, but ain't no chains was gonna hold her. She run all the way from Georgia to be free in Spanish Florida, and her son don't intend to leave her bones here alone. You know my men. They gonna be free, or they gonna die. You all talk o' not given up the land. Hell, we'll give up all the land in Florida, but we ain't gonna give up our freedom. You all talk about bein' great warriors. Ain't no man fights for his land like a black man fights for his freedom."

Phillip nodded, satisfied with the answer. "Gator John speaks with a strong heart." He looked to Abee-Aka, who had been chanting in an almost inaudible voice while rearranging snake bones with a stick. "Does The Breath Giver offer guidance, old friend?"

Abee-Aka did not look up. "Hesaketa-Mese weeps for his children. Many years of hardship are ahead, many tears must be shed before we are at peace. Of the two paths before us, one will be easier to walk but will blacken our hearts forever, while the other will be harder to walk but will make our hearts proud." Phillip nodded. The Breath Giver rarely gave clear advice.

He then turned to his son, who had thus far been silent. "Kachi-Hadjo, my son, you have said nothing."

The young chief looked at each man in succession as he pondered their arguments. "There has been much truth spoken, but it is all false.

30

Chalo Emathla says the land in the west is good. Perhaps it is, but the Creeks will take the best of it, and we will have only those places they do not want. He says the treaty is good, that the white man will pay us well. The white man only *promises* to pay us well. When has the white man ever kept his promise? Asi-Yoholo says we have guns and lead and powder. We do, but we cannot make more, like the white man can. When our powder kegs are empty, where will we get more? He says we have three warriors for every soldier. Yet who will replace our warriors when they are slain in battle? If we kill a hundred soldiers, the white men will send five hundred to replace them. Gator John says his black warriors will stand beside their red brothers. Will they stay if the white man offers them freedom in the west?" An image of his daughter came into his mind. "I will fight because I want Kitisci-Haasi to grow up in the land where the blood from her naval strings first stained the earth. Yet I fear the blood of her heart will stain it too, and that she will die young and without her father. Halek Tustenuggee does not fear war. Kachi-Hadjo does, but if my father says we must fight, then Kachi-Hadjo will fight as hard as any man."

"Well spoken, my son." The discussion went on for several more hours, each man presenting his point of view or trying to undermine the view of another. Individual warriors approached the fire and spoke their minds. Finally, when he felt there was no more to be said, Phillip stood up. The decision was made. "We will tell the Agent Thompson this: We will not move our homes to this western land. They will see that the Seminole is not afraid. Yet we will not go on the warpath until the soldiers come into our lands in search of our women and children. Then we will fight, but we will send our women and children into the swamps and hammocks where the soldiers cannot follow us. We have but one hope: We must pray that the white man will tire of searching for us where he cannot go. Perhaps then we can sign a new treaty that will let us remain."

Asi-Yoholo and Tustenuggee both let out a piercing war whoop and most of the assembled warriors followed suit. Chalo Emathala turned away, his head lowered. Abee-Aka continued his chanting, his eyes closed and his hands raised skywards. Gator John looked straight into the eyes of Kachi-Hadjo. The closest of friends, each knew what the other was thinking. *Abee-Aka gave us two paths to choose from. We have chosen the path of pain and sorrow.* There really was no other choice.

~~~

Maria put down her sewing and looked out the window. It had been one day since her father had led the soldiers away from the house and out of St. Augustine. He was such a strong, loving man. She would miss him terribly. She also knew it would be many months before she saw him again. Between the impassable roads and the hostile Seminoles, overland travel was becoming both difficult and dangerous.

As she watched Nettie and Nero tidy up the parlor, thoughts of another man came to mind. At first she had thought Lieutenant Sparkes to be a rather naïve, all-too-proper young man, the sort who would find army life disappointing and soon be on his way. As the day had progressed into evening, however, her opinion had changed. He was, indeed, naïve, but he also was quick to grasp a new reality. And yes, he was very proper, but it was a sincere propriety, not the veneer that new Academy graduates soon lost. There was something more to the young man, and it intrigued her.

As Nero walked by, Maria tried to sound as casual as possible when she asked him, "What do you think of Papa's new lieutenant?"

"Right fine young man, Miss Maria. Strong, good lookin', and maybe a decent head on them shoulders."

Nettie's ears perked up and she strode over, giving Nero a slight push, an indication that he should be moving on. Her eyes fell sternly upon Maria's. "Now ain't you just a wee bit shy of bein' a lady to go about thinkin' o' young men, fine as they may be? You best not let your Pappy hear you talkin' like that. Massa Colonel like to put you in irons an' shut you away, then have that poor young fella flogged jus' for saying 'Good mornin' Miss Maria.' You know how your pappy be, Missy."

Maria sighed. Yes, she did know how her father could be.

4

June 23, 1835
Seminole Agency, Ft. King
E. Florida Territory

To:
Mrs. David Kilgour
Cincinnati, Ohio

My Dear Sister:

We arrived at this place yesterday afternoon after the most arduous journey, every afternoon spent in the fiercest of rainstorms. Thanks must be given to the Lord that not one of us was struck down by lightning. Our woolen uniforms, already heavy with sweat, became like lead when soaked with rain. The road from St. Augustine to Picolata was tolerable, and the steamer trip from Picolata to Palatka, approximately twenty miles, was uneventful. Past there, however, was pure wilderness. The road, what little there was of it, passed through bogs and pine barrens, much of it under several inches of water. The wagons frequently became mired, and the men spent many exhaustive hours pushing and pulling them through the mud. In some places trees were felled to make a corduroy road. Much was our joy at arriving here, and a warm room, be it no more than a crude wooden blockhouse, never felt so welcoming.

The post itself is a wooden stockade of moderate size, with blockhouses at opposing corners and a large storehouse in the center with a lookout tower perched high atop it. There are a few outbuildings, but no town of any sort. The forest has been cleared from around the fort, but not much more than a musket shot's distance. Beyond that is woodland, most of it tall pine with an occasional oak grove. By and large the land is pleasing to the eye, but the soil is sandy and unsuited to agriculture, and will never support a great population. The garrison consists of but one company, many of whom are on the sick list. There are at least a thousand mosquitoes for every man, and my hands, neck, and ankles are covered with their welts. *Considering it all, it becomes obvious as to why General Clinch has chosen to spend the summer in St. Augustine. If I had my way, I would join him.*

Alas, I must report that my military career may begin with an actual war. There is much talk of the Seminoles taking to the warpath, and all whom I have spoken to consider them a formidable enemy. Just in the past few weeks, both an Indian and a soldier have been killed, though the colonel thinks full hostilities are some way off. Fear not for my safety, however. I am surrounded by stalwart men, and it is believed that the Indians will more likely run and hide than dare to face us in actual battle. Most likely we will spend the majority of our time tracking the red devils into their hiding places than actually exchanging shots with them.

My fellows here are few, and for the most part very likable. Col. Wooster is somewhat distant, but professionally so. I feel that in time he will warm to me as much as a colonel can to a lieutenant. Lt. Smith is a most cordial fellow and will no doubt be my closest companion for the coming months. Already our mess is a most jovial one. Dr. Weightman is a jolly soul and is often accompanied by his orderly, a young Englishman of quick wit and ready smile. General Clinch, who departs in the morning, is a robust old man, well loved by all. Then there is Genl. Thompson, the Seminole Agent. He is not an army man, his rank being from the militia during the late war with Britain. His is a thankless job, being an advocate for the Indians but in the employ of the government. Being caught betwixt the two, he tries to please both, but can satisfy neither. The burden wears upon him, making him at times disagreeable.

Do not expect to hear from me often, dear Emily. Because of the dangers, there will be few mail riders passing here. If the rains continue, as they shall for the entire summer I am told, the roads will become quite impassable.

Give my best to David and the children,

Your most affectionate brother,
Jacob

Sparkes could hear a small cheer arise from inside Fort King as word spread through the post that Colonel Wooster's column was approaching. Even the rain could not dampen the spirits of men who knew they would soon be heading for the comforts and pleasures of St. Augustine. The column split as it passed through the gate, with the enlisted men making for the warmth of the barracks, while the officers turned toward the east blockhouse.

Sparkes stepped ahead of the colonel and swung open the heavy wooden door of the blockhouse. It may have been daylight outside, but it was dark inside. Light entered the room only through small loopholes cut in the log walls. It was, after all, a fort, and defensibility came before comfort. From inside the room, Sparkes heard a voice call out. "Leave it open, Lieutenant. The rain should be coming to a halt soon." A man rose from a chair at the back of the room, normal in height, but a bit expansive in girth. A full head of white hair stood atop a face that carried a broad smile. There could be little doubt that this was General Clinch. Stepping around a table, Clinch moved towards Sparkes as he greeted Wooster. "Colonel! I see you've brought the rain and a new officer. May we be rid of the former and welcome the latter." Sparkes stiffened and began to salute, then realized the general's hand was extended. Clinch smiled as the pair shook hands. "This is not the Academy, Lieutenant. We are much less stuffy here on the frontier. Save such formalities for when the enlisted men are present. Welcome to the dear old Fourth Infantry."

Wooster stepped up to make the introductions. "If I may, General, this is Lieutenant Sparkes, the new second officer of Company 'B'. Lieutenant: General Clinch." He then nodded to Smith. "And I believe you remember Lieutenant Smith."

Clinch nodded as he grasped Smith's hand. "I am gratified the Senate confirmed your promotion to First Lieutenant, Mr. Smith. Good officers such as yourself are hard to find." The general then reached out his hand to Dr. Weightman. "Good to see you again, Doctor. We have urgent need of your services. The regimental surgeon for the Second Artillery is at Fort Drane, and we have quite a number of men who are in need of medical attention at this post. I'll need you to advise me as to which of those men can risk the trip to St. Augustine. Not a one of them would give up the chance of getting out of here, no matter how close they might be to the grave. The thought of a crowded tavern and a willing wench is a powerful curative." As he spoke, two men emerged from the shadows at the back of the blockhouse. Clinch continued with the introductions. "Mr. Sparkes, this is Captain Vance, Company 'F', Second Artillery, and General Thompson, the Seminole Agent."

Greetings were made all around. For some there were new acquaintances, for others, they were welcoming old friends.

When all formalities were finished, Clinch eased back, letting the table take his weight. His face became serious. "We received a bit of distressing news this morning, I'm afraid. Private Dalton--the express rider from Tampa Bay--was found murdered about fifteen miles from here."

Wooster nodded. "Indians, sir?"

"I would suppose, unless some of these damn squatters have taken to scalping white men."

"Do we know who did it?"

Clinch shook his head. "I would imagine either Asi-Yoholo or Halek Tustenuggee. Doesn't really matter. They've gotten satisfaction for the warrior killed at Black Swamp. They'll be quiet for awhile, though I wish they would take to killing squatters instead of my soldiers."

Thompson stepped forward, obviously agitated. "As I said, General, I feel strongly that we should take some sort of action to punish these murderous savages."

Clinch sighed. He had experienced this conversation earlier. "Mr. Thompson, I have forty men at this post, a third of which are on sick list. Until I receive reinforcements, there is little I can do."

Thompson continued to press the matter. He stepped closer to Clinch, his tall frame allowing him to look down on the general. "You have an additional thirty men here now. Send them out and bring Micco Nopy in. That should get the savage's dim-witted attention!"

Sparkes looked past the agent and into the eyes of Captain Vance. The captain winced, shook his head slowly, and then rolled his eyes. Sparkes got the message.

Clinch slapped his hand on the table. He was frustrated at his lack of ability to deal with the Indians and certainly didn't need anyone making the situation worse. He held his temper, but let his displeasure be known. "Mr. Thompson, *your* job is to talk the red men into emigrating to the new Indian Territory. *My* job is to protect the people of Florida in the event your efforts fail. Considering what little success you seem to have had in accomplishing your task, I see no advantage in complicating mine by following your advice."

Thompson looked about the room, hoping for support from the newly-arrived officers. None was forthcoming. Wooster and Smith had too much respect for Clinch to question his judgment. Sparkes was too new to the Territory to express an opinion. Thompson huffed and turned to leave. "This shall not go unpunished!"

Clinch and the other officers watched as Thompson stormed from the blockhouse and crossed the muddy parade grounds. The general shook his head. "Whatever he does, it will only make matters worse."

Lieutenant Smith smiled. He couldn't resist making light of Thompson's suggestion. "Shall I take the men and bring Micco Nopy in?"

Captain Vance laughed. "Micco Nopy is too sick to travel. Micco Nopy is *always* too sick to travel." Everyone in the room laughed, with the exception of Sparkes. There was obviously something about this Micco Nopy fellow that he didn't understand.

Wooster's eyes followed Thompson as the agent passed through the fort's gate, the rain pouring down on him. After Clinch left for St. Augustine, Wooster would have to deal with the agent. It was not going to be easy. Thompson may have been a good militia officer and may have served with distinction in Congress, but he knew nothing of the Indian character. It was a common problem with Indian agents: As political appointees, they received their positions because of who they knew, not what they knew. The colonel turned back toward Clinch. "Have there been any other signs of hostilities?"

Clinch shook his head. "This isn't war; it's simply Indian justice. Still, it should be taken as a warning. Upon my arrival in St. Augustine, I shall send yet another letter to the War Department asking for more troops. Perhaps they'll send some this time."

Vance smiled. "I would be surprised, sir."

Clinch nodded. "So would I, Captain. Still, we must endeavor to strengthen our forces as best we can. The 'talk' from old Phillip seemed clear enough." He looked at Wooster, informing him of the Seminoles' decision. "They won't go." Letting the news settle in, Clinch walked behind the table and sat down. "At any rate, gentlemen, that is not our present problem. I cannot, in good conscience, ask another man to risk his life carrying the mails between here and Fort Brooke, or, for that matter, here and St. Augustine. I am afraid, Colonel, that you are going to be rather cut off here, at least until we get some reinforcements. Do not send any express riders to Tampa Bay, and only to St. Augustine when absolutely necessary. If you must communicate with Fort Brooke, dispatch a well-armed mounted squad to Fort Drane and from there the message will be carried to the Suwannee, where it will travel by boat to Tampa Bay. The long way around, to be sure, but it is all that is available to us. I will send provisions under armed guard whenever possible, but with the roads beginning to flood, that may not be very often."

Wooster wondered about using the Ocklawaha River, which passed close to the fort and fed directly into the St. Johns. "What about the water route, sir?"

Clinch shook his head. "There are so damn many snags in that river that a canoe couldn't make the passage. With all the hostiles about, I wouldn't risk a work party."

Wooster nodded and stood tall. "We will make do, sir."

"Of that, Colonel, I have the greatest confidence. As for reinforcements, the best hope I can give you lies with the two companies of artillery now at Key West under Major Dade. If I can convince the Administration that the Indians are more of a threat than the Cubans--who are no threat at all--perhaps they will allow me to transfer those men to Fort King. For now, Colonel, simply be on your guard."

~~~

The rain had stopped and a warm meal had been eaten. Coffee cup in hand, Wooster rose from the table and motioned to Sparkes. "Shall we explore the environs, Lieutenant?" Sparkes had learned that even in camp, Wooster liked an after-dinner stroll. As Sparkes turned toward the door, the colonel raised a hand. "Pistol and sword, Mr. Sparkes. These are dangerous times, you know."

When both men were armed properly, they left the fort and headed for the sutler's cabin, about a quarter mile off. The regimental merchant did a brisk trade with the Indians, though by his own admission it was primarily in gunpowder and whiskey. A good portion of the whiskey also went to the soldiers of Fort King, a trade General Clinch could regulate, but never stop.

It had been a week since Sparkes had reported to the colonel, and in that time he had become more at ease with the man. "If I may say, sir, the general and Mr. Thompson seem rather at odds."

"Thompson is a fool, Lieutenant. He treats the Indians as if they were no more intelligent than children. Probably believes it, too." He stopped and looked Sparkes in the eye, making his point clear. "Never underestimate the cunning of a red man, Mr. Sparkes. He is lord of the forest and damn well knows it. The only way we can ever beat the Indian is with superior numbers. We don't have that at the moment."

The more Sparkes heard of the situation in Florida, the more concerned he became. "General Clinch mentioned a possible strike at the Seminole strongholds. Are the two hundred men at Fort Drane sufficient for such a task?"

"Nowhere near enough. If it does come to war, the governor will have to call out the militia. *Then*, Lieutenant, you shall learn the true meaning of 'worthless.'"

Sparkes was surprised by the statement. "Worthless, sir? Did you not command a company of militia at Niagara?"

"By the time we fought at Niagara they were militia in name only. Strong discipline under General Scott had made them into real soldiers. When the British opened fire we lost over ten percent of our men, yet our line did not falter. We pushed on, lost even more men, then fixed bayonets and charged. Not a man thought of his own safety or of turning tail. Raw militia would have broke and run at the first volley."

Sparkes was beginning to understand. "If I may say, sir, on first impression, the soldiers at Fort King do not appear all that well disciplined."

Wooster smiled. "They are the dregs of the earth, Lieutenant. They are addicted to the bottle, quick to draw the knife on anyone who crosses them, and respect nothing save the lash. If they put their mind to it, any one of those men could earn a dollar a day on the outside, a far cry better than the eight dollars a month the army pays them."

Sparkes had wondered about that. "Then why do they stay, sir?"

"We feed them, clothe them, shelter them, give them good companions, and give them absolutely nothing to worry about. Within limits, we even allow them to be drunken and blasphemous. All they have to do is be here, work occasionally, and, once in a great while, get shot at." Wooster's smile broadened. "What more could a man ask for?"

"A home, sir? A family?"

The colonel let out a laugh. "That, Mr. Sparkes, is why most of them are here. A home and a family are usually what causes a man to be drunken and blasphemous."

The pair continued to stroll in silence for a while, until Sparkes broached the next question. "What sort of man is General Clinch, if I may ask, sir?"

"The finest, Lieutenant. It is largely through his efforts that war has not broken out here in Florida. He is one of the few white men the Indians actually trust. The only misgivings I have concerning the general is his battlefield experience. He spent the whole war with Britain sitting behind a desk in Washington. Not of his own choosing, of course, and a more honorable man would be hard to find. Still, he's only led troops in battle one time, and in truth, the navy won that one for him."

"When was that, sir?"

"At the Negro Fort. After the war with Britain, the English turned over a fort on the Apalachicola to runaway slaves. You can rest assured the slaveholders in Georgia weren't happy about that. Anyway, Florida was still a Spanish colony at the time, but Clinch was ordered to invade and destroy the fort with the help of a navy gunboat or two. When we got there, one of the gunboats got off a lucky shot that struck the fort's powder magazine." A sad look came over Wooster's face. "The earth shook with such force that I almost lost my footing. The upper half of some slave woman landed nearly at my feet. Not the sort of thing one easily forgets."

Sparkes thought he understood. "The hand of God, no doubt."

Wooster gave Sparkes a stern look. "Never place the hand of God on the battlefield, Lieutenant. The slaughter of war is an indiscriminate thing; the saints are butchered along with the heretics."

Sparkes nodded. If anyone understood the horrors of war, it was certainly the colonel. "The general mentioned his children, sir. What of his family?"

"A sad tale, Lieutenant, and proof of his devotion to duty. His wife-- a fine, delicate lady--passed away little less than a year ago, leaving eight children without a mother."

"Where are the children now?"

"With their grandparents in Georgia. Of course, the general immediately tendered his resignation so that he might retire to his plantation and raise his children, but President Jackson prevailed upon him to remain in Florida until the Seminoles were removed. So the general remains at his post, cheerfully ready to fulfill his duty, no matter how long it takes, and no matter what the personal cost. That, Lieutenant, is the sign of a true soldier."

By now the two men had reached the sutler's cabin. Passing through the open door, they walked up to a crude counter. A balding man with no front teeth turned to greet them. "Colonel Wooster! I'd heard ye be back. St. Augustine too busy for ye, was it?"

"Not a drop of good whiskey there, Mr. Rodgers. A glass of your finest for Mr. Sparkes and myself. Has trade with our red friends been good of late?"

"Aye, a bit too good in some ways. A lot more powder and a bit less whiskey. General Thompson talks of stopping the sale of powder to the heathens, but I don't know. They might not take kindly to that."

"Mr. Thompson does seem to know exactly how to infuriate our red friends, doesn't he?"

"Aye, that he does. I told him: 'Better watch your back around old Asi-Yoholo. He won't forget the time ye locked him up,' I said."

Wooster looked around, through the window, and into the woods. "We'd better all watch our backs, Mr. Rodgers."

5

Hesaketa-Mese, Giver of Breath! Hear the words of Chalo Emathla!

I come to you with a heavy heart, and like the fallen tree that has been in the water for many summers, it shall not rise again. Five moons have passed since my brothers and I met in council to give answer to the Agent Thompson. The time has now come when the white men say we must leave our homes. The council says we shall not go to this new land beyond the great waters, and war has been decided upon.

I know the warpath well, but I do not wish to walk it this time. I have the trophies of many battles outside my lodge, but they bring me no pleasure. It is the happiness of my people and the laughter of the little ones that brings the most joy to my heart. Yet can my people be happy when they are driven from their homes and must live in the watery swamps and dark hammocks? Can the women be happy when their men are dead? Can the little ones laugh when their mothers are unable to feed them? This war may be an honorable thing, but it is foolish. The Seminole will be driven into the sea, and our names shall disappear from memory.

If I stay with my people and fight, what good shall come of it? If I die the death of a great warrior, who of my people will be left to remember? When the war is over, all my people will be dead or scattered like the poorly sown seed. What of my children? My daughters are young and pleasing to the eye. Will the white soldiers not ravage them when there are no warriors left to defend them? What of the people of my village? They look to me for protection. I may kill many soldiers, but I cannot kill them all. Like the ants in a rotting piece of wood, you can crush many of them, but there are always more. I have always believed that the warrior fights to defend his people. I fear that if we fight this war, it will destroy us.

To my brothers in council I have given my word; I have told them that I shall not leave this land. To break this trust will bring dishonor upon my name and the forfeiture of my life. It matters little. If I fight the white man, I will surely die before this war is over. If perish I must, I would rather it be at the hands of my brothers.

I pray to you, Hesaketa-Mese, to protect my people, for it is to the happiness of the children yet born that I look. If my life be taken, but my people live, my spirit shall be content. I must break with my brothers and lead the people of my village to this new land. Many will perish along the path and on the great ship, but with the help of you, Breath Giver, the Seminole may survive the cold winter and like the grass that has turned brown but turns green again in the spring, we shall grow healthy in the land of the sunset.

It was late November, and the air was comfortably cool. The leaves on the trees had lost the vibrancy of their summer color, but few of them were bare, and there was no great color change, as seen farther north. To those who had suffered through the oppressive heat and torrential downpours of July, August, and September, this was the most welcome time of year. It was not the time to think of leaving one's home.

Yet that was the subject on nearly every Seminole's mind. The Great Father in Washington had given them until the beginning of the white man's new year to gather for emigration to the west. The council had defied the order, but had otherwise taken no action, and neither had the army. The land was at peace and no blood had been spilled, but no one expected it to last. Red, white, or black, everyone was waiting for someone to pull the trigger.

Chalo Emathla wanted no part of the upcoming war. Yes, the white men were in the wrong. What right did they have to tell the Seminole to leave his home? Yes, the pride of the Indian had been insulted yet another time. But does pride win wars? Yes, there would be much honor and many trophies to be gained in this war. But would honor and trophies feed the children? Yes, the council was right in calling for war, but it was the wrong decision.

It had been a hard choice, but Emathla had concluded that he must lead the people of his village away from the coming war and out to the new lands in the west. He had sold his cattle to Agent Thompson, gathered his followers, and was on the path to the embarkation camp at Fort Brooke on Tampa Bay. He had done all this as quietly as possible; to break with the council meant the forfeiture of one's life.

Emathla stopped along the path and held up his hand, a signal for his people to also stop. At his side were his two daughters, followed by nine warriors and about two dozen women and children. The warriors looked anxiously about, while most other eyes were on Emathla. He looked off into the deep woods that surrounded the narrow road and smiled sadly. "Come forth into the daylight, my friend. You may stalk like a panther, but you do not smell like one."

There was a movement from the trees and Asi-Yoholo emerged, accompanied by a dozen warriors. Rifles were raised on both sides, but with a motion of their hands both leaders ordered the weapons lowered. Emathla stood calmly in the path, waiting for Asi-Yoholo to speak. The young leader looked nervous, not sure he wanted to go through with the task he had given himself. In the end, he had no choice but to confront his old mentor. "Where does the mighty Chalo Emathla go? Does he flee to the white man's fort in fear? Better he should stand before the walls of the fort and brave the soldiers' muskets like a true warrior."

Emathla would not be shaken by mere words from an unproven leader. "I have braved the soldiers' muskets and their long knives many times. I have led better warriors than Asi-Yoholo to their deaths."

"Speak not to me of your bravery in the past. Today I see only a coward and a traitor to his people."

Emathla spoke softly but firmly, motioning with his arms as he made his argument. "Does a coward walk through the forest in full daylight with only a few close friends? Does a traitor lead his people into a hopeless war? I shall not be party to this senseless war with the whites. Wisely or not, we have signed the treaty. As men of honor, we should abide in it."

Asi-Yoholo flared. "Men of honor? How can a man of honor make peace with the white snakes? What do they know of honor?"

Emathla sighed. There was no use arguing. "I have spoken my mind and made my decision. I must now lead my people to their new homes in the west. I must leave the bones of my ancestors and seek new burial grounds beyond the great river. Our leaving this land is like the coming of winter; it cannot be stopped."

Asi-Yoholo laughed. "You have spoken *your* mind? Does Chalo Emathla speak for the nation?" He then became very serious. "The council has met. They have declared that our people will not be herded like cattle to the west. They have placed a sentence of death upon the man who breaks faith with his nation. Does Emathla say he will not take up arms against the white man?"

"No longer shall I raise the rifle to my eye or bring my scalping knife to the brow of a slain enemy. I will not try to prevent this war, but I will not take part in it. I seek nothing more than a life of peace for my children. If this be a crime, then let it be so."

Searching for justification, Asi-Yoholo saw it in the form of a pouch hanging from his old friend's sash. With the speed of a coiled snake, his hand flew to the pouch, ripped it loose, and held it aloft. Raising his voice for all to hear, he shouted, "To wish for peace is no crime, but to take the white man's gold is. How many cattle did you sell to the white man? How many warriors would they have fed?"

For the first time in their confrontation Emathla was slightly shaken. Standing on principal was one thing, but taking money, no matter how well deserved, was another. "We will need the gold in our new homes. It is fair payment for what we are to abandon here."

"We will need no gold because we will not abandon our homes!" Asi-Yoholo emptied the coins into his hands and threw them into the forest. "The Seminole sells his lands for blood, not gold! Let the hogs of the forest root for your gold. Asi-Yoholo will have none of it!"

Regaining his composure, Emathla stared calmly at his adversary. The two men had been close in years past. Indeed, Emathla had helped raise the young man after his mother's murder. Yet Emathla knew that no matter what the bond between himself and Asi-Yoholo, the young man's thirst for revenge was too strong to overcome.

A look of pain came to Asi-Yoholo's eyes. "I ask you again, old friend: Do you stand beside us or do you take the side of the white man? I have no stomach for the taking of your life. Join us. Avoid the doom that has been placed upon you."

Emathla shook his head. It was too late. "I have spoken. I will say no more; I will fight no more. Do what you must or let us pass."

All of Asi-Yoholo's brave talk had come to naught. He reached for his knife, but could not draw it. If the older man would fight or flee, he could kill him. But Emathla did neither. He just stood there, no emotion on his face. Asi-Yoholo's hand relaxed. He began to turn away.

There was a slight movement in the trees, then the loud crack of a rifle. Emathla gripped his chest and fell to the ground as his daughters screamed. From behind a tree stepped Halek Tustenuggee. Approaching the lifeless body, he shook his head. "He is but the first good man to die."

~~~

Sparkes entered the blockhouse, removed his hat, and took a seat on the crude chair that was positioned across the desk from the colonel. "Good afternoon, sir."

"Good afternoon, Lieutenant. Did you have an eventful patrol this morning? I thought I heard shots."

"Nothing unusual, sir. The normal rattlesnake and an alligator. Gives the men some sport."

Wooster nodded and took another sip of coffee. "Anything else?"

"The usual, sir: Plenty of Indian sign, but no sign of Indians." Wooster knew the meaning. The Seminoles were out there, they were watching, but they were not showing themselves. It was like sitting on a smoking volcano, waiting for it to erupt.

It had not been an easy summer. The rain, the heat, the insects, and the disease had all been expected and in one way or another had touched every man at the post. Wooster himself had passed out from heat exhaustion one day. Lieutenant Smith, along with a good portion of the entire command, had been incapacitated by fevers at one time or another. Four soldiers had succumbed to those fevers. Private Thatcher had literally gone mad, running from the fort to the Silver Spring, throwing himself into the cooling waters where he drowned, an odd smile on his face. Sparkes's one outburst had been more comic relief than anything else. Taking a rolled-up newspaper, the lieutenant had gone on a mission to kill every mosquito in the blockhouse. He had failed miserably, but everyone enjoyed a much needed laugh at the attempt.

Those, however, had been normal difficulties. Troubles with the Seminoles had only made things worse. Although there had been no violence, the threat was pervasive. On those few occasions when an Indian would visit the fort, the meetings would be tense. The casual friendliness that had once existed between the soldiers and the natives had disappeared completely. Everyone knew a war was coming, but no one knew when.

Wooster had one bit of advice for Sparkes: "We had best keep the sport shooting to a minimum, Lieutenant. We're trying to avoid a war, not start one. That rustling in the bushes may be a Seminole, not a deer. If nothing else, we need to conserve powder."

The conversation was interrupted by shouts from within the parade ground and the sound of boots running up the steps of the blockhouse. A soldier appeared in the doorway. "Six Indians approaching, sir! They seem to be carrying a litter."

Wooster and Sparkes came quickly to their feet, stepped out of the blockhouse and onto the parade ground. The colonel looked around and caught the eye of a sergeant. "Bigelow! Take ten armed men and go to the Silver Spring. I believe you'll find the doctor and Lieutenant Smith there fishing. Corporal! Have your men at the ready on the palisades! This may be a ruse." When all was in readiness he ordered the gate opened.

Through the portal came four warriors carrying a crude litter bearing the body of Chalo Emathla. Close behind came his two daughters. As the sergeant and his ten men left, the gate was shut. Wooster bellowed, "Bemrose!" With the doctor off fishing, the hospital steward was the only man who might be able to help. One of the warriors began to speak in Muskogee, the native tongue of the Seminoles. Wooster threw up his hands in frustration. "Primus!"

Bemrose ran up to the litter and tore Emathla's blood-soaked shirt open. He shook his head. "Blimey, Colonel, right through the 'eart. Been gone awhile, 'e 'as. Nothing left but to bury 'im."

Primus, an old black man dressed in an odd mixture of Seminole, military, and civilian clothing, approached. He immediately began conversing with one of the warriors; then turned to the colonel. "The Injen says they was stopped by Oziyola and Hatta Tustenukkee on the trail to Ft. Brooke. Mathla and Oziyola argued some, then Tustenukkee shot Mathla. They brought him here to see that he gets buried proper and hopes you will see to his chillen here. They say that's what ol' Mathla would o' wanted." The warrior spoke and again Primus interpreted. "He wants to know if you be done with them, Massa Colonel. Says they gots to get back to their people."

Wooster kicked a clod of dirt. "I would imagine. Not likely to tell us much more anyway."

After a word from Primus and a few words to Emathla's daughters, the four warriors turned towards the opening gate. As they walked through they were met by Agent Thompson, who was rushing in. The lead warrior looked with disdain upon the agent and muttered something in Muskogee. He then spat on the ground and walked on. Thompson slowly approached the litter. Wooster looked at the agent, then at Sparkes and Bemrose. He had seen it coming and been powerless to stop it. The killing of Emathla was a sign that the time for reason had passed. War was now inevitable. He shook his head sadly. "The last voice of moderation has been stilled, gentlemen. Once again we find ourselves going into an Indian war without the wherewithal to fight it. Florida will suffer, my friends, and there is nothing we can do about it."

Wooster's sad expression changed to one of anger, and he began to pace back and forth. The savages, both Indian and white, would have their war. There was nothing either he or any other reasonable person could do to prevent it. Seething, he looked at Sparkes. "Blood will flow, Lieutenant, and make no mistake about it: It is on our hands." He took a deep breath and looked down at the lifeless form of Emathla. Wooster had always held the chief in high regard, impressed by his quiet wisdom. Like his dead friend, Wooster knew that anger and frustration would accomplish nothing. "Prepare a burial detail, Mr. Sparkes; full military honors. It is the least we can do for a man of peace and a great warrior." He then looked at Thompson, who was pondering the fate of Emathla's weeping daughters. "Your first orphans of war, Mr. Thompson. There shall be more."

6

St. Augustine
12th October, 1835

To:
Lt. Jacob Sparkes
Ft. King

My dear Lieutenant,
    Thank you for your letter of the fifth October. I can scarce believe that it will soon be four months since my father left St. Augustine. It is good to hear that he is well. If not for your letters, I would be unaware of his true state of health. I fear that if he were on his deathbed he would not tell me. I do hope my writing to you does not cause you undue embarrassment. I am well aware of my father's protective nature. Indeed, I am sure he has demanded that you allow him to read this, something that he would tell me is a very improper thing to do. . . .

    The colonel frowned, then muttered, "Damn girl." Wooster had taught Maria to think for herself, and she occasionally found annoying ways to remind him of that fact. He folded the letter and handed it back to Sparkes.

    The lieutenant, standing in front of the desk, knew better than to crack a smile. Still, he couldn't resist reminding Wooster of one pertinent fact: "I did not initiate this correspondence, sir." That much was true. Upon receiving insufficient communication from her father,

Maria had written to Sparkes, hoping for more detailed news from Fort King.

The colonel huffed. "I don't see you doing anything to discourage it." Not that Wooster wanted the letters to stop. He had always found it difficult to express himself on paper. He could convey his feelings better through Sparkes than he could with his own hand. If nothing else, Maria's letters would be a welcome respite from the growing tensions with the Seminoles. It was mid-December, three weeks since Chalo Emathla was killed, and everyone on the frontier was waiting for the war to erupt. The warmth of Maria's letters would help lighten the day.

In the months since Sparkes had become the colonel's aide, he and Wooster had grown accustomed to one another. The young man knew where the line was in their relationship, and the most dangerous section of that line centered on Maria. He also knew he could push at that line, just a little bit. "Perhaps if the colonel were to write more openly to his daughter, she might not feel the need to solicit information from his aide."

"Mr. Sparkes, if I could write a legible, intelligent sentence, I wouldn't need an aide. Just tell her I am fine, Fort King is as tedious as ever, the road more dangerous than before, and that she will not be coming here." Wooster knew that if he were to write a letter, those were close to the exact words he would have used. Sparkes would make it sound so much better. Wooster also realized that the correspondence would draw his daughter and the lieutenant closer, and it concerned him. If it had been any other officer he would have put a stop to it immediately. With Sparkes, it was different. The young man's moral integrity was beyond reproach. If Wooster had to worry about anyone's actions, it would be his daughter's. She could be quite independent and obstinate when she cared to be. Still, it was a risk he felt he could manage. At the first sign of trouble the lieutenant would find himself transferred to the Wisconsin Territory.

The colonel gave a slight wave of his hand. "Go read your letter in silence." Sparkes took a seat nearby as Wooster began to open his own mail.

. . . .Please reassure him that my concerns are for him, and not for you (though I do wish you the best of health).

There is still much talk here that the Indian war will soon be upon us. On what evidence these speculations are based I cannot tell. Rarely is a warrior seen, and never a squaw or a child. The most distressing news comes from the plantations along the St. Johns, where they report numerous Indian signs. There is great fear among the planters that should a war commence, hundreds of slaves will join the Seminoles. Many of the planters and their families have fled to the city and have brought their negroes with them. That, of course, has given rise to the great fear that the negroes will somehow take up arms and slaughter all of us here in St. Augustine. If such be the case, I would rather they join the Indians. General Hernandez has placed a strict curfew over all the negroes in the city, fearing that some of them are delivering supplies and information to the Indians. He drills the militia regularly, though I fear there is not a true soldier among the lot. Indeed, one nearly killed Mrs. Morris when his musket discharged unexpectedly. Still, General Clinch assures me we are perfectly safe here, and I have always placed the greatest faith in his judgment.

Please tell father that Nettie slipped while coming down the stairs last week and seems to have broken a rib. She is in much pain whenever she is forced to exert herself, so Nero and I have taken over many of her duties. She protests vigorously that I should not perform such tasks, but it is no more than the wife of any common soldier would do, and certainly not beneath me. For the meantime, it amuses me that I do the work of the servant and she rests, doing little more labor than the mistress of a fine house. Still, knowing the sensibilities of our southern neighbors, I confine my labors to the interior of our home, so as not to arouse their suspicions or their ire.

Do give my love to father, Lt. Smith, the good doctor, and dear Mr. Bemrose.

Nettie's most obedient servant,
Maria

Sparkes folded the letter and placed it in his coat pocket, then related the news of Nettie's injury to the colonel. Wooster winced. "I hope she has the presence of mind not to let the neighbors see her doing servant's work. They'll think we're damn abolitionists or that Nero has staged some kind of uprising." He then returned to reading his own mail.

There was quite a bit of it. Because of the threat of hostilities, the mail had not been brought from Fort Drane for over three weeks. Most of the mail consisted of routine paperwork, the sort Wooster would eventually hand over to Sparkes. One letter, however, was from General Clinch. He read it over twice, shaking his head. When he finished he looked up at Sparkes. "Find Smith and Thompson, Lieutenant."

In a matter of minutes the two men, along with Sparkes, were standing before the colonel's desk. Wooster looked disgusted and spoke in a sarcastic tone. "It seems that someone in Washington has at long last woken up to the fact that we are about to have an Indian uprising down here. The War Department has asked the governor to call out the volunteers, to which His Excellency has concurred, ordering up five hundred men for the extremely long duration of *one month*."

Lieutenant Smith shook his head. "It'll take them a month just to get organized."

Wooster continued. "As soon as possible we are to proceed with our men to Fort Drane, where we will join with the volunteers and General Clinch, who is on his way there from St. Augustine. From Fort Drane the combined force will head south, cross the Withlacoochee, and invade the Seminole villages in the Cove. According to the 'Great Fathers' in Washington, all threat of hostilities should be over by New Year's. Lieutenant Smith, you are to remain here at Fort King, in command of the post, with a small garrison of the sick and the lame."

Sparkes snickered, Smith moaned. Thompson took issue with the tone of Wooster's voice. Since the colonel's arrival, the two men had gotten along, but just barely. Thompson was particularly annoyed by the fact that Wooster, like Clinch, refused to call him by the title of "General Thompson." In the end, however, there was nothing he could do about it: Thompson's days as a soldier were long over. For the moment, the best the agent could do was show some indignation at the colonel's satirical remarks. "You show little faith in our forces or our elected officials, Colonel."

"On the contrary, Mr. Thompson. I have complete faith in the ability of our volunteer forces to somehow embarrass the army, and even more faith in the fact that our elected leaders have absolutely no idea what is going to happen here. The entire excursion will be a grand waste of time, if not worse."

"You don't believe the savages will stand and fight?"

Wooster was becoming irritated. "They are *not* fools, Mr. Thompson, and they'll certainly not be standing idly by as we march into their villages. They'll be nipping at our heels the whole time, out of sight or just out of musket range." There was a point he needed to make, a fact that Thompson and his superiors in Washington seemed unable to grasp. "The war won't be ending when those volunteers' enlistments are up, damn it, it will barely have started!"

Smith was concerned. "Will I have enough men to defend this post, sir?"

A very worried look came over Wooster's face. "Relief has been dispatched, Mr. Smith, but I fear you may never see it. General Clinch has ordered Major Dade and two companies of Artillery from Key West to Fort Brooke. When they arrive, they are to proceed up the military road and relieve this post."

Sparkes took a breath. The military road was little more than a dirt path through the heart of the Seminole homeland. Two companies would number barely one hundred men. If the Seminoles cared to, they could bring a thousand warriors against the soldiers. "Just two companies, sir?"

Wooster nodded and bit his lip. "And may God be with them."

~~~

General Richard Keith Call looked out over the assembled troops of the Florida Mounted Volunteers. True, there was nothing military in their appearance, but that, he felt, was of little consequence. Uniforms didn't win battles. These were the grandsons of the Minutemen who had fought in the Revolution. They were also the sons of the men who had fought alongside Andrew Jackson at New Orleans. Faced with an Indian uprising, "Old Hickory" had called them to duty once again, and they had responded with enthusiasm.

Call was confident. He had been at Jackson's side in 1814, when they had slaughtered over six hundred Creek warriors of the Red Stick faction at Horseshoe Bend in Alabama. He had also accompanied Jackson during the Seminole War of 1818, when the army had destroyed numerous Seminole, Mikasuki, and refugee Red Stick villages in north Florida. Some of the chiefs he was about to face in Florida were the same men he had faced a generation earlier. The American force of arms had crushed the Indians back then and would crush them again, nearly twenty years later.

As Call looked proudly upon his force, an old friend, Col. Thomas Warren of Jacksonville, approached. Warren could sense what Call was thinking. "We got us a right fine bunch of boys here, R. K."

Call was in full agreement. "Four-hundred-eighty-nine at last count, all mustered in and itching to lift a few scalps of their own." For Call and the other Florida frontiersmen, an Indian war was a personal matter. Unlike the regular army, they were not carrying out the government policy of Indian removal; they were protecting their own homes and families. An Indian war was not a matter of national policy; it was a matter of life and death.

For that very reason, Floridians were suspicious of the federal government's motives. Warren gave out with a sarcastic laugh. "I hear General Clinch says we're not supposed to hurt no Indians, just round 'em up for shipment out west."

Call favored a more direct approach and saw little use for government interference in a purely local matter. "Jackson ought to let us Floridians handle this our own way. Hang a few chiefs and skin a few squaws, and before you know it the damn redskins will be lining up on the docks asking for passage to the Indian Territory." Call's disdain for the federal government extended to the army as well. "It's a waste of good tax money to keep all them damn regulars around the territory. Few things are as worthless as a regular army man." If the government was going to spend money, Call had a much better use for it. "I hear they brought two companies of artillerymen up from Key West. What the hell they know about fighting Indians? They ought to send them damn regulars back to their forts and leave the militia to guard the settlements. Our boys could use a little of that Washington money these days." Call may have been a general in the militia, but he was also a politician. The voters liked it when their representatives were able to bring federal dollars their way.

Warren had another concern. "How many niggers you think the Indians got with 'em?" Call shared his friend's interest. Both men were plantation owners and slaveholders. As far as they were concerned, Seminole villages were nothing more than safe havens for runaways. Removing the Seminoles would remove a threat to the plantation economy.

Call gave a quick shake of his head. "Don't know. Maybe two, three hundred men folk and just as many women and pickaninnies. You can bet that every slave catcher from here to North Carolina will be following the army, placing a claim on every negro we get hold to. Might see if I can grab a few for myself. Price of slaves being what it is, a man could make a quick thousand or two."

A look of resolve came over Warren's face. "Tell you one thing, R. K.: I don't care how much he might fetch, if I see a nigger with a gun, that's one dead nigger."

~~~

Kachi-Hadjo looked at Gator John. The tall black man was cleaning his rifle for the third time that day. "It will not fail you, my friend. It never has."

John shook his head and smiled. "Never feared that, ol' frien'. I jes' likes to take care o' her. I figure she's the only thing 'tween me an' slave chains."

Kachi-Hadjo could not imagine John in chains. The man would die first, and would no doubt take a few white men with him. Or at least he assumed it would be that way. The truth was that few of the younger warriors, himself and John included, had ever participated in a war. The Seminoles had been living in an uneasy state of peace with the Americans for the past seventeen years. There had been numerous confrontations with the whites, but no real shooting had broken out. Still, it had been easy to see who the real leaders were and who the most stalwart warriors would be. Gator John would be both.

The war they were waiting for might be only a few days away, when the New Year's deadline arrived. Rumors had been abundant concerning the gathering and possible movement of troops, both from Fort Brooke at Tampa and from Fort Drane to the north. But rumors were just that. Until somebody made a move, the only thing anyone could do was make preparations.

Kachi-Hadjo turned as he heard the approach of a rider. A young warrior rode swiftly into the village and swung off his mount as he neared the center of the group of thatched huts. Once on the ground, he called out for Micco Nopy. Out of the largest lodge stepped the chief, accompanied by Abraham, his closest advisor.

Kachi-Hadjo and John, along with all the other villagers present, began to gather around the rider and the chief. When Micco Nopy came close, the rider breathlessly made his announcement: "The soldiers have left the fort at Tampa Bay. They are traveling the road to the Agency at Fort King."

Halek Tustenuggee spoke before anyone else had a chance. "How many soldiers are there?"

The rider reached into a pouch and drew forth eleven bundles of small sticks. Everyone knew that each bundle contained ten sticks. There was no need to announce the total; each stick represented a man with a loaded musket.

Micco Nopy looked nervous. The council had agreed that if a large group of soldiers entered Seminole land they would be attacked. Yet Micco Nopy was in no hurry to see the war begin. He had grown relatively prosperous in the past decade, both from his large herds of cattle and from the surplus produce of the many slaves he owned. Try as he might, he could not envision any outcome to the war that would not cost him dearly. He had wanted to do like Chalo Emathla, sell his cattle and take his slaves out west, but the opportunity never arose. Considering Emathla's fate, it was probably a good thing it hadn't.

The thought of war was distressing to Micco Nopy, not only because of his own potential losses, but because of what it would do to his people. If the white men prevailed, the Seminoles would wind up destitute, forced to live in a hostile land. Should the Seminoles prevail, it would only be after a long and deadly conflict that would claim many lives and result in the loss of what little wealth they had. Either way, there was no happy ending.

There was also the problem of the blacks who lived among them. Many were his slaves, but they were also his brothers and sisters. Unlike the whites, a Seminole never mistreated his slaves. For the most part, their only duty to their masters was to hand over a portion of the produce from their fields. Otherwise they were free to do as they pleased. True, the presence of these people was always a sore spot with the whites, but the blacks had been loyal to their Indian friends and masters, and the Seminoles would remain loyal to them.

All of these problems weighed heavily on Micco Nopy's mind. It was easy for the others to call for war. They were not the chief. Caught in a no-win situation, Micco Nopy looked desperately for a way to avoid either inevitability.

Abraham sensed what his master was thinking. "Maybe the soldiers are jus' going to the Agency. Maybe they ain't gonna try to gather us up."

Kachi-Hadjo shook his head. He knew Micco Nopy's talent for procrastination. If the chief wasn't pushed, the opportunity to surprise the whites would be missed. "The Agent Thompson said we have until the beginning of the white man's new year to gather our people and board the ships for the journey to the new land. That time is but a few days away. These soldiers may be on their way to the Agency, but they will soon come for our women and children. They must be stopped now."

Gator John was in agreement. "We all done heard the reports of hundreds of white men gathering at Fort Drane. Them soldiers leaving Fort Brooke will either join with them at Fort Drane or the white men will split up and come at us from different directions. Either way, we gots to stop 'em now."

Halek Tustenuggee nodded. "The time for sharpening the scalping knife has passed. It is time to use it."

Micco Nopy was getting desperate. If he could somehow stall the inevitable, perhaps an agreement with the whites could yet be reached. "We must wait on Asi-Yoholo."

Gator John disagreed. Asi-Yoholo and his band had gone to Fort King to kill Agent Thompson. If they were successful, the government would see it as an act of war and begin to hunt the Seminoles in their homes. "If we don't get them soldiers before Asi-Yoholo kills Thompson, we may never get the chance."

Tustenuggee was more to the point. "Is Micco Nopy afraid of war?"

Abraham came to his master's defense. "Micco Nopy only wants to wait for Asi-Yoholo 'cause we wants to face them whites with all o' our warriors."

Kachi-Hadjo held his tongue. He would not openly disagree with the chief. He also knew it was nothing more than a stalling tactic on the part of Micco Nopy.

In reality, Micco Nopy would have preferred Asi-Yoholo *not* be at the battle. In Micco Nopy's eyes, the brash young chieftain was nothing more than a refugee Red Stick; he was not from the line of Cowkeeper, the first great Seminole leader. Micco Nopy felt vulnerable, his own power lessening as Asi-Yoholo's grew. Micco Nopy also feared the influence of Kachi-Hadjo. Unlike Asi-Yoholo, Kachi-Hadjo was of proper lineage and one of the few men who would be considered as a replacement for Micco Nopy. Hopefully that would not happen anytime soon. Still, in times of crisis, someone might not care to wait for Nature to do its work.

Micco Nopy wasn't the only one concerned about the head chief's status. Abraham was even more vulnerable. His influence within the tribe was tied directly to that of his master. Should Micco Nopy be deposed, Abraham would be just another black Seminole. Worse, perhaps. As Micco Nopy's closest advisor, Abraham had gathered a few enemies of his own.

Kachi-Hadjo understood all this, but harbored no ambition to replace the head chief. For the moment he would lend his support. "Micco Nopy is right. We should wait for Asi-Yoholo and his warriors.

But we cannot wait forever. Once the soldiers cross the last river, it will be difficult for us to surprise them."

Abraham asked, "What if Asi-Yoholo ain't here by then?"

Kachi-Hadjo snapped, "Then he does not collect any scalps." He then reconsidered his hasty answer. "We will wait until the soldiers reach Small Pond, and no longer. The long knives will feel safe if they reach Small Pond. They will think that because we have not attacked them at the river crossings, we are afraid of them. We can surprise them at Small Pond."

Micco Nopy tried another approach. "What of the soldiers at Fort Drane?"

Kachi-Hadjo already knew the answer. "There are but two ways they can attack us if they come from the north. They must either cross the Withlacoochee far to the west to attack our homes in the Cove, or they must attempt to meet with the soldiers coming from Fort Brooke. We must be ready for both." He then looked to Micco Nopy. Kachi-Hadjo had given the chief an opportunity to take command. Would he grasp it?

The chief had backed himself into a corner and knew the only way to survive was to walk boldly out of that corner. He also saw an opportunity to temporarily remove two of the men who might challenge his leadership. He looked to Tustenuggee. "We must have three warriors to face each soldier if we are to meet them in open battle. We have near twice that number with us now. Tustenuggee will take half our warriors and watch the ford of the Withlacoochee. If the whites come, he must stop them and send word for the rest of us to join him."

Tustenuggee wasn't happy. "I do not wish to miss this battle. There will be many soldiers to kill."

Kachi-Hadjo put a hand on Tustenuggee's shoulder. "It will be a long war. There will be whites enough to kill."

Micco Nopy then turned to Kachi-Hadjo. "After the battle Kachi-Hadjo will go to my brother, Micco Phillip, and with his Mikasuki warriors they will drive the whites from the sugar fields east of the St. Johns. This will free many slaves and they will join us. It will also force the white men to protect their plantations and their towns and not attack our villages. When they see how strong we are, they will ask for peace and allow us to remain in our homeland."

Kachi-Hadjo agreed with the strategy but doubted the end result. Never before had the white men been stopped so easily. In a way, he had sympathy for Micco Nopy's dilemma. Both men understood the likely outcome of the war. Micco Nopy, with more to lose, was still desperate to find an alternative. Kachi-Hadjo had passed that point and had decided to place his fate in the hands of the Breath Giver. As far as he could tell, there was no other choice.

~~~

Major Francis L. Dade surveyed the landscape through the cold morning mist. To his right was a small pond, surrounded by a field of tall grass. To his left was an open pine woods, the ground covered in thick palmetto bushes. He and his 107 men were five days out of Fort Brooke and about half way to Fort King. The most dangerous part of the trek was behind them. The river crossings and thick forests were in back of the soldiers, and open pine woodlands lay ahead. If the Seminoles hadn't attacked them at the river crossings, they probably wouldn't attack at all. For all practical purposes they now were safe.

Dade wasn't sure why the Seminoles hadn't attacked. The Indians certainly had superior numbers. Every night, as they camped, Dade and his men could hear the warrior's whoops and calls of derision. Dade had told his men not to worry: "The Indian you hear isn't the one who will kill you." Now, as the threat of ambush diminished, Dade relaxed. He allowed the men to button their great coats over their cartridge boxes in hopes of keeping out the winter wind. He pulled in his flankers and brought the advance guard closer to the main body.

Captain Gardiner, his second in command, was concerned. "Is it wise to pull the flankers in, sir?"

"Fear not, Gardiner, the danger has passed." The men had maintained their discipline throughout the march and Dade appreciated it. The only grumbling had been over the fact that they had left Fort Brooke two days before Christmas and had likely missed a hearty celebration. Stopping his horse, Dade rose up in the stirrups and addressed the troops. "Have a good heart, lads! Our dangers and difficulties are now over, and as soon as we arrive at Fort King you shall have three days rest and keep Christmas gaily!" They were the last words he spoke.

~~~

It was a beautiful afternoon. The cold air of morning had dissipated with the bright sun of a cloudless day. Agent Thompson and Lieutenant Smith had just finished their afternoon meal and had decided on a stroll. As they exited Fort King, Smith voiced his reservations. "Are we sure this is wise, General? The woods have been extraordinarily quiet of late."

Thompson shook his head. "We cannot remain holed up in the fort forever, Lieutenant. If the Seminoles had meant to kill us, they could have done it long before today." He motioned toward the sutler's shack. "You don't see Mr. Rodgers cowering in the fort, do you? He sleeps quite unmolested in his cabin every night."

Smith was not totally convinced, but could offer no argument. As the gate closed behind them, Smith took a breath. "I just don't feel safe."

From behind a bush, Asi-Yoholo smiled. The time for revenge had come.

7

1 January 1836
Ft. Brooke, Tampa Bay

To:
Maj. Genl. Gaines
N. Orleans

Genl.

It is with deep regret that I must inform you of the most melancholy tidings that herald this new year. On 23 December last, Maj. Dade, accompanied by 107 officers and men of Compy "C", 2ⁿᵈ Arty and Compy "B", 3ʳᵈ Arty, departed this post for Ft. King, under orders of Genl. Clinch to relieve said post. At sunset yesterday, one of Dade's men, Pvt. Ransom Clark, Compy "C", returned to this post in the most wretched state, crawling on hands and knees, his clothing soaked with blood, and his body seriously wounded in several places. His survival can be seen as nothing short of miraculous.

The man is quite lucid and informs me that on the 28ᵗʰ, perhaps an hour after sunrise, the column was attacked by what must have been the entire Seminole Nation. In the days previous to the attack, Dade and his men had made four river crossings with no interference from the savages and having entered more open country, presumed themselves safe from attack. At the first shot from the hidden Seminoles, the gallant Dade was slain. The Indians then rose from their concealment and fired upon the entire column. By this fire, nearly half the force was cut down. Now under the command of Capt. Gardiner, the men took cover and returned an effective fire upon their attackers. The six pounder was unlimbered and used to good effect, eventually forcing the enemy to disengage and move some distance off.

During this respite, the wounded were attended to by the good Dr. Gatlin. Cartridge boxes were recovered from the fallen, and a small breastwork was erected for the protection of the wounded. In addition to Maj. Dade, Lt. Mudge was also slain early in the action. Lts. Henderson and Keais were severely wounded at the same time. Capt. Gardiner, Lt. Basinger, and Dr. Gatlin were at this point unhurt.

Before an effective breastwork could be completed, the enemy resumed his attack, advancing with deliberation, remaining well concealed behind trees and shrubbery. Over the course of several hours they advanced, killing each man in his turn. Lt. Basinger was the last officer to fall. By mid-afternoon, there appeared not a man alive among the two companies. Pvt. Clark, so severely wounded as to appear dead, saw the Seminoles cautiously enter the breastwork. They stripped the dead of weapons and valuables, but did the slain men no injustice. They were followed by a large group of Negroes, who committed unspeakable atrocities upon the bodies of our brave fellows. Those who were found with life still in them were cruelly dispatched. Of the 108 officers and men, only Pvt. Clark and another private, DeCourcey, remained alive. At nightfall they left the scene of horrid death and began a painful journey back to Ft. Brooke. The following day they were seen by a Seminole rider. They split, but DeCourcey was overtaken and slain. Clark managed to take cover and elude his pursuer. With much difficulty Clark continued his arduous journey, and by the grace of God, arrived safely at this place. Whether he shall survive his wounds is most difficult to say. The doctor believes there is a ball lodged in the man's lung, which is impossible to extract.

I have given orders for this post to be placed in complete readiness for an Indian attack. Pickets are being erected and all unnecessary personnel placed aboard vessels bound for Key West. Among them are the widows and children of the fallen. I have also dispatched word to Commodore Dallas of the Navy, presently at Havana, pleading for what succor he can provide. Until such time as our defenses are complete, we are much in danger. Our force numbers little over a hundred, and many are sick. Our supply of munitions may not be sufficient to repel a prolonged attack. We are also burdened by the presence of a large number of civilians who have taken refuge among us. Our provisions cannot last long. There are also encamped nearby several hundred Seminoles ready for departure to the west. Although they profess no willingness to engage in hostilities, we cannot be entirely sure of their intentions now that war has truly commenced.

If it be in your power, please dispatch aid to this beleaguered Territory as soon as it may be gathered. The Seminoles will no doubt be emboldened by their victory and may attempt the capture of this post. We also fear for the safety of our fellows at Ft. King, having had no communication from Col. Wooster for nearly a month. *May providence protect them.*

Your most obedient servant,
Alexander T. Belmont,
Major Commanding.

Gator John woke up slowly. The first sensation he felt was warmth on one side and cold on the other. As he opened his eyes, he saw the dark hair of an Indian girl just inches from his face. He took a deep breath, hoping she wasn't the wife of some jealous warrior. Then he realized just how much his head hurt. He smiled. It had been a great celebration, one that equaled the great victory they had scored over the white soldiers. The night had been capped by the arrival of Asi-Yoholo from Fort King with the scalps and bullet-hole-riddled coats of Wiley Thompson and another white man. Yes, it had been a celebration none of them would easily forget.

Rising slowly, so as not to disturb the woman, John stepped out of his hunting lodge. The sun was high, nearing midday. Eyes half closed, he staggered toward the thin smoke of a dying fire and the seated figure of Kachi-Hadjo. Kitisci-Haasi, Kachi-Hadjo's daughter, approached, bearing a cup of hot tea. She was a wisp of a girl, only in her seventh year, shy, but always quick to break into a smile. Although her name meant Red Sun, everyone called her Ki-Tee. Kachi-Hadjo, who was often called Mad Panther by the whites, thought it appropriate, knowing that in the white man's language "Kitty" referred to a small cat. True to his Mikasuki tongue, he pronounced the word differently than the whites, putting emphasis on the last part of the name.

John drank the tea slowly and kept his eyes closed, the bright sunlight making his head hurt even more. He had tasted this brew before. It was something Abee-Aka cooked up to make the headache go away. Kachi-Hadjo smiled. "Good whiskey makes for a bad morning."

John moaned. "I thinks them soldiers be the lucky ones. Their pain be over." The soldiers. The words brought images to his mind, pictures of men screaming and dying, terror and anger in their eyes. The gravity of the situation struck him. He looked at Kachi-Hadjo. "You know, ol' frien', we done started a war we can't win."

The chief nodded slowly. "It is as it must be. Like a great storm, the white man comes and sweeps all that lies before his path. If your home is threatened by the winds, do you not do what you can to protect it, knowing that the storm may take it anyway? Thus must it be with the Seminole. The white man would take what he wishes and leave nothing for the red man. If we fight the good war, perhaps we may save some small part of this land for ourselves. It is a small hope, my friend, but I would rather live with a small hope than with none at all."

John nodded then turned his head to the west. He thought he could hear the sound of an approaching horse. Kachi-Hadjo gazed in the same direction, as if his eyes could penetrate the thickly forested surroundings. More out of habit than from fear, he also reached for his rifle.

The rider emerged from a well-worn path, moving at an easy gait. Kachi-Hadjo relaxed as he saw the man; it was one of Tustenuggee's warriors. As the messenger rode through the large encampment, he took time to relate his news to groups of warriors that had gathered in one place or another. By the time he reached Kachi-Hadjo and Gator John, both men had already surmised the nature of the intelligence. Kachi-Hadjo spoke before the rider could say a word. "The white soldiers come from the north?"

"Many hundreds of them."

"Are there more soldiers than we have warriors?"

The rider shook his head, but not very emphatically. "We have more, but not many more."

Gator John asked the next obvious question. "Where they headed?"

"For the ford in the river. They mean to attack our homes in the Cove. Yet they move with the speed of a gopher tortoise. They shall not reach the ford for two more days." The rider looked up as several men approached. Among them were Micco Nopy and Abraham. The messenger related the news for at least the tenth time, but this time in the greatest detail. Micco Nopy listened intently then conferred with Abraham in a hushed voice.

Their discussion completed, the head chief let his decision be known. For once, Kachi-Hadjo was in full agreement. "We will gather at the south side of the ford of the Withlacoochee. We will not let the white men pass the river. They will see we mean to defend our homes." As decisive as Micco Nopy sounded, he had not abandoned his usual languor. "We must use the remainder of the day to rest and to prepare for battle. We will leave in the morning." Having said his piece, Micco Nopy turned and strode toward his lodge. Like the others, he had celebrated well into the night. He would spend most of the day resting and little of it in preparation.

~~~

An old black man stood by the north bank of the Withlacoochee River, surrounded by a dozen officers and a few enlisted men. Among them were Generals Clinch and Call, Colonel Wooster, Captain Vance, and Lieutenant Sparkes. They all looked longingly toward the heavily-wooded south bank of the river, some twenty yards distant. General Clinch turned to the black man. "I do not see a ford, Primus."

Primus rubbed his chin. "It gots to be roun' heres some'eres, Massa Gen'ral." He also felt the need to defend himself. "I done said, Massa Gen'ral, I ain'ts been down this here road for some times now, an' my memory ain't what it used to bein'. Still, I knows its here some place." With that, the slave started to walk eastwards along the riverbank.

Colonel Wooster called out to his sergeant. "Bigelow! Take some men and follow the lost soul." At the same time, Captain Vance ordered another party to search to the west.

General Call, in command of the volunteers, turned to Clinch. "Perhaps this is a futile mission, General."

Clinch tensed slightly but did not let his annoyance overrule him. "I am well aware that today is December thirty-first, General, and that your volunteers' enlistments end with the coming of the new year, but until that time they are under my command and I will use them to pursue the enemy. We cannot let the murders of General Thompson and Lieutenant Smith remain unavenged. If the Seminoles mean war, then we must take it to them."

The past four days had been especially trying for Clinch. On the twenty-eighth he had left Fort Drane with 250 army regulars accompanied by 500 Florida Volunteers. Call had voiced opposition to the campaign from its outset. He would rather have used his volunteers to scour the Alachua region. Although most Seminoles had fled the area, Call and the volunteers felt the Alachua offered a better chance of rounding up Seminole cattle and stray slaves and of finding villages to burn. On the twenty-ninth, an express rider had arrived from Fort King with news that Agent Thompson and Lieutenant Smith had been ambushed while strolling outside the fort on the previous afternoon. From that point on, Clinch's mind had been firm. The third day had been a slow march with constant bickering between the regulars and the volunteers. It was now mid-morning on the fourth day. There were still six or seven hours of daylight remaining and Clinch meant to make something useful come of the trip.

Sparkes looked about with extreme uneasiness. With Smith left in charge at Fort King, and now dead, command of Company "B" had devolved to Sparkes. It was a responsibility he was ill prepared for, irregardless of the four years spent at West Point. Colonel Wooster and the commanders of the other companies had been helpful, but the duties and the paperwork had become overwhelming. The threat of actual combat only heightened a growing sense of panic.

His thoughts were interrupted by the sight of Sergeant Bigelow, Primus, and another soldier coming downriver in a canoe they had found. It was a battered old cypress dugout, but it was large enough to carry seven or eight men. Clinch, Wooster, and Call gazed at the vessel, each seeing it in a different way. Clinch spoke first, almost excited. "The river is narrow, gentlemen, and the canoe is long. We could have a sizable number of men across in short order."

Call objected immediately. "My men won't cross the river without their mounts, and no horse could ride in *that*."

Clinch shot back, "Then build a bridge, damn it! You have axes and the trees are plentiful. In the meantime, the regulars can secure the opposite shore." No one gave thought to the idea of *ordering* the volunteers to dismount and cross the river in the canoe. Clinch knew as well as anyone that as volunteers, they could always un-volunteer if orders were given that were not to their liking.

Wooster shook his head slowly. The thought of splitting their force with nothing but an old canoe connecting the soldiers with the safety of the northern shore was unsettling. He would rather the volunteers spend their time looking for the ford than building a bridge. Still, he was reluctant to question Clinch's plan; he had too much respect for the old general. Perhaps a word of warning would be enough to make the general reconsider. "We should be cautious, sir. That canoe may have been too easily discovered. The first men across will be in extreme danger. Indeed, we may all be until the entire force is across."

Clinch nodded, but did not take the hint. "Then proceed with caution, Colonel."

Wooster motioned for Sparkes to follow him, but then hesitated for a moment. Was the lieutenant too inexperienced? Then an image of Sparkes's father came to mind. Was there another reason Wooster was reluctant to send the young man across the river? The colonel quickly dismissed the doubts from his mind. Sparkes was a soldier and was as qualified as anyone to reconnoiter the opposite shore. "Select two good men and take them to the other side. Fan out and look for Indian sign. If you see any of the savages, open fire then run like hell back to the river. We'll be covering you from here. If it looks safe, then we'll bring the rest over. Be careful!" He then added an afterthought: "And don't shoot each other!"

Sparkes approached his men, selected his crew and boarded the canoe. In a matter of moments the boat was across the river and the men were disembarked. In silence, Sparkes motioned for his men to spread out. Each man had his weapon at the ready and his finger on the trigger.

Sparkes moved directly inland, perpendicular to the river, following a well-used path. The forest was a mixture of mostly oak and bay with an occasional pine, not too thick, but certainly dense enough to hide an Indian war party. His eyes attempted to look at every spot an

Indian could be hiding. He looked for moccasin prints, but the ground was covered by dead leaves with little exposed dirt. After traversing about fifty yards, he came to a large clearing. He entered it slowly, his eyes darting from tree to tree, expecting to see a Seminole behind each one. Never in his life had he felt so exposed. Something moved to his left, and he quickly turned towards it and raised his pistol. He immediately recognized one of his own men and relaxed. Then a twig snapped behind him. He spun around, only to see the other soldier emerge from the opposite side of the clearing. Sparkes gave the man an inquisitive thumbs-up. The soldier nodded in the affirmative. Sparkes then motioned them back towards the river. If all three had found the clearing with no sign of Indians, it was likely safe.

Within an hour, the entire force of regulars was across the river and resting within the clearing. As the regulars crossed, the volunteers commenced their bridge building. Several tall trees were felled and placed across the gap, and a number of volunteers were busy with the task of leveling and lashing them together. Others were busy splitting logs to use as a crude deck for the bridge. If the Seminoles were nearby and unaware of the army's presence, the sound of innumerable axes had certainly brought the fact to their attention.

Wooster had been one of the last men across the river, having stayed behind to direct the crossing. As he entered the clearing, he looked nervously at the surrounding woods and then to the men, relaxed in small groups with their muskets stacked. It was a dangerous situation. The soldiers used old, smoothbore, flintlock muskets, most of them made over twenty years earlier during the war with England. The Seminoles used rifles, many of them only a few years old, gifts given to the Indians at the signing of the treaty of Payne's Landing. The spiral grooves that had been machined into the barrels of the rifles resulted in a weapon with far superior range and accuracy. Muskets were acceptable when fighting a "civilized" opponent like the English, in battles where the opposing lines stood facing each other and exchanged volleys. When fighting an enemy hidden within a forest, the muskets put the soldiers at a decided disadvantage. The colonel turned to Sparkes. "Form the men, Lieutenant. I do not like this."

Sparkes motioned for the men to get up and ready their weapons. "Did you see something, sir? The general *has* dispatched scouts."

Wooster gave a quick shake of his head. "Here we are, on the hostile side of a river, with nothing save a leaky canoe between ourselves and our reinforcements."

"They are, sir, attempting to build a bridge."

"Would as soon swim as to trust a bridge built by volunteers. Especially those whose enlistments are to end at midnight." Wooster shook his head in disgust. "Thirty day enlistments! What idiocy!"

"We've seen no sign of Indians, sir."

Wooster was not convinced. "That is when I worry the most, Lieutenant. Where are they? They're not at Fort King. They've already killed Thompson and Smith. Not much use for them to lay about there. Have they run into Dade? Are they gathered at the ford, not realizing we have no idea where the damn ford is? When you don't know all the possibilities, you have to prepare for every one of them."

"Perhaps Major Dade never left Fort Brooke, sir."

"One can only hope, Mr. Sparkes, but I doubt it. Give Dade a hundred men and a set of orders and he would march into hell." Wooster took one more look around. "Keep a sharp eye out, Lieutenant. I think it is time I had a talk with the general."

The colonel had taken no more than two steps before a shout was heard, followed by a gunshot. Almost immediately, the surrounding woods erupted in gunfire and soldiers began to fall. Sparkes stood stunned, unable to move as his men dove for cover. A rifle ball tore through his cap, removing it from his head. He looked about in panic, not knowing where the firing was coming from. A firm hand grabbed his shoulder and spun him around. It was the colonel. "Form the men and return fire! Keep them together! Don't let them break ranks! I've got to get to the general!"

Sparkes wasn't sure what to do. His eyes fixed upon a soldier with blood streaming from his head. Frozen, Sparkes watched as a panicked soldier ran by. Suddenly he heard the far-away voice of his grandfather reciting a line that he often used whenever troubles mounted: *Never mind the bullets, son. Just get the job done.* As another fleeing soldier passed, Sparkes reached out and grabbed the man's collar, then pushed him in the direction of the rest of the company. Drawing his sword, he began shouting at the men. Disciplined soldiers, the company immediately followed orders and calmly formed a line. When all were ready, a volley was fired and the guns quickly reloaded.

Wooster, running surprisingly well for a man with a limp, quickly reached Clinch. "General! We must order a bayonet charge!"

Clinch wasn't sure. "We don't know how many are out there! Could be hundreds!"

"Doesn't matter, sir! They'll cut us to pieces if we stay like we are."

"Should we fall back?"

"They'll cut us down at the river! We must go on the offensive!"

Clinch hesitated. Then a rifle ball passed between him and Wooster. "Make it so, Colonel."

Wooster ran back across the clearing in the direction of Sparkes. As he ran he shouted orders to the officers and men he passed. Ranks began to form as bayonets were fixed. One by one, the officers raised their swords and the lines advanced towards the trees. Sparkes and the men of Company "B" were ready by the time the colonel arrived. Wooster smiled and drew his sword. "Gather up your courage, lads! Charge!"

The men began to shout and yell as they ran toward the nearest edge of the forest. Sparkes could see a puff of smoke ahead and a Seminole turn to run. At the same moment, he felt a stinging in his left arm. He looked down, saw the blood, but kept running—it was nothing. Then he stopped, gasping for breath. He coughed, tasted blood, and then fell to the ground.

~~~

Kachi-Hadjo was breathing hard. It seemed as though he had worked harder today than on any other day of his life. He and the other Seminole warriors had spent the morning in preparation for the defense of their homeland. Trees that had been felled the previous day had been placed strategically, while paths were cut through the thick woodland. Guns had been cleaned and rifle balls molded. Powder was passed out and scalping knives sharpened. The purifying Black Drink was taken, prayers were said, and war paint applied. Scouts had been sent to the ford to keep watch for the approaching army. All was in readiness.

Then it was discovered that the white men had somehow missed the ford and were attempting to cross farther downriver. With little order in their march, the Seminoles began to move to where the white army was gathering. By the time the Indians reached the place, many of the soldiers were already across. With as little noise as possible, the warriors attempted to surround the small clearing where the army was gathering.

Before the encirclement could take place, one of the Indians was spotted. With too few men in place and too much distance between them and their targets, the Seminoles found themselves with less of an advantage than they had enjoyed against Major Dade a few days earlier. Kachi-Hadjo and the other chiefs tried to rally more men to the front, but when the soldiers fixed bayonets and charged, all order within the Indian ranks disappeared. Not that his men had thrown down their weapons and fled in panic, but most had seen the wisdom of retreat. A Seminole warrior would never be a disciplined soldier; each man fought as he saw fit.

Kachi-Hadjo and his men had not fled the battlefield, they had simply moved out of range. As the day progressed, they trailed the army as it retreated toward the river, taking the occasional shot when it seemed opportune. Many of the enemy had been wounded, but few had been killed. At the range that most Seminoles fired from, the balls were nearly spent when they hit their target.

Kachi-Hadjo withdrew from his memories of the battle and looked about. To his right were the bodies of the dead warriors. One of them had been no more than a boy, anxious to make a name for himself as a fearless warrior. He had tarried too long as the whites charged and had tripped on a vine as he retreated. Three soldiers had caught up with him and had stabbed him repeatedly with their bayonets.

To Kachi-Hadjo's left sat the wounded warriors. Thankfully, there were few. Foremost among them was Asi-Yoholo, who had suffered a ball in his forearm. Abee-Aka forced a poultice into the wound, placed a large leaf over it, and bound it all as best he could. He chanted for some few minutes then blew his breath over the bandage. Without a word, he moved on to the next patient.

Kachi-Hadjo stepped over to Asi-Yoholo. "We did not fight well today. Each warrior fights his own war and does not obey the command of his chief. When the soldiers put their knives on the barrels of their rifles and run at us, each warrior thinks that all those white men are running only at him. He does not rely on the strength of the warriors at his side. If we are to win this war, we must learn to stand against the white soldiers."

Asi-Yoholo didn't care to hear the criticism. "Had the white men crossed the river at the ford, they would not have been so lucky."

"Can you be so sure? What if the soldiers had run across the ford? Many had horses. Would our warriors have stood their ground?"

Asi-Yoholo tried to dismiss the notion. "Would you have our warriors stand in a line to be shot, as the soldiers do? The Breath Giver has given us a victory today. Are you not happy with his gift?"

"The Breath Giver laid a feast before us, and we did but nibble at it. The white men are no more than hurt. They will be back."

~~~

The memories were vague: Officers and soldiers shouting. The moans of wounded men. Being carried across the river over a makeshift bridge. Resting in the back of an ambulance wagon. The searing pain in his side.

By the time Sparkes was fully cognizant, the sun had set. The army had made camp beside a narrow stream, where the surgeons and their orderlies were busy tending the wounded. The young man opened his eyes and saw Colonel Wooster standing above him. General Clinch approached, a pained look on his face. "Do we have a return on the casualties as yet, Colonel?"

"Four dead, sir, fifty-nine wounded. We were fortunate. The scouts noticed the red devils before they could approach close enough for their shots to have full effect. Dr. Weightman believes most all will recover."

"Pray that he is correct." Clinch looked down at Sparkes and gave him a warm smile. "Six months out of the Academy and already collecting lead, Lieutenant? The army has invested considerable funds in your education, young man. Try to live long enough for us to get our money's worth." He then looked back at Wooster. "What did the good doctor say?"

"The ball hit the lieutenant's lung, but did not fully penetrate, so he was able to extract it. There was also a slight wound to the arm. Mr. Sparkes should recover fully."

"Wonderful! Rest easy, Lieutenant. It's going to be a long war, so there is no reason to hurry back to duty." He began to turn away. The expression of deep pain returned to his eyes. "Let me know if any of the men take a turn for the worse. I shall be in my tent, writing dispatches."

After the general was out of earshot, Sparkes commented, "Defeat seems to weigh heavily upon the general."

Wooster gave the wounded officer a look of mock disdain. "Defeat, Lieutenant? Never utter the word. Read the papers in a month and you'll think we scored the most signal of victories. By the time our dear general retires he'll be known as 'Old Withlacoochee.'" There were other things Wooster wanted to say, things that were better left unsaid. He respected Clinch too much to dwell on the old soldier's faults. He would have handled the whole campaign differently, but that had not been his decision to make. He was just a colonel; Clinch wore the star.

There was something else on Sparkes's mind. He remembered his moments of confusion and panic when the first shots were fired. "Did I do my duty, sir?"

Wooster smiled and put a hand on the lieutenant's shoulder. "You fell while leading the charge, Lieutenant. No more can be asked of any soldier."

Wooster turned to leave but Sparkes took hold of his sleeve. "Sir, can you tell me how my father died?" Wooster couldn't refuse. The young man's brush with death had earned him the right to know. Still, Wooster couldn't tell him the whole story. It wasn't time yet.

The colonel pulled up a nearby camp stool, set his coffee cup on the ground, and took a deep breath. "We were at Fort Erie, of course, and the British were doing their best to overrun the place. The fighting was close and the situation doubtful. General Gaines had vowed we would never surrender, and every man among us was of the same mind. Just when it looked as if we might be able to hold them off, they were able to bring a cannon to bear on a vulnerable portion of the wall. They kept pounding at it until finally there was a breach, and fifty or more Redcoats rushed the opening. If they had made it through, they'd have taken the day. Your father, bless the man, took ten or twelve men and held that opening. Not a one of those Redcoats made it in alive." Wooster stopped as the memory unfolded in his mind. "I never saw a man fight with such passion. It was as if God had given him that hole in the wall, and there was no way on Earth that he was going to part with it. In the end, it was a bayonet in the back that brought him down." The colonel stood up. "When I say your father died a hero, Lieutenant, I mean it. There are far too many 'heroes' in this army, and few of them deserve the title as much as Erastus Sparkes."

Sparkes was surprised. "I've read the reports, sir. They all indicate that he died in the explosion that breached the wall, not in its defense."

Wooster nodded. "It was not an intentional oversight. Quite simply, I was the only officer who saw what had happened, and I was so badly wounded that no one bothered to ask me for my report. The way the bodies fell, it was impossible to tell who died when. I tried to correct the reports after I read them in the papers, but by then it was too late. The only thing people cared to talk about by that time was Jackson at New Orleans."

Their conversation was interrupted by the approach of hospital steward Bemrose and a soldier with a bandage on his leg who hobbled along with the help of a crude crutch.

Wooster greeted the men warmly. "Mr. Bemrose! I hear you have been performing miracles. Dr. Weightman has been most glorious in his praises."

"I do me best, sir. I'll not let a man pass on, if it be in me power to stop it."

"Of that I am sure, my friend. You have need of something?"

"This man 'ere, sir, says 'e saw something you might should know about, sir."

Wooster gave the soldier a quizzical look. "You have something to report, son?"

"One of the Indians, sir. I saw a sash on one of them I could swear belonged to Major Dade. The red one with the strange gold weave. Never seen another like it."

"You served with Major Dade?"

"Three years, sir. I know it were that sash."

Bemrose cut in. "Other men said they saw uniform coats, sir. I fear something bad 'as befallen the good major, sir."

Wooster nodded. "So it would seem. I thank you both for this information, troubling as it may be. Pray that our fears prove to be unfounded."

Sparkes was unsure of Wooster's meaning. "Our fears, sir?"

"I would expect that Major Dade and the one hundred men who were being sent to the relief of Fort King have met with some great disaster, Lieutenant. This unfortunate little war seems to have gotten off to a very bad start."

8

18 January 1836
Ft. Drane, E. Fla. Terr.

To:
His Excellency
Genl. Andrew Jackson
Pres. of the U. States.

Genl.,

After mature deliberation, I feel it is my painful duty to resign my commission as an officer in the United States Army. As you are no doubt aware, the death of my wife has left our eight children without parental care for more than a year. Although I had reluctantly agreed to maintain my position until the removal of the Seminoles could be effected, there appears to be little hope that the goal will be accomplished in the foreseeable future. Feeling that I have too long imposed the care of my children upon my late wife's parents, I request that I be allowed to leave the service and return to my home in Georgia. I will remain at this post until 1 February, when I will turn command over to Col. Wooster of the 4th Infy., who will command until such time as a senior officer arrives in the theatre of war. While yet in command, I will pursue the enemy with vigor using the very limited means at my disposal.

In consideration of the many fond acquaintances I have made in this Territory, I feel it incumbent upon my honor to request that all possible aid be dispatched to Florida as soon as conditions allow. The state of the Territory is indeed unfortunate. The frontier inhabitants have abandoned their homes and fields and crowded into the fortified places for protection. Many who were well situated are now utterly dependent upon the military for sustenance. Isolated homesteads have been overrun and their inhabitants cruelly murdered. The Territory's prosperous sugar plantations have all been destroyed, thus eliminating

Florida's most important industry. In addition, hundreds of slaves have been freed from these plantations and have joined the Seminole ranks. As a result, there is much fear that a general slave uprising may occur. Finally, there is no road in Florida that is safe to pass over, except by the most commanding force. If a large, well-equipped army is not soon brought to bear against the Seminoles, it may be decades before the Territory can regain its prosperity and the population grow to the point where Florida may enter the Union.

I must also take this opportunity to suggest that as much as practicable, regular troops be used against the Indian enemy. The conduct of the Florida Mounted Volunteers during the action at the Withlacoochee River was not equal to the standards of good military service. Initially, there was much complaint about undertaking the mission against the Seminoles, and much louder complaint when asked to cross the river to actually attack the enemy. If, when our forces were attacked, had the volunteers been on the same side of the river as were the regulars, we could have taken the battle to the enemy and perhaps defeated them, thus bringing this war to a swift conclusion. Thankfully, through the heroic efforts of our men, and most notably the skilled leadership of Col. Wooster, we were able to rout the vastly superior enemy force and reach safety with little loss of life.

Wishing you the best of health, I am, with deep respect,

Your Most Obedient Servant,
Duncan L. Clinch
Brig. Genl. Comm., Fla. Terr.

It was a small homestead, but she was proud of what she and her husband had accomplished. The cabin was well built, the crops in the field were doing well, and the stream was running clear. True, they were not wealthy, but they were self-sufficient and owed not a penny to anyone. She smiled. It had been cold the previous week, with a touch of frost. Today, as she hung the laundry to dry, the sun was warm and the sky a bright blue. There was little more she felt she could ask for.

As she hung her husband's shirt, her foot reached out and gave a cradle a slight touch, setting it into a rocking motion. Hopefully the baby would keep sleeping. She turned and looked to her other son. "Jeremy, take that nasty old stone out of your mouth! T'ain't no tater!" She laughed to herself; he was such a good boy.

As she reached into the basket for another shirt, she heard a rustling in the nearby woods. Before she could turn to see what had made the noise, there was the crack of a rifle and an Indian war whoop. She screamed as she saw Jeremy fall to the ground. Lifting the infant swiftly from the cradle, she fled towards the cabin. At the sound of her scream, her husband burst out the cabin door, shotgun in hand. No sooner had his foot touched the ground than several more shots rang out, killing him instantly. She kept running for the cabin, hoping to find safety within, but before she could reach the door, a bullet entered her back, then another. She fell to the ground and the crying infant rolled away from her.

Into the open stepped Halek Tustenuggee and two dozen warriors. They walked carefully up to the woman and her husband and prodded them with the muzzles of their guns, making sure they were dead. As the warriors went on to ransack the cabin, Tustenuggee looked down at the woman. She had a soft face and beautiful hair. Drawing his knife, the chief reached down, took hold of the hair, and made a swift cut around the scalp. Holding the trophy aloft, he let out a victory cry. He rolled the woman gently onto her back, placing her in what looked to be a comfortable position. He then reached for the wailing infant and placed the child delicately upon his mother's bosom. He looked at the pair for a moment then brought the mother's arms into a final, loving embrace of her child. The infant stopped crying.

~~~

The plantation owner had known the attack would come, but had waited too long in deciding what to do. Like many of his neighbors he had sent his family to the city, but had remained on the land, hoping to somehow save his fortune. There had been few options, and none of them were good. First off, he could expect no help from the army or the militia; there were simply too many plantations to protect. Some planters that had attempted to mount a defense had either been killed or had barely escaped with their lives. A few had acknowledged the inevitable and had abandoned their land, hoping that with no whites around, the Indians would have no reason to attack. A few others had hoped their good relations with the Seminoles would protect them. In all cases, the plantations had been destroyed.

The attack came at midday. The plantation was one of Florida's largest, but the Indians treated it with no more respect than if it had been the smallest. Over fifty warriors surrounded the house from a safe distance, firing at anything that appeared in the windows. The owner armed his most trustworthy slaves, but they soon fled, leaving only himself and the overseer to protect the house. With a feeling of helplessness, he watched as the large brick sugarhouse went up in flames. The work of a lifetime and the fortune it had brought were being reduced to ash.

Outside the plantation house, Kachi-Hadjo sat on a stump and lit a cigar that had been taken from the last plantation he had attacked. He was in no hurry. There would be no one to come to the white man's aid. It was better to take the time and make sure the sugar house was destroyed completely. He wanted to drive the whites away and give them no reason to return. He didn't even care if he killed any. He just wanted them gone from his homeland.

Over at the slave quarters, Gator John strolled calmly, a curious look on his face. How could his fellow blacks live like this? Why didn't they rise up and kill their masters? He would die before he let someone whip him or put him in chains. Yet many of these slaves bore no signs of being whipped and none wore chains. Why had they simply not fled? He watched as his black warriors went from cabin to cabin, calling for the people to come out. Some had already emerged and were jumping and dancing, excited to be free. Others had to be forced out, literally pulled from their crude shacks. Were they afraid to be free? Some were crying and begged to be left with their master. A tear came to John's eye. They had been slaves for so long that they had lost the yearning to be free.

The plantation owner watched from a second story window as the chimney of the sugar works collapsed into the flames. He saw his slaves dancing and throwing torches into their shacks. He heard rifle butts pounding on the door of the house, then the blast of a shotgun. A moment later he heard rifle shots and war whoops from the room below. His heart sank: the overseer was dead and he was now alone. He heard soft footsteps coming up the stairs. Moments later, a warrior stood at the doorway to the room, his fierce eyes surrounded by red and black war paint. He saw the scalping knife in the Indian's hand. He heard other Indians tearing through the cabinets and drawers in the rooms below him. There was no escape.

The Indian watched as the plantation owner raised a pistol, but instead of pointing it at the warrior, the white man put the muzzle to his own lips. Would the white man really blow his head off, rather than fight? Curious, the warrior stepped up to the man. The white man was trembling and sweating and stared at the Indian with wide open eyes, but seemed unable to pull the trigger. Disgusted at the white man's lack of courage, the warrior turned to leave. Such a weak man could keep his scalp. Let him burn with his home. Then he felt pity for the man. He turned, wrapped his hand around the white man's, and helped him pull the trigger.

~~~

The captain of the militia troop spat on the ground then placed another wad of tobacco in his mouth. Turning in his saddle, he surveyed his small band of men. There were half a dozen of them to escort two wagons from Fort Drane to Fort King. They were one of the more uniform of the militia units, though not in a military manner. All wore tattered brown clothes and all were mounted on skinny mares. Not a one of them could read or write, and none of them had a full set of teeth. And all of them, to a man, thought this was the easiest twenty dollars a month they would ever earn.

Was the captain afraid of the Seminoles? Not really. *Hell, yeah,* he thought, *them damn Indians done ambushed that idiot Dade then forced old Clinch to run back to Fort Drane, but hell, them was baby-faced regulars. There ain't no Indian alive can stand up to a Florida Cracker.* The captain smiled as he listened to the men talk. One of them had already decided on a small "bonus" he would receive: "I hope ol' O-See-Olee got him a good lookin' sister, cause when I get holda that red bitch I gonna have me some fun. I gonna take her to my cabin and use her all night 'til they ain't none left, then I gonna skin her and cut her up and feed her to the hogs. Lawdy! I gonna have me a good time!"

The militiaman never finished laughing. From the side of the road a warrior rose and fired at the man's chest. Before he could fall from his horse, thirty other Indians appeared and opened fire on the other militiamen. Three were killed instantly, and the other two turned their mounts in hopes of making an escape. Both were shot in the back as they fled. On the first wagon, the teamster lay slumped in the seat, a bullet hole in his head. The driver of the second wagon, momentarily safe while the Indians reloaded, jumped from his seat and fled into the nearby swamp.

Asi-Yoholo lowered his rifle. He watched as his warriors gathered the horses and tore through the wagons. He looked down at one of the dead militiaman, the one who had joked about ravaging "O-See-Olee's" sister. "I have no sister. The white man killed my mother before she could bring me one."

~~~

Major General Edmund Pendleton Gaines looked at the young officer who stood before his desk. First Lieutenant Horatio MacDuff was a tall, sharp-edged man with an unruly crop of dark red hair and a thick moustache. With the exception of the moustache, Gaines had looked much the same thirty years earlier. Now, as an old man, the hair was white and the sharp features were best described as "gaunt." The most noticeable thing about MacDuff, however, was the large, medieval-looking sword that hung by his side. Gaines then looked at the orders that had brought the man to New Orleans. "A transfer from the Second Infantry to the Fourth? You don't like the north, son?"

"No sir, the north was fine. It was a certain major in the Second that I didn't like, sir. Or should I say he didn't like me?"

Gaines chuckled. He knew exactly to whom MacDuff was referring. He looked again at the monstrous sword. "And I suppose you are going to tell me that you are a direct descendant of Shakespeare's MacDuff."

"Aye, sir, that I am." It was an odd accent, a strange combination of deep southern drawl and Scottish brogue.

Gaines's eyes narrowed. "I thought MacBeth killed all of MacDuff's heirs."

The lieutenant had to think fast. For some reason, no one had ever caught that major flaw in his tale. He smiled. "Aye, sir, but the great Lord of Fife remarried and had many more little chickies."

The general laughed. "Welcome to the Western Department, Lieutenant. We'll send you down to Colonel Wooster and the Fourth as soon as possible, but for the moment, I could use you here. As you probably know, the Texians are attempting to free themselves from Mexican rule. There is some fear in Washington that we may be drawn into the conflict, and the War Department has instructed me to be ready to march at a moment's notice. In the meantime, you can make yourself useful at the arsenal. Lieutenant Betters succumbed to the fever last month and his replacement won't arrive for some weeks yet, so at present the place is under the command of a drunken old sergeant. A good man, mind you, but not the most organized fellow in the corp. Just see what you can do to get things into shape for Betters's successor. You'll find sleeping quarters there and after you're settled in take some time to sample the pleasures of New Orleans. I doubt you'll find much pleasure in Florida."

A playful look came across MacDuff's face. "Aye, sir, that I shall. I do have some old female acquaintances I should . . ."

He was interrupted by a loud knock at the door. A soldier came in, breathing hard, as if he had been running. He handed Gaines a letter. "From the captain of the *Merchant*, sir. He says it's extremely urgent, sir."

Gaines tore open the seal and began to read. It was from Major Belmont at Fort Brooke. As he read, he looked again at the date. The news was almost two weeks old. When he was finished he set the letter down gently and looked up at MacDuff. "Major Dade and over one hundred men have been wiped out by the Seminoles."

The only thing the lieutenant could say was a somber "Yes, sir." Then he thought to ask, "Who was with him, sir?"

Gaines didn't have to look at the letter to recite the names. The army was small, with only a few hundred officers. He knew each of the fallen men personally. "Gardiner, Keias, Mudge, Henderson, Basinger, Dr. Gatlin." There was an awkward silence for a few moments before Gaines came suddenly to his feet. "We have work to do, Lieutenant! Copy this letter and catch the next steamer for Baton Rouge. Find the governor and tell him to call out the Louisiana Volunteers. Then find Major Riley at the barracks and tell him to gather every available man and await my orders. We are going to Florida, Mr. MacDuff!"

"What about Texas, sir?"

"There *might* be a war in Texas, son. There *is* a war in Florida."

9

To:
Chester and Emma MacDuff
Spartanburg County, S. Carolina

Dear Mother and Father,

As you can see, I am on the move once more. As you have no doubt heard, there is war with the Seminoles, and your son, the "Warlike Harry," is about to be in the thick of it. I had no sooner arrived in New Orleans when word was received of Dade's massacre. Genl. Gaines immediately put out the call for volunteers and gathered what regulars were available in the vicinity of Louisiana and Mississippi. Preparations were completed with amazing swiftness and we were able to embark for Tampa Bay within a fortnight. The good citizens of Louisiana were not lacking in their patriotic fervor, supplying us with over 800 volunteers and immense quantities of supplies for the troops and the suffering inhabitants of Florida. With regulars, our total force is over 1,100 men. I trust the Seminoles shall be taught a quick and bloody lesson.

We march in the morning for Ft. King, where it is rumored provisions will be waiting. Although we brought large quantities of stores with us, much of it has been used to feed the garrison here and to relieve the hunger of the civilians who have fled to this post for safety. So great was the need at this place that we have but one week's rations left, just enough to last us until we reach Ft. King. We will be traveling the same road as Dade's ill-fated band, and I fear we will be the first white men upon the scene since that horrible day. I pray that our comrades may be recognized. Basinger, especially, was a good friend of mine at the Academy.

When we arrive at Ft. King I will hopefully find Col. Wooster and learn of my permanent posting. For the moment, you may post my mail to Ft. Brooke. It will *find me by and by.*

While in New Orleans I was able to purchase a boy by the name of George for a very good price, due to his former master's poor luck at cards. He is about twelve years of age, and a strong little fellow. When next I see Charleston I should be able to sell him at a good profit. In the meantime, it will be good to have someone to tend to my baggage while we are on the march.

Fear not for my safety. The cowardly savages might well have slaughtered a hundred unsuspecting poor souls, but will no doubt think twice before taking on a thousand men who are forever at the ready. Perhaps, with luck, I can use the old family blade to cleave a few redskin necks.

My love to all,

Your peripatetic son,
Harry

General Gaines and his army were five days out of Tampa when they came upon the gruesome scene of Major Dade's battle. MacDuff, riding at the head of the advance guard, could tell, simply by the smell, that they were getting close. As he came around a slight bend in the road his progress was stopped by a corpse lying in the middle of the pathway. After ordering a pair of soldiers to move the body aside, he rode on. He soon came upon a pair of dead oxen off to the side of the road, still in the yoke. A slight change in the breeze blew the stench in their direction, and one of the soldiers behind him fell out of line and began to vomit. After passing a few more victims, MacDuff came upon the little breastwork Dade's men had erected for their defense. The structure had, in truth, become a slaughter pen.

As MacDuff looked about, he could understand the soldiers' hopeless situation. The Seminoles' initial volley had killed or wounded half of Dade's force. If the force had suffered only minor casualties, Captain Gardiner, then in command, could have rallied the men, gone on the offensive, and possibly fought his way to safety. Their chances would have been slim and their losses severe, but some of them might have made it through. The moment they built that breastwork, however, their fate was sealed. There was no chance of rescue and no chance of escape. Yet what choice would Gardiner have had? The number of wounded had been too great. He couldn't leave them to the mercy of savages, he couldn't carry them onward, and he couldn't bring himself to administer a *coup de grace* to the severely wounded. So they all died together. MacDuff shuddered. Could he have done any different?

Within and around the breastwork the slain men lay about in a haphazard manner, their skin dark and taut. Some had been stripped, others had been mutilated. All had been ravaged by carrion feeders. A line from *Julius Caesar* came to MacDuff's mind: *Cowards die many times before their deaths. The valiant never taste of death but once.* After dismounting, he carefully entered the enclosure. Propped against one corner were the remains of an officer. MacDuff drew closer. Even the shriveled skin could not hide the handsome features. It was his good friend Basinger.

General Gaines quietly rode up to the breastwork, his head shaking slowly. "Have the men remove the bodies with care, Lieutenant, and dig a grave within the confines of this breastwork. We will inter the enlisted men here. The officers will occupy a grave near the spot where Dade fell."

MacDuff looked about. It would be a painful task. He began to motion for the men to come forward. For some reason, it did not seem proper to shout orders in such a hallowed place. Catching sight of his young slave, MacDuff beckoned him forward. "Give me a hand with Lieutenant Basinger, George." The boy's eyes widened; he really didn't want to touch a decomposed dead man. One look from his master forced him to overcome his fears. He had learned quickly that while MacDuff was usually an easy-going master, his commands were not to be ignored. As MacDuff placed his arms carefully under the dead man's shoulders, George gripped Basinger's trousers just above the ankles. With the utmost care, the body was lifted over the low walls of the enclosure and placed gently upon the earth. The other soldiers followed the example and before long there were nearly sixty bodies arranged neatly on the ground.

In total silence, the men went about the business of digging the grave. When it was deemed large enough, the bodies were gently laid to rest and the dirt placed over them. As the last spadefull of dirt was thrown onto the mass grave, several of the soldiers knelt to say a prayer.

A short distance further down the road, a smaller grave was made for the six officers and the doctor. Someone had noticed that the Indians had wheeled Dade's cannon into the nearby pond. A detail was sent to pull it out of the water and remove it from its carriage. The weapon was then buried muzzle-down to mark the foot of the officers' grave.

On the road beside the breastwork a group of musicians began to form ranks. Behind them, the remainder of the regulars fell into line. The Louisiana Volunteers stood by as solemn spectators, most with their heads bowed and hats removed. General Gaines mounted his horse and came before the musicians. MacDuff could tell the general was having a difficult time giving the order to commence the ceremony. Clearing his throat, Gaines took a deep breath. "March!" The drummers began to beat a slow cadence while pipers played a melancholy dirge. They marched three times around the breastwork then headed up the road toward Fort King. They would complete the journey Dade had begun.

~~~

Colonel Wooster took a sip of coffee and looked at the red haired officer who had just ridden into Fort Drane. "And what, Mr. MacDuff, leads General Gaines to think we might have sufficient provisions here at Fort Drane?"

MacDuff shrugged. "He lives but in hope, sir. We had believed supplies would be waiting at Fort King, but found that none are expected for at least a week, if not longer. The general requests only enough to allow him to return to Tampa Bay with his thousand men. Whatever you can spare is most urgently needed."

Wooster was not the least bit surprised by this turn of events. Washington had been warned that war was on the way, but had done absolutely nothing to prepare for it. "And what does the general intend to do with his thousand men once they reach Fort Brooke?"

A sly grin fell across the lieutenant's face. "He intends, sir, for the war to be over. He will march for the ford of the Withlacoochee and invade the enemy strongholds. With luck, sir, he will meet the Seminoles and put an end to this uprising."

"Well, I hope he finds the crossing easier than we did, though I suspect he'll get no farther." Wooster looked at the two letters MacDuff had handed him. One had been Gaines' request for provisions; the other had been a set of orders from the War Department assigning MacDuff to Wooster's Fourth Infantry Regiment. "Did General Gaines give any instructions as to your own disposition?"

"He said only that I am now under your command, and that he was glad to have delivered me safely to the seat of war."

Wooster smiled. He and Gaines had been close friends since 1814 and the war with Britain. Rising from his chair, he strode over to the window and looked across the parade ground. He shook his head in disbelief. Sergeant Bigelow, his thin frame leaning against a post, was making advances toward one of the settler women who had taken refuge in the fort. If her husband found out, there would no doubt be trouble. It wouldn't be the first time. The presence of the destitute refugee settlers among the soldiers was beginning to be a problem. Just three days ago, one of the civilians had murdered his wife after discovering she had been with one of the soldiers. Wooster had turned the murderer over to the civil authorities and had ordered one hundred lashes for the soldier. "Sergeant!" Bigelow spun around. "Find the commissary officer and bring him here!" The sergeant turned to say farewell to the lady. "On the double, Sergeant!" Wooster turned back to MacDuff. "The general may not be pleased with the quantity nor the quality, but he will have all that can be spared, and his men shall be eating no worse than we are."

Wooster moved to his chair and motioned for MacDuff to take a nearby seat. "Had any experience fighting Indians, Lieutenant?"

"A little, sir. Just a few small skirmishes. No scalps lost on either side."

"Well, we've already had two major battles here and neither one has gone our way, so any experience will be appreciated. As it is, your appearance is most fortuitous. Company 'B' is, at present, nearly without an officer. Captain Boyle left the army last year and, as you know, Lieutenant Smith was killed at Fort King along with Agent Thompson. Second Lieutenant Sparkes is a fine enough lad but is still recovering from the wounds he received at the Withlacoochee. So unless the War Department sees fit to send another captain, Company 'B' is yours."

"Thank you, sir. Where is the company posted?"

"They're here. Generally, they remain with me. The regiment is somewhat split at the moment, as I suspect it will be for some time to come. Companies 'A and E' are also here at Fort Drane, 'C' is at Fort King, 'D and G' are on the Texas border with Lt. Col. Foster, and 'F' is at Fort Brooke with Major Belmont. Bigelow is your sergeant, and he'll assemble the men for you. Sparkes is in the hospital and can bring you up to date on the paperwork."

MacDuff came to his feet and rendered a salute. "Thank you, sir. They shall serve you well."

"They shall certainly have the opportunity, Lieutenant. I fear there is going to be considerable toil and little glory in this war."

~~~

A few days later General Gaines was gazing across the Withlacoochee River, wishing he were on the other side. Captain Vance came to his side. "This is the same place we came to with General Clinch, sir. Never did find the ford. I see the Indians have destroyed the bridge the volunteers made."

Gaines nodded. "Well, let's find the ford before the damn redskins find us." He looked about and motioned to a pair of nearby officers. "Prince, take your company and look to the east. Izard, you look to the west." He then turned back to Vance. "The river is narrow enough that we could build another bridge, but I don't want to give away our presence by chopping down trees. Hopefully we'll find the ford before long."

The parties had been gone for no more than fifteen minutes when shots were heard toward the west. Gaines quickly dispatched Vance with a company of men to investigate and lend support if needed. After several anxious minutes the soldiers returned, carrying a bloody and screaming Lieutenant Izard. As the wounded man was set on the ground, a surgeon ran to his side. After examining the officer for a few minutes, the doctor slowly stood up. He looked at Gaines and shook his head. "The ball has entered his skull. There is nothing I can do for him."

Shots suddenly rang out from across the river. Soldiers ran to the bank and immediately began to return fire. Gaines began to pace up and down his line, shouting orders. "Take cover behind the trees, you fools! Choose your targets carefully!" As the minutes passed, the war whoops from the south side of the river became more numerous, the fire more intense. Gaines realized that exchanging shots across the river would accomplish nothing. He was also astonished by the number of Indians that seemed to be gathering on the other side of the river. "Fall back to the pines! Form a perimeter!"

He was now faced with a dilemma. The Indian force was large, certainly large enough to prevent his crossing the river. He could not go forward, and he *would not* go back. There was but one thing to do: "Break out the axes! Build a breastwork!" Gaines wasn't sure what would happen next. Would the Indians cross the river and attack his force? He hoped so, but doubted it. Rarely did red men take on whites in open combat. Would they place his breastwork under siege? It would be unusual, but certainly not impossible. It was also his greatest worry. His men only had three or four day's worth of minimal provisions.

The soldiers worked quickly, fearing that sooner or later the enemy would cross the river and attack them. A hundred axes cut into the tall pines, bringing them crashing to the ground. Limbs and branches were removed, and the trunks moved into a line. Supports were dug into the ground and the trees stacked one atop the other, parallel to the earth. It was a large enclosure, big enough to contain a thousand men, their horses, and the baggage wagons. Although only four or five logs high, the breastwork would be sufficient to repel any Indian attack.

The work was but partially completed when the Indians made their first assault. It was half-hearted and from a distance, more for the purpose of confining the white men than for killing them. Still, it was enough to tell Gaines what he needed to know: The Seminole force was formidable and was intent on keeping him under siege. He also knew that the Indians had no idea what to do next, other than prevent his army from leaving.

By nightfall the breastwork was almost complete. It was given the name Camp Izard in honor of the dying lieutenant. Periodically the doomed man would scream in agony, his mangled brain unaware of where he was or what had happened to him. The camp, filled with the hum of men speaking in low voices, would become suddenly silent, except for Izard's wailings. Everyone prayed that he would mercifully pass on, but no one had the heart to hasten the departure.

As moonlight replaced sunlight, Gaines paced back and forth through the camp. Suddenly he stopped and smiled. He saw a way out. "Lieutenant Prince! Get a piece of paper and a pencil! We need to send a runner to Wooster."

As the lieutenant took a seat and readied his pencil, Gaines dictated a short letter:

29 Feb. '36
Camp Izard

Wooster,
We have reached the crossing of the Withlacoochee opposite where Clinch had his battle. We were met by a large Seminole force, perhaps the entire Nation. We have erected a large breastwork and will remain within, in hopes of keeping the enemy concentrated. Proceed with all dispatch and with all available men to this place. Approach with stealth, and we may be able to crush the enemy between our forces. Our provisions are near gone. Bring what you can, so long as it does not cause delay.

Gaines

From inside the tent that served as the hospital at Fort Drane, Sparkes leaned forward in his chair, his attention focused on a loud noise outside. He could hear the colonel swearing from far outside the gates of the fort and realized the voice was getting closer. Hospital orderly Bemrose, who was examining the nearly-healed wound in Sparkes's side, offered some good-natured encouragement: "Not to worry, sir: You're already wounded, 'e won't 'urt you. Blimey! The old man's mad."

Sparkes had no idea what could have gone wrong. The colonel had received an urgent request from General Gaines and had spent the previous day in preparation for a rescue mission. Now, only an hour before departure, something had turned the colonel into a loaded cannon.

Storming into the building, Wooster threw a letter onto a table and paced back and forth about the room. Sparkes and Bemrose waited silently, having no idea what to say. Suddenly the colonel stopped and looked straight at Sparkes. "I am against dueling, Lieutenant, but for the good of the service, they really ought to allow those two to square off and end it here and now!"

Sparkes was more confused than ever. He motioned for Bemrose to hand him the letter. He read it once, realized he'd missed something, then read it again.

3 March 1836
Camp Barnwell, St. Johns River
Volusia, East Florida

To:
Col. Wm. A. Wooster
Commanding Fourth Infantry
Fort Drane, East Florida.

Colonel:
It has been brought to my attention that Maj. Gen. Gaines, Commanding Officer, Western Department, United States Army, has, contrary to orders, brought a force into the Territory for the purpose of engaging the Seminole Indians. I feel it my duty to inform you, so that you may be properly apprised of the chain of command, that the President of the United States, the honorable Andrew Jackson, has appointed yours truly, Maj. Gen. Winfield Scott, Commanding Officer, Eastern Department, United States Army, to conduct the war in Florida. As such, you will understand that Maj. Gen. Gaines is an interloper upon this command, and should immediately vacate the theatre of war.
In the event Maj. Gen. Gaines requests assistance from you or those under your command, such assistance is to be denied. As soon as preparations are complete, I will proceed to Fort Drane to take active command of the war. Hold your men in readiness and make all necessary preparations for the glorious

upcoming campaign.
    Yours, with the highest respect,

Winfield Scott, Major General,
Commanding, Army of Florida

Sparkes now understood Wooster's frustration. The two most influential men in the army had issued seriously conflicting orders. To disobey either one was unthinkable. He handed the letter to Bemrose. The little Englishman read, then began to chuckle.

Wooster was not amused. "I fail to see the humor in this situation, Mr. Bemrose."

"Aye, sir, but only because you're the fox caught a-tween the 'unter an' the 'ounds. For the rest of us common dogs, it does bring a wee smile." Sparkes also smiled, but only when the colonel's back was turned. Wooster paced a bit more then sat on a bench, shaking his head.

Gaines and Scott had been bitter rivals since the War of 1812, and their careers had closely paralleled each other's. Both had risen to prominence in battles along the Niagara frontier in 1814. Both had been severely wounded and had nearly lost their lives. Both had been promoted to Brigadier General on the same day. Both had received brevet promotions to Major General, the army's highest rank, within days of each other.

And that was where the similarity ended. Gaines was a man of few words and quick to take action. He loved the frontier life and the casual society that went along with it. Scott was a man who loved military pageantry and studied intensely the science of European warfare. By the end of the war with Britain, both Gaines and Scott had reached the top of the nation's military establishment. As far as the army was concerned, both men were equals. Gaines was given the Western Department, which dealt mainly with Indian uprisings, while Scott was handed the Eastern Department, which was concerned primarily with defending against potential European adversaries. Each man was where he belonged, but each man wanted to be in charge of it all. By 1821 only one man outranked them: Jacob Brown, who held the post of Commanding General.

When General Brown died in 1828, a simmering rivalry became a bitter feud. Scott declared himself senior to Gaines because his brevet rank of Major General had been awarded slightly earlier. But brevet rank carried a stigma: Because the holder of brevet rank did not receive the actual pay of that rank, it was viewed as being more honorary than real. Gaines countered that because his name was above Scott's on the alphabetical list of Brigadier Generals, he outranked Scott. Acrimonious letters filled the newspapers and opposing politicians took sides. Fed up with the petty squabbles, President John Quincy Adams bypassed the pair and gave the position to the next man in line, Alexander Macomb. The feud didn't end, however, it simply went underground.

And so it came to pass that Wooster found himself at the center of a feud he wanted no part of. Gaines, trapped at the Withlacoochee and low on food, had ordered Wooster to come to his aid. Wooster could not refuse. Scott, knowing his rival was also in the area, ordered Wooster not to render any aid to Gaines. It was an order Wooster could not ignore. The colonel was a man in the middle, and he didn't like it.

Despite it all, Wooster respected both men deeply, which only added to his frustration. As a young officer in 1814, Wooster had fought alongside both generals on the Niagara frontier. Both men had befriended him and both had taught him valuable lessons he would never forget. Under normal circumstances, he would have followed any order either man had given, no matter what the consequences.

Wooster looked at Sparkes. "Did they tell you how to handle this sort of situation at the Academy, Lieutenant?" Sparkes shook his head. The colonel then turned to Bemrose. "And do you, Mr. Bemrose, possess any strange potion that might make me appear dead until after these two lock horns and leave?"

"I do, sir, but the last time a bloke tried it, 'e never woke up."

There was a knock at the door. Standing at the opening was MacDuff. "Does the colonel have any instructions for the men?"

"Tell them to stand down." He shook his head slowly, not quite believing he had been placed in this position. "And tell that express rider to find another mount and to rest up as best he can. I'll have a response for General Scott shortly."

For the rest of the day, Wooster paced about Fort Drane, either in the officer's quarters or over the parade ground. He'd dispatched the express rider back to Scott with a plea to let him go to the aid of Gaines, but a response was days away. As much as he didn't like it, when it came to the conflicting orders, he was duty bound to obey the one from Scott, mainly because the president had placed Scott in charge of the war. There was also the practical matter that once Gaines left Florida, Wooster would be serving under Scott, perhaps until the war was over. He did, after all, have a career to protect.

When morning arrived, Sparkes found Wooster still pacing. As the colonel poured the lieutenant a cup of coffee, the door to the quarters opened and MacDuff walked in. "The men are assembled, sir. Any orders for the day?"

Wooster took a deep breath. The troops were awaiting his command. It all came down to something both Gaines and Scott had told him: Indecision kills. "Tell the men we depart for Camp Izard in an hour."

MacDuff turned crisply and went back to the waiting soldiers. As he strolled across the parade ground they could hear him shout, "Look lively, lads! We are but marchers for the marching day! Ah! We few, we drunken few. We band of bastards."

The colonel turned to Sparkes. "I can't leave a thousand men to starve or be slaughtered. To hell with Scott's orders. He had no knowledge of the situation when he wrote them." He smiled slightly. "Draft a letter to Scott. Tell him we proceed to the *rescue* of General Gaines, and that we are sure he would not wish us to delay when there are the lives of a thousand United States soldiers at stake. He won't be too upset if the record shows that we are going to save the helpless General. Gaines won't really care, so long as we show up before the Indians storm the breastworks."

Sparkes took pen in hand and wrote swiftly, but with all the flourish that the fastidious Scott would expect. Wooster looked it over, nodded his approval, and scratched his signature upon the paper. There had been no real choice: He could sit and wait for Scott, or he could go to war.

As the sun set on yet another day at Camp Izard, General Gaines reluctantly took a small piece of meat that was offered him by the cook. He wasn't bothered by the fact that it was horseflesh, but rather by the fact that it had once been part of his favorite horse. As a leader he knew that it was important to set the proper example. Two days after the last rations had been consumed, Gaines ordered that his own horse be the first to be slaughtered. The volunteer officers, many of whom truly loved their mounts, had no choice but to follow suit. Gaines had little sympathy for them. They had squandered their rations on the first two days of the siege, thus creating a shortage for everyone. Gaines hoped relief would soon arrive. There was talk of auctioning off the sergeant's dog.

Though he did not show it, the general was worried. Why hadn't Wooster come to his aid? He had sent three messengers; he could only hope that at least one had gotten through. It was now a week and a day since the army had become trapped at Camp Izard. The Indians had made several attempts to draw the soldiers out and had even set fire to the surrounding grass in hopes of forcing the situation. None of it had worked. Starvation, however, might force the army to act.

But what could Gaines do? Early in the siege he could have attacked the enemy or at least fought his way clear and retreated to Fort Drane. Now, with his men emaciated and a portion of his ammunition spent, he faced the very real possibility of his entire command being slaughtered by the Seminoles. Surrender was something Gaines could not even contemplate. Never before had an American army surrendered to an Indian nation, and he was not going to be the first general to do so. He wasn't all that sure what would happen in such a situation. The Indians would not take prisoners, and Gaines had no authority to negotiate a new treaty with the Seminoles. There was, in truth, nothing he could offer them, other than to retreat, but he could not guarantee that another general wouldn't continue the war. He was trapped.

~~~

The five chiefs stood apart from the other warriors, hoping to keep their differences to themselves. Halek Tustenuggee was the most positive as to what to do. "Storm their little pen. The walls are only three or four logs high. Even the smallest Seminole can jump over it. The white men are weak; they have nothing to eat but their horses. Great shall be the number of scalps we lift."

Micco Nopy was, as always, cautious. "We would lose many warriors, and the whites would come back stronger. We should just leave. The soldiers will not know we are gone, and they cannot chase us. We will be able to get the women, children, and old people far away before they can threaten us again."

Gator John shook his head. "We should let them skinny white boys go, then attack 'em when they is clear 'o the fort."

Asi-Yoholo had a more ambitious plan. "We should talk to the white men and make them sign a paper that gives us the land below this river. This will make the third time we have beaten them. They will have learned that the Seminole cannot be driven from his land."

Kachi-Hadjo bit his lip. There was, in reality, no good plan of action. "If we attack, as Halek Tustenuggee would have us do, we will lose too many warriors. The white men may be weak, but even a dying man's rifle can kill you. If we simply flee, as Micco Nopy suggests, the white men will soon follow us and destroy our homes. Gator John says to let them leave, but I do not think they will until more soldiers come to bring them food and protection. Such a time cannot be far off for we have seen at least two riders leave their camp. Asi-Yoholo believes they will sign a treaty allowing us to live in peace. They may, but as with all the white man's treaties, it will mean nothing." The other chiefs grumbled, but could not argue with Kachi-Hadjo's logic. "I believe we should withdraw to the other side of the river and leave the soldiers be. They know they have been defeated. Killing them will gain us nothing. If we return to the other side of the river, we will have time to prepare for the next time the white men come. If the Great Father truly wants peace, he will let us know."

The discussion, sometimes heated, lasted well into the night. No one could prevail. Finally, a decision was reached that seemed to please no one and everyone at the same time. As Kachi-Hadjo had suggested, most of the warriors would cross back to the south side of the river to begin preparations for a future defense. Micco Nopy would lead the women, children and old people to the Big Swamp, where they would be safe. Asi-Yoholo would hold a parley with the white men, more for the purpose of buying time and gathering intelligence then in hopes of coming to some agreement. If the white men wouldn't talk, then Tustenuggee could lead a nighttime assault on the breastwork. If the soldiers tried to flee, Gator John and his black warriors would be waiting to intercept them. It was a decision that had been made to please the council, not defeat the whites.

After the council broke up, Kachi-Hadjo began to realize why the Seminoles would never defeat the army. Although he had little use for the ways of the white man, at times he understood their value. The soldiers had many leaders, but no two were equal and there was always one headman who made the decisions and who everyone obeyed. It was different with the Indians. Micco Nopy may have been the head chief, but decisions were always made in council. For the most part, if a chief or a warrior didn't like the plan of the council, he didn't have to obey it. It was a great way to live, to be free to act as one wished, but it was no way to win a war.

~~~

Colonel Wooster and 300 men had been traveling through the night, moving as quietly as humanly possible. The procession stopped when it reached a small clearing near a slow moving creek, the same place where Clinch's army had gathered to tend their wounded after the battle on New Year's Eve. After appointing a detail to remain with the horses, provisions, and baggage, Wooster ordered his men to check their weapons and prepare to resume their march. It would be dawn when they arrived at the Withlacoochee, and he had no idea what he would find there.

When ready, the force moved on in total silence. The men's muskets were loaded and bayonets were fixed. To prevent accidental discharge, a small leather pouch covered the flints. The soldiers' white cross belts, always a conspicuous target, had been rubbed in the dirt to make them less visible in the moonlight. Wooster wanted his arrival to be a complete surprise.

Even in the dark, the path was easily followed. A thousand men had passed this way a little over a week before, clearing away the surrounding brush and trampling down the forest floor. Wooster's main concern was that the Indians might be guarding the path, expecting the arrival of reinforcements. He could only hope the Indian sentries were asleep.

After an hour had passed and the sun had risen enough to light the landscape, Wooster knew he was getting close to Gaines's camp. Suddenly a shot rang out. The colonel had no choice but to assume that an Indian sentry had spotted them. Without hesitation, he drew his sword and yelled, "Charge!" It had been prearranged that if they were spotted anywhere near the camp, the army would immediately go on the offensive. What they would find when they emerged from the woods was anybody's guess, but at least they would not be caught standing still, waiting to be shot.

As the bugler sounded the charge, the soldiers entered the clearing, running and shouting, looking for targets. Wooster saw a group of Indians retreating into the morning mist. They were almost out of range and nearly into the surrounding forest. He ordered the foremost company to open fire. The men stopped momentarily, aimed, and fired. It was impossible to tell if they had hit anyone, but at that distance, it was unlikely that they had done any real harm.

Wooster saw a number of men leap over the breastwork and come running toward him, their arms waving. He recognized one of them as Captain Vance, the artillery officer who had been with them during Clinch's battle. Wooster ordered his men to come to a halt. He was shocked at the sight of Vance, who appeared to have lost at least fifteen pounds. Vance stopped, out of breath. "Thank God you're here, sir." He then looked toward where the Indians had fled. "The danger's past, sir. We were holding a parley."

The colonel ordered his men to take up defensive positions within the surrounding woods. He did not want the enemy to return. Runners were sent back to the rest of the troop, ordering them to come up with the provisions. He then went into the camp to see General Gaines.

The general was sitting on a campstool when Wooster approached. Gaines, like everyone else in the camp, looked exceptionally thin. He didn't bother to get up; he just waived Wooster to a nearby stump. "Welcome to Camp Izard, Colonel. You just missed the parley."

"My apologies for running them off, sir."

"No matter. If they're sincere, they'll be back. I wasn't all that convinced they were serious in the first place. Hope you brought some food with you."

"Mostly cattle, but also some corn and bread and forage for the horses. Whatever I could gather quickly."

"Well, we certainly need it. The men are too weak to march at the moment. We'll let them fatten up for a day or two then make for Fort Drane. Any word on supplies?"

"They've arrived at Fort King, sir." Wooster then took a deep breath. "And General Scott will be there soon."

"Gave old Fuss and Feathers the command, did they?"

"Yes, sir." Wooster looked about. "Any casualties, sir?"

Gaines nodded. "A few. Worst loss was Izard. He approached the river and one of the damn redskins put a ball right through his skull. Poor man lasted for six days, crying out and wailing like a madman." Gaines shook his head. "He was a damn good officer, a likeable young man."

"Yes, sir, he was. Every fallen soldier was a good man."

10

March 25, 1836
Ft. Drane
Florida Territory

To:
Mrs. David Kilgour
Cincinnati, Ohio

Dearest Emily,

My sincerest apologies for not having put pen to paper sooner. I am happy to report that by the Grace of God my health is much improved. My chest wound is well healed and will leave but a small scar. The wound in my arm never was much to speak of and has long since ceased to bother me.

All is in a flood of activity here in preparation for the upcoming campaign. Genl. Scott has come to Florida with over 5,000 men. Most are volunteers, and all seem anxious for the march to begin. With us here at Ft. Drane are mostly the Volunteers from Georgia. Waiting at Tampa are several companies of regulars and quite a few Alabamians. Coming from the east will be a large contingent of S. Carolina Vols. and a few regulars. There is little doubt that such a large force is more than adequate to subdue the enemy, which cannot bring more than a thousand warriors to the field at one time.

Perhaps the only man who did not welcome the arrival of Genl. Scott was Genl. Gaines. As you may know, the pair are old enemies. Indeed, from the appearance of the area around Ft. Drane, it might have seemed as if the nation had two armies. To the east of the fort was the camp of Genl. Scott, while to the west was that of Genl. Gaines. Not once did I see an officer of one camp pass to the other. Were it not for the presence of the two generals, many of the junior officers would have been happy to have socialized with old friends from the other departments, but just as with Whigs and Democrats, the lines are drawn, and reasonable men dare not cross it. In truth, most of the senior officers under Genl.

Scott are Whigs, whilst those under Genl. Gaines are Democrats, so now you see how it is: Between the pride of old soldiers and the stubbornness of politicians, we waste more time waging war amongst ourselves than against the Indians. Not to speak ill of Genl. Gaines in any way, but it was certainly a relief when he and his followers departed.

Genl. Scott's plan appears quite likely to bring the war to a swift conclusion. Genl. Eustis will depart from Volusia, on the St. Johns, and drive west to Peliklikaha, a Seminole Negro village to the east of the Cove. Col. Lindsay will move north from Tampa Bay and take position at Chocochatti, a large Indian town south of the Cove. These two columns will prevent the Indians from escaping the Cove. The "Cove," I ought to tell you, is the area west of the Withlacoochee River, which is north of Tampa Bay. It is a land of numerous swamps, lakes, islands, and peninsulas, and is where the Seminoles have built their strongholds. On the day when Genl. Eustis and Col. Lindsay are in place, our column, commanded by Col. Wooster and accompanied by Genl. Scott, will enter the Cove from the north and drive the Seminoles into the hands of the other two columns. Thus surrounded, the Indians will have no choice but to surrender.

Have no fear for my safety on this campaign, dear sister. Our force is overwhelming and, God willing, we shall not be surprised again. With any fortune at all, my next letter shall be informing you of the end of this sad little war and hopefully of my departure from this most unpleasant of territories.

Love always, and my best to David and the children,

Your most affectionate brother,
Jacob

Sparkes set his pen down; the daily weather report for Fort Drane would have to wait. He was out of ink and about to fall asleep. Colonel Wooster had taken every available man on the mission to relieve General Gaines, leaving Sparkes in command of a handful of sick and wounded men. Few of the men were fit to do anything more than stand sentry duty, so very little actual labor was taking place. All in all, it had been a boring three days.

It wasn't much of a fort to protect. In truth, it was nothing more than a hastily erected wall of pickets around the main buildings of one of General Clinch's several Florida plantations. The closest thing to a blockhouse was the two-story overseer's house, and most people considered the fort as nothing more than a post erected to protect the general's sugar works. Whatever the reason for its initial construction, the post had turned into the main staging area for the war.

The lieutenant leaned back in his chair and closed his eyes. Even though it was not yet noon, it would have been so easy to fall asleep. He yawned, and his head began to nod. The faint sound of drums and horns fell upon his ears. It was a strange way to begin a dream, but he didn't mind. Suddenly there was the sound of shouting and someone running up the house steps. Sparkes looked up to see Bemrose standing in the doorway, a sly smile on his face. "Blimey, sir, you've got to see this!"

"See what, Mr. Bemrose?" He then realized that the music he had been listening to while drifting off to sleep had not been in his head. Bemrose nodded toward the second story of the building. Both men quickly climbed the stairs and looked out the window. Sparkes's eyes widened. "Call the men to order, damn it! It's General Scott!" He then took another look out the window. It was a sight to behold. There was the general, riding at the front of the column, sitting tall in the saddle and attired in his dress uniform, followed by a small but well-equipped marching band. Beyond the band came a series of wagons, followed by what seemed to be an endless line of soldiers.

By the time Scott's column had gotten close enough to the fort to necessitate the opening of the gate, all the men who were healthy enough to bear arms were assembled on the parade ground. First through the portal was Scott, still on horseback, followed by a contingent of officers of every rank. The general was the tallest of the officers, made taller by his large cocked hat topped with a row of white feathers. To the east of the fort the troops, numbering well over a thousand, began to set up camp. As Scott and the other officers dismounted, a wagon came into the fort. Sparkes, standing at attention in front of his men, noticed a young woman sitting at the front of the wagon. Then his eyes widened: it was Maria. She was a bit taller and with a slight bosom, but the face and hair were the same.

As Scott approached Sparkes's small group of soldiers, the lieutenant snapped a salute. "Welcome to Fort Drane, General. Second Lieutenant Jacob Sparkes in temporary command, sir."

Scott passed a critical eye over the men. "Is this your entire command, Lieutenant?"

Sparkes swallowed. The general did not look happy. "Yes, sir, with the exception of those who are in the hospital. Colonel Wooster left only the sick and wounded."

Scott looked the men over again. "Damn fine group of men, Lieutenant. Damn fine. I always have the highest regard for those wounded in battle, I do. Were you the officer who took a ball in chest at the Withlacoochee?"

"Yes, sir."

"Are you healing satisfactorily?"

"Yes, sir." Sparkes began to relax.

Scott nodded his approval. "Good. We'll soon have a glorious battle with these red devils. I wouldn't want you to miss it." He looked about the fort. "You may dismiss the men." Sparkes nodded to Bemrose, who shouted out the order. "Show me to the hospital, Lieutenant. I always make it a point to visit the wounded."

Maria approached as the general began to turn away. "Lieutenant Sparkes, it is so good to see you again. Are you still troubled by your wounds?"

Sparkes bowed slightly and kissed the hand that was offered. "No, Miss Maria, I am near fully recovered. Your father had to leave *someone* in command, and I suppose I was the least useful."

It was a short visit to the hospital. Most of the wounded were recovering nicely, while those who were in the most danger were those suffering from disease. No matter how deadly the battles might be, it would always be the Florida climate that would prove more deadly.

After a short inspection of the fort's facilities and a conversation relating to Sparkes's needs as to medical supplies and provisions, Scott and his retinue proceeded to their camp to oversee the erection of the tents and the care of their horses. From one of the wagons, a pair of soldiers unloaded Maria's baggage and brought it into the overseer's house. As they left there was an awkward moment of silence as Sparkes, Maria, and Bemrose stared at each other, unsure of what to say.

It was Bemrose who finally said what he and Sparkes were thinking. "Blimey, miss, the old man's gonna go off like an overloaded 'owitzer!"

Maria dismissed the notion with a wave of her hand. "On hush now, Johnny, he'll do nothing of the sort. I'm sure he'll be very glad to see me."

"Aye, miss, I'm sure 'e will, right after 'e tosses me and the lieutenant into the stockade for letting you get off that wagon. I'd best get over to the 'ospital and fetch me gear."

Sparkes was confused. "Why are you . . . ?"

Bemrose rolled his eyes. "Begging your pardon, Lieutenant sir, but I'll not be the one to tell the colonel that you and Miss Maria were the only two people spending the night in this house. I'll probably have to tell him I slept at the foot of the stairs with a loaded musket."

Both Maria and Sparkes were shocked. "Mr. Bemrose!"

"Begging both your pardons, but Lieutenant Sparkes can't leave you unguarded 'ere at night, an' I can't leave you unguarded 'ere alone with Lieutenant Sparkes. Not that I expect anything the least bit improper would go on, but it don't matter a wee bit what I think, it's what your father will think that concerns me, it is."

Sparkes and Maria both knew the young Englishman was right. Although there was absolutely no romantic connection between them, the colonel's mind might well invent one. It was best to let Bemrose play the chaperon. Sparkes motioned toward the staircase. "Your father's room is up there. Mr. Bemrose and I will be sleeping downstairs."

Bemrose nodded. "Aye, an' me with me loaded musket."

They all laughed slightly before falling into another awkward silence. Maria changed the subject. "Your wounds, Mr. Sparkes. Are they healing well?"

"Very satisfactorily, Miss Maria. Dr. Weightman and Mr. Bemrose have been most attentive."

She then said something shocking, at least to the lieutenant's ears. "May I see the wound?"

"I, uh, I . . . I don't think that would be proper, Miss Maria."

She shook her head and smiled. "Mr. Sparkes, ever since I was a little girl I would accompany my mother when she visited the sick and injured. She felt that as an officer's wife, it was her duty to look after the men in my father's command. After her passing, I vowed to do the same. Since this dreadful war has started, not a day has passed that I have not visited the hospital in St. Augustine. Now that I am here, the sick and wounded at Fort Drane shall receive equal attention. Are you not among those wounded?"

"The wound is near healed, Miss Maria."

She again shook her head. "I shall judge that for myself, Mr. Sparkes. Lift the shirt, please."

Sparkes squirmed. "Miss Maria . . ."

"Is the wound in your chest, Mr. Sparkes?" He nodded sheepishly. "My mother once said, 'If it's above the belt or below the knees you needn't worry, dear. There's nothing there that's dangerous.'"

Bemrose finally settled the matter. "You may as well bare it, sir. She'll give you no peace until she looks upon it with her own eyes."

Sparkes raised his shirt reluctantly. Maria's hand moved gently over the reddened flesh that surrounded the last signs of the wound in his side. A curious look came over her face. "A small little musket ball caused such a large wound?"

Sparkes shook his head. "Most of the damage was done by the good Dr. Weightman as he probed for the ball. He had little choice. Had the ball remained, it might well have festered."

She laughed. "If the Seminoles do not kill you, the surgeon surely shall."

Sparkes held his breath as her finger slowly outlined the scar that was forming. She seemed enthralled by the healing process. "Why do we heal so swiftly? Why does our flesh not remain as it is, leaving a gaping hole?"

"Because God intended it so."

She gave a swift shake of her head. "That is no answer. How can we learn the secrets of Nature if we attribute all the mysteries of life to the incomprehensible will of God? You might as well say that the dog barks because that is what dogs do."

Sparkes now understood how Maria had managed to convince General Scott to bring her along on the march from St. Augustine to Fort Drane. He could imagine the conversation between the tall, commanding Scott and the delicate young woman. Scott would have given Maria every logical reason why she should not travel with his force across the hostile territory. Maria would have politely refuted every argument. The general wouldn't have stood a chance.

~~~

The march from Camp Izard back to Fort Drane had been a long, slow trek for General Gaines and his force. The men were still weak from the lack of food and there were several wounded or sickened soldiers who could not be rushed. In truth, Gaines had been in no hurry. He had known General Scott would be awaiting their arrival, and Gaines wasn't looking forward to the confrontation.

As Fort Drane came into view, Gaines looked at Colonel Wooster, who walked by his side. The colonel smiled slightly. Neither man was surprised at what they saw. Arrayed in front of Fort Drane was a military band, standing at attention and attired in dress uniforms. When the band caught site of the approaching column, the drum major raised his baton and the music started. Gaines did his best to ignore them. Wooster gave the bandleader a slight nod of acknowledgement as he passed.

"I suppose he brought his traveling library," Gaines said in a low voice that only Wooster could hear.

Wooster nodded. "And his French wines."

Gaines laughed. "I don't suppose he'll be offering *me* any of that."

A small city of tents stood beyond the musicians. The fact that they were not arranged in neat rows signified they were the dwellings of the volunteers. Many of the volunteers began to gather, staring as the regulars marched by in neat columns, tired and worn, but still with a military bearing. It had been two weeks since Gaines and his men had left Fort King. All of the men showed the effects of over a week without sufficient food. A few, too weak to walk, were carried on litters.

The regulars were followed by the Louisiana Volunteers. They walked in loose groups, mostly by companies, and occasionally chatted amongst themselves. There appearance was more haggard than the regulars. Lacking the discipline of the regulars, they had refused to ration their supplies at the beginning of the siege. As a result, they had suffered worse when the food ran out.

Wooster had dispatched MacDuff and his company ahead with instructions for those at the fort to prepare a hearty meal for the incoming men. One by one, the Georgia Volunteers left their camp, tin plate in hand, and approached the men from Louisiana. Before long, each man would be eating well and be in the company of one of his fellow Americans. The colonel felt good.

The regulars marched through the gate and into Fort Drane. They were greeted first by three cheers from the fort's garrison and the regulars who had accompanied Scott, then by the sight of tables laden with food. Gaines turned to Wooster. "Colonel, you may dismiss the men." No sooner were the words out than the men broke ranks and headed for the tables. Gaines and Wooster then turned toward the overseer's house. Standing in front of it was a group of officers. At the center of the group was General Scott, still attired in his dress uniform. There was a smile of satisfaction on his face. He obviously enjoyed seeing Gaines return in defeat.

Gaines looked anything but defeated. "General Scott: It is a pity you came all the way from the comforts of New York with so many men just to conclude negotiations with the Seminoles."

"Negotiations, General? The battle has yet to be fought. Not fought at all, I would say."

Gaines was putting on his best face. As with Clinch, he would not admit that the Seminoles had bested him. "Come now, General. I have met the enemy and they have agreed to cease hostilities if allowed to remain below the Withlacoochee. White men will never live in the south of Florida. Grant the Seminoles a reservation in the southern swamps, and they will cease to be a threat. I see little reason to pursue this war any farther."

Scott cast the notion aside. "*You* may see no reason to continue the war, General, but President Jackson does. My orders are to crush the Seminoles and to accept nothing short of unconditional surrender. No conditions, General. Every last one of them shall be removed from Florida. Every last one, I say."

An argument might have erupted, had not a small feminine form stepped forward. Wooster stood in shock. The last face he had expected to see was that of his daughter. The girl then ran to her father and threw her arms around him. "Father! It has been so long! Nearly a year!"

Wooster wasn't sure if he were pleased or not. He was truly happy to see her, but he had certainly not given her permission to come to Fort Drane. Yet with so many other officers around, there was little he could say. "This is, my dear, a pleasant surprise. How did you get here?"

Scott answered the question. "Brought her with me, I did. St. Augustine is full of scallywags, it is. Full of them. Not a proper place for a proper young lady, I say. The child should be with her father. A child should always be with her father, I say."

Sensing a way to avoid an embarrassing confrontation with Scott, Gaines stepped forward and took Maria's hand. "Dear child, how you have blossomed! Close to a full-grown woman now." He smiled at Wooster. "You had better keep a sharp watch over this fair child, Colonel. She's bound to catch the eye of some young lieutenant." Wooster took a quick glance at the assembled officers, looking for Sparkes. He found him, almost hiding at the back of the group.

Maria curtsied as the general kissed her hand. "My pleasure to see you again, General. Will you be with us long?"

"No longer than necessary, my dear. My mission here is finished. I will leave it to my esteemed colleague to take care of the final details." Scott huffed, but said nothing. Gaines came to attention. "Duty calls, my dear. I have sick men in need of attention. May my staff and I have the pleasure of your company at our evening meal today? The food and the company may be simple, but the conversation will not be the least bit stuffy, I assure you."

"It would be my pleasure, General."

"Excellent! I shall send an officer to escort you at the appointed hour." He turned back to the assembled officers and looked straight at Scott. "Good day, gentlemen. Give my best to Micco Nopy *and* the President, when next you see them."

Scott huffed again as the general passed out of earshot. "War is over! Ha! The war shall not be over until we say it is, Colonel. Crush the red devils, we will. Crush them."

Wooster was not so sure, but held his tongue. "It is good to see you again, General. I thank you for bringing my daughter. I should have sent for her earlier, but our lack of troops had prevented my being able to provide an adequate escort."

"My pleasure, Colonel. Pleasure indeed."

As Wooster and a few other officers stepped onto the porch, an old slave who had been sweeping the floor was forced to step aside. MacDuff waved the back of his hand at the old man. "Out o' the way, boy."

The colonel was curious as to how Scott intended to crush the Seminoles. "Your plan of attack, sir. Have you completed the arrangements?"

"Yes I have, Colonel, I certainly have. Quite simple, really. Elegant, I would say. Yes, elegant." The general then began to lay out his plan, describing in great detail how the two columns under Lindsay and Eustis would move in from the south and east, and how he and Wooster would then come from the north, trapping the hapless Indians in a three-way vise. Wooster nodded, voicing his agreement at every important point. Inside, his stomach churned. The plan would never work.

~~~

Later in the evening, as the fort's garrison was retiring for the night, the old slave who had been sweeping the floor walked towards the woods, a bucket in hand. As the darkness of the forest enveloped him, he stopped to empty the bucket. From behind a tree stepped another black man, this one dressed in Seminole clothing. The two spoke for a few minutes, clasped hands, and parted. As the slave returned to the fort, Gator John moved deeper into the woods.

11

To:
Mrs. David Kilgour
Cincinnati, Ohio

My dear sister,

   It is with a sad and angry heart that I write to tell you that Genl. Scott's "Grand Campaign" has been a miserable and utter failure. We left this place on the 26th of March with full enthusiasm for the glorious battle ahead, with our men in precise military order and accompanied by the general's marching band. Confidence was in our hearts, for no savage nation had ever stood against so large and well-equipped a force as had been gathered here in Florida. Remarkably, such is still the case, for no savage nation presented itself to us. They simply fled without giving battle, melting into the impenetrable swamps and hammocks. The difference in the enemy's attitude is best exemplified by the fact that we crossed the Withlacoochee with ease and suffered no challenge, this at the same place where I received my wounds on New Year's Eve and where Genl. Gaines had been held under siege for over a week.

   The disappointment is, I must admit, my fault entirely. I was so taken with the grandeur of Genl. Scott and his enthusiasm that I failed to see that which was right before my eyes. When I expressed my grand expectations for the decisive battle that would soon take place on the banks of the Withlacoochee, Col. Wooster quietly informed me that there would be no battle. With our forces having met such resolute resistance near that very place twice before, I refused to believe him. I could not imagine that the savages would so easily abandon the ground they had fought so desperately to defend only a few weeks earlier. I should have known. More than once the Colonel has told me, "We fight to conquer, the Indian fights to *survive."*

As for the Colonel, he was not the most jovial companion during our travels, finding himself under the command of a militia general of the Georgia Mounted Vols. For a career officer of twenty-four years continuous service to be commanded by a politically appointed state officer is insulting, especially for one as skilled as Col. Wooster. What made this situation especially galling was that Genl. Dill had served under the Colonel during the Seminole War of 1818 as a <u>sergeant</u>! Mind you, Genl. Dill is a fine gentleman and an adequate soldier and was careful not to insult the Colonel's pride in any way, yet there was much muttering under the Colonel's breath, along with the use of a number of terms that are not fit to place in a letter to my sister. To be fair, however, most of the Colonel's invective was reserved for those astute members of Congress who allow such a system to exist.

Upon crossing the Withlacoochee, Genl. Scott split the column, one wing to proceed to the west of the cove and establish a fort, and the other, ours, to move down the west bank of the river, to the east of the Cove. Both wings were to meet at Chocochatti, where Col. Lindsay was to be waiting, and where the Seminoles were supposed to oblige us by making a stand. We passed through the Cove with no resistance until the morning of the 31st. On this day there occurred the only significant fight of the entire campaign, one in which your brother played his small part.

We were proceeding in tight formation along a path through a somewhat open grove of large oak trees, a company of Georgia horsemen in the lead. Ever watchful, the Colonel directed me to ride up and warn Genl. Dill to be wary of the hammock to his right, fearing an enemy ambush. Suddenly, before I could even spur my mount, rifle fire erupted from the hammock. Several of the volunteers were slain, a number were wounded, and more would have suffered had the hammock been closer to the path. As expected, the Georgians scattered in confusion, being undisciplined, as volunteers tend to be.

The Colonel, with no thought of speaking to the General, instantly ordered a bayonet charge. Being out of musket range, we did not waste our loads, but ran at our best speed until we entered the hammock. The Colonel, MacDuff, and I, being mounted, rode ahead of the men, our swords drawn, and our paths often crossing, so that we would present a more difficult target to the enemy. The red devils must have been truly surprised at our swiftness (or fearful of MacDuff and his broadsword), for all we saw were their fleeing backs. Having routed our foes, we could have stopped, but the Colonel would not hear of it. On we pressed, passing through the hammock and entering a swamp, with water often to our waists. Still, we did not stop. For close to two miles we ran, not stopping until we reached the banks of the river. As is always the case, the slippery redskins had managed to disappear completely. I must admit, dear Emily, that there is a certain thrill to leading such a charge, to putting oneself in front of the enemy and forcing him to *flee. The thoughts of personal danger leave you, and you feel naught but pure exhilaration. I now better understand why Grandfather spoke so warmly of his years with General Washington.*

Our battle over, we continued on for another two days with no further sign of hostiles. On the 2nd we arrived at Chocochatti, but found it deserted and with no sign of Col. Lindsay. Genl. Scott, with the other column, had arrived the previous day and was quite perplexed as to Lindsay's whereabouts. The good colonel arrived the following day, five days after the date which had been appointed him. It appears there had been considerable trouble with the Alabama Volunteers, mainly over the size of the whiskey ration, and their progress from Ft. Brooke was not what it should have been. Col. Lindsay also reported that except for burnt-out bridges, he had seen no sign of the red men, which is not to be marveled at, when one considers that in order to communicate our advance to the other columns, Genl. Scott ordered a cannon to be fired at noon every day of the march—as if the musicians had not given the savages warning enough!

Genl. Scott now decided that the Seminoles must be gathered between Chocochatti and Peliklikaha, where Genl. Eustis was supposedly waiting. Abandoning Chocochatti, which we burnt, we headed northeast towards Peliklikaha. Col. Wooster could not imagine why the Indians should be waiting for us there, but Genl. Scott could not be deterred. He had come for a great battle and was determined to have it. As it happened, the only force we met was that of Genl. Eustis, proceeding to Ft. Brooke after having found Peliklikaha deserted and not an Indian in the neighborhood. They, too, had been delayed, not by bickering over whiskey, but by unmapped lakes and sand hills in the center of the peninsula, which were able to bog the wagons down as surely as any swamp. As with all of us, they had seen little sign of the enemy. Being short on rations, we all turned our direction toward Ft. Brooke, where we arrived on the 7th of this month.

After little rest and with minimal provisions, Genl. Scott once again put us on the march. Col. Lindsay was to scout the area around Tampa Bay in hopes of finding at least some enemy, whilst Genl. Eustis, accompanied by Genl. Scott, was to return to Volusia, hopefully encountering the Seminoles along the route. This I doubt that any serious action will take place, and I suppose the valiant Genl. Scott is resting easy in St. Augustine as I write. Our unhappy little band was to once again pass through the Cove, destroy what Indian resources we might find, and return to Ft. Drane.

This we did, and without much incident, which was fortunate, for I suffered much from a fever whilst on the march, and the passage was often hampered by cold air and heavy rains. On the 19th we arrived at Ft. Cooper, which Genl. Scott had earlier erected deep within the Cove. The garrison was quite thrilled to see us, our arrival having lifted a siege that had been in place by the Seminoles for near two weeks. We then proceeded here to Ft. Drane, arriving this morning. The temerity of these savages is best shown by the fact that they had the gall to attack even this post, one of the strongest in the territory. They inflicted little damage and but one minor casualty, for which we were thankful, for among the occupants is the Colonel's daughter, Maria. (Lt. Sykes informs me that she is quite handy with a pistol.)

So it is that over 5,000 well-provisioned men have tramped through this god-forsaken swampland in a futile attempt to engage a foe that will not stand and fight. How many millions of our national treasure has been wasted on this campaign, one cannot imagine. Colonel Wooster is thoroughly disgusted, as am I. Genl. Scott may well be a great tactician when it comes to fighting the likes of Wellington or Napoleon, but he knows nothing of Indians.

Having now arrived at Ft. Drane, we find that we are once again to take up the line of march. Genl. Scott, having decided that all interior posts will be unhealthy during the summer, has ordered that this post be abandoned. As soon as we are rested and the post's property can be packed and loaded upon wagons, we are to once again cross the Cove and remove to Ft. Brooke. So you see, the army is in retreat and the Seminoles shall rule the interior for months to come. We are, I feel, whipt again.

If all this were not bad news enough, we have been informed that General Call, who waited on the north bank of the Withlacoochee whilst we were being attacked on New Year's Eve, has now been appointed Governor of the Territory, and will most likely be given command of the war upon Genl. Scott's departure. I fear, dear Emily, that we are in for a long war, and if I am to remain here throughout, my end must come eventually, either by rifle ball or by disease. Pray for me.

My apologies for such a long and tedious letter. Hopefully, should we reach Ft. Brooke in good health, my spirits will recover and my next letter will be one that will bring a smile to your face. Love to all,

Jacob

Major General Thomas Jesup watched the summer sun set behind the forested, rolling hills of northern Alabama. As the bright orange light flashed through the tops of the trees he pondered his situation. He had attained the highest rank in the army, yet he was still receiving senseless orders from inept superiors. He shrugged. Unless your name was Andrew Jackson, there would always be inept superiors. It was the nature of life in the military. The only person who knew how to do things properly was the man who inhabited the mirror. Incompetence started at the top, with politicians harboring grand ideas and simple stupidity. The incompetence filtered down the chain of command, finding its way to officers who sought glory in the most inglorious manner, by slaughtering their fellow humans and destroying the homes of the helpless. In the end, it all fell upon the shoulders of the simple soldier, who followed orders without question and gave his life for a purpose no one really understood.

Jesup smiled. In truth, he could not complain. He had been the army's Quartermaster General for almost eighteen years, and it had been an enjoyable position. He was a man who loved efficiency and orderliness. Keeping the army organized was a challenge he thrived on. It was also one of the few positions in the army that allowed him to live a quiet, settled life without fear of having to uproot his family every few years and move to a duty station at the god-forsaken fringes of the civilized world. Whenever he tired of life in the capital he could declare the need for an inspection tour and leave the tedium of Washington City behind.

This time, however, the mission was quite different. The Creek Indians of eastern Alabama were resisting removal to the west, perhaps inspired by the successes of their cousins in Florida. With Gaines busy along the Mexican frontier and Scott bogged down in Florida, President Jackson found himself running out of two-star generals. Other than Commanding General Macomb, who *never* left Washington, Jesup was the only one left. The fact that he was a staff officer and not a field officer was of little concern. Jesup had seen bloody fighting during the war with England and had distinguished himself in battle. At any rate, it was a short-term assignment. The Florida War was slowing down for the summer and as soon as matters were secure down there, Scott would take over the war against the Creeks.

Fortunately (or unfortunately, as it now appeared to Jesup), Scott had concluded his Florida campaign sooner than expected and was now in Georgia, ready to take command. Always the grand tactician, Scott laid out a plan that called for two columns to converge upon the Creeks from opposite directions, much like the plan he had used in Florida, but with one less column. Jesup feared the result would be the same, but kept that view to himself. Scott was, after all, the senior officer. The new plan called for Jesup to remain in northeastern Alabama and take command of the forces there, while Scott gathered his own forces in southwestern Georgia. When all was in readiness, the two columns would move toward each other and surround the Creek villages and towns.

And that had led to Jesup's present problem. He was now in Alabama and ready to commence operations, but Scott was still in preparation, weeks from being ready to take the field. Jesup could have relaxed and waited, but events were not going to permit it. He had received word that the Creek warriors were gathering nearby and preparing to attack several white settlements. Jesup could wait on Scott or he could go on the offensive. There was really little choice: The settlements had to be protected.

The general turned to his chief of staff. "Colonel Stanton, send an express rider to General Scott, informing him that we are commencing offensive operations. Present hostilities give us no choice."

Stanton smiled. "We'd best not move too swiftly, sir. We may end the war before the general is ready to start it. He might not be amused."

"And if I stand idly by while homesteaders are slaughtered, the president will be even less amused. President Jackson holds a grudge for a lifetime; General Scott will get over it in a year or two."

Stanton nodded. "There is another thing to consider, sir: If we end the war too swiftly, the president might put *you* in charge of the Florida War."

Jesup laughed. "Then you had better pray that Governor Call rounds up the Seminoles this autumn. Otherwise . . . Well, I hear Florida is quite lovely in the winter. No snow, warm breezes from the tropics, friendly natives."

~~~

Even in the midst of war it was a festive occasion. The warriors drank and bragged about their exploits. The women tended the cook pots and chatted endlessly. In an open field a bare tree had been erected, a notch carved into the bark near its top. In the field beneath the tree young men and women played, fighting joyfully over a small leather ball. The men and boys carried cupped sticks, which they used to pass the ball to one another or to hurl it toward the notch in the treetop. The young women and girls used their hands to accomplish the same task. The fact that no one hit the target seemed not to matter. It was an opportunity to be carefree and to mingle with members of the opposite sex. As the men and women reached and wrestled for the small ball, they often tumbled on the ground, giving them an opportunity for a fleeting intimate contact. It was obvious that the ball game was not the only sport being played.

Nearby was the remnants of a large campfire with a small whiff of smoke drifting skyward. Around it danced a line of men and women moving snake-like around the fire. The old medicine man at the head of the line shook a rattle and led the chant. The women wore turtle shells filled with small stones on their ankles, which supplied the rhythm for the dance. Occasionally a couple that had been observing either the ball game or the dance would leave the area and disappear into the surrounding brush.

This year the Green Corn Ceremony had been especially festive. There had been many battles with the whites, and most all had been counted as victories. True, the Seminoles had been driven from their homes in the Cove and the Alachua Prairie, but that had been expected, and with the whites having abandoned many of their forts, the Seminoles were returning to those homes. The Indians were feeling proud. They had fought to remain in Florida, and in that they had been successful. The festivities had also been an opportunity for the scattered bands and clans of the tribe to reunite. The army had forced many of the Seminoles to take refuge in hidden hammocks or swamps and to avoid the more exposed pathways. Families that had been separated were once again able to come together without fear of the white man's army.

There was also much tribal business to be discussed. In order to replenish their supplies of powder and lead, the Indians needed to trade with the Cuban and Bahamian fisherman who came to the islands in the south of the peninsula. The elders needed to hold court, to decide disputes between tribal members. Supplies of salt and corn and other essentials, having become scarce because of the loss of many of their villages, needed to be fairly rationed. Yes, it was a festive and busy Green Corn Ceremony, but it was also a somber one. They had lost many warriors in battle, many of their blacks had been captured and sent into slavery, and a large number of their homes, cattle, and horses had been lost to the whites. For every shout of joy, there was an accompanying tear of sadness.

Kachi-Hadjo sat outside his temporary shelter, his daughter Ki-tee nestled under his arm. He had not seen her since the families had been forced to leave the Cove. Eight summers had passed since her birth, six since her mother had gone to the ancestors. There were many reasons Kachi-Hadjo had chosen to fight the white men, but foremost among them was his daughter. Yes, he wanted to protect his homeland. Yes, he hated the white settlers who insulted the red men, and yes, he despised the white officials who lied and cheated the Indians, but most of all, he simply wanted to protect Ki-tee.

It was unusual for a widowed Seminole father to remain so close to his child. By custom, when a Seminole woman died, her sisters, brothers, or other members of her clan would raise the child. The father, who had been living with his wife's clan, would go back to living with his own clan, and the close ties would eventually fade. Kachi-Hadjo had broken with tradition and had remained with his wife's clan so that he could be near Ki-tee. The move had caused some talk, but no one had possessed the nerve to question Kachi-Hadjo's motives.

The girl looked up into her father's eyes. "Is the war over, father? Can we build our lodge in peace this winter?"

Kachi-Hadjo shook his head. "No, Ki-tee, we cannot. The white man rests, for he is weak and cannot fight when the air is warm and the ground is wet. The white men are like the flocks of birds that come in winter. They are here only when the weather suits them. When the air is cool and the land is dry they will return, and we must fight again."

The girl began to sob lightly. "I am afraid when you are gone, father. I am afraid the white man will kill you or that you will be sent far away and I will never see you again."

The young chief shook his head. "Be strong of heart, my child. There are many paths ahead, and only the Breath Giver knows which one we shall follow. If we fight the good war, perhaps we can make a peace with the white man that will allow us to remain in our homes. That is what we wish for. If we do not fight well, we will grow tired of this war and go to the west, where life will not be as good. I do not wish this. The bones of our mothers are buried in these sands. They speak to me often, and I do not wish to leave them. Perhaps we must fight until the Seminole is no more. I cannot say. Only Hesaketa-Mese can say. You must have faith in His wisdom."

Ki-tee sniffed, tried to suppress her sobs, and curled up under her father's protective arm. He held her tight, staring at a small stand of cypress trees nearby.

Gator John approached, a bottle of whiskey in his hand. He took a seat on the log next to his friend and began to smooth Ki-tee's dark hair. Kachi-Hadjo smiled. "You have left the other chiefs, my friend. Do you tire of their company?"

John chuckled. "Tired of their boastin'. Ol' Tustenuggee and Asi-Yoholo keep countin' scalps and each time the number gets bigger. Think they gonna wipe out the whole damn 'Merican army. A man get foolish when a man get drunk."

"Your black warriors have taken many trophies this past winter. They have fought well."

"Ain't often a black man gets to cut the flesh off a white man. Usually the other way 'round. Best take the opportunity whiles we can. Don't expect it gonna last much longer. The white man gonna be back big this winter. We done put the shame to him, and ain't nothin' the white man like less than bein' shamed by the black man and the red man." Kachi-Hadjo nodded. The soldiers had gone for the summer, off to fight other Indians or to rest at the forts near the sea, away from the forts farther inland, where the soldiers became sick and many of them died. But the summer would not last forever. The soldiers would be back.

John took a drink from his bottle and handed it to his friend. "Best rest up good and enjoy the summer. It gonna be a long, hard winter, ol' frien'."

17 October 1836
Ft. Drane, Fla. Terr.

To:
Gen. Roger Jones
Adjt. Gen. U. S. Army
Washington City

Sir:

   *As Regimental Surgeon, I am happy to reply to your request for a full Report
of the Medical Department of the United States Forces in the Florida Territory for
the Period beginning 1 May 1836 (after the Re-assignment of troops following the
close of Genl. Scott's campaign) until the end of September. As it is quite Lengthy,
I will Summarize for your Benefit. I must also point out that these Figures are
only for the Army and do not Include those from the Marines, Volunteers, Militia,
or the Naval forces that are manning several Posts in addition to patrolling the
Coast. Their rates of Illness will, by Reason, be similar to that of the Army.*

   *Of the 1,383 Men of the Regular Army on duty in Florida, close to two-thirds
of them, 859 men, were reported on Sick List during this Period. Many of these
Men were in the Hospital due to Malaria or Yellow Fever. Thankfully, the
Incidence of Cholera was low this Year. Dysentery and Diarrhea were also very
Common. Twenty-seven suffered Gunshot Wounds, four of those at the hands of
Fellow Soldiers, three from Civilians, the balance from the enemy. Four died of
their wounds. We counted 123 who Succumbed to their illnesses (14 Officers, the
balance Enlisted). In candor, I must also report 3 Suicides (1 Officer, 2 Enlisted.)
For the sake of their Families, I feel it only Proper to withhold their Names. We
also lost 7 men to Drowning, 5 to other Accidental Misfortunes, and 1 to
Lightning.*

   *As you can see from the above Figures, the normal level of Medical Staffing is
totally Inadequate for the Conditions encountered in Florida. As you are aware,*

new Units are arriving in Florida on a Weekly basis, and soon our Troop strength is expected to be more than Triple what it was at the time of this report. I would most Respectfully suggest that the number of Surgeons with each Unit be Doubled, and that two large Hospitals be erected and fully staffed, one at Tampa Bay and one at St. Augustine. In the field, Tents and Cots and Moskeeto Bars are a necessity for the Sick and Wounded. Medical supplies will also be Desperately needed in the coming Campaign. As always, Anti-Diarrheal Suppositories are in continual demand, especially when the Army is on the March. Quinine will be required in large quantities during the next Summer sickly season, should the War continue. Indeed, should the War continue for several Years hence, as many have predicted, we may face the Embarrassing Prospect of having lost a greater number of men to Disease than are the number of Seminole Warriors that presently populate Florida.

General Scott's order to abandon the Interior Posts for the Summer, though perhaps Premature and over-reaching, was, I believe, a Correct one. In those Posts which were abandoned lastly, Fever spread quickly and with Deadly effect. Still, it is Unfortunate that every Summer we shall be forced to give up what we have Gained the previous Winter. Upon re-occupation, we found this Post utterly destroyed, as were the Buildings of the surrounding Plantation and Sugar works (the property of Gen. Clinch). It is but sad Consolation to learn from captured Indians that those who entered the Forts upon our departure also Suffered greatly from Fevers, having breathed the same Malignant Vapors as did we.

> Respectfully,
>
> > Your most Obedient Servant
> > Dr. R. Weightman
> > Surgeon, Fourth Infantry

P.S. In an unrelated Matter, but one in which I am sure the Sec. of War and the President will find of Interest, Gov. Call's "Grand Armee of the Militia" returned to this Post this morning, having Failed in its attempts to engage the Enemy. From the reports of Col. Wooster and others, it seems they arrived at the Withlacoochee only to find it too Swollen to ford. This should not have been Unexpected, in consideration of the Fact that the Rainy Season has just recently ended. To make matters worse, it appears as if the Gov. did not think to carry Axes, thus preventing the Men from building Rafts or Bridges. Having insufficient Supplies, the Gov. attempted to locate Gen. Read's depot near the Mouth of the Withlacoochee, but could not, being unaware that the Supply Steamer had come to Grief on the Bar and sunk. The Gov., undeterred, plans to resume his Grand Campaign as soon as Conditions allow.

> > R. W.

The soldiers pushed through the swamp at a steady pace, not running, but certainly with a sense of urgency in their steps. Occasionally they would catch sight of their quarry fleeing before them, always out of musket range and rarely stopping to look back. It was hard to tell how many of the Indians there were, but there was no doubt that the force was considerable. It was also obvious from the items that had been discarded that women and children were part of the group. Warriors did not carry cook pots and dolls.

It was a large swamp, wide, but not deep, with numerous small islands scattered throughout. Known as the "Wahoo Swamp," it was a favorite haunt of the Seminoles. The trees were predominantly cypress, their needles turning slightly brown as autumn came upon the land. Hampered by the water, the muck, and the hidden cypress knees, the men pressed on as best they could, holding their muskets and cartridge boxes well above the water. Whenever they saw a small stand of swamp maples or oaks they would gravitate in that direction, knowing the water was slightly shallower. It was exhausting labor, but the thought of capturing the enemy kept them moving.

Wooster, at the head of his men, spent as much time looking backward as he did forward. *Where was the damn militia?* His regulars were advancing with good speed, but they could not keep up such a pace indefinitely. There were limits to human endurance. And that was why he kept pushing. The Seminoles faced those same limits. If one of the militia units had kept reasonably close behind, Wooster could let his men rest while another unit kept up the pace. By allowing several units to alternately advance the front, the distance to the enemy would eventually be closed. A large portion of the Seminole Nation was within their grasp.

It had been a frustrating campaign. They had left Fort Drane in mid-October and marched to the Withlacoochee, only to be turned back by a swollen river and a lack of axes. Then they had marched to the coast, only to spend wasted days looking for a supply depot that wasn't there. Trudging back to Fort Drane, more time was wasted as Governor

Call's militiamen leisurely went about the task of re-supplying. By the time the army crossed the Withlacoochee, over a month had been lost.

As Wooster shifted his gaze from front to back, he realized the distance between him and the Seminoles was less than the distance to the lagging militia units. That in itself was dangerous. If the enemy turned to fight, his soldiers would be outnumbered and it would take quite a bit of time for reinforcements to arrive. If they arrived at all. Reluctantly, he ordered his men to slow the pace. Breathing hard, he knew he was reaching his own limits. He would not, however, call a halt. He would not let the enemy escape.

The colonel looked across the ragged line of soldiers as they waded through the knee-deep water. At the far right of the line was MacDuff, both hands tightly gripping his broadsword, clearing a path where none had existed before. The other soldiers went around minor obstacles; MacDuff went through them. At the far left was Sparkes, stepping nimbly over rotting logs and around clumps of ferns. They were good officers, Wooster thought; the type of men the army needed, if only the army could keep them. Service in Florida had become so onerous to young officers that they were resigning their commissions in record numbers.

On they pushed, hoping the Indians would tire of the pursuit. The women, children, and old people *had* to be slowing them down. Very soon the Seminoles would have to make a stand. If only the damn militia would come forward.

~~~

Kachi-Hadjo looked over to Gator John. They both knew what the other was thinking. Their people could run no more. If the soldiers were not stopped, they would soon be within reach of the women, children, and old people. Kachi-Hadjo had been watching the whites closely. They had tired, they had slowed, but they had not stopped. He also knew that there were many more whites farther behind. If his warriors were going to make a stand, it had to be now, before the rest of the soldiers arrived.

The Seminole forces had just crossed a shallow stream. It wasn't much of a stream, perhaps ten or twelve feet wide, but it was just deep enough that the soldiers could not run across it. That meant that while the soldiers were in the stream they would be exposed, making them good targets. All Kachi-Hadjo needed was time; a few hours. If his warriors could somehow make a stand and keep the whites on the opposite side of that stream, there was a chance his people could escape. If they could just hold out until dark.

Kachi-Hadjo called out to his warriors, telling them to come back, that it was here that they would have to stand and fight. John called out to his blacks, ordering them to take up positions behind the tall cypress trees. Other chiefs echoed the call, bringing their men up to the front. Each chief shouted encouragement, pointed out the best places to take cover and the best places to steady the rifles so that they could kill the most whites. Kachi-Hadjo looked at the stream, then at the sky. Was the Breath Giver with them?

~~~

Wooster called a halt at the first sound of enemy gunfire. He ordered the men to spread out behind the cypress trees and return fire, but only when they saw a target. Both forces were well back from the stream, very much aware that the person who ventured too close would soon lose his life. For the moment, both sides were holding the other in place. The whites couldn't advance, while the Indians had no choice but to hold their ground. If he had possessed more than one company of men, Wooster would have charged across the opening. Yes, there would be some casualties, but the stream wasn't that wide and there was heavy cover right up to its banks. Once the first soldiers were across, those behind them would be relatively safe. The Indians would be concentrating their fire on the soldiers closest to them.

Wooster felt hamstrung. If he had been allowed to bring the entire Fourth Regiment the battle would have been over by now. Instead, he was under the command of a civilian governor and forced to work with a thousand undisciplined militiamen. Indeed, the only reason he was there was because President Jackson had insisted that Governor Call take at least one company of regulars and a senior officer on the campaign. Wooster was beginning to wish he had appointed Major Belmont to the task.

Ever so slowly, the militia forces began to gather around him. Wooster began to pace nervously. If they moved swiftly, the battle could be quickly won. A militiaman came up to his side. "The Guv'ner wants to see you. Somethin' 'bout a council o' war." A council of war? What was there to discuss? Form the men, fix bayonets, and then tell the bugler to blow "charge!" Everything else was in God's hands.

Wooster followed the militiaman back to a small rise where Governor Call had gathered his senior officers. There was General Read and Colonel Warren of the Militia, and Major David Moniac, commander of the Creek Indian Volunteers. For many years there had been bad blood between the Lower Creeks and the Seminoles, and it had been easy to find warriors to fight against their cousins in Florida. Still, it surprised Wooster that the Creeks were so eager to aid the whites: Several months earlier the Creeks had risen against the government, attempting to forestall their own deportation to the west. They had failed, and when this war ended, Moniac and his people would be herded west.

Call looked hesitant. For some reason, the stream seemed a formidable barrier. He looked at Read and Warren then shook his head. "I don't know . . ." He then turned to the colonel. "What do you think, Wooster?"

The colonel couldn't believe he was having to point out the obvious. "If we cross now, Governor, we stand a good chance of ending this damned war. Their women and children cannot be far ahead of them."

General Read was always quick to support the Governor who had appointed him. "We have no assurances of that, Colonel. For all we know the families are several days removed from us."

Wooster knew better. "The Indians wouldn't be making a stand if they didn't have to. My God! What have we to lose?"

Colonel Warren cast a glance at the stream. "We gonna lose men, Colonel! Them damn redskins is well dug in and ain't gonna be easily uprooted. I can't go back to Jacksonville and face a bunch o' widows without givin' 'em good reason for their men folk bein' dead."

"What the hell did they think they signed up for? A picnic? This is war, damn it!"

Moniac gave Warren an angry stare. The Creek officer had been the first of his race to attend the Military Academy and was known to both Indians and whites as a fierce warrior. "A true soldier fights for the *chance* of victory. He does not ask the odds. A brave people do not mourn their dead, they honor them."

Knowing their argument was weak, Read suggested another excuse to Call. "I must remind the Governor that our provisions are near exhausted. If we cross that stream we obligate ourselves to several days of pursuit in order to locate and secure the women and children."

Wooster was quick to respond. "If we cross that stream *right now,* the war will be over by this time tomorrow. If ending this war means going hungry for as much as a week, it is well worth it."

Call did not like being backed into a corner. "But where do we cross the stream, Colonel? For all we know, it might be ten feet deep."

Wooster was about to lose his temper. Raising his hand, he pointed at the unseen Seminoles across the water. "*They* got across!"

Read responded just as emphatically. "*They* know where the damn ford is!"

The governor could see the situation getting out of hand. "Gentlemen! We ain't gonna argue amongst ourselves. We need to figure out how deep that stream is. How can we do that without risking our men?"

Read offered that they might throw stones into the creek with lines attached. Warren suggested casting spear-like branches into the water.

Moniac was disgusted. On the previous day his own son had been severely wounded while leading a scouting party. To him, all such talk sounded like the voice of cowardice. "Does my son lie dying for having defended such women and children as I see before me? Stones and sticks? A true warrior finds the depth of the water by *walking into it!*" Picking up his rifle, he motioned to his warriors.

The Creeks worked their way slowly to the stream, moving from tree to tree, taking what cover they could. Wooster motioned to MacDuff and Sparkes. He wasn't sure what the Creek chief intended, whether it was to dash in and dash back, or to actually engage the Seminoles. If Moniac did gain the other side, Wooster wanted the regulars to move swiftly in support. If the regulars charged, the militia would have no choice but to follow. Call and the other two militia officers stood in silence, not quite believing the Indian would act so rashly.

Both sides continued to exchange shots as the Creeks advanced toward the stream. Shouting a fierce war cry, Moniac and a dozen warriors ran toward the stream as the remainder of his warriors kept up a covering fire. The Seminoles returned fire, killing two of the warriors before they reached the water. Moniac made it half way across then suddenly lurched, cried out, then slipped beneath the surface. Leaderless, his warriors fell back.

Call looked toward the stream. "Can anyone see him?"

Read shook his head. "Not a sign of him, Governor."

Warren was quick to reach the conclusion that the governor wanted. "Must be deeper than it looks. If we wade in now, all our men will end up like that."

Call was happy to agree. "The hour is late, gentlemen. Make camp. We will attempt a crossing in the morning."

Wooster was ready to follow in Moniac's steps. "Governor!"

Call would not be deterred. "Colonel, that is my decision. If the redskins are as close as you say, we'll catch them in the morning."

~~~

The sun was rising behind Gator John as he watched the soldiers cautiously enter the water. The night had passed, and his people were safe. He now wanted to know if the whites would pursue them any farther. He observed a group of soldiers carrying the body of the slain Moniac. There, he thought, had been a brave warrior. Long would his name be remembered. One by one, the soldiers waded across the stream and began to penetrate the Seminole side of the swamp. They soon turned and went back to their camp. There would be no pursuit.

~~~

Wooster and MacDuff looked up as Sparkes entered the tent. The colonel asked the obvious question. "Did they find the major's body?"

"Yes, sir."

"How deep?"

"About three feet."

"And I trust we have easily gained the opposite shore?"

"Yes, sir."

The colonel looked at his two subordinates. He sighed and shook his head. "We could have ended this war today, gentlemen. We could have restored peace to this land. Even the Seminoles would have been better off."

Sparkes attempted to offer some hope. "Yes, sir. Lord willing, perhaps we can take up the pursuit today."

It was MacDuff's turn to shake his head. "No, we shall not. The Governor has ordered us to Fort Brooke."

Sparkes took the cup of coffee that was offered by MacDuff's servant then took a seat on a camp stool. All three had nothing to say. All three had wanted the war to end. It made absolutely no sense. Sparkes didn't understand. "Why, sir? Why not pursue the enemy?"

Wooster took a deep breath. "Because, Lieutenant, the governor is a politician. As soldiers, we must look far into the future to realize our true goals. Politicians look no farther than the next election. For us the risk was worth taking. For him it was not."

MacDuff closed his eyes and probed his memory, looking, as was his habit, for some wisdom from The Bard. "Our doubts are traitors, and make us lose the good we oft might win, by fearing to attempt."

Sparkes began to understand. His grandfather had been given the name "Steady Silas" by General Washington because of his ability to complete any task assigned. If there were need for a bridge to be built or cannon to be moved, Steady Silas would get it done. He simply didn't know how to give up. Sparkes's own father, it seemed, had inherited that trait. He had not let the British through that breach in the wall. Sparkes now understood why they had acted that way: Completing the immediate task helped assure the long-term goal, even if that goal wasn't well defined. His grandfather hadn't been building bridges; he was building a nation. His father wasn't defending a fort; he was defending his country and an unborn son he didn't even know he had. It was a deep sense of duty that had driven them, a character trait that Sparkes hoped he could adequately emulate. For the moment, though, he had but one question: "Now what?"

Wooster shook his head. "I have no idea, Lieutenant. There are too many changes afoot. We have a new president coming into office, along with a new Secretary of War. Not that I expect much of a change in policy; both Van Buren and Poinsett are Jackson men and will dance to the old man's tune. What we need most is a new general."

An unbidden thought ran through Wooster's mind: *Just give me the chance. Make me that general.* He knew better. General's stars weren't handed out like sugarplums at Christmas. He had been close to achieving that goal more than once, but his quarry always turned into a falling star, enticingly bright, then disappearing. The vagaries of the military establishment always seemed to conspire against him. Either Congress had changed the rules or the promotion had gone to someone else. Or, like today, the opportunity to prove his worth had been taken away by an inept superior. In one respect, he knew that his longing to be a general was nothing more than vanity. A brevet promotion to Brigadier General would not increase his pay by a single cent. What it would do, however, was open up opportunities. Above all, it would give him the opportunity to end this horrid war.

December 31, 1836
Fort Wooster
Hillsborough River

To:
Miss Maria Wooster
Ft. Brooke

Dear Miss Maria,

   Good tidings for the coming New Year! The Colonel sends his love and hopes that you were able to hold Christmas in a joyous manner with those in company at Ft. Brooke. For us, the day provided a welcome respite from the incessant sound of saws and axes upon wood, hammers upon nails, and the myriad other noises that accompany the construction of a frontier fortification. Following breakfast, your father allowed that I might read the first and second chapters of St. Matthew for the men's benefit, there appearing little chance of any other religious observance on that most holy of days. Indeed, there had been some grumbling among the men as to the unfortunate circumstance of Christmas falling upon a Sunday this year, thereby depriving them of an additional day of rest, one they feel most sorely entitled to. I suppose I shall hear the same refrain tomorrow.

   The weather being exceedingly pleasant, the men turned to their day's labor with energy, knowing the sooner the task was completed, the sooner their time would be their own. Had it not been for the necessity of hanging the massive gate upon its hinges, the Colonel would have given the troops the entire day to themselves. As it were, the task took little more than an hour, after which the men turned to their leisure pursuits, aided by the extra Gill of liquor provided by the Colonel. In addition to the usual games of chance and skill, much time was devoted to fishing, hunting, and to bathing in the river. The anglers' endeavors were richly rewarded, the men catching fine strings of perch, bass, and other species in which this river abounds. Indeed, George has fed us so much fish of late that I fear we may soon find it as tedious as the dry beef and hard bread that is our normal fare.

Your father and I both look forward to returning to Ft. Brooke, but please do not expect us soon. Although we seem to have traded our pistols and swords for spades and axes, we both agree with Genl. Jesup that this is the proper way to conduct an Indian war. By building permanent posts in the Indian territory and sending out detachments to harass the Seminoles, we may soon force them to capitulate. As you can tell from the heading of this letter, we have completed the fort that will guard the crossing of the Hillsborough. The General has honored your father by ordering it to be named Ft. Wooster, but let it be known that both the Colonel and I have decided that in reality it is bearing *your* name! Our work here being nearly completed, we proceed forth in a few days' time to erect a similar fort at the crossing of the Withlacoochee. No longer will we find our bridges burnt soon after they are built.

The extent to which our government is willing to commit the nation's resources to this war has become evident in the amount of supplies that are to be stored in the two posts that we are building. Each fort will store over 50,000 musket and rifle cartridges. That is over 100 bullets for each Seminole we are likely to face! At that rate, if we just shoot blindly at the woods, we stand a good chance of exterminating the red devils! We have also been told to prepare to store 50,000 rations and 5,000 bushels of corn at each post. Just yesterday, Col. Freeman and 200 of his Marines arrived, escorting a train of 30 wagons. They were loaded mostly with hay and oats for the horses, 110 of which arrived last week. The inability to find good forage for the horses when in the field is a continual problem. The Georgia Horsemen that have been sent out on patrol invariably return with emaciated mounts, many so weak that they must be destroyed.

I find it difficult to believe that a year has passed since I received my wounds at Genl. Clinch's Battle. The events we have seen! Dade's men massacred. Clinch driven off from the Withlacoochee, Gaines under siege at Camp Izard, Scott and his grand, failed campaign, and Gov. Call with his timid militia. It seems that we have put our best against the Seminoles and have nothing to show for it. Had you told me such would be the case when I first came to Florida, I could scarce have believed it.

Whilst we see the construction of these forts as necessary, we are also anxious to resume pursuit of the enemy. General Jesup has informed us that upon completion of the fort at the Withlacoochee, we will once again enter the Cove in hopes of removing the final bands that are hiding within. Unlike their experience with Gov. Call, the Seminoles shall discover that this time the army will not hesitate.

The Colonel believes that with good fortune, we will return to Ft. Brooke near the end of January, or, at the latest, mid-February. If there are any changes, we *will keep you apprised. In the meantime, the Colonel wishes to extend his best wishes to Nettie and Nero and especially to you. To that, I add my own good wishes.*

Yours most respectfully,
Sparkes

Hidden behind a stand of palmettos, Kachi-Hadjo watched as the wagon train passed. It seemed to never end. No sooner had one wagon gone over the stout wooden bridge than another quickly followed. Each wagon was guarded by four soldiers, their muskets at the ready, with bayonets fixed. He looked across the river at the fort. In each of the tall blockhouses a sentry kept watch over the bridge and the surrounding landscape. With only eighteen warriors at his disposal, Kachi-Hadjo could do nothing. True, they might kill a few soldiers, but the wagons would not stop and the fort would not disappear.

He looked longingly at the wagons. Some were open, and he could see what was inside. There were fat, round barrels in some, bales or sacks in others. Sometimes he could guess their contents, other times he could not. Was it flour, sugar, salted pork, or gunpowder? It didn't matter: He would have been happy with any of it. Other wagons were covered, and he wondered what was concealed within. Perhaps there was enough food in there to feed his band for a month. Or perhaps it was filled with powder and lead. With such supplies, he could continue to fight for the entire winter.

He looked at the wagon that had just come off the bridge. It appeared that a bag of corn had fallen over and opened, allowing the dry, yellow kernels to pour slowly out the back of the vehicle. The soldiers who were walking behind the wagon saw the kernels falling to the ground but did not bother to set the bag upright. Kachi-Hadjo fought back the urge to shoot the soldiers. It angered him that they were content to waste the corn while his daughter went hungry.

The sight of the endless train of wagons and the thought of Ki-tee being hungry brought sadness to Kachi-Hadjo's heart. Despite the Seminole victories of the past year, the white men would not be deterred. For every soldier they had killed, twenty more had been sent. For every homestead that was burnt, a fort was erected. For every wagon destroyed, another hundred came. There seemed no end to the amount of effort the white men would spend to remove the Seminole from his home.

Kachi-Hadjo could sense a change in the way the white men were waging the war. In the past the soldiers had come in strength, but they had come expecting a quick victory. They had traveled far to attack the Seminole villages, but they had always carried all their supplies on their backs. Kachi-Hadjo knew that the lack of food had stopped the white armies just as effectively as the Seminole bullets. He also knew that the white man had learned from his mistakes. The new general, the one called Jesup, understood what had happened in the past. Now, when his army moved into Seminole territory, he built a fort and kept it well supplied. Before, when the soldiers came, the Seminoles could fight, hide, and then return to their homes after the soldiers left. Now the soldiers would never leave. They would come from the forts, hunt for the Seminoles, then return to the forts to rest and gather more supplies. Fort by fort, patrol by patrol, the soldiers would cover Florida, leaving the Seminole no place to live. Kachi-Hadjo did not need Abee-Aka, the great medicine man, to tell him what the future would be. He saw it in every wagon that passed in front of him.

And yet he was not about to give up the fight. If the white men could adapt, so could he. If his people could not live where the white man was, they would have to learn to live where the white man couldn't. The white men could build forts to house their soldiers, but the settlers could not live in those forts. They would have to build their own homes on their own land in order to grow their crops. The Seminoles could not attack the forts, but they could attack those isolated homesteads. The soldiers could patrol the roads, but they could not always travel in large groups. There would always be the lone wagon or the small group that would fall prey to a Seminole war party. It was Kachi-Hadjo's only hope: If the white men could not live on the land or if they could not travel between their towns, then perhaps they would make peace.

He knew that everything depended on the white man's resolve. How long would the Great Father in Washington be willing to send so many men and so many supplies to such a poor land? Would he tire of this war in one year, two years, or as many as five years? Would he keep fighting for ten years? Kachi-Hadjo knew that he would have to ask that same question of his own people. Who could hold out the longest?

~~~

Shouting at the top of her lungs, the Seminole woman ran as fast as she could through the early morning mist. Behind her came three men on horseback and forty-two soldiers on the run. Sparkes spurred his mount, overtaking and passing the fleeing Indian. The path ahead was clear, and he didn't need her to show him the way. Through a small stand of trees he galloped, followed closely by MacDuff and Colonel Wooster. Swords drawn, they passed through the trees then broke into a clearing. Ahead of them was a small village. Sparkes turned immediately to the right and MacDuff to the left, encircling the village in hopes of cutting off any escape by the startled natives. Wooster kept his course, bearing straight for the central fire pit. He saw a warrior running for the woods, and immediately took off in pursuit. The warrior, knowing he could not reach the safety of the forest, turned to face his pursuer, a war club held menacingly in his right hand. Wooster didn't hesitate. In his long military career he had faced worse dangers than a war club. Galloping forward, he held his sword high. Moments later, the club and the hand that had held it were both lying on the ground. The warrior gazed in disbelief at the bleeding stump that had replaced his hand. Wooster turned his mount and slowly approached the wounded man.

By now the rest of the company had reached the village, cutting off any chance of escape by the natives. Frightened Seminoles ran about in all directions, but few were lucky enough to make it safely into the nearby woods. The women, encumbered by children and unwilling to leave their possessions, could do nothing. In a matter of minutes, the village was secure. Pointing his sword at the warrior he had just wounded, Wooster called out to the hospital orderly. "Bemrose! Bind his wounds before he bleeds to death!"

Blood flowing from his right wrist, the warrior picked up the fallen club with his left hand and swung wildly at anyone who tried to approach. Wooster rode slowly toward the man, his sword pointing downward. The unsteady warrior raised the club again, looking anxiously around, hoping for aid or the magical appearance of an escape route. Once again the colonel swung his sword. This time the blade cut into the head of the club, tearing the weapon from the warrior's grip. The Indian let out an anguished cry and then collapsed.

A woman tried to break through the cordon of soldiers and go to the wounded man. Screaming, she fought the soldiers as they forced her back. Wooster nodded at the soldier in charge. "Let her go to him, Corporal. I have no wish to add to her misery." He turned to Sparkes, a sad look on his face. "A brave warrior has been reduced to nothing more than a crippled Indian, a burden to his people when they will be least able to care for him. Better if I had killed him outright."

The colonel looked around at the village. The soldiers were going from hut to hut, making sure no one was hiding within. They pointed toward the center of the village, motioning the people into one group. For those that refused to cooperate, a slight poke of the bayonet made them realize the futility of their situation. Wooster sighed. This was the third such village they had found in the past week, and the process was becoming routine.

The colonel's expression suddenly turned angry. Across the village he saw Sergeant Bigelow motioning a terrified young woman toward one of the huts. Spurring his mount, he soon reached the sergeant and hit the man with the flat side of his sword. "Mr. MacDuff! Two dozen lashes for the sergeant when we return to camp!" He then cast his eye over the entire company. "We will *not* engage in dishonorable acts! Should any man violate an Indian woman, I'll have him shot."

Sparkes asked the next question with some hesitation. "Shall we burn the village, sir?" The small huts were solid and well built, the garden well tended. It seemed a waste to destroy something that had required such effort and care.

The colonel nodded. "The only way to restore the peace is to quicken the destruction." If Wooster had any complaint about Sparkes, it was his lack of enthusiasm for destruction. There was no other way to put it. A soldier's business was to kill and to destroy. Battles weren't won by being considerate of your enemy. The time for such feelings was after the fighting had stopped. In the heat of battle, a soldier had to have no reservations about the task at hand.

Wooster called out to MacDuff, who was using the point of his massive sword to convince a warrior that it would not be wise to attempt an escape. "Lieutenant! After the prisoners are secure, find their cattle and their stores. Take what's worth having and destroy the rest. Gather what cook pots and blankets you feel they'll need. They'll have use of such things in the embarkation camp." He then had another thought. "Let them take as much food as they can comfortably carry. They don't much like hardtack and army beans anyway."

Sparkes looked at the woman who was crying over her wounded husband. "'Tis a pity it had to come to this, sir."

"It always is, Lieutenant." The colonel looked weary and troubled. "Do you remember the preacher's sermon last Sunday, Mr. Sparkes?"

"Yes, sir."

Wooster then attempted to mimic the preacher, but there was no humor in his voice. Instead, there was a tone of bitter contempt. "The advance of civilization cannot be stopped! The savage must give way before the plow and the steam engine, for he does not use the land in the way the Lord intended! We cannot expect them to understand this; we can only force them to accept it!" Sparkes could say nothing. He had heard the same sermon and had accepted the preacher's words without question. He looked upon the small cabins and the cultivated fields that were about to be put to the torch. They were not that different from those of a white settler. He now understood the colonel's anger: God had nothing to do with it. It was nothing more than the greed of the white man. He also came to the painful realization that his own presence in the army made him an instrument of that greed.

The woman who knelt over the wounded warrior began to wail, beating her chest. The look on Bemrose's face made it clear that the man had not survived. Sparkes turned his mount and looked away. It wasn't the loss of blood or the colonel's sword that had killed the man. The guilt belonged to the land speculator, the politician, and yes, even the preacher, who had misrepresented the word of God in order to justify stealing the red man's land and destroying his way of life. Sparkes also knew a portion of that guilt would reside in his own soul forever.

The colonel lowered his voice, his head shaking slowly. "They are like children, Lieutenant. They cannot understand that what we do is for their own benefit." Both of them knew better.

14

To:
Mrs. David Kilgour
Cincinnati, Ohio

Dear Emily,

It is with the happiest of hearts that I write to inform you that this miserable little war is soon to be over! Yesterday, with much pomp and ceremony, Micco Nopy, the grand king of the Seminoles, came in to place his mark upon the Capitulation, stating that he and his people will give up this land and move to their new homes in the west. It was an exceedingly entertaining day. Accompanying Micco Nopy was his chief counsel and interpreter, the black Abraham. Also present was his brother-in-law Jumper, heir-apparent to the Seminole "throne." Many other lesser chiefs were present, all dressed in their finest regalia. You would have thought they were signing a treaty declaring <u>they</u> had won the war! The only thing lacking was the presence of the Mikasuki chiefs (Phillip, Mad Panther, and Medicine Man Sam). Also absent was Ossiyola, but Genl. Jesup feels confident that all will obey the command of their head chief. The Colonel, ever cautious of the red man's promises, is not so sure, but I feel that this time he may be in error.

One must give full credit to Genl. Jesup for his vigorous pursuit of the war since taking command in December. The speed at which forts were built and the manner in which detachments conducted the offensive shows a determination to bring the war to a swift and definite conclusion. Unlike Genl. Scott, who planned everything and accomplished nothing, Genl. Jesup has given his commanders much latitude and flexibility of movement. Above all else, he has given us the supplies and material needed to take the war to the Seminole heartland. If there is the report of a Seminole war party or village, a company is sent to investigate. In this manner, we have given the enemy little time to rest and he is now ready to give up the fight.

Yet there is more good news: Should this wicked war be terminated, the Colonel says he will request duty at the Recruiting Depot at Lexington, Kentucky! If the request is granted and I remain his aide, I shall be stationed a short ferry trip across the river from your home! I look forward to introducing you to the Colonel and Maria. I am sure you would find their company as enjoyable as I have.

Need you hear more? The Colonel has recommended both MacDuff and I for brevet promotions. Should they be approved it will mean little, for with brevets there is no increase in pay and MacDuff will still command the company and I shall be his underling, but I am happy with that. Perhaps in time I shall have my own company or a second lieutenant I can order about.

I must close for now, dear sister, as the steamer is about to depart for New Orleans and the mail soon closes. Give my love to David and the children, especially little Jacob. It was so kind of you to give him my name. Before too long perhaps I shall hold him and will even, if requested, volunteer to change his diaper. Love, always,

Your most affectionate brother,
Jacob

Spirits were high at Fort Brooke. Spring had come and peace had settled over the land. As if they needed yet another reason for revelry, Colonel Wooster had invited his staff and General Jesup to join him in a celebration of Maria's sixteenth birthday. The simple wooden table had been covered with a white linen cloth, and chairs had been gathered from other officers' quarters to replace the usual benches. Seated at one end of the table was General Jesup, looking dignified in his dress uniform. At the opposite end was Maria, the guest of honor, wearing the best dress she had brought from St. Augustine. It was nothing fancy, fashioned from a cream-colored fabric with thin beige stripes, highlighted by a brocade collar and waistband. The colonel sat to his daughter's right, while Major Belmont, Wooster's second in command, sat to her left. The Major was accompanied by his wife, a red-cheeked, kind-hearted woman with a sly twinkle in her eye. Across the table sat Dr. Weightman, who was already feeling the effects of too much wine.

The party was completed by the presence of Sparkes and MacDuff, who were positioned on either side of the general.

The colonel looked up as Nettie and Nero cleared the table. "A fine repast, as always, Nettie. The turtle soup was excellent."

"Somethin' special for the special guests, Massa Colonel. Bes' as I could do here. Sho' be glad to get back to St. Augustine an' a proper kitchen."

Wooster nodded. Everyone in the room wanted to be anywhere but where they were. "That shall hopefully be soon. The Seminoles continue to come in, though not as swiftly as we might like."

Major Belmont chuckled lightly. "Did we actually expect them to come in any faster?"

Jesup smiled. "I have come to believe, Major, that Indians consider procrastination a noble virtue."

MacDuff expressed a concern that all felt. "I, for one, would feel more assured of their removal were there more squaws present."

Dr. Weightman's eyes rolled. "The excuses I have heard! I could swim to New Orleans in less time than these squaws take to walk from the Okeechobee, wherever *that* may be." They had all heard reports of a big lake somewhere in the south of Florida, but none had ever seen it.

Mrs. Belmont shook her head. "They *are* quite pitiful looking. I do hope they find peace in the west."

Sparkes beamed with pride and confidence. "Well they shall certainly find none here. The general keeps the patrols in the field constantly. Surely they must realize that it is futile to continue their struggle."

Wooster smiled. He had dealt with Indians for over twenty years. As much as any man in the army, he understood them. "An Indian does not fight for logical reasons, Mr. Sparkes. He fights because his heart tells him to, not his mind. They must *feel* that the cause is lost, not be *told* that it is."

Maria had accompanied her father to the Indian camp on the opposite bank of the Hillsborough when he had gone to meet with Micco Nopy and some of the other chiefs. Something had seemed strange to her. "I have seen very few sentries at the Indian camp, General. What is to prevent them from leaving?"

"In truth, my dear, nothing. They have come in of their own volition and have given their word as to emigration. I must admit I entertain the same fears as you do, but I feel I can do little to actually secure them. Were I to build a stockade about the camp or cordon it off with a large number of soldiers, the remaining fugitives would never come in. When dealing with these children of the forest, one must maintain a level of trust."

Mrs. Belmont asked the next question. "When do you expect them to embark for the west, General?"

"It is difficult to say, Mrs. Belmont. Hopefully, within the month. The transport ships should be arriving before long, but I cannot commence the loading until more of the families come in. My greatest concern is the presence of the slave catchers. They hover about like so many vultures, ready to snap up the first unwary negro. As often as I run them off, I find they have returned, bearing writs from this judge or that judge, demanding permission to scour the Indian camp for runaways."

MacDuff laughed. "Aye, one of them came up to me this morning, waving his legal papers in my face, demanding to be allowed to enter the camp. I said, 'Go right ahead, lad, just see that gentleman right there,' and pointed him in the direction of old Halek Tustenuggee. It didn't take but one look for that old catcher to decide he needed the hair on his head more than he needed to catch some fool runaway."

Belmont nodded in agreement. "If it were just runaways they were after, I might be inclined to provide them an escort. But they'll grab anyone whose skin is a bit too dark or whose hair isn't perfectly straight. If they snatch up an Indian, that camp will be cleared in a day."

There was a moment of silence as everyone contemplated what would happen if the peace broke down. As soldiers, these men all dreamed of war. Now that it had begun, however, they were as anxious as anyone for it to be over. This was not a war that was being fought for some glorious cause. It was the sort of conflict that chewed men up and spit them out, wasted and broken, a war brought on by greed, not patriotism. Everyone at the table knew that if the Seminoles fled the camp, the war would continue with no end in sight.

Jesup used the lull in conversation to change the subject to something more festive. He set his wine glass down and reached into a leather bag lying on the floor by his chair. From it he withdrew two pieces of paper, both rolled up and tied with a ribbon. He handed one to MacDuff, then one to Sparkes. "Gentlemen, these arrived from the war department last week. I decided that tonight would be the proper time to hand them to you." The general smiled as the young officers untied the ribbons and unrolled the papers. It was their brevet promotions, signed by President Van Buren and Secretary of War Poinsett. The general then stood up and raised his glass. "May I be the first to salute *Captain* MacDuff and *First* Lieutenant Sparkes. May these promotions lead to many more earned in the defense of our glorious nation." Good wishes were expressed by the others at the table, and both young men responded with appreciation.

As Jesup took his seat, Wooster arose, smiling broadly. "Nero! Might we have our glasses filled? I believe there are other toasts in order." When Nero had finished the task, Wooster held his glass aloft. "Let me propose the first toast of the evening to our honored guest: To my beloved daughter Maria, on this, her sixteenth birthday. May each year add to her wisdom, as well as her beauty. Indeed, may she grow as lovely and as wise as her dear mother, who is no doubt looking down upon us with pride in her heart." Glasses touched, and a "Here! Here!" or a "Bravo!" was voiced by all.

Jesup, as the senior officer, offered the next toast. "To the lovely Maria and to the United States of America! May they both prosper and attain all the happiness that God may bestow upon them." Again the glasses clinked and the sentiment was agreed upon.

Major Belmont rose and cleared his throat. "To the gracious Maria and to the United States Army. May they both be blessed with the success that they most assuredly deserve."

Mrs. Belmont kept her seat but raised her glass. "To this sweet child Maria and to her dear father. May the man who someday takes the daughter's hand be as kind and generous as the father. And . . ." she smiled, looking to her husband. "May he be an officer as handsome as my wonderful husband."

Maria laughed. "An officer? I have little hope of that. Father has frightened them all off! Indeed, I would suppose *First* Lieutenant Sparkes stands under the threat of a court-martial should he so much as touch my hand."

The colonel smiled and nodded. "I have already chosen the firing squad." It was an automatic response from Wooster, something he was expected to say. Yet a thought nagged at him: She had mentioned Sparkes as the one who should be worried not to touch her hand.

MacDuff looked across the table at Sparkes. "Well, Sparkes, it seems we've been put on notice: The fairest lady at Fort Brooke is beyond approach."

Dr. Weightman rose, an uncharacteristically serious look on his face. "To the charming Maria and to the Territory of Florida. A brilliant blossom in the 'Land of Flowers.' As did Eve of Genesis, she dwells in a true Garden of Eden." He then broke into an elfish grin. "Eden it must surely be, for there is certainly no shortage of serpents!"

As the laughter died, MacDuff came to his feet. As he rose, Mrs. Belmont called for "A short recital, Captain. I have heard you would be the actor, if not for the uniform."

MacDuff nodded. "At least in the army they pay you, no matter how poor your talents." He closed his eyes, searching for the proper line. He then smiled, raised his glass to Maria, and gave a quick performance. "Oh! She doth teach the torches to burn bright. It seems she hangs upon the cheek of night like a rich jewel in a Seminole's ear; beauty too rich for use, for earth too dear! Did my heart love 'til now? forswear it, sight! For I ne'er saw true beauty 'til this night."

The guests applauded as MacDuff bowed and then took his seat. Wooster laughed. "A line I am sure he has used often on the young ladies of this nation." MacDuff smiled and nodded. It *had* served him well.

As junior officer, Sparkes was the last to make a toast. For the entire evening he had wondered what he would say. Maria was no longer the simple girl he had met two years earlier. In that time she had begun to show the signs of becoming a woman, both in body and in mind. Through letters and through time spent together in the colonel's company, they had become close. He needed to express his affection for her without sounding romantic. After all, she was still a child and more than that, his commanding officer's daughter. He took a breath. "I now see the true disadvantage of my lowly rank in this grand army. My superiors have used all the terms synonymous with womanly perfection and have stolen all the usual objects that one might raise a toast to. Being at such a loss, I offer the simplest of salutations. To my dear friend Maria: Long life and happiness. I could wish no more for anyone. May the smile upon your face never diminish." Maria smiled warmly at Sparkes; it was the best toast of the night.

Wooster gazed at his daughter. She was growing up and there was nothing he could do about it. "Does the object of all this adoration wish to propose a toast of her own?"

Maria raised her glass. She wasn't sure what to say. Who did she want to extend good wishes to? Then she realized who it was. "To the Seminoles. May they find peace in their new homes. They and the people of this Territory have suffered enough."

Everyone nodded in agreement and offered a simple "Amen."

~~~

Weeks passed and the Seminoles came and went from the embarkation camp in a steady trickle. Some brought every possession they had, while others seemed to wander about, furtively moving from tent to tent, speaking in whispers and often leaving before dawn. Then, late on an evening in early June, something happened. A group of chiefs sat huddled in the darkness, protected from prying eyes by the shadows of the tents. At one side sat Micco Nopy, looking nervously from man to man. Next to him sat Abraham, trying to decide the best course of action in a dangerous situation. Across from him were Asi-Yoholo, Halek Tustenuggee, and Gator John. In hushed but defiant tones Asi-Yoholo made his case. "We shall talk no more! We must lead our people from this camp before the moon rises. The white sentries must not see us."

Micco Nopy may have been uneasy, even fearful, but he felt obligated to protest the manner in which he was being addressed. "We shall talk as long as your chief sees fit! I shall not be ordered about by low men such as you. Where is my brother, Micco Phillip? In his counsel I place the most trust. Why has he not come from the Big Swamp?"

Gator John supplied the answer. "Phillip be sick. Speaks only of dyin', not travelin'."

"And what of his son, Kachi-Hadjo?"

John shook his head. "Kachi-Hadjo stays with his father. He ain't gonna say nothin' 'til the fate of Micco Phillip be spoken."

Tustenuggee spat on the ground. "What more is there to say? The Seminole shall not leave his home. The chief of the Seminoles is as bound to the will of the council as was Chalo Emathla. Does Micco Nopy wish to share the grave of Emathla?"

It was clear to Micco Nopy that Tustenuggee was not making an idle threat. Yet still he hesitated, and for good reason. The plight of many Seminoles was mirrored in his own situation. There was no future for them in Florida. In the west there would at least be the chance to make a new life. The stubborn pride of a few angry men might very well lead to the extinction of his people. It was a valid argument, but he made the mistake of voicing that argument in personal terms, not those of the tribe as a whole. "Am I not bound by the paper I marked with General Jesup? I have sold my cattle. My village has been burnt. Many of my slaves have been stolen. What is left for me here?"

Asi-Yoholo scoffed. "I care little what remains for Micco Nopy! Our women and our children are starving while Micco Nopy remains fat." In a gesture that everyone could see, the angry young chieftain moved his hand to the handle of his scalping knife.

Micco Nopy turned to Abraham. "My friend, your counsel has always been wise. What says Abraham?"

The chief's counselor pointed out the obvious. "Abraham thinks these Injens gonna kill Micco Nopy if he don' go with 'em."

Gator John felt the situation was about to get out of hand. Even though he was in full agreement with Asi-Yoholo and Tustenuggee, he would not let them harm the chief. The stability of the tribe had to be preserved. "Gator John gonna allow no hand be touchin' his chief. If Micco Nopy wanna go west, let Micco Nopy go west. We got no place for cowards here."

It was a challenge Micco Nopy could not ignore, though he wished he could. "Let no man say Micco Nopy is a coward. Let them say he led his people to a new land where the water is sweet and the hunting is good."

John would not hear of it. "The water be foul and the game be all shot up by the Creeks. Ain't no place for the Seminole out west. Let the Injen say Micco Nopy made war upon the whites like no one ever seen."

As he heard the soft cry of a baby coming from a nearby tent, Micco Nopy tried his final argument: "Have not our children suffered enough? Do our women not cry for the babies they have lost?"

Asi-Yoholo could not contain himself. "Our women cry for revenge! Has not my own woman been forced to scavenge corn from the discarded sacks of the white man? Has she not melted lead for rifle balls and loaded my rifle while we were in battle? Is Micco Nopy less a man than this woman?"

John looked at Abraham. He knew it was the one voice the chief would listen to. "How many of our black brothers been got drug away by the slave catchers since we come here? How many more they gonna steal when we get out west?" He smiled and poked Abraham in the shoulder. "You gonna look good in chains, ol' frien'."

It was a point Abraham could not ignore. Turning to Micco Nopy, he said, "Gator John be right about that. Them Creeks out west gonna take whatever you got. Might be better off stayin' here."

John pressed his advantage. "Micco Nopy might be our chief, but if he goes west, he gonna be our chief no more. He gonna be just another Injen without a home, livin' off the white man. If Micco Nopy stays, he gonna be remembered as the greatest chief the Seminoles ever had, the chief the white man couldn't drive from his home. What say Micco Nopy?"

Once again, as had happened before the attack on Major Dade, Micco Nopy was being forced into something he didn't want to do. It would have been so much easier to please the white man and take the boat to the west. Still, it was obvious that he had no choice. If he refused, either Asi-Yoholo or Tustenuggee would take his life. "Let no man call Micco Nopy a coward. Let no man say Micco Nopy was driven from his homeland by the whites. Come! We must lead our people away from this place. The moon will soon be rising."

15

June 5, 1837
Ft. Brooke, Tampa Bay

To:
Mrs. David Kilgour
Cincinnati, Ohio

Dearest Emily,

As you will no doubt have read in the papers, this miserable war is upon us once again. Three days past, the Indians, some 600-700 of the red devils, fled camp and returned to the wilds with no warning whatsoever. You can have no idea of the disappointment and anger felt by all present at this post. There was not a man among us who did not look forward to leaving this accursed Territory. Ten days from now will mark the second anniversary of my coming to this unholy place, and now I fear that I will never leave it alive. There are times I feel compelled to resign my commission. Perhaps it is the thought of the sacrifice made by our father that keeps me in the service.

I must, of necessity, keep this letter short. We have been in the saddle constantly since the escape and have returned to post to rest our mounts and refill our haversacks before once more taking up the chase. Both Col. Wooster and Maj. Belmont are determined to run the enemy down, no matter where they have fled. Genl. Jesup is beside himself and has offered his resignation. We can only hope the War Dept. does not grant his request. The treachery of the Indians cannot be blamed on him. The fault lies most properly with the slave catchers and other designing whites that prowled about the camps looking for any monetary advantage that might be gained. There are, in truth, many whites who do not wish to see the war come to a conclusion. All are living fat off the gov't. purse and are loathe to see it end.

As you see, dear sister, my plans to be with you this summer are now all dashed. Any thought of the Colonel being transferred to Kentucky can be *forgotten. I had so looked forward to seeing you, David, and the children again, and especially to look upon little Jacob. Perhaps a furlough can be arranged, but this seems doubtful, as so many troops have already left the Territory.*

My best to all,

Jacob

Lieutenant Isaac Ingram, United States Navy, looked out over his command, peering through the slight morning mist. The cannon were in good order, the Marines at the ready. He closed his eyes and sniffed the air, trying to smell a familiar salt breeze or hear the soft flapping of the canvas. He couldn't. The wooden walls that stood before him were not those of a sloop-of-war, but of Fort Wooster. Instead of sails fluttering in the breeze, there was a solitary pennant hanging limp from a flagpole. Instead of trading broadsides with British frigates, he was standing guard over a bridge. It was not the sort of warfare he had expected when he joined the navy.

Indeed, fighting Indians had been the farthest thing from his mind when he took to sea. His imagination had been filled with the tales of glory that had come out of the numerous naval battles fought during the war with England. When war with the Seminoles broke out his ship was in dry-dock at the Navy Yard in Pensacola. As it put back to sea the ship was ordered to Tampa Bay. Upon its arrival off Fort Brooke, half the crew was put ashore and many of its cannon off-loaded. The cannon and the crew now guarded several forts, while the ship patrolled the coast, ever on the lookout for smugglers bringing weapons and supplies for the Seminoles.

Like all good sailors, Ingram longed to be at sea. Still, this was where he was needed, so he did his duty without complaint. The army was altogether too small to fight a major war without some outside assistance. Of the 7,000 men of the regular army, half of them were serving in Florida, leaving the east coast, the western frontier, and the contentious borders with Canada and Mexico severely undermanned. Volunteers and militia were used, but they tended to be expensive and unreliable. The navy, however, had a surplus of manpower, and

Commodore Dallas was more than happy to lend some of his men to the army. Thus it was that Ingram found himself in command of a fort on dry land. Above the fort's gate was a sign that identified the structure as "USS Ft. Wooster."

The fort was situated about twenty yards from the Hillsborough River, which was not an especially wide or deep river, but impossible for wagons or horses to cross. A stout wooden bridge had been erected over the river, strong enough for any traffic that might cross it. The fort was large, close to one hundred feet on each side and constructed of tall, straight, pine pickets that were pointed at the top. Loopholes had been cut into the pickets to allow gunners to fire from behind the protection of the walls. At opposing ends of the fort were a set of two-story blockhouses, both of which had a clear view of the bridge. At the corner of the fort closest to the bridge was a small wooden door known as the sally port, from which a cannon could be fired and troops dispatched to secure the bridge in case of attack.

In the months since the Indians' flight from the embarkation camp, Ingram had been expecting an attack on the bridge. He understood the importance of the span. An immense amount of military traffic moved along the road from Fort Brooke to Fort King. Thousands of tons of supplies and hundreds of horses had crossed over that bridge in the past month alone. If the Seminoles could succeed in destroying the bridge, the war effort could be seriously hampered. Because of that Ingram kept ammunition alongside the sally port cannon at all times. He also kept four marine sharpshooters posted in the blockhouses, and two sentries on the bridge whenever visibility was low. The Seminoles might attack the bridge, but they would never destroy it.

~~~

Kachi-Hadjo and Gator John had been watching the bridge for over a week. It needed to be destroyed. If they could disrupt the soldiers' movements for a week or two it would give the remainder of his people time to move south. The army was operating at will throughout the Cove, forcing the Seminoles from the homes they had lived in for decades. Their only hope of survival was to flee to the lands in the south, places the white man had not yet gone.

Burning the bridge would not be easy. They would have to move fast, and they would have to attack at night. From the time the sentries were killed until the time the soldiers began to fire on the warriors attempting to light the fire there would be but a few minutes. There were other problems. The rainy season was upon them, so the bridge was damp, as was much of the tinder that could be gathered nearby. Just bringing fire to the bridge would be difficult. Building a fire near the bridge was impossible; it would be easily spotted from the fort. Gator John had seen the solution: The sentries kept a small fire near the fort. It would take but a few seconds for a warrior to run up to the fire and pick up a burning stick. The big problem was the four soldiers who stood watch from the two blockhouses. Running to and from the fire would leave the warrior dangerously exposed.

For the task of running to the fire John had chosen his most agile warrior, Tommy August. He was a small black man, more of a boy than a true warrior. John had told Tommy not to worry: The soldiers used old smoothbore muskets, and the chances of them hitting him were slim. Neither man really believed it. Other warriors were given tasks that matched special talents. The best riflemen would fire on the blockhouses in an attempt to prevent the soldiers from shooting Tommy. The best archers would kill the sentries. If the sentries could be slain without firing a shot, Tommy would stand a better chance of making it to their fire. Other warriors waited nearby, some with their rifles at the ready, others with bundles of grass and twigs mixed with gunpowder. It was a complex plan, one that required precise timing and more than a little luck.

About two hours before sunrise the warriors began approaching the bridge. The six archers crept as close as they could, taking position so as to have a clear shot at the sentries. Tommy August and the warriors who carried the tinder crouched behind them, waiting for the signal from Kachi-Hadjo. It was planned that while Tommy ran to the fire, the other warriors would spread the tinder over the bridge. With luck, one touch from Tommy's burning branch would ignite the mixed-in gunpowder, and the blaze would start.

The archers waited patiently, their bow strings lightly drawn. Kachi-Hadjo watched the sentries, knowing it was their habit to occasionally leave their posts at opposite ends of the bridge and come together at the center. He smiled as the soldier closest to the fort put down his weapon, went to the fire, stirred the embers, and poured two cups of coffee. The soldier returned to the bridge and walked toward the center of the span, one of the cups held out. The other soldier shouldered his musket and came to meet him halfway. They met, sipped their brew, and turned toward the fort. Kachi-Hadjo whistled. Six arrows flew to their mark.

One of the sentries fell to the deck of the bridge without making a sound. The other screamed, took a few steps, then also fell. Kachi-Hadjo could hear shouts from within the fort and realized that total surprise had been lost. As the archers threw down their bows and picked up their rifles, Tommy ran onto the bridge and toward the fire. Kachi-Hadjo ordered his men to hold their fire. The soldiers in the fort knew something had happened, but didn't know what. Tommy was probably safe until he reached the fire. Then the soldiers would see him.

Close behind the runner came the men with the tinder. Each had an appointed section of the bridge to cover with the sticks, dry grass, and gunpowder. As they were spreading the fuel, Tommy reached the fire. Behind him he could hear the Seminole rifles open fire, forcing the soldiers in the blockhouses to take cover. Feeling it worth the risk, he took a moment to choose a stout branch with a strong flame at its end. Taking hold of the branch, he turned for the bridge and ran as fast as he could.

~~~

Inside the east blockhouse, a Marine stood back as Seminole bullets struck near the narrow window of the structure. He saw the small black man pick a burning branch from the sentries' fire. Ignoring the enemy fire, he rested the muzzle of his long rifle on the windowsill. He had been trained to fire from the tall mast of a sailing ship; firing from a solid building was much easier. With a practiced eye he tracked the small figure as it sped toward the bridge. When the man was several paces from the span the Marine squeezed the trigger. The runner fell and the branch tumbled away.

~~~

Gator John was on his feet in an instant. Running onto the bridge, he sped past the warriors who were spreading the tinder and made for the burning branch. As he bent down he heard the crack of a rifle from one of the blockhouses and almost immediately felt a sharp pain in his leg. He stumbled momentarily, but quickly regained his footing. Picking up the branch, he hobbled toward the bridge. As another bullet whistled by his ear, he threw the branch onto a pile of tinder. The gunpowder flashed and the grass broke into flame. Sparks flew from the gunpowder and another bundle ignited. John winced in pain and was about to fall when he felt the strong arm of Kachi-Hadjo wrap around him. The chief supported his friend as the pair ran for the safe end of the bridge. As they stepped onto the dirt they heard shouts from the warriors, telling them the sally port of the fort had been opened and the cannon was about to fire. Having little choice, Kachi-Hadjo threw John to the ground then fell next to him. He had barely reached the ground when the cannon boomed and a swarm of grapeshot flew across the bridge.

~~~

As a group of sailors worked to reload the cannon, Lieutenant Ingram led a squad of Marines out the sally port and toward the bridge. It was no different, he thought, than when he had been a young midshipman and had led a boarding party during a battle with pirates. Behind the Marines came armed sailors and yet more seamen, these carrying buckets of water. Once again, their naval training was being put to good use. Because of the dangers of a fire at sea, every ship kept full buckets of water close at hand to douse any fire that might start. More out of habit than anything else, Ingram had ordered buckets kept along the wall near the sally port. It had been a wise precaution.

~~~

The charge of the Marines caught Kachi-Hadjo completely by surprise. He had expected the soldiers to fire from behind the walls of the fort, giving time for the timbers of the bridge to catch fire. He ordered his warriors to fire, but only two of the soldiers fell. The others kept coming. Knowing he could not hold the bridge, he ordered his warriors to flee into the woods and attempt to stop the soldiers' advance. With his arm around Gator John, he made for the nearest clump of trees.

~~~

Ingram ordered the Marines to take station at the foot of the bridge in order to give cover to the men who were extinguishing the flames. As the Seminoles fired, one of the Marines fell wounded. Ingram looked behind; the flames were almost out. He ordered his men off the bridge and into more protected places along the riverbank. The bridge was secure; his men had done their duty.

~~~

Kachi-Hadjo and his warriors slowly fell back into the woods. The soldiers were not pursuing them. It was the bridge that was important, and both he and the white officer knew it. For today, at least, the bridge would remain standing.

16

September 12, 1837
Ft. Brooke, Tampa Bay

To:
Mrs. David Kilgour
Cincinnati, Ohio

My dearest sister,

I cannot thank you enough for the wonderful weeks spent with you and your family whilst on furlough this past summer. My return voyage down the Ohio and Mississippi was quite pleasant; the beauty and vastness of our nation always astounds me. The passage from N. Orleans to Tampa Bay was uneventful, with but one minor squall to mar the fine weather. As it is, I will soon be aboard ship again, this time bound for St. Augustine. The Colonel has been ordered there and I, of course, go with him. MacDuff and the company shall remain here with Lt. Col. Belmont (who has received his brevet after the unfortunate passing of Lt. Col. Foster). I shall write to you as soon as we arrive safely in the old city.

Words cannot express the happiness I enjoyed whilst in your company. After two years in this land of savages and loathsome reptiles, it was a pleasure to spend my furlough in a civilized portion of the realm. I now return quite refreshed and ready to continue with this burdensome duty. I do thank David for the offer to join him at the store, but feel that I have an obligation to the nation, the army, Col. Wooster, and to grandfather to see this war through.

Although our hopes have been dashed before, I now feel this war may end with the coming campaign. The number of men at Tampa is astounding, and more are on the way. General Jesup says that more than half the regular army will be in Florida, about 4,000 men. In addition, there may be some 5,000 volunteers from throughout the nation. Already I have seen men from as far away as Pennsylvania and New York. Whilst in St. Louis, I heard tell of a regiment of Missouri Volunteers gathering for the trip. In N. Orleans I met with Col. Zachary

Taylor, who is bringing the 1st Infty. to Florida. Surely, such an army has not been raised by this nation since the late war with Britain. One would think that we were off to conquer Mexico City or some other foreign capital, rather than a batch of ragged savages.

The General's plan for this coming campaign is ambitious, but is the only plan which offers some chance of success. He intends to divide his force into several moving columns that will sweep through the peninsula from top to bottom, driving the Seminoles before them. From the coasts the Navy will penetrate the southern rivers, forcing the Indians inland and preventing them from attaining the southern swamplands known as the Everglades. As these columns press southward, posts and supply depots will be built, thus keeping the troops supplied and in motion, depriving the enemy of any opportunity to rest. By such means we hope to exhaust the red men and force them to surrender. Wish us luck. If the war does not end with this campaign, I know not what we shall do.

One can certainly see a marked difference in the attitude of Genl. Jesup since earlier this year. The flight of the Indians from the embarkation camp in June has caused a hardening in his feelings toward the red men. He has issued the order that any Indian who comes in to parley under a white flag is to be immediately taken prisoner. The Colonel questioned this policy, saying it appeared as a violation of the rules of war and might in fact discourage negotiation, but the General insisted, pointing out that the Seminoles signed a capitulation in March that obligated them to emigration. The time for negotiation, the General believes, has long passed, and the white flag will now guarantee them nothing but safe passage to the west.

Once again, dear Emily, I thank you for the wonderful days spent in Cincinnati this summer. It was a joy to hold little Jacob. I am sure he will grow into a fine lad someday. Give him a kiss from his Uncle, and my best wishes to David, Lizzy, and Kenneth.

Your most affectionate brother,
Jacob

A brilliant orange sun began to rise above the calm sea as the small naval vessel, propelled gently by the autumn wind, inched its way along the east coast of Florida. Sparkes stepped out on deck and took in the salt air. Most of the time he hated Florida, but at times such as this it could be an enchanting place, with the sparkling white sand beaches, the lush green foliage along the shore, and the crystal clear water. Looking about, he noticed Maria at the starboard rail, her eyes fixed on the eastern horizon, her dark hair flowing in the wind. A beautiful day and a beautiful lady, he thought, then caught himself. As natural as they might be, such thoughts were not wise to contemplate. There was too much honor at stake.

As he walked up beside her, Sparkes tipped his hat. "Good morning, Miss Maria. You have arisen early."

"'Tis a habit of mine that had to be abandoned while at Tampa Bay, Mr. Sparkes. From our balcony in St. Augustine one can see the sun rise over Anastasia Island. It was a sight I never tired of. Every morning I would rise early enough to view it."

"You might have substituted the sunsets at Fort Brooke. The beauty of God's work is equal, both in the morning and the evening."

She nodded, but disagreed. "They were beautiful indeed, but a sunset seems to symbolize an end. The sunrise always fills me with the promise of a new day."

"I have heard tell that the Seminoles feel much the same. Because the sun dies in the west they feel the lands in the west are a place of death. Perhaps that is why they resist removal so strongly."

Maria gave a short laugh and joked, "One can never reach the west without the west moving yet farther west, and are they not now in the west in relation to someplace farther east?" She sighed and the smile faded. "No, Mr. Sparkes, the Seminoles fight because they are a proud people and love their homes." She turned her head back toward the rising sun and asked, "Is there any special wish you have for this new day, Lieutenant?"

He shook his head. "Whilst aboard ship I wish for nothing more than for the Lord to grant me a safe passage. This coast is home to the skeletons of many a fine vessel. I have no wish to find myself ashore in such an inhospitable place. How many good seamen have lost their lives when wrecked upon this beach? How many widows wait for the sight of a familiar mast that will never appear?"

Maria looked down at the ship's spreading wake. She wanted to know more about this man. She was being drawn to him and she knew it. "I have heard you speak often of your sister, Mr. Sparkes, but never of your mother. Is she no longer alive?"

Sparkes looked at the rising sun. "'Tis not a happy story, so I do not often mention it." He then took a slow, deep breath. "After the death of my father, Mother returned to the home of her own father, the pastor of a large and wealthy congregation near Boston." Sparkes realized that such a description did little to paint a true picture of his maternal grandfather. "In the mind of her father, the Wrath of God was always more important than the Love of God. There was certainly little love in their home."

Sparkes stopped for a moment, trying to recall the stories his sister had told him. The events he were about to relate had all happened while he was still an infant. They were also something he had never truly fathomed himself. "By some sort of maniacal logic that I cannot begin to understand, *her* father believed that the death of *my* father was God's punishment for sins that my mother must have committed." He then corrected himself. "Mother's sin, I suppose, was nothing more horrid than marrying a gentleman of arms."

"But your father was a hero!"

"That, it seems, was a matter of opinion. As far as the old preacher was concerned, my father had abandoned his wife to run off and find glory on the battlefield."

Maria was becoming angry. "And he calls himself a man of God?"

Sparkes shrugged. "That will be for the Lord to decide in the end." He continued with his story. "One Sunday, whilst I was still nothing more than a suckling babe, and for reasons I shall never know, the good pastor began to berate my mother before the whole congregation, and in a most degrading manner."

"For what? And before the whole congregation? What could your mother do to defend herself?"

Sparkes smiled broadly. He was about to relate his favorite part of the story. "She didn't have to. Unbeknownst to the pastor, Grandfather Sparkes was in the congregation, having come to Boston on business the previous day and with plans to pay a visit to his grandchildren in the afternoon. Barely was the sermon finished before old Silas came to his feet in defense of my mother's honor. Tapping his cane loudly on the floor, he paced back and forth along the center aisle of the church, giving his own sermon, enthralling the congregation with tales of duty, forgiveness, and God's love. At the end of his little 'talk' he stood before my mother and extended his hand, saying 'Nine children has my good wife brought into this world and all have felt the unconditional love of our home. This fine lady shall be the tenth.' Ah! It must have been a grand sight. If only I had been of an age to comprehend it. If it was fated that I should lose my father, than the Lord more than compensated by allowing my sister and I to be brought up in the home of Grandfather and Grandmother Sparkes, with all the aunts, uncles, and dear cousins that gathered around them."

Maria didn't understand. "I see little sadness in the story, only a just redemption."

Sparkes's smile faded as the memory became darker. As if called for, a cloud moved in front of the rising sun, removing its warmth from their faces. "Had but the tale ended thus. My mother, it seems, could never be free of the feeling of shame that her father had placed so firmly within her mind. She stayed with us in Providence for perhaps a year, then, on the coldest of days, she simply left. Never again did we hear of her, though grandfather later learned that she had been seen upon the wharfs of Providence late that night. Perhaps she gave her life to those frigid waters or perhaps she took passage on some far-bound vessel. I cannot say."

Maria wanted to reach out and hold his hand, but thought better of it. Her father might come on deck at any moment. "I'm so sorry." It sounded thoroughly inadequate. Feeling sorry was not enough, but at the moment there was little else she could do or say.

The pair stood in silence for some time, watching the water slip by. Sparkes turned to Maria. "You are fortunate to have known both your parents. What sort of woman was your mother?"

"Mother had never been a woman of strong constitution. When first married, father was stationed on the frontier and life was difficult. Mother was constantly ill. Every few years there would be a change in posting and each station proved more difficult. The long winters of Maine were especially hard on her. Father requested a transfer to St.

Augustine in hopes that the mild climate would prove more suitable to her health. Before the orders reached us, she passed away."

The revelation brought another question to Sparkes's mind. "Does your father regret having chosen to devote his life to the army?"

Maria shook her head. "Oh, no. He loves the army. He also loved mother deeply. At first I thought he held the army responsible for her death, but I was mistaken. If he blames anyone, he blames himself for asking her to join him in that life. Indeed, when she died, it was the army that provided the most solace. His fellow officers were like brothers and their wives became beloved aunts to me."

"Yet he often rails against the army."

She laughed. "Perhaps I should be more specific. He loves the military life. He hates the army. He despises the low pay, the lack of promotion, the senior officers who conspire against one another, and the fools in Washington who supervise the entire affair. You do not know how often he has threatened to resign his commission. I think he remains in the army only because he knows no other life and could imagine nothing better."

"I sense the colonel sees a good deal of your mother in you and wishes to protect you from her fate."

Sparkes had touched a nerve. "While I may have the face of my mother, Lieutenant, I also have the strength of my father. The life of an officer's wife would not kill me." She then gave Sparkes a long, pointed look. "Indeed, I would be honored to be wed to a gentleman of arms."

~~~

Kachi-Hadjo did not want to smile, but he had no choice. Playful Otter could make anyone laugh. Indeed, she was one of the few Seminole women who could even make Halek Tustenuggee crack a smile. There was but one other time that Kachi-Hadjo could recall seeing a sad look upon her face: It was when her husband had been slain fighting the white men at the Wahoo Swamp. Yet she had recovered quickly, refusing to let her spirit be broken. Kachi-Hadjo admired that.

The young woman sat down next to Kachi-Hadjo and looked at Ki-tee, who was sleeping soundly despite the mosquitoes buzzing about her head. With a caring hand she brushed the insects away. She turned to the young chief and went straight to the point. "Why do you not lay with me?" It was a good question, and one he could not answer easily. She knew he was having difficulty, so she helped him. "Do you find me unattractive?" He shook his head and smiled. "Do you feel you would be dishonoring my husband?" Kachi-Hadjo shrugged; that was part of the problem, or at least a good excuse. Playful Otter looked at the sleeping girl. "Do you feel it would dishonor Ki-tee's mother?"

Kachi-Hadjo gave a quick shake of his head then changed it to a nod. She was being honest, and deserved as much from him. "It has been five years since the bite of the snake took her life, yet I think of her often." He reached out and took Playful Otter's hand. "You have been good to Ki-tee, you have cared for her while I have been away fighting the white man. You have slept in my lodge, and I have treated you like a sister, because I cannot yet treat you like a wife."

She leaned toward him and put a gentle hand on his cheek. "I do not seek a husband, nor do I wish a brother." She was smiling, but a tear ran down her face. "I wish only to lose this emptiness in my heart."

Kachi-Hadjo wiped the tear from her face. He had been at war for almost two years. He had killed many white men, and he had burnt many of their homes. He had seen white women scalped and their babies' heads smashed. He had seen warriors killed in battle and had found Seminole villages burned to the ground. He had seen Indian women who had been raped and babies that had been run through by the bayonet. He knew how she felt.

Playful Otter reached down and began to lift Kachi-Hadjo's shirt. He did not try to stop her. He, too, had an emptiness in his heart.

17

7 October 1837
Ft. Marion
St. Augustine

To:
Maj. Genl. Thos. S. Jesup
Commdg. Army of the South
Ft. Brooke, Tampa Bay

Genl.:

It is with great pleasure that I inform you of the capture of Micco Phillip and thirty-eight of his Mikasuki tribesmen, the result of an operation two days' march south of this place. This most fortuitous occurrence came about when Genl. Hernandez produced a slave who had lately fled Phillip's camp. For a modest bounty (being reunited with his woman), he offered to lead us back there.

Using the utmost caution and stealth, we approached the camp under cover of darkness. Praise must be given to the men of Comp. "C", 2nd Arty, for strict adherence to silence and discipline. Moving with care and often lying on the damp earth, they encircled the camp with nary the snap of a broken twig. On my command (a pistol shot), they arose as one and stormed the camp. The surprise was complete. Not another shot was fired.

Even in captivity, Phillip retained his dignity. He offered to surrender himself for emigration if his people could remain. When I told him that all his people must go to the west and that they would be happy there, he asked if I truly believed that. As a show of respect I did not bind him, though I did feel it necessary to restrain the warriors. He and his people are, at present, housed within Ft. Marion.

Phillip has asked to see his son, Cachi Hadjo. For what purpose I cannot say, other than in some vain hope of affecting an escape. Nonetheless, I shall send a *runner, offering a parley. Perhaps some good may come of it.*

It is only proper that I mention that in this action much credit must be given to Lt. Sparkes for the manner in which he commanded the men of the company, their own captain being seriously indisposed. Although it was I who commanded the expedition, Lt. Sparkes was given the task of deciding upon the disposition of the troops and the precise manner in which they were to be deployed. In the absence of Capt. MacDuff, who is detached to Lt. Col. Belmont, he has shown himself to be a most capable officer.

Preparations for the coming campaign are progressing quite well. Genl. Hernandez has formed the militia into an adequate fighting force, and I am happy to report the arrival of the Tenn. Vols. under Maj. Lauderdale, 500 men strong. I will, of course, keep you apprised of any developments as may concern Cachi Hadjo or Phillip.

With deepest regards,

Your Most Obedient Servant
Wm. A. Wooster
Col. Commg. 4th Infty.

Colonel Wooster paced back and forth in front of the small fort located near a marshy creek a few miles south of St. Augustine. The autumn air was cool and refreshing, but he took no notice of it. Darker thoughts occupied his mind. General Jesup's latest order was troubling and seemed to go beyond the limits of good judgment. When Kachi-Hadjo arrived for the parley he was to be taken prisoner, irregardless of the white flag that flew nearby.

The colonel turned as Sparkes stepped from a wooded path into the clearing in front of the fort. Standing silently, he waited for the lieutenant to approach. "Are they coming?"

Sparkes nodded. "Yes, sir. Asi-Yoholo, Kachi-Hadjo, Gator John, and about ten warriors just stepped out of their canoes at the landing. Shall I form the men?"

Wooster nodded his approval, but inside, his stomach churned. The capture of Asi-Yoholo, Gator John, and Kachi-Hadjo would make Jesup ecstatic, while the Northern press and Whig politicians would be furious. Wooster feared he would be caught in the middle of an acrimonious debate. "Let's get this foul work over with." Shaking his head, Wooster took a seat behind a small table. *My God, I hope this ends the war. That may be the only way I can live with the shame.*

Some minutes passed before the three chiefs, followed by their warriors, stepped out of the woods. In the lead was Kachi-Hadjo, a white cloth tied to the barrel of his rifle. As they walked toward the table they passed through two columns of soldiers, standing at attention, their muskets at their side. Kachi-Hadjo noticed that the bayonets were fixed. The trio came to a halt a few feet in front of the table, the warriors behind them. "I have come at the summons of my father, Micco Phillip. Is he well?"

Wooster nodded. "He is well. He wishes you to join him."

Kachi-Hadjo knew better, but was non-committal. "We have come to talk of these matters."

Wooster was impatient, but didn't want to scare the Indians off. Except for Kachi-Hadjo, they all looked wary. "The time for talk is over. You must surrender. It is for the good of your people."

Kachi-Hadjo shook his head slightly, staring at Wooster. He did not like the colonel's tone. "The council will decide what is good for our people. It is not for the white man to say."

The colonel looked at Asi-Yoholo. The chief looked pale and weak. He was obviously ill. "The council has been false. Micco Nopy gave his word to go to the new land in the west, but then left the camp at Fort Brooke. What does Asi-Yoholo have to say to this?"

Asi-Yoholo's voice was barely audible. "There was great sickness at the camp. It was an unhealthy place. There were also many slave catchers who stole our black brothers. General Jesup broke his word and did not protect us from them."

Wooster could not deny the truth of the statement but saw little relevance in the fact. Camps were always troubled with sickness, and slave catchers, as obnoxious as they might be, had every legal right to collect fugitive property. "What of the Negroes you promised to return to their owners? You have delivered none of them."

Gator John spoke up. "Ain't no Negroes 'cept Seminole born or Seminole slaves. All dem what 'scaped from the plantations done

gone." It was not entirely true, but in general, correct. Most of the freed
plantation slaves had found life in the Seminole camps too arduous.
They weren't used to the constant travel, making camp in damp
swamps, and living off unfamiliar foods. For many of the escapees, they
had simply traded one form of drudgery for another. They also realized
that even if the Seminoles won their fight to stay in Florida, the hunt for
escaped slaves would never cease. In the end, most of them left the
Seminole camps, looking for something that suited them better. Some
had gone farther into the swamps, searching for rumored villages where
other runaways had gathered, while others escaped to Cuba or the
Bahamas, either on small trading vessels or by dugout canoe. Still
others had returned to their masters, trading the risky unknown for the
security of bondage.

Wooster was becoming angry, more at the circumstances than at
the Indians. He had been placed in a situation he wanted no part of and
had been ordered to perform a duty that would stain his reputation. He
felt as betrayed as he knew the Seminoles would feel. Still, it was at
them that he directed his anger. "The Seminoles speak lies. We shall
have no more of it!"

John turned to Kachi-Hadjo. Something wasn't right. "Best we be
goin', ol' frien'. Ain't no talkin' gonna be done roun' here." Asi-Yoholo
and Kachi-Hadjo nodded in agreement and began to turn. Wooster
pounded his fist on the table. It was the prearranged signal Sparkes had
been waiting for. A shot was fired from within the blockhouse. The two
columns of soldiers immediately swung their muskets up, pointing
them at the Indians. The gates to the fort flew open and a company of
soldiers ran out, their weapons at the ready. The Indians had nowhere
to run.

Kachi-Hadjo tore the white cloth from his rifle and threw it to the
ground. "So this is what the flag of peace means to the white man. The
white man has no honor."

John voiced his agreement. "We done knowed that."

Wooster looked at Asi-Yoholo. Both men saw the look of relief in
the other's eyes. It was over.

~~~

The following morning Wooster sat at a desk in a half-empty storeroom at Fort Marion. It was a simple table, used by the commissary officer to keep record of the receipt and distribution of supplies at the fort. Across from the colonel sat Kachi-Hadjo, a guard at either side. The chief had a look of disdain on his face and his words reflected the feeling. "Why should I speak to a man who dishonors the white cloth? What words of his can I now believe?"

The colonel smiled slightly and nodded. It was a valid question. "Mad Panther should speak to me because I command this post and therefore have considerable influence over the welfare of his people while they are here. You must understand that I wish them no harm."

The chief huffed. "Then why do you keep us in a dark cell where the air is damp and unhealthy and the sun does not shine? Asi-Yoholo and my father are not well. If they do not see the sun they shall die. The Seminole cannot live without the sun."

Wooster nodded again. He had wronged these people and he wanted to somehow make up for it. "Your people shall have the freedom of the parade ground during the daylight hours and shall have full access to the ministrations of our doctors. I wish your people to be as healthy as possible for the trip to their new homes."

Kachi-Hadjo gave a sly smile. He did not trust the white colonel, but he could work with him. "Of that we shall say more later. We do not want the white doctor. We wish to use our own medicines."

It was Wooster's turn for a sly smile. "Would you like me to send for Medicine Man Sam?"

The chief laughed. "Abee-Aka is not as foolish as I was. He will not get close enough to a white man to let himself be taken prisoner. I know some of the ways of the medicine man. I shall gather the plants and bring them to my father, who is wise in the ways to prepare them."

Wooster also laughed. The two men seemed to have reached a common understanding. "Taking you prisoner under that wretched flag has soiled my reputation quite enough, thank you. I'll not have it further soiled by letting you out of this building and having you escape. No, my friend, in here you must remain." His face became more thoughtful. "I will, however, allow you to send forth some women to gather what plants you require."

Kachi-Hadjo nodded; the preliminary sparring was over. "How long do you plan to keep my people here?"

Wooster shrugged. "Until the rest of your band comes in and we can arrange passage to your new homes in the west."

Kachi-Hadjo gave a defiant shake of his head. "We shall not go to this new land. Our homes are here."

The colonel was almost apologetic. "The choice is no longer yours. Your chiefs have signed the treaties. Your people must remove."

The chief leaned forward. "Would the colonel honor a treaty that was forced upon him by the muzzle of a musket? Would he honor a treaty that was full of lies? Do not speak to me of treaties. These strange marks that the white man puts on paper mean nothing to the Seminole. The red man cannot trust that the words of the interpreter are the same as the words on that paper, yet you hold this treaty before us as if the Great Spirit had spoken these words and they are never to be doubted." Kachi-Hadjo settled back in the chair but kept his eyes on the colonel. "There is much the white man has promised in these treaties, yet the Seminole has seen little of it. Why should the Seminole honor his part of the bargain when the white man will not honor his? Had the Seminole truly intended to go to the west, we would not have needed a treaty. We would have gathered our people and gone to your forts to await the ships." He then made his final point: "All treaties are worthless once the war begins."

It was all very true and there was nothing Wooster could argue against. The Indians *had* been treated unfairly. The treaties *had* always been interpreted in the white man's favor. There was, in reality, only one argument available. "The treaties do not matter, my friend, and they never have. They are nothing more than the words that tell us what we already know. The white man will have this land, and the Seminole cannot stop him. The most the red man can do is ask for what few gifts we will give him in return for this land. You can fight, but you cannot win. The power of the white man is too great. You may be as strong as an oak, but even the strongest tree must fall before a great wind. Mad Panther may not like these truths and I may not like these truths, but we cannot deny them."

Kachi-Hadjo was surprised. No white man had ever spoken so honestly to him. "If Wooster does not think the red man should be forced from his home, then why does he fight? I have often heard the soldiers speak of how they hate this land, how they long to be where they were first born. If the white man has no use for this land, why not leave it to those who love it? We ask for nothing more than a small piece to live upon, far from where the white man will build his home. The white man will never place his home in the south of this country. He and his woman can grow nothing but sickly children there. Leave the land to us. It will be difficult, but we will survive."

The chief had another point to make. "The white man says this is his land. We do not agree. The Great Spirit does not give the earth to anyone; he only lets us walk upon it. You may own your musket and I may own my hunting knife, but no man may own the earth or the rivers that flow upon it. I have heard it said that the Spanish sold this land to the Americans. Who gave it to them to sell? This is the land the Great Spirit has made for the Seminole to walk upon, and where we can bury our dead. We must fight to keep it."

Wooster stared straight into the chief's eyes. "And I must fight to take it from you. I am a soldier. I do not decide what is to be. That is for the Great Father in Washington to do. When the council decides to go to war, do you question their authority? You and I may be leaders, but we are not the Great Father or the council. We must do what they command us to. It is our duty. We are no more than weapons, like the musket or the rifle. What if you and I were to take the tomahawk and the sword, go outside this room, and fight to the death? Would this war be over tomorrow?" Kachi-Hadjo could not answer. The colonel was right. Wooster relaxed. "I brought you to this room to ask what we could do to make your people more comfortable. As I said, we wish you no harm."

"We will need more blankets."

"They have already been called for."

"Your food is not fit for slaves."

"You will eat as well as my men do." The two men smiled at each other. For the moment, at least, the war was over.

~~~

Several weeks passed during which Kachi-Hadjo and the colonel achieved a certain level of trust and mutual respect. Although the idea of being a captive was galling, Kachi-Hadjo had to admit that his people were being treated well. Nearly every morning the colonel would come to the fort, and the two men would walk the parade grounds or stroll atop the walls of the fort, the colonel inquiring as to the health and comfort of Kachi-Hadjo's people. One time, the pair had peered over the wall, looking at the ground below. Wooster had read Kachi-Hadjo's mind. "Brewster!" he had said, calling out to a nearby sentry who carried an especially fine rifle. "See that yellow flower across the moat?"

"Yes, sir!" In one fluid motion, the sentry snapped the rifle to his eye and fired. The flower disappeared. Kachi-Hadjo had understood the meaning of the demonstration: If he were to try an escape, he had better not do it when Brewster was on duty.

In appreciation of the chief's cooperation, Wooster had invited Kachi-Hadjo to attend a ball that was being given in honor of the newly arrived Tennessee Volunteers. As the chief and his four armed guards entered the large stone building, Kachi-Hadjo looked around, hoping to see where the food and whiskey were kept. Someone had called the building a "church," one of those places where the white man worshiped his gods. After all the time he had spent in St. Augustine in his younger years, Kachi-Hadjo still wasn't sure how many gods the white men had. They said there was only one, some pitiful man who had allowed himself to be nailed to a wooden cross. Kachi-Hadjo could never understand how a god could be nailed to a cross. Still, there appeared to be other gods. For one thing, the Spanish had their Cat-lick gods; a father, a son, a Great Spirit, and the mother of them all. As near as he could tell, most of the Americans didn't like the Cat-licks. Then there were the fishermen called Greeks. These people seemed to worship the same god as the Americans, but for some reason the

Americans looked down on them, saying they didn't worship the true god in the right way. Then there were the ones called Jews. The whites seemed to despise them the most, even though the one Jew Kachi-Hadjo had met was a wealthy white man who had been treated most cordially by his white neighbors. In truth, Kachi-Hadjo wasn't even sure the Jews had a god. More than once he had heard the whites call them "godless Jews." He doubted it was true. All too often he had heard his own people referred to as "godless savages." The more he learned of the white man, the more he realized that they knew nothing about the Breath Giver or any other god.

Kachi-Hadjo smiled contentedly as he looked around the church. Benches were stacked against the wall while men and women in their finest clothes moved about the floor. Black men in equally fine clothing passed between them, carrying trays of food and drink. In one corner of the room a few men played musical instruments, some of them blowing into horns while others drew bows across strings. He had to admit that he liked the sound, though he missed the simple rhythms created by the rattles and drums of a Seminole dance. He noticed that at every entrance a pair of armed guards stood by, muskets at their side. He also noticed that every officer carried his long-knife. Kachi-Hadjo may have been the guest of honor, but he was still a prisoner.

The chief marveled at the women's clothing. How long did it take to get into those hooped skirts with the narrow waists? More important, how fast could they get out of them if they needed to relieve themselves or if their men wanted to use their pleasures? When the opportunity arose, he would have to ask one of the ladies. The men's clothing was almost as impractical, especially the uniforms of the army chiefs. No wonder the white men fought so poorly. They would be tired just from carrying all the clothes they owned. Not that the chief didn't appreciate high fashion. He had worn his best shirt for the occasion, his finest beaded sash and matching shot bag, along with his most colorful turban topped with his longest ostrich feathers. His red woolen leggings had bright blue trimmings and on his chest were three silver gorgets. Around his upper arms were silver bands tied with exceptionally long strips of buckskin. As far as he could tell, he was the finest dressed man at the party.

The chief turned at the sound of a familiar voice. It was the colonel, who had just entered the building. On Wooster's arm was a lovely young woman. Next to them was the one called Sparkes. Kachi-Hadjo moved in their direction, a smile on his face. Wooster was the one white man he could laugh with. As he made his way toward the trio, Kachi-Hadjo grabbed an *hors devours* from a tray carried by a black waiter. Popping it into his mouth, his expression turned to one of slight distaste. Finding another waiter, he took a small glass of whiskey and downed it. He shook his head as he came up to Wooster and the others. "The colonel has good whiskey, but the food is fit only for women. If your soldiers eat no better than this, the Seminole warriors shall have little to fear."

Wooster bowed his head in acknowledgement. "With Mad Panther removed from the fight, my soldiers will have less to fear."

"We shall see, Colonel. A Seminole warrior does not need a chief to tell him how to fight. It is the way we are raised. When I was but a newborn, the white men burned my village. When I nursed at my mother's breast there were tears and blood mixed with the milk. Yet I have tried to teach my daughter Ki-tee to dream of the day when we shall be able live in peace with the white man. The time of peace will come some day. The Great Spirit will not allow the war to go on forever. He will soften the heart of one side or the other. Maybe both." He then looked at Maria. "Is this the child of the colonel?"

Wooster nodded. "My daughter, Maria."

Kachi-Hadjo turned to Sparkes. "She is very pretty, my friend. You shall enjoy planting the seed of many children with her before she gets old and wrinkled."

Sparkes almost dropped the glass he was holding. He quickly turned to the colonel. "Sir. . . . I, I . . ."

Maria came to his defense, taking Kachi-Hadjo by the hand. "Thank you for the kind compliment, Chief Kachi-Hadjo, but you are mistaken. The Lieutenant and I are simply friends."

The white men are such fools, Kachi-Hadjo thought. *They cannot see what is right before them.* It had been different when he met Ki-tee's mother. Micco Phillip had not been pleased. She was from a weak clan, and her father had been a timid warrior. Kachi-Hadjo had cared little for the arguments. He had made up his mind, and he would have her. In battle or in love, he could not be stopped. It still saddened him when he thought of how few years they had shared. He gave a serious look to Sparkes then smiled at Maria. "The lieutenant should open his eyes. You will make a fine wife." Maria returned the smile. She was thinking the exact same thing.

~~~

More weeks passed, and as the air grew colder the confinement in Fort Marion became more tedious for Kachi-Hadjo and his people. The colonel had been called away, and the new commander of the fort was much less friendly. As the days passed, Kachi-Hadjo began to formulate a plan of escape. Finally, the time to act had come.

It was dark in the cell, almost too dark to see, but that suited Kachi-Hadjo's purposes just fine. The cell was a large room, originally designed as a storeroom built into the massive walls of Fort Marion. The arched ceiling rose perhaps twenty feet from the ground and covered a room that was just as long and half that in width. Within the room were twenty-five people, most of them warriors but also a few women. At one end of the room was a door that led out to the parade ground. At the other end, near the ceiling, was a small window, a few feet high, but less than a foot wide. Across it were two iron bars. Otherwise, there was no opening into the room. It may have been designed as a storeroom, but it served very well as a prison.

Under the window was a stone platform, raised a foot or so higher than the floor. On it sat the three chiefs, Micco Phillip, Asi-Yoholo, and Kachi-Hadjo. At the opposite end of the cell Gator John looked through the small window in the door and saw a Seminole woman giggling as she flirted with the guard, who occasionally offered her a sip from his flask. John smiled, then turned and proceeded to where the chiefs were sitting. Kachi-Hadjo whispered, "Which of the women has chosen to sleep with the guard tonight? She sacrifices much."

"Pond Lily was happy to. She says she be ugly. Drunken white man the only man she can get."

Kachi-Hadjo smiled. "Ugly Indian woman probably the only woman drunken soldier can get." His smile disappeared as he turned to Asi-Yoholo. Kachi-Hadjo was close to pleading. "Will you not come with us? Your strength will return once you are outside these sickly walls."

Asi-Yoholo shook his head. He knew the truth. His great strength, both in body and in spirit, had left him, never to return. He was wracked by fevers, tormented by chills. For him there was no future. "Where the white man's bullets have failed, the white man's sickness has triumphed. I have not the will to continue this fight. The flame of war I pass to you." It took some effort, but Asi-Yoholo stood up and embraced his old friend. "Soon I shall see the Breath Giver, and I shall ask him why he has abandoned us so. I wish you well, my friend."

Although Kachi-Hadjo and Asi-Yoholo had often argued in council, each held a deep respect for the other. Asi-Yoholo's life had been a hard one; his losses to the white man greater than anyone should have had to bear. It was disheartening to see such a great warrior laid low by common disease. A valiant leader should die in battle or as an old man, surrounded by his family, not in a prison, surrounded by enemies. The two men embraced again. Kachi-Hadjo looked into the weary eyes of Asi-Yoholo. "Long shall all men speak the name of Asi-Yoholo. The torch of the War Spirit may have passed to others, but long shall we remember the man who first set fire to it. Good-bye, my friend."

Kachi-Hadjo turned to his father. This would be the most difficult parting of all. "It pains me much to leave you here. Will you not join us?"

Phillip shook his head. Like Asi-Yoholo, he knew it was impossible. What disease had done to the younger man, time had done to Phillip. The constant moving from camp to camp that had taken place since the beginning of the war had exacted a heavy toll on the once invincible leader. It seemed as if he had aged ten years in the past two.

"I cannot, my son. I am an old man. I would but slow you down. Let the old ones pass, as all must do in their time." His eyes beamed with a fading pride. "I have killed many whites in my years. I have taken many trophies. That is enough for any warrior. I have led my people for many years, and they have prospered in spite of the white man. That is enough for any chief. Just as the old buck must make way for the young buck, so must the aging chief. Be wise, my son; lead your people well. May The Breath Giver be with you."

Kachi-Hadjo embraced his father, a single tear flowing down his cheek. Both knew it would be the last time they would see each other. As the other warriors said their farewells to the chiefs, Kachi-Hadjo moved to the back wall of the cell. It was time.

Standing on the low platform, two tall warriors hoisted Kachi-Hadjo up onto their shoulders. The chief pulled a knife from his belt and wedged the blade between two stones. Finding a handhold, he lifted himself up and stood on the handle of the knife, then reached up to a ledge beneath the narrow window. Taking hold of one of the bars in the window, he hoisted himself up to the ledge then rested for a moment. He then began to remove loose pieces of plaster from around the other bar that bridged the narrow opening. As he removed the pieces he tossed them down, where they were caught in a blanket. Finally, he removed the bar and handed it down to Gator John. Not a noise was made. In the background could be heard the chatter of Pond Lily and the guard.

From below, the end of a short rope was tossed up to Kachi-Hadjo. Reaching for it, he almost lost his balance, and the rope fell to the floor. Taking a deep breath, he signaled to have the rope tossed again. This time he caught it. Gator John then tied a chain of blankets to the rope. Kachi-Hadjo pulled it up and tied it off to the remaining bar. Taking a final look into the eyes of his father, he took a deep breath, held it for a moment, and then forced it all out. The opening looked too small to pass through. Extending his arms above his head, he put them through the opening. Once the arms were through, he carefully poked his head through, his eyes closed. He took another breath, exhaled fully, and pushed against the outer walls with his arms. As his chest passed through the opening, his skin was torn by the sharp fossilized shells that made up the stone walls. Closing his eyes, he kept working his way out. As Kachi-Hadjo's hips reached the opening, he looked down and saw the earth some thirty feet below. Finally, his hips came through. Extending the blankets beneath him, Kachi-Hadjo lowered himself to the ground.

One by one, eighteen other warriors and two women repeated the task. Last to come was Gator John. When he was about ten feet from the ground, the blankets parted, sending him tumbling to the earth. All the Indians held perfectly still. Agonizing seconds passed. No soldier appeared along the top of the wall, none came from the guardhouse. Kachi-Hadjo motioned to his people and they moved off into the darkness. Inside the cell, Asi-Yoholo and Micco Phillip sat in silence. The only sounds they could hear were the grunts of Pond Lily and the drunken soldier.

18

December 24, 1837
Camp Basinger, Kissimmee River
Somewhere in the God-forsaken Middle of Florida

To:
Mrs. David Kilgour
Cincinnati, Ohio

Dear Emily,

I take pen in hand to wish you the Merriest of Christmases and, by the time you receive this, the most joyous New Year. Never could I have imagined I would be sending Christmas greetings from such a place as this. Indeed, never could I have imagined that this war could possibly last the two years it already has. I grow very weary of it, Emily, but the task is not yet done, so I shall persevere. Soon, perhaps, this accursed war will end.

We are, at present, camped along the banks of the Kissimmee River, which flows down the backbone of the peninsula and into the great Lake Okee-Chobee, which we believe we shall reach tomorrow. I say "we believe" because none of us are entirely positive where this giant lake is or, for that matter, that it actually exists. Our total knowledge of this part of Florida comes from our Indian and Negro guides, who have often proven less than reliable. At times I feel akin to Capts. Lewis and Clarke on their great journey to the Pacific. Indeed, this land is so poorly known that Capt. Vinton of the Topographical Engineers has almost gone through all the paper he brought for the purpose of drawing and mapmaking.

Our column, close to a thousand men strong and under the command of Col. Zach. Taylor, 1st Infty., left Tampa Bay just short of a month ago, making our way more or less due east. Much of the march was through impassible terrain, sometimes allowing us to make little more than five miles a day. We erected our first post at Pease Creek, and our next when we reached the Kissimmee. I know not which is harder on the men: The dull, laborious march or the physical difficulties of erecting a fortification. From there we turned south, following the course of the river. The terrain here is low and wet, making for slow progress. If we had attempted this trek during the summer, with its incessant rains, the passage would have been impossible.

We have erected one other post, Ft. Kissimmee, and will soon make this camp a permanent depot. By leaving these posts manned and well supplied, we hope to deprive the enemy of all rest and refuge, in hopes that he will tire and find it to his advantage to surrender. Already in our march down the Kissimmee, we have taken in portions of the bands of Jumper and Alligator, two powerful chiefs of the Nation. Captured Indians tell us that the main body of Seminoles is not far ahead, and we are anticipating a battle in the near future. If we can affect a resounding victory over the savages, perhaps the war will end.

Our force is the largest of the seven columns moving through the Territory. At the moment we are over eight-hundred men strong, having left about two-hundred men to garrison the posts we have erected along our path. Somewhat less than half of the force belongs to Col. Taylor's First Infantry, with the rest divided about equally between Col. Wooster's Fourth Infantry, Lt. Col. Thompson's Sixth Infantry, and Col. Gentry's Missouri Volunteers. Our plan is to split when we reach the lake, with Col. Taylor and the bulk of the troops going east to join the columns under Genl. Jesup. Our regiment shall then head west to meet up with Col. Smith on the Caloosahatchee, which reportedly drains the lake to the Gulf of Mexico.

Whilst nearly all the officers of the army are in agreement with Genl. Jesup's conduct of the campaign, there is much talk of his questionable use of the white flag. As you have no doubt read in the papers, much vilification has been heaped upon the general for his capture of Ossiyola and Kachee-Hadjo (Mad Panther) under that flag, and the criticism has increased since the escape of Kachee-Hadjo from Ft. Marion. (Thank the Lord that the Colonel and I had left St. Augustine prior to the escape, or the blame would have been placed on us.) Such criticism has not deterred the general in the least from continuing with the policy. Soon after our departure from Ft. Brooke, we learned that head chief Micco Nopy had been taken during negotiations with a delegation of Cherokees sent down by the Govt. in hopes of ending the war. Genl. Jesup felt the Cherokee effort to be useless and elected to take the Seminole leaders whilst the opportunity presented itself. Although most of us abhor the practice as a violation of the rules of war, we reluctantly accept it as a means to bring this most inglorious war to a swift conclusion. An honorable conclusion would have been preferable, but we have long since passed the point where such a thing is possible.

I must close for now, the day is dimming. I know not when this will reach you, for it must make its way back to Tampa Bay before heading to New Orleans and hence up-river to you. I was gladdened to hear that little Jacob has recovered *from his illness. The little boy is so dear to me. Give my respects to David, and hugs to Lizzy and Kenneth.*

> *Your most affectionate brother,*
> *Jacob*

Colonel Wooster let his mind wander as his horse paced alongside the mile-long column of troops. *Always second in command.* Zachary Taylor was no more experienced than Wooster and had received his promotion to colonel on the same day. "Taylor," however, came before "Wooster" in the alphabetical register of army officers, which therefore rendered Taylor the superior officer. *Damn! Why don't they alphabetize by first names?* Time after time, some small technicality had stood between Wooster and promotion. Still, it was better than serving under a militia officer.

Not that there was much chance of promotion in this unpopular war. In a few days, when the column split, Wooster would be in command of his own force. Then, he dreamed, perhaps by some strange bit of providence he would come upon the main body of Seminoles. A great battle would ensue, and Wooster would be victorious. The surviving warriors would surrender and the women and children would be captured. The war would end, and he would be made a general. Wooster shook his head. *Damned unlikely.*

The colonel's reverie was broken by the approach of Captain MacDuff on horseback. "Colonel Taylor wishes to see you, sir." Wooster spurred his horse, and the pair rode toward the head of the column, past hundreds of soldiers on the march. At times the line moved snake-like, taking the path of least resistance, avoiding watery depressions or small stands of cypress.

Within minutes the two officers reached the head of the column, where they found Colonel Taylor sat astride his horse, his wide-brimmed straw hat shading his eyes from the sun. Beside Taylor were Colonel Gentry of the Missouri Volunteers and Lieutenant Colonel Thompson of the Sixth Infantry. Standing on the ground before them was an old Indian and a young black man who was serving as interpreter. As Wooster came alongside, Taylor removed his hat and wiped his brow. "And a most Merry Christmas to you this morning, Will." Taylor and he had been friends for almost twenty years, but it was unusual for them to greet each other by their first names when on duty or with other officers and enlisted men present. Something had put Zachary Taylor in an exceptionally good mood.

"And likewise to you, my friend, though I could think of better places to observe the day."

"Or a less fitting way." Taylor looked down at the Indian. "The old man says the Seminoles have embodied in a hammock a few miles ahead of us and propose to give us battle."

"How many?"

"Maybe three hundred." Taylor shook his head. "Not that I suppose he can count that high or would likely tell us the truth if he knew it. At any rate, tell your men to prepare to advance. If the redskins mean to take us on, I mean to give them the opportunity."

~~~

Two hours later, five horsemen stood at the edge of a watery bog filled with sawgrass. Colonel Wooster and the four captains of the Fourth Infantry surveyed the scene, awaiting the signal to advance. Wooster bit his lip and shook his head. He didn't like the situation nor did he like the orders. The situation was bad enough. The Indians had taken up position in a dense hardwood hammock along the north shore of Lake Okeechobee. Looking beyond the hammock, Wooster was amazed at the size of the lake. It reminded him of the first time he had stood on the shores of Lake Erie, knowing there was an opposite shore but unable to see it.

The Indians had picked the perfect place to make their stand. The branches of oak, bay, and swamp maples intertwined to form a thick canopy over the hammock. Near the ground, short bushes, ferns, and saplings covered the earth. Fallen logs and entangled vines would make progress difficult. Many of the Seminoles had climbed into the trees, choosing positions that afforded them an excellent perspective of the field the soldiers would have to cross.

As formidable a stronghold as the hammock was, the sawgrass swamp in front of the hammock posed an even bigger problem. The sharp teeth of the long, stiff sawgrass blades would tear into the soldiers' uniforms, slowing them down. The water and mud would delay them even more. Well within range of the Seminole gunners, the soldiers would find it almost impossible to move with any rapidity. The casualties would be horrific.

Taylor's orders were no less obnoxious. The first column to face the Seminoles would be the Missouri Volunteers. Taylor had a strong dislike for volunteers, and these young men were going to pay the price for that animosity. When the volunteers broke, which was fully expected, the Sixth Infantry would take up the advance. This bothered Wooster, for although Thompson was a good officer, he was no Indian fighter. He would march into the hammock as if he were going up against a battalion of British regulars. The column would march straight and slow and never flinch. They would be cut to pieces. When that occurred, it would be Wooster's turn to advance. What bothered Wooster the most, however, was that almost half the force, Taylor's own First Infantry, was being held in reserve. For what? Did Taylor expect the Seminoles to bring in reinforcements?

To Wooster, it was all a show. Taylor wanted to win the big battle of the Florida War. He wanted his men to charge into the hammock and crush the Seminoles. The newspapers would love it, and Taylor would get his general's star. Militarily, it was all a waste. Wooster had argued that what they ought to do was capture the women and children. Bypass the warriors and leave the Missouri regiment to keep them bottled up in the hammock. Just because the Indians had offered an invitation to battle did not mean it had to be accepted. Forget the glory; win the war. Taylor would hear none of it. The bright glow of a general's star had blinded him.

~~~

Kachi-Hadjo looked down from the tree at the approaching American army. The soldiers numbered twice as many men as the Seminole warriors, but for some reason, almost half of them were staying back. Why didn't the white chief send in all his men? Did he plan on sending them after the women and children? He had no idea, and it really didn't matter. The battle was about to begin. It could not be called off now.

The whole idea of making a stand against the army was questionable in the first place. Halek Tustenuggee had argued for it; he wanted more scalps. Abee-Aka had argued against it; he put his faith in his medicine and his ability to stay hidden. In the end, everyone had turned to Kachi-Hadjo. With Asi-Yoholo dying in a far-off prison, and with the other major chiefs also taken prisoner, leadership had devolved to Kachi-Hadjo. He didn't want the job, but he could not refuse it. The Breath Giver decided these things, not mere chiefs.

Kachi-Hadjo had pointed out that there was no guarantee the white men would actually fight. He had simply assumed they would be too proud to pass up the opportunity. There was certainly no guarantee that the Seminoles could inflict serious damage to the white army. There was also no guarantee that the warriors could escape when the time came to retreat. The chiefs were risking everything in hopes of nothing more than slowing the Americans down. The army was closing in on the women and children. If the soldiers weren't stopped, if only for a day, the war would be over. Their way of life, even their Seminole identity, would be lost.

~~~

At the rear of the American army, Zachary Taylor stood tall in his saddle and waved his straw hat. A bugle sounded, and drums began to beat out the march. With sword held high, Colonel Gentry of the Missourians stepped forward, with one-hundred and twenty men close behind. Into the sawgrass they strode, a quarter of a mile from the hammock. Instead of staying abreast, they formed into irregular columns, falling into lanes that had been trampled down by the Seminoles. MacDuff shook his head. "Don't they realize the redskins want them to go down those paths? They shoot the one in front and reload while the next one stumbles over his dead comrade."

Wooster watched intently as Gentry urged his men on. "There, Mr. MacDuff, goes a courageous man."

"Aye, sir, and a doomed one."

~~~

Kachi-Hadjo waited. No one would fire until he did. He looked the soldiers over carefully. These men were not in uniform, but were wearing the clothes that any white man might wear. He smiled. They were not true soldiers. They would never reach the hammock. He watched their ragged line breakup as the men moved into the paths the Indians had made for them. His eye caught site of their commander, a handsome, proud man marching in front and waving his sword. Kachi-Hadjo rested his rifle in the notch of the tree and aimed at the man. For every white man that fell, Ki-tee and Playful Otter would be able to move a little farther toward safety.

~~~

The Missourians stumbled through the sawgrass until they were within fifty yards of the hammock. Suddenly there was a war cry and the trees erupted in puffs of smoke and points of flame. One of the first to fall was Colonel Gentry. Sparkes watched and shuddered at the sight. The Indians were gunning for the officers. Two more of the leaders fell, including Gentry's son. Almost leaderless and blocked by the men who had been shot at the front of each column, the volunteers stopped. Some of the men tried to hide in the sawgrass, while others would take the occasional shot, firing blindly into the hammock. Some tried to carry their friends to safety. Others stood frozen, unable to think. Sparkes could hear Wooster shout, "Move, damn it! Don't just stand there, you fools! Move!" It was a wasted effort: The volunteers were simply too far away.

The few remaining officers and some sergeants managed to form the men into a line. A disorganized volley was fired at the hammock. The Seminoles fired again with uncommon order and precision. The remaining volunteers looked about as their fellows fell into the swamp. With almost every officer dead or wounded, there was no one left to urge them on. When a Seminole bullet zipped into the mud at his feet, one of the volunteers dropped his musket and ran. Most of his fellows were not far behind. Wooster couldn't blame them. Everyone had told them how glorious the battle would be. No one had told them how horrible it would be.

Wooster turned to his officers. "Go to your companies, gentlemen, and await my orders. Fix bayonets and tell each man to look to the muzzle flashes and observe where in the trees the Seminoles are hiding. I want no wasted volleys. Also observe where the men of the Sixth make the most progress. There will be shallow areas in that swamp that will allow us to gain the hammock quicker." He then tapped the leg that had been wounded by the British so long ago. "And tell them if they can't keep up with an old man with a butchered leg, then they should take a seat with the volunteers!"

~~~

Gator John smiled. The first wave of white men had been no match for the Seminole warriors. If that were the best that the soldiers could do, the day would go down as a great Seminole victory. He also knew that those first white men had not been real soldiers. The regular soldiers were forming a line and marching toward the hammock. They would not be so easily turned away. Still, he wondered why so few were coming. Why didn't the whole army advance? He shrugged. He could kill but one white man at a time.

~~~

Wooster stayed in the saddle as he watched the Sixth slowly advance. It was a perfect line, as even as in a dress parade. It was a chilling sight to behold as the men bravely marched to their doom. A wry thought came to Wooster's mind: *At least they're trampling down the sawgrass.* He kept his eye on Thompson, the commander of the Sixth. Wooster had advised him to fix bayonets and charge before the Seminoles opened fire. He knew the advice would not be taken. Thompson might order the men to move at double time, but in the heavy sawgrass it would make little difference. Thompson had spent too many years studying European tactics under Winfield Scott.

The bravery of the common soldier never failed to impress Wooster. Unlike the officers, who could expect fame, glory, and promotion to result from conspicuous acts of valor, the enlisted man had everything to lose and nothing to gain. He would march straight forward to his death for no grander purpose than the knowledge that somehow, in the incalculable calculus of war, his passing might somehow provide a better world for those that would follow him. It had little to do with character, something that was not the common soldier's strong suit. In the end, it was discipline and loyalty to his comrades-in-arms that allowed the soldier to face almost certain doom. Thompson and Wooster's men were in reality no different from the volunteers who had panicked and ran. They were simply better trained. They knew that the war could not be won until the final battle was fought. Defeat would gain them nothing. Only through victory could the killing be stopped. It was all a grand and noble foolishness that Wooster could not fathom but never ceased to admire.

Thompson's men were still marching in close file when the Seminoles opened fire. Once again, the natives targeted the officers. First to fall was Lieutenant Center, clutching the base of his neck. Then Captain Van Swearingen wheeled around and fell face down into the water. The line stopped as the soldiers raised their muskets and took aim. Thompson's sword dropped, and a perfect volley was fired. The men calmly but quickly reloaded as the Indians began to fire another round, dropping soldiers from one end of the line to the other. Then, to Wooster's relief, he saw the men begin to fix bayonets. Finally, Thompson was going to order a charge.

The order never came. Before the command could be given, a rifle ball tore into Thompson's abdomen. Another penetrated his skull. Wooster closed his eyes. He and Thompson had known each other since 1814. Without orders, the Sixth remained frozen. Yet unlike the volunteers, the men of the Sixth did not break ranks. One by one, the soldiers took aim, fired, and reloaded, seemingly oblivious to the men who fell around them. The only officer still active was Captain Noel, who ran back and forth in back of the line, shouting orders and encouragement, telling the men to take cover behind fallen comrades or large clumps of vegetation.

~~~

Kachi-Hadjo jumped from his tree and began shouting at the other warriors to do the same. They had killed or wounded many soldiers, but the white men would not be stopped. It was time to move deeper into the hammock, to prepare for the next wave of soldiers. They must not let the enemy get too close. They must leave time to escape.

~~~

Without waiting for orders from Colonel Taylor, Wooster vaulted from his horse. With sword drawn and held high, he burst through his own line. "Run, damn you! Run to the aid of the Sixth!" The men of the Fourth cheered and charged into the swamp, Wooster at the lead, a pistol in one hand, his sword in the other, mowing sawgrass aside as he ran. The going was easier for them than it had been for the previous regiments. The sawgrass was matted down and pathways were clearer. Still, to say they were running swiftly would have been an exaggeration. As they approached the rear of the Sixth, the Seminoles began to fire at them, but with little effect. The Indians were falling back and taking less careful aim. Besides, moving targets were harder to hit. Once they passed through the ragged line of the Sixth, Wooster shouted, "Volley!" Each man stopped on his own, found his target, fired, and then resumed his running, loading as he ran.

As Wooster reached the edge of the hammock he saw a Seminole fleeing through the tangled forest. It was Kachi-Hadjo. Leveling his pistol, he fired. The ball lodged into a tree not three inches from the Indian's head. The soldiers passed into the hammock, stepping over fallen trees and tripping over hidden vines. Wooster called a temporary halt. "Take cover! Form your companies! Keep together!" The men began to move cautiously about, finding trees closer to their officers, taking time to fire when they saw a target. When order was fully restored, Wooster shouted, "Advance!" Suddenly, to his left, an Indian jumped out of a tree and atop a soldier's back. As the two men fell to the ground, the Indian brought his tomahawk crashing into the soldier's skull. Just as swiftly, Wooster spun around and plunged his sword into the warrior's back, twisting the blade maliciously as the Indian screamed in agony.

The American line moved slowly forward as each man ran from tree to tree, exposing himself as little as possible. The Indians were doing the same, only in reverse. As Wooster's men reached a small stream, shots were fired at them from the right. The colonel ordered MacDuff and

Sparkes to move in that direction. He then heard other sounds behind him. It was Noel and the remnants of the Sixth, along with a handful of the Missouri Volunteers, coming to join the fight. On they pushed for over an hour, advancing slowly through the dense vegetation. The Indians were retreating, but not running. Far off to his left, Wooster heard cheering. It was Taylor's First Infantry entering the hammock from the flank, safely clear of the main action.

~~~

Kachi-Hadjo stopped paddling and let the canoe drift. He could see the soldiers gathering on the shoreline, some of them firing futile shots at the fleeing Seminoles. Behind him, a warrior gave out with a piercing yell, taunting the soldiers. Kachi-Hadjo was less jubilant. Yes, they had stopped the whites, but only temporarily. At best, the battle had been a draw. The war, he knew, was far from over.

~~~

MacDuff and Sparkes were standing on the shore of Lake Okeechobee when Wooster caught up to them. A few soldiers knelt on the beach, firing shots that fell far short of the departing canoes. The colonel turned to MacDuff. "Take your men and scour the edges of the hammock. There may be some stragglers who were left behind. Mr. Sparkes, come with me." They walked slowly back through the hammock toward the sawgrass swamp, noting casualties as they proceeded. As they exited the hammock Wooster asked, "How many Indians do you think faced us, Mr. Sparkes?"

Sparkes shrugged. "Three-fifty, four hundred, maybe." Then, in a more disappointed tone, "Not more than a dozen killed." The two men then began to pass through the sawgrass. The dead and wounded were everywhere, being carried off or helped from the field. Dr. Weightman and Bemrose darted about, tending to the wounded, their trousers cut to ribbons by the sawgrass, their legs lacerated. Wooster stared at the body of his old friend Thompson, who had been hit at least three times; twice in the stomach, once in the head. There was blood all over his face. The colonel bent down, cupped some swamp water in his hands, and began to gently wash Thompson's face. For all practical purposes, the Sixth Regiment no longer existed. He stopped and looked around, and then closed his eyes. Almost a third of the men who had crossed the swamp were either dead or wounded. "They beat us, Sparkes; whipped us fair and square."

Sparkes's eyes narrowed. "Sir?"

"Oh, that's not what they'll print in the papers, but it's true nonetheless. Colonel Taylor will claim a great victory, saying we charged the Indians in their fastness, routed them, and held the disputed ground at the end of the day. Isn't that how we measure military victories?"

"So I've been taught, sir."

Wooster looked back at the hammock, out toward the lake. "Look at it from their side, Lieutenant. All they wanted to do was stop us, to give the squaws and the old people time to get away. They've done it. The volunteers and the Sixth are destroyed, and the Fourth will have to tend to the wounded and get them back to Tampa. Half of our force is gone or out of action for weeks. So tell me, Mr. Sparkes, who is the winner here?"

Sparkes nodded. "Yes, sir, I take your meaning. A rather hollow victory, I suppose. Still, I've been in the army long enough to know that Colonel Taylor will soon be *General* Taylor."

Wooster nodded and began to walk toward dry land. Sparkes was right. Taylor had gone for the glory. The safe bet would have been to bypass the warriors and send the main force after the women and children. But Taylor had wanted a battle. He had kept the First Infantry in reserve so he could use them to pursue the fleeing families, assuming the other regiments would deal quickly with the warriors. Taylor, however, had miscalculated on the skill and determination of the Seminoles. The Sixth and the volunteers had paid the price of that miscalculation, while Taylor would still reap the rewards. Wooster would have been disgusted were it not for one nagging question: What if the alphabetical register of officers had listed "William" before "Zachary"? What if he had been in charge? Would he have taken the more prudent path, or would he too have gone for the star?

19

To:
Miss Maria Wooster
St. Augustine, E. Florida

Dear Maria,

Greetings from the inhospitable salt marshes of southern Florida. The Colonel sends his love and has asked me to write. He is well but is recovering from a cold, which I believe I am soon to be suffering from myself. We are camped near an ocean inlet, our tent pitched upon a large shell mound that Dr. Weightman believes was built as a temple by some long extinct tribe of enlightened savages. Mr. Bemrose says it is nothing more than a refuse heap.

The fighting has ceased for the time being. There were two battles fought near here in January, but neither of much consequence. In the first, Lt. Powell of the Navy happened upon a large force of Seminoles, no doubt remnants of those we fought at Okee-Chobee. Being surprised and outgunned, Powell beat a hasty retreat back to his boats, losing a number of men in the action. Several days later, unaware of Powell's battle, our own force met the same Indians near the same creek and fought a running battle for an hour or two. As always, the savages melted away, and the result was a few lives lost on both sides and much powder spent.

The army is now resting comfortably enough. Indeed, rest we must. The men are exhausted from the long march and the battles. Most of the men, myself included, are dressed in tattered uniforms, the result of passing through the wicked sawgrass. Many of the men are without serviceable shoes, and both the Colonel and I are left with nothing but our riding boots. We look forward to the supply ships, which should arrive here most any day.

Two days past, the senior officers of the Corp met with Genl. Jesup on the subject of terminating the war. All are in agreement that the Seminoles have been beaten and that it would be folly to pursue them any further. Indeed, there are few Seminoles left to fight. Of the perhaps 5,000 who dwelt in Florida at the commencement of the war, at least 3,000 have been captured and sent to their new homes in the west. Hundreds must surely have died as a result of the war. There are, at present, several hundred camped nearby, calmly awaiting negotiations. They are in a most miserable state and have asked for nothing more than permission to live peacefully in the Everglades. By the most generous calculations, that would leave little more than a thousand still in the peninsula, nearly all of whom are scattered and destitute within the swamps of the Everglades. Many of those are women and children, or the very old. If left alone, they will not be a threat to the white man, for no one but a Seminole could live in the lands south of Okee-Chobee. Except for some small towns that might grow along the coast, white men will find it impossible to dwell in great numbers in south Florida. Why not let the savages have it?

One wonders how they continue to hold out. Almost all their leaders have been captured. Micco Nopy, Micco Phillip, Jumper, and Abraham are on their way west. News has just reached us that Ossiyola is dead. The only powerful chiefs that remain are Kachee-Hadjo, Halek Tustenuggee, and old Medicine Man Sam. Of those, only Halek is a true threat. Both Kachee-Hadjo and Sam will do their best to avoid us.

Whilst the general is in agreement with all this, he fears Mr. Van Buren and Sec. of War Poinsett will find peace a difficult pill to swallow. They have pledged to remove all Indians from the states east of the Mississippi and will be reluctant to modify this policy for the sake of the Seminoles. Such a decision would not be popular politically, and our leaders in Washington are, unfortunately, political people. Still, the effort must be made, and Genl. Jesup has written a letter to the Sec. of War suggesting the war be terminated. We can only hope the proposition is viewed with favor. We cannot calculate the years, the wasted lives, and the national treasure that would be lost in a futile attempt to remove the Seminoles from the trackless Everglades.

Both the Colonel and I hope that all is well with you and our friends in St. Augustine, and kind wishes are sent to Nero and Nettie. Soon, perhaps, we will join you. Should our attempts at peace fail, we must soon quit this place anyway, as it will no doubt be unhealthy during the summer months. Tonight we go to the nearby Seminole camp for some sort of festivity. For the moment, at least, there is peace in Florida. Pray, dear Maria, that it lasts.

With much love from your father and deep regards from myself,

Your Most Obdt. Serv.
Sparkes

Secretary of War Joel Poinsett picked a wilting red leaf off the plant that grew near his desk. The plant was a direct descendant of one he had brought from Mexico while serving as United States Ambassador to the newly independent nation. It was an odd thing, with large red leaves surrounding the small cluster of yellow flowers. As a naturalist, such things intrigued him. Why didn't other flowers do this? What made the Poinsettia so different?

A clerk stepped through the open door. "Sorry to disturb you, Mr. Secretary, but a messenger from General Jesup is here."

Poinsett knew it was something important; routine correspondence almost always went through the Adjutant General. He gave a quick nod and said, "Show the man in."

A well-dressed lieutenant stepped up to the desk, bowed slightly, snapped to attention, and held forth an envelope. "First Lieutenant Thomas Linnard, sir, with respects from Major General Jesup."

The Secretary smiled. "At ease, Lieutenant. Are you finding the weather in Washington City agreeable?"

"Not really, sir. I'd rather forgotten what snow looked like."

Poinsett nodded. This was the third winter in Florida for many of the nation's soldiers. He wondered how many more winters the lieutenant would have to spend there. Taking the letter, he broke the seal and glanced through the text. Looking at the date, he shook his head. Even with the advent of steamships and railroads, it still took two weeks for a letter to travel from the seat of war to the capital.

He read the letter carefully then set it down. He wasn't sure if he liked what he saw or not. Jesup was asking him to declare the war at an end. The general's arguments were certainly good: Most of the enemy killed or captured and on their way west; the remnants scattered throughout the Everglades and a threat to no one; would take years to catch the rest; would be an enormous waste of blood and treasure; all his senior officers in agreement.

It would be wonderful to end the war. It had lasted much longer than anyone had anticipated and was proving a very deadly, expensive, and unpopular conflict. When he had taken office a year earlier, the war appeared to be ending. The Seminoles had just signed a capitulation and appeared to be ready to board ship. Then the whole agreement had fallen apart, and he had been forced to raise the largest peacetime army the nation had ever seen. Even the navy was in on it. There was nothing he would like better than to say the war had been won under his watch.

It had also turned into a very unpopular conflict. The opposition Whigs in Congress were starting to make noise about the money spent and the lives lost. They also had the nasty habit of tying the war to the issue of slavery, something Poinsett's fellow southerners did not appreciate. Yet what surprised Poinsett most was the growing number of people who had become sympathetic to the Seminoles. There was a sense among many Americans that it was a cruel, unnecessary war, waged against a people who were gallantly attempting to defend a homeland that white men would never find attractive. The capture of Asi-Yoholo under that damned white flag and his death while in captivity certainly didn't help. From the very beginning the war had gone badly and now the citizenry were becoming impatient. Even Taylor's victory at Okeechobee had lost its luster. People were pointing to the number of casualties and complaining about Taylor's remarks concerning cowardly Missouri Volunteers. Yes, it would certainly be good to end the war.

He also knew it was not going to happen. He could already hear all the voices that would demand the war be carried to its ultimate conclusion. The Florida Congressional Delegate would be the first at his door, demanding that every last Indian be removed from the Territory. Florida, of course, was not paying the bill. He could also hear the Governors, Congressman, and Senators from Georgia, Alabama, and South Carolina complaining about all the slaves that were fleeing to the Seminoles. Poinsett always wondered how a handful of fugitive slaves could find the Indians when 9,000 soldiers couldn't. He could also hear, whispering into Congressional ears, the innumerable contractors and suppliers who kept the army fed, armed, and on the move. They would loathe losing those lucrative contracts.

Poinsett could also hear the voice of Andrew Jackson. The old man had a special hatred for the Seminoles. At least once a month Poinsett would receive a letter from The Hermitage, carrying on about how embarrassing the war had become. Once again, Poinsett would be reminded that Jackson could raise an army of fifty women and conquer the Seminoles within a week. The Secretary admired, almost worshiped, Jackson, but as each year passed, the old man became harder to deal with. If the war went on for another five years, as some were predicting, Jackson would become impossible.

About the only voice Poinsett could not hear was that of President Van Buren. The man in the White House had almost ignored the war. The president understood politicians and money men. He understood military men very little and Indians not at all. Out of courtesy, Poinsett would have to consult with the president, but he already knew what the response would be: "I wonder what Old Hickory would do?" That would be followed by, "Do what you think best, Poinsett."

Now that the subject had been broached, it could not be ignored. The secretary would have to write Jesup, telling him that the war would be prosecuted to the bitter end. Jesup wouldn't like the reply and would ask to be relieved. That was acceptable. He had probably done all that he could. It would be a smaller war from this point on, and a two-star general was no longer necessary. A one-star would be enough. Probably Zachary Taylor. Let him earn that star he was about to get.

The words were already forming in the Secretary's mind. It is the settled policy of this nation that the Seminoles will be removed. . . . It was a simple fact of American politics: There could be no compromise with an Indian nation.

~~~

Summer had arrived, and the army was making its usual retreat from the "unhealthy" interior of Florida. Much of the Fourth Infantry had been moved north from the Everglades with orders to ready the interior posts for abandonment and then consolidate along the coast. As his company marched away from Fort King, Sparkes turned in his saddle and took a last look at the fort. Would it still be there in the fall?

This year, with the war having moved south, there was the hope that there would be too few Seminoles around to burn it. At any rate, it would not be completely abandoned. A small local militia unit would keep an eye on the post and passing army patrols would visit occasionally. The war wasn't over, but its nature was changing.

The administration's refusal to end the war had been a bitter, though not unexpected, pill for the army in Florida to swallow, and there had been an immediate drop in morale among both officers and enlisted men. When they had been actively campaigning against the Seminoles there had been the hope that their toil and suffering would bring an end to the war. Now, with no end to the war in sight, all the hard work, sickness, and death were meaningless. They had begun to feel like Fort King: abandoned.

The appointment of Zachary Taylor as commander of the Army of the South, as it had come to be known, had especially rankled Colonel Wooster. As far as he could tell, Taylor had been rewarded for getting all those good men killed at Okeechobee and allowing the Seminole women and children to escape. To some small degree, Wooster blamed Taylor for the war not being over. He was also somewhat jealous. Wooster wanted to be the one with the general's star, the one with the opportunity to end the war.

Wooster also feared that Taylor had no idea how to end the conflict. "Old Rough and Ready," as Taylor liked to be called, was not sure and steady. Place a well-defined enemy in front of Taylor and he'd fight tooth and claw to defeat it. The Battle of Okeechobee had suited him perfectly. A cunning, amorphous antagonist like Kachi-Hadjo would baffle him. How could the army defeat someone who wouldn't come out and fight?

In a way, Sparkes was happy that Wooster, Dr. Weightman, and a portion of the company had left for St. Augustine a week earlier, taking the sick and the company paperwork with them, leaving him, MacDuff, and about twenty-five men to finish closing down the fort. Hopefully the colonel would be in a better mood after returning to his home, Maria, Nettie, and Nero.

As the company trudged along, Sparkes took notice of what he considered the only benefit of the war: After three years of improvement and maintenance, the major roads in Florida were much easier to travel than when he had arrived in the Territory. His first trip to the interior had been along this same road and much of it had been under water, even at the beginning of the rainy season. Now, a month into the summer, it was high and dry. It was also a shorter trek. At the commencement of the war it had been a fifty mile march to Palatka on the St. Johns River, where they would often have to wait days for an old steamer to arrive. Now it was a thirty mile march to the depot at Gerry's Ferry on the Ocklawaha, a tributary of the St. Johns, where newer, faster steamers made regular visits.

It had been a leisurely, two-day march to Gerry's Ferry, and as the company waited for the slave laborers to finish loading the steamboat, Sparkes began to feel sick. The illness started out as a mild fever accompanied by an intense backache, but by the time they boarded the boat, it had worsened and begun to alternate between periods of intense shivers and severe vomiting. Bemrose checked Sparkes's pulse and noticed that the lieutenant's heart rate had slowed. It was something the hospital orderly had seen before. "It's the Yellow Fever, sir, if I'm correct. We'd best get you and the others to Dr. Weightman as quick as we can." Bemrose understood the gravity of the situation: Sparkes was the fifth person out of the twenty-five men in the company to take sick.

For Sparkes and the other patients it was a slow, agonizing trip down the Ocklawaha and St. Johns. Bemrose and the men who weren't ill did their best to make their friends comfortable, but beyond that, there was little they could do. Upon reaching Picolata, MacDuff commandeered a wagon and rushed the five diseased men to Dr. Weightman at the hospital in St. Augustine. By the time they arrived, two of the men were showing signs of recovery, but Sparkes and the other two were getting worse. Their skin had taken on a yellowish hue, and all were suffering severe abdominal pains. Within hours of reaching the hospital, Sparkes was vomiting dark blood. The other two men were no better. All had nose bleeds; one was even bleeding from around the eyes. All of them felt as if they were about to die.

A day after their arrival, Bernolak, the Pole, succumbed to kidney failure. Besides the pain, the only other constant was the care. The doctor and the orderlies did what little they could by administering medications they knew would have minimal effect and giving the men water and soup whenever they could take it. If care alone could have cured the men, all of them would have recovered speedily. As it was, there was no choice but to let the disease run its course. When it came to actually curing the disease, the doctor was as helpless as the patient.

Assisting the hospital staff was another tireless worker. Since the war's beginning, Maria had visited the sick and wounded on a daily basis, rendering aid and comfort in any manner available. She visited each man in turn, talking softly of home, wiping their brows, emptying chamber pots, changing soiled linen, and giving them sponge baths to the limit that propriety would allow. It was dirty work and she had often been sick herself, but she had never shied away from the task. If her father could put his life on the line for these men, so could she.

After the arrival of Sparkes and the others, Maria's visits continued with little change in routine. She would go to the first bed and minister to whomever was there, then proceed to the next bed and do whatever needed to be done for that patient. Yet she always managed to end her visit at Sparkes's bed and spent just a few more minutes in his company. More than anything, she prayed the fever would break.

~~~

Kachi-Hadjo sat by a pond, cutting strips of buckskin to use as fasteners for a new pair of leggings. It was a hot afternoon, but not as bad as most summer days. The skies were cloudy, and a small rain shower had passed through earlier in the day. It was a quiet time, affording him an opportunity to reflect and to plan. For the third year in a row, the soldiers had departed at the end of their winter campaign, driven from the land by insects, disease, and rain. On a nearby patch of grass lounged Gator John. Both men were silent. Both had much to say.

Kachi-Hadjo broke the silence. "Gator John is quiet today. His mind is troubled."

John nodded slowly, his eyes fixed on the clouds above. "Ain't no hiding it, ol' frien'. I done paddled up the creek so far I done run out o' water. I jus' ain't lookin' forward to another year o' fightin'."

"I, too, had hoped the war would end, that we could live in peace. After the battles of Okeechobee and Loxahatchee there was talk from the white men that peace was near. As always, it was lies. The white man will not stop until the last Seminole is dead or beyond the great water."

"Hear tell they got them a new gen'ral in charge. Same damn fool what led the fight at Okeechobee."

Kachi-Hadjo shrugged. "It makes no difference who is big chief; all take orders from the Great Father in Washington. The Seminole must fight longer before the Great Father tires of war."

"White man ain't been fightin' too hard lately; just enough to keep us hidin'." He sighed. "Gettin' tired o' hidin'."

Kachi-Hadjo looked into his friend's eyes. "I feel a weariness in the voice of Gator John."

John shook his head slowly. "Don't know; maybe time for me to quit this war. Hear tell that the gen'ral gonna guarantee my freedom if I go out west. Most o' my people already there."

Kachi-Hadjo had always known that eventually it would come down to this moment. The blacks were fighting for their freedom, not the land. General Jesup had understood this and had begun to offer freedom in the west for those blacks who turned themselves in. If Gator John stayed in Florida, that chance for freedom in the west would be lost. Kachi-Hadjo didn't want to lose his closest friend, but felt he owed it to the man. "The black Seminoles will need a strong chief in the west. You should go. This is now the red man's fight."

The black man's voice wavered slightly. "You been my frien' since we was babies, Kachi-Hadjo. Gonna be hard to leave you here."

The Indian tried to look on the bright side. "Perhaps it will be better if the black man goes west. The slavers will leave us alone if the black men are not here. Maybe they will tell the Great Father in Washington to leave the Seminole be, that we no longer keep their slaves."

John knew better. "Won't do no good. The white man gonna want *all* this land an' ain't gonna suffer no red man to set foot on it."

"Then the Seminole must hide until the white man grows tired of looking for us."

"Why don' you give it up, ol' frien'? Your people gonna need good chiefs out west, jus' like mine." It was a futile suggestion, but he made it anyway.

Kachi-Hadjo stood up and stretched. "The bones of my mother and the mother of Ki-tee are buried in these sands. I cannot leave them until their spirits tell me so. They will tell me when they are free of this land, when they are free to join the spirits of those who have gone with their loved ones to the west. Until then, I must fight to stay with them."

John nodded. He picked up a handful of sand and let it slip through his fingers. "Somethin' I ain't never understood, ol' frien': Why the Injen so attached to the land? Ain't nothin' but dirt. Hell, might be better dirt out west." He laughed. "I guess everybody sees it different. The red man sees spirits in the land, the black man sees fields o' corn, and the white man sees somethin' to take away from somebody else." He stared out into the pond. The land was a good thing to fight for, but freedom was even better.

Kachi-Hadjo walked down the path that bordered the pond, leaving Gator John to his thoughts. He wasn't surprised that John didn't understand the Indians' attachment to the land. He wasn't sure he understood it himself. He gazed at a nearby pumpkin patch. It was not so much that the ground his mother was buried in was sacred, it was the fact that her spirit was now part of that ground. When the pumpkin's roots spread through the soil they were drawing in some part of the spirit of his mother. The love that she had given him while she was alive was now going into that pumpkin. Yes, the pumpkins might grow out west, but they would not be nourished by his mother's love.

As he strolled along the periphery of the pond he spooked a turtle, which slid off the fallen log it was sunning itself on and into the water. Kachi-Hadjo looked at the ripples, then thought of the turtle shell rattles that Ki-tee had been fashioning earlier in the day. He had no way to explain it, but the sound of that rattle came not from the small stones inside the empty shell, but from the spirit of the turtle that had once lived inside. He looked at a large cypress tree. When it was but a seedling it had begun to draw life from the waters of that same pond. When it died it would be made into a canoe, returning some of that life to the waters it traveled over.

He began to notice all sorts of things that were commonplace to his eyes but very dear to his heart: A small purple flower. A black and yellow butterfly. A green lizard. He knew the names and habits of each. A small alligator swam lazily through the water. He thought he heard the cry of a panther and the croak of a frog. He looked down the path, to where it turned off into the woods and out of sight. He knew where it went, and all the things it passed, both great and small. No, John did not understand. It had nothing to do with dirt. Kachi-Hadjo wasn't fighting for the land, he was fighting for the life that came out of that land and permeated every part of his being.

Kachi-Hadjo smiled. Up until that moment, he had been fighting because he felt a certain duty to his people. Now he understood why it was so important for his people to remain in their homeland. Their lives, and his, were part of this land. His ancestors' spirits were part of that pond, part of every tree that his eyes fell upon, part of every creature that walked upon this beloved land. To remove the Seminole from his homeland would be like removing the snail from its shell. Half of the creature would be nothing more than a slug, unprotected and doomed. The other half would be a hollow shell with no purpose to its existence. All of a sudden, he felt an immense amount of pride. Here was something worth fighting for.

~~~

The morning sun felt good as Sparkes relaxed on the balcony of the colonel's home in St. Augustine. He would enjoy it while it lasted. Within an hour or so, when the sun's rays began to heat the humid atmosphere, the air would become warm and thick and any physical exertion would lead to instant perspiration. Later, in the afternoon, the thunderstorms would come, cooling things for awhile, but leaving the air feeling like a Roman steam bath. These early morning hours, with the cooling breezes coming in from the ocean, were to be savored whenever possible. It made one feel good to be alive.

After little more than two weeks in the hospital, Sparkes's fever had broken. When Dr. Weightman informed the lieutenant that he could continue his convalescence at the barracks, Maria had insisted that Sparkes finish his recovery at the colonel's home. Wooster had noticed the extra attention his daughter had been paying to the young man, but there was little he could say to prevent Sparkes from moving in. As the colonel's aide, the lieutenant had always maintained quarters in the colonel's residence whenever they were in St. Augustine.

So it was that Sparkes found himself enjoying the sunrise on the colonel's balcony, a blanket covering him from the slight chill of the morning air. As the sun rose above the treetops on Anastasia Island, Bemrose stepped out onto the balcony. "Good morning, Lieutenant, sir. Rather nice to be out of the 'ospital, isn't it?" Sparkes nodded as the steward checked his pulse and felt his forehead. "The fever seems to be well broken, sir. Should be fit as a fiddle in a fortnight, I should think."

"As always, Mr. Bemrose, your ministrations have done much to restore my health. I have heard that Dr. Weightman is thinking of recommending you for the College of Surgeons. You should take him up on the offer. You would make a fine doctor."

"Don't know, sir. Don't know as I could take all that schooling. Could 'ave been a chemist in England now, I could, but couldn't sit still when I was apprenticed."

Sparkes could appreciate the young man's honesty, but, like the doctor, he had been impressed by his intelligence. "What were you and Dr. Weightman discussing yesterday? Something about the cause of malaria?"

Bemrose shook his head. "Ah, the doctor and 'is 'malignant vapors.' Now what in the name of Good King George are those? You breathe them in, 'e says, and you get sick. Well then why, I ask ye, ain't we all dead? When the fever breaks out, we all should get it, 'cause we all breathe the same air. It just don't make no sense."

Sparkes smiled. "And you have a better suggestion?"

The young man lit up, obviously proud of his theory. "Mosquitoes, sir." Sparkes gave him a skeptical look. "The way I see it, sir, when you 'ave the sickness, there's something in your blood. One of them damn mosquitoes comes along and bites you and sucks it up. Then 'e goes over to someone else, bites 'im, spits it back out, and that fellow gets sick. It would explain why only some of us get sick, why its worse when the rainy season is 'ere and the mosquitoes are thicker, and why it's so much the worse when we're 'oled up in the forts."

"And what exactly is in the blood, Mr. Bemrose?"

"Little animalcules, I'd say. Those little things you see swimming around when you look through one of those microscopes. I've seen drawings in some of the doctor's books, I 'ave, and . . ."

Their conversation was interrupted by the arrival of Maria, bearing a tray with a tea service on it. "Should the lieutenant be out in this brisk morning air, Mr. Bemrose?"

"The day is warming nicely, ma'am. The fresh air will do the lieutenant good, I think. Is the colonel about, ma'am? I 'ave the weekly medical reports for 'im."

"He has already left for the day, Mr. Bemrose. You may find him at his office in the barracks."

"Very well, ma'am, then I'll be on me way. Do 'ave a good day, sir. I'll leave you in the young lady's kind care. And remember, sir, it's the damn mosquitoes, it is." The young Englishman ran down the stairs, exited the front door, and was out in the street in no time. Passing in front of the house, he looked up at the balcony. "You rest easy, sir! Fit as a fiddle in a fortnight!"

Maria laughed. "He is such a dear man." She poured Sparkes a cup of tea.

Sparkes took the cup and said, "Thank you, Miss Maria."

Setting the tray down on a nearby table, she turned and stood before him. In the weeks since he had taken sick, she had grown much closer to him. She had seen him near death, and it had frightened her. She had watched other soldiers die and had felt the loss, but the potential loss of Sparkes had made her tremble at night. Their conversations by his sickbed had been polite, but had also been heartfelt. The only thing that frightened her more than the thought of losing him was the realization of how much she cared for him. She had also come to the realization that while the fear of losing him was something she could do nothing about, the fear of becoming closer to him was a fear she could conquer.

The first thing she needed to do was get past the wall of propriety that stood between them. "Must you always call me *Miss* Maria? We have been acquainted for over three years now, Lieutenant. I do believe we know each other well enough to dispense with such formalities."

Sparkes smiled nervously. He knew where the conversation was going and didn't want to follow that path. He tried to deflect the question with one of his own. "Would you then go to calling me 'Sparkes,' as my colleagues do?"

"Might I not use your Christian name?"

He then thought to lightheartedly evoke the one power that might end the conversation. "Certainly not in front of your father."

A look of frustration came over Maria's face. It had been the wrong thing to say, but Sparkes's recently-fevered mind hadn't been quick enough to realize it. "Oh, my father! He guards me better than Fort Marion guards this city. Does he think I shall forever remain a child?" She looked Sparkes straight in the eye. Could she say it? "Does he think I shall never fall in love?"

Sparkes was now very worried. She had crossed a line, one from which there was no backing away. "You should not be speaking of such things, Maria."

She would not be stopped. The feelings had been building for too long. She reached down and took his hand. "Should I not speak my heart, Mr. Sparkes?" She had to help him overcome his fear of her father. She also felt there was something he was not yet ready to admit. "Do you not see me as something other than a *Miss* Maria?"

Sparkes looked away, searching his mind for the proper response. She was right, and he knew it. For the past few weeks she had been in his mind more than anything, even more than thoughts of his own survival. When the fever had been the worst, he had fought to stay alive to please Maria and to see her another day. At any number of times, the agony had been so great that he hadn't cared if he lived or died. He had just wanted the pain to end. It was only during Maria's visits that the suffering left his mind. Her comfort had kept him alive and had bound her to his heart. It was a reality he could not ignore.

Yet he had to. It wasn't just the two of them. There was the war, the army, her age, and above all else, her father. He was truly torn. Should he speak from the heart or from the mind? As usual, the memory of his grandfather supplied the answer. *Honor your word, son: The only arrow worth a damn is the one that flies true.* He would be honest, but he would not cross the same line that she had. He would not say the word that could not be taken back. "It matters little what my thoughts may be. It would dishonor both you and your father were I to act upon my feelings." He looked back into her eyes. "Until such time as honor will allow it, dear Maria, I shall speak no words nor take such actions as would encourage those feelings from you. Your father has placed his trust in me; I cannot misuse him."

She let go of his hand and took a deep breath. The softness left her face, replaced by one of deep resolve. "Then patience shall have to fortify my heart, Mr. Sparkes. If these feelings must be held within, then most dearly shall I hold them. So confined, they shall only grow stronger." Picking up the tray, she left the balcony.

~~~

From behind his desk Colonel Wooster closed his eyes and bowed his head. His window faced his home, the balcony in clear view. Although he had not heard the words, he could tell what had been said. It was, he knew, his own fault. In being so protective of Maria, he had forced her to reach out to someone else in order to find her freedom. The colonel also knew that he had done little to prevent the romance. He hadn't needed to keep Sparkes so close, almost as one of the family. Once again, the vision came to mind: The Redcoats, the bloody bayonet, and the cannon fire. Yes, he owed this young man something. But did he owe him his daughter?

20

October 12, 1838
St. Augustine

To:
Mrs. David Kilgour
Cincinnati, Ohio

Dear Emily,

This may be the last you hear from me for some time, as we will be departing this place in the morning, with Ft. Brooke as our destination. It will be good to once again take to the field. It has been a most tedious and lengthy summer, especially since I was so long abed with the fever. I am thankful, however, to be alive; so many of our fellows did not survive. It anguishes me considerably to think of all the good men lost to disease. If a man must die in wartime, let it be by the hand of an enemy, not some malignant vapor that cannot be defended against.

Once at Ft. Brooke, I know not what we shall be doing. Genl. Taylor has ordered us there, but has yet to confide in us his plans for the winter campaign. Of one thing we are certain: The campaign will in no way resemble that of previous years. The War Dept., whilst urging us to pursue the war, has given us but half the troops we had under Genl. Jesup. This may be enough to guard the frontier or perhaps invade the Everglades in search of the Seminole hideouts, but certainly is not sufficient to do both. The one advantage is that we shall no longer have to bother with the Volunteers and much of the militia.

For the most part, the countryside has been quiet and one might wonder if there is actually a war taking place. The Indians are no doubt resting and gathering in their crops, preparing for another year's fight, and have been disinclined to show their faces. The settlers have returned to their homesteads and have planted their crops, many of which have been harvested. The winters being exceedingly mild, they have planted a second crop and will, in the spring, harvest again. Were it not for the war, Florida might well prosper, supplying various

213

fruits and vegetables to the north during the winter months. Sadly, should this pattern of peace in the summer followed by war in the winter repeat itself every year, this inglorious war will never end, and all of us—soldier, settler, and Seminole—will continue to suffer immeasurably.

Pardon me, for I complain too much. 'Tis the tedium of war and nothing more. In truth, it is actually quite lovely and agreeable at present. The air has cooled noticeably, and we are now entering that most delightful time of year in Florida. Were I a wealthy man with the freedom to live where my cares wished me to, I would spend the summers with you in Cincinnati and the winters here in St. Augustine (provided, of course, this damnable war were over).

I am sorry to hear that little Jacob is ill. I trust that with your love and good care he will speedily recover. Tell him I pray for his most rapid return to good health and that Lizzy and Kenneth remain free of disease. Also extend my appreciation to David for once again offering me a place in his business. I would gladly accept, for I have tired of this war and the military life, but there are personal matters here that I cannot yet resolve, which keep me tied to the army and to this place.

Your most affectionate brother,
Jacob

She had begged, almost demanded, to go with her father, but he had been firm. Maria was to remain in St. Augustine during this winter's campaign. There was both sorrow and anger in the tears that ran down her cheeks as she watched Wooster and Sparkes mount their horses. She remembered the widows of the men who had fallen at the Battle of Okeechobee. Would this be the year that she would share those same feelings of loss? Could this be the campaign from which one of them did not return? She remembered that nearly every officer of the Sixth Infantry had been killed in the battle. Death was indiscriminate. It could take one, or it could take many. Could she survive if both her father *and* Sparkes were to perish? She turned and placed her head onto Nettie's bosom and was enfolded in the cook's comforting arms. Nero rubbed her hair as she sobbed.

Wooster looked straight ahead as the horses turned the corner onto St. George's Street, making their way toward Fort Marion and the assembled troops. Out the side of his eye, Wooster saw Sparkes look back in the direction of the house. He knew what the young man was thinking. "It was for the best, Lieutenant. With the offensive soon to begin, we may not be at Fort Brooke for long. I would not want her to be there alone."

"Yes, sir, I fully agree." Sparkes knew there was more to it than that, but did not want to mention it.

It had been an interesting, almost dangerous summer once the fever had passed. Maria had been as proper as ever when in the presence of others, but on those rare occasions when she and Sparkes were alone, even for a moment, she had used the opportunity to remind him of how she felt. Sometimes it would be a look, while at other times it might be a touch. On one occasion, when he was seated at his desk, she had bent over and whispered in his ear, "I shall have thee, Mr. Sparkes." Another time she had stood behind him and run her finger down his back, moving it slowly from one side to the other, making big "S" curves from his shoulders to his belt line. On every occasion, he had done and said nothing, a response she seemed content with. It was a game she was playing, but he had no idea what the rules were.

Unfortunately for Sparkes, Maria's father had decided to play his own game. The colonel had avoided mentioning anything about the budding romance between his daughter and his lieutenant while in St. Augustine. He could handle Sparkes. He wasn't sure he could handle Maria. With the pair separated, the problem was temporarily put aside. Knowing Sparkes still had the tearful departure on his mind, Wooster said, "Our going to Fort Brooke will also serve to remove you from her presence, Mr. Sparkes."

It was a statement Sparkes could not ignore, as much as he wanted to. He also knew the colonel well enough to know that a simple "Yes, sir," would not be accepted. Like an Indian ambush, it had to be confronted. "Your meaning, sir?"

Wooster kept his eyes dead ahead. "My daughter's affections toward you have not gone unnoticed, Lieutenant."

Sparkes looked about, hoping someone would magically appear to interrupt the conversation. No one did. "Sir, I have done nothing to ..."

Wooster raised his hand, gesturing for Sparkes to be silent. "Your honorable behavior has not gone unnoticed either, Lieutenant."

Sparkes was relieved, but only slightly. He still had no idea where this exchange was headed. Would he have to take a transfer to the wilds of Maine, or was he expected to ask for Maria's hand in marriage? Once again, he tried to say as little as possible. "Thank you, sir. I assure you ..."

Wooster again motioned the young man to silence. "I have no worry of that, Lieutenant. Still, I am afraid these matters place me in a most difficult situation. Were I to have you transferred to another post, it would only serve to drive a wedge between my daughter and me. She can be quite headstrong when she cares to be, Mr. Sparkes."

"Yes, sir, I have noticed that."

"To dismiss you from my staff for no obvious reason would cast a shadow over my daughter's reputation. I am sure there are enough tongues wagging. Were I to send you away without good cause, unfounded rumors would multiply."

Sparkes was at a loss as to what to say. The best he could do was to reassure the colonel of his good intentions. "I would do nothing to bring your daughter's virtue into question, sir."

Wooster turned and looked Sparkes in the eye. "So what *will* you do, Lieutenant?"

Sparkes shrugged slightly. Wooster smiled. Both knew the colonel wasn't expecting an answer at the moment. The winter campaign wouldn't end until April. The situation might very well resolve itself before then. It was enough that the matter was now out in the open. The time for serious discussion would come later. By removing Sparkes from Maria's presence, Wooster was giving the young man time to think.

Sparkes wasn't the only one who needed time to think. The colonel had known for many years that his daughter would one day catch the eye of some ambitious young officer. There were two things he feared: First, that the officer would see her as nothing more than a vehicle to gain favor with a superior officer. Second, that Maria would suffer the same privations that her mother had. Wooster had always counted on his ability to scare off any undesirable suitors. What he hadn't counted on was Sparkes. From the very beginning he had sensed that Sparkes might be the one to capture Maria's heart, but Wooster had actually done little to prevent their coming together. He wasn't sure why. Sparkes was a good officer, but he was neither a natural-born warrior, like MacDuff, nor wildly ambitious, like Zachary Taylor. He could make a career of the army, but would probably never rise above Major. In the end, Wooster had to admit that it had more to do with Sparkes's father than anything else. He and Erastus Sparkes had been like brothers. What better man for his daughter than his closest companion's son?

There was another thing he liked about young Sparkes: He was utterly trustworthy. The need to separate the pair had less to do with Sparkes than it did with Maria. She was the impetuous one. As reliable as Sparkes might be, however, there were limits to any man's will power. A dark thought entered Wooster's mind: Sparkes's devotion and trust might evaporate if the young man ever discovered what had really transpired at Fort Erie so many years ago.

The pair rode on in silence for awhile, letting their thoughts run free. Midway through town they turned onto a side street, past a row of slave shacks. As they passed one of the buildings they heard a woman crying softly. The sound caught both men's attention, and they turned to see where it was coming from. Through an open window they saw a young slave girl, pretty, and barely in her teens. As one trembling hand worked to fasten her ragged dress, the other wiped away a tear. The door of the shack opened and a white man appeared, tucking his shirt into his trousers. Wooster recognized him as Mr. Handly, a local merchant. Touching his hat, as if they had met anywhere else in St. Augustine, Wooster called out warmly. "Good day, Mr. Handly. Do give my regards to your wife and children."

The merchant looked up quickly, mumbled a greeting, and hurried on.

There was an agitation in Wooster's voice that Sparkes had never heard. "Curse every damn slaver that ever lived, Sparkes. They shall be the ruin of us yet."

"Yes, sir." It was all Sparkes could think of to say.

Wooster carried on. "It stains the best of us, Lieutenant. Handly's reputation within the business community is without question. His family is as dear to his heart as my daughter is to mine. Yet nothing, it seems, prevents him from sampling a new *aquisition*."

Sparkes felt the time was at hand to ask a question that has always bothered him. Almost apologetically, he put forth his query. "If I may ask, sir, are not Nettie and Nero your slaves?" No one had ever said they were, but the inference had always been there.

There was a profound sadness in the colonel's answer. "It compromises us all, Lieutenant." As a career military officer, Wooster had learned it was best to keep his political views to himself, especially on the subject of slavery. Today, however, he felt a need to explain. "When Maria was born we were posted in New Orleans. It had not been an easy birth, and my wife's delicate condition necessitated us acquiring servants." He looked at Sparkes and shook his head. "There are, Lieutenant, no white domestic servants for hire in all of Louisiana. You must either purchase or hire a slave, or you must do without."

Sparkes nodded; it was no different in Florida. "I should think I would rather hire a slave than own one."

"Does it make any real difference? The man is still in bondage. You are using his services, and he gets nothing out of it. Worse yet, the owner, who does nothing, receives the fruits of the servant's labor. There is also the matter of loyalty. If you were paying a free laborer, he might feel he owes you something in exchange for the money you've paid. What obligation does a slave fell if he receives nothing from you?" Wooster let the question sink in then continued his tale of Nettie and Nero. "About the time I was considering this situation, a fellow officer was being transferred north and let it be known that Nettie and Nero were for sale. It was, I assure you, a most difficult decision to make. I have always abhorred slavery, and recoiled from the thought of becoming a slave owner myself. In the end, it was necessity, and the callous talk of others, that led me to become a slave holder."

"The talk of others, sir?"

"Another officer, a young captain from Alabama, sat calculating their worth, separated or together, as house servants or as field hands, in Louisiana or Mississippi, all as if they were nothing more than a bale of cotton, and all while they were standing right there. Although I could ill afford it on a brevet Major's salary, I paid the price, fully intending to free them when I no longer needed their services." He saw the questioning look in Sparkes's expression. "For some reason, the opportunity never seemed to arise. Either my wife was ill or Maria needed looking after while I was gone on duty, or I had simply gotten used to their presence. In a way, it's like any other form of property: You can't bring yourself to just give away something you paid good money for, and I certainly wasn't going to sell them down the river."

"Could you free them now, sir?"

Wooster looked annoyed. "To what end, Lieutenant? To make myself feel more righteous? How would they make their way? What would they do? Slavers are evil men, Lieutenant, and a free Negro in a slave society has no security. As long as I hold the papers, they're safe." Sparkes nodded. In his own way the colonel was fighting the system, protecting a pair of blacks who had become dear to him. "They're getting old, Mr. Sparkes. What better life can they hope for? The best I can say is that they are free to ask for their freedom. They know I would grant it in a minute."

Sparkes realized that the trust between him and the colonel was deepening. "I have never heard you speak so passionately on the subject, sir."

Wooster shrugged. "Something in the innocence of that slave girl reminded me of my own daughter, I suppose." He glanced back at the girl's shack. "Or my own guilt."

Sparkes was at a loss for a proper response. "I understand, sir. I pray that I am never forced to own a slave."

The look of annoyance returned to the colonel's face. "Do you think you are untouched by slavery, Lieutenant? Do you dare question the practice in front of MacDuff or any other fellow officer from the south? George may be MacDuff's slave, but he cooks your meals and tends to your mess no differently than his master's. Slavery is like a foul-smelling carcass we do our best to ignore, hoping the putrid odor will disappear. Someday, Mr. Sparkes, the stench will rise to consume us all, including those who thought they were untouched by it. No, Lieutenant, we are all compromised."

~~~

Kachi-Hadjo was glad the council was over. It had been a contentious meeting and tempers had flared. Everyone was on edge, arguing over how to conduct the war against the whites. In the end, Kachi-Hadjo and those who felt as he did had prevailed, but just barely. Angry words had been spoken and would not soon be forgotten. The solutions they had reached were only temporary. Unresolved matters would no doubt come back to haunt them.

Even the meeting place reflected the tension. They had come together in an isolated hammock, as well concealed as could be expected in mid-winter, when many of the trees had lost a good portion of their leaves. The chiefs had gathered in a temporary camp instead of a permanent village in hopes of keeping the council hidden from any army patrols or spies. So many Seminoles and blacks had surrendered or been captured that it was becoming difficult to trust anyone who happened to wander into camp. Few of the spies were willing traitors. The blacks, threatened with being sold into slavery, were especially vulnerable to coercion. Even independent-minded Indians found themselves in difficult positions when family members were held by the army. Kachi-Hadjo shook his head. If the whites couldn't destroy the Seminole way of life with bullets, they would find some other way.

The men in attendance were all capable chiefs, but few were truly experienced. It saddened Kachi-Hadjo to think of how many good men were no longer with them. Micco Nopy and Abraham were far to the west, in the new Indian Territory. Asi-Yoholo had died in prison, and Micco Phillip had perished while on the trip west, buried in a white man's cemetery, far from those who loved him. Other, less important but highly respected leaders were also gone. Chalo Emathla had been the first to die, before the war had started. Gator John and most of his black followers had surrendered, taking the government's offer of freedom in the west. Blue Snake, Coahadjo, Jumper, Alligator, and many other leaders had surrendered or been captured. Uchee Billie, Waxe-Hadjo, and a host of others had been slain in battle. Of those who held prominent positions when the war began, only he, Abee-Aka, and Halek Tustenuggee remained.

Yet the tribe was not leaderless. Younger men had stepped in to take the place of those who were no longer present. Chitto Fixico, Hospetarke, and Otulke were all fine leaders and eager to carry on the struggle. The most prominent of the new leaders was Holata Bolek, head of the Alachua band. As the nephew of Jumper and a relation of Micco Nopy, Bolek was from the line of Cowkeeper, which made him eligible to be head of the Alachuas and, indeed, all of the Seminoles. Unfortunately, it was a position that many people thought Kachi-Hadjo should have.

Such differences of opinion were the primary reason the council had been called. At the beginning of the war, all the bands had fought as one. As the conflict had worn on, however, old animosities had begun to surface. The deepest divide was between the two largest tribes of the nation, the Mikasukis and Alachuas. Between personal, clan, and tribal rivalries, it was becoming increasingly difficult to hold the nation together.

Fortunately, there was no real rivalry between Kachi-Hadjo and Holata Bolek. Kachi-Hadjo had earned his position as head of the Mikasukis through his actions and by being the son of Micco Phillip. Bolek's rise as head of the Alachuas was more surprising. He had always been quiet and thoughtful, and had rarely spoken his mind when in council. On the battlefield he had performed adequately, but never with great bravado. He was a man always seen, but never noticed. As the war had progressed, however, things began to change. As the other leaders of his line were either killed or captured, Bolek became more prominent. He began to lead war parties and to speak out in council. He began to gain respect. In some ways his ascension was by default. In others, it was inevitable.

The reason there was little rivalry between the two men was because neither one cared to be the Micco, or head chief. Both men seemed to understand that the time for petty politics would come after the war was over. For now, such concerns were a dangerous distraction. If the Seminoles were successful against the whites and retained a homeland in Florida, there would be plenty of time for people to stake out leadership positions within the tribe. If they lost the fight, it really wouldn't matter.

The biggest disagreement within the nation came from the two other most powerful men in the two tribes, Abee-Aka of the Mikasukis and

Halek Tustenuggee of the Alachuas. Abee-Aka, the cunning old medicine man, believed that the best way to defeat the whites was to not fight them at all. He argued that the Seminoles should take refuge within the hidden hammocks and islands of the Everglades and avoid all confrontation with the enemy. Sooner or later, the whites would no longer perceive the Indians as a threat, and the red man would be allowed to live in peace.

Halek, as the Tustenuggee, or War Leader, of the Alachuas, held the opposite opinion. He was determined to make war upon the whites until they returned Seminole land and brought his people back from the land in the west. He was also unwilling to admit that it was an impossible goal. For men like that, the eventual outcome of the war was secondary to the need to vent their anger and frustration on the whites. What made matters worse was that both men were charismatic leaders who inspired a large following of warriors.

Unfortunately, the position of Abee-Aka was just as untenable as Halek's. The whites would never accept the presence of the Seminoles in Florida unless they had to. They would always be covetous of Indian land, no matter how worthless that land was. They would always believe that the Seminoles were harboring runaway slaves, whether the Seminoles did it or not. And they would always fear Indian war parties, no matter how peaceful and reclusive the Seminoles tried to be. The best that Kachi-Hadjo and his people could hope for was to force the Great Father in Washington into signing a treaty he would actually abide by. The only way they could do that was to continue to fight a defensive war, to prove to the white men that they were not going to leave their homes. It was a slim hope, but it was the last hope they had.

~~~

Winter had passed and the spring of 1839 had arrived. The weather had brightened, but the mood at Fort Wooster had not. Inside the blockhouse, MacDuff threw a tin plate against the blockhouse wall, sending the food in all directions. George immediately began to clean up the mess. MacDuff shook his head in disgust. "Three years and you still can't cook worth a damn, can you?"

George looked to the floor. "Never says I could, Massa Mac." George had matured since MacDuff had won him in a card game and was now a healthy young man of fifteen years. Although he despised being a slave, George did his best to keep his master happy. The young slave knew what he was worth at auction and was aware that if MacDuff intended to make a sizeable profit, now would be a good time to sell, while George was at his prime. Indeed, more than a few of the slave catchers who hung around the larger army posts had made MacDuff offers, but the white officer had always turned them down, saying he could get a better price elsewhere. George shuddered at the thought of becoming a field hand on a large plantation and conspired as best he could to prevent MacDuff from selling him. Taking care of the white officers may have been demeaning, but it was considerably better than chopping cotton.

MacDuff shook his head. It wasn't George's fault that he was in a foul mood. His own mother's cooking would have tasted no better. In reality, it was nothing more than simple boredom. He had spent the whole winter at Fort Wooster, accomplishing nothing and doing nothing to bring the war to a close.

George's eyes widened as MacDuff pulled the old family broadsword out of its scabbard. The captain swung the blade lazily, carving a figure-eight pattern in the air. "Where's that damn bottle of whiskey?"

"You and Massa Sparkes done drained it las' night, Massa Mac."

MacDuff yawned. "Really? I don't remember that." He shrugged and put the sword away. He sat down, trying to think of something to do. There was no paperwork to be filled out, no reports to be sent to Washington. The storehouse was full, locked, and guarded, and the leaky roof had been fixed. The unofficial business looked even less promising. The last bottle of whiskey was empty, the only women within ten miles were the unwashed, toothless wives of squatters, and the bow for his fiddle had snapped when he'd accidentally sat down on it. And it was only three in the afternoon.

Noises from outside the blockhouse began to command his attention. It sounded as if a rider had just come into the fort. Suddenly the door burst open and Colonel Wooster stormed in. He looked about the blockhouse, obviously upset about something. "George! Get me some coffee!" The colonel turned to MacDuff. "Where's Sparkes?"

"Out on patrol, sir. Some report of Indian sign." It was an almost daily occurrence: A settler thought he saw signs that Indians were in the area, and a patrol from the fort would be obliged to check out the report. Nine times out of ten, it amounted to nothing. Once in awhile they would find signs of a Seminole camp, but it was usually several days old. Most aggravating were the times when they would thoroughly explore an area, find it totally free of Indians, only to hear of an attack in that same vicinity a day or so later. The army was doing all it could to protect the countryside, but no one's life seemed to have been saved.

MacDuff knew that Wooster had just ridden in from Fort Brooke, twenty-four miles away. Something must have happened in Tampa that was still bothering the colonel hours later. It probably had nothing to do with Sparkes. When the colonel was angry, he liked to vent his frustrations on Sparkes. The lieutenant never took it personally. Both parties knew that Wooster wasn't angry with his lieutenant, but rather with the circumstances they were all forced to put up with. The war had become thoroughly frustrating to them all, and they all understood the occasional need to release their anger. MacDuff did it by yelling at George. Wooster did it by yelling at Sparkes, and Sparkes did it by yelling at some enlisted man. It was what someone called the "chain of annoyance." Unfortunately, with Sparkes out on patrol, MacDuff realized that he would have to suffer the slings and arrows of outrageous military bungling. He sighed: It was all part of the job.

Wooster paced the room, stopping only to drink the coffee that George had brought him. He then wheeled about and looked straight at MacDuff. "A year, damn it! A whole year wasted!"

"Sir?"

"Did we not, at this same time last year, ask the War Department to declare this inglorious war over?"

"Aye, sir. As I recall, General Jesup's arguments were most logical."

"We damn near begged them, didn't we?" MacDuff nodded, but said nothing. "And how did Poinsett and those other melon-heads in Washington answer us? Indian Removal was the 'Settled Policy'! No discussion! No compromise! Every last one of the red sons-of-bitches has to be gotten out, no matter what it takes!" MacDuff understood the hidden meaning in Wooster's words. Whenever the colonel started to curse the Indians, it was to prevent himself from mentioning too many of his superior officers by name.

MacDuff attempted to calm the colonel down. "We *have* tried, sir."

The remark had the opposite effect from what MacDuff had hoped for. Wooster's near-empty coffee cup sailed across the room, hitting the log wall with a metallic clang. George quickly grabbed a rag and went to work on the cleanup. "No we have not, damn it! We have sat on our asses the whole damn winter waiting for General Taylor to go on the offensive, and he never has." Wooster resumed his pacing for a moment then stopped again. "Do you know what we've accomplished in the past year? Would you like a list?" MacDuff said nothing. It wasn't the sort of question he could say "no" to. "We've built a thousand miles of roads, innumerable bridges, and a hundred little blockhouses for the population to run to whenever the damn savages show their ugly red faces."

MacDuff had to admit that Wooster was correct. For the past six months Taylor had set his men to the business of building defensive works throughout the more populated areas of the Territory. The general had divided the northern half of Florida into twenty-mile squares and had erected blockhouses near the center of each square. Roads and bridges were constructed between each post and a garrison was maintained at each. The whole effort had made north Florida more habitable, but had done nothing to remove the Seminoles.

Wooster went back to his pacing then stopped to ask another question. "How many Indians have we killed this winter?"

MacDuff answered with a bit of embarrassment. "Perhaps a dozen, sir."

"And how many settlers have the Indians killed?"

The next answer was even more embarrassing. "Considerably more than a dozen, sir."

Like a lawyer who had just clinched his case, Wooster pounded his fist onto a nearby table. "A ringing success, Captain! And now that the summer sickly season is about to come upon us, we can assume that an order will soon be issued to abandon all those posts and cease the offensive operations that have never begun!"

MacDuff was confused. Something was missing from Wooster's tirade. "What does this have to do with General Jesup's request to end the war, sir?"

"We've wasted a year, damn it! We've brought no peace to this Territory, we've spent millions of dollars the treasury does not have, and we've lost or ruined hundreds of lives."

MacDuff was still confused. Wooster's complaints were everyday aggravations, something they had all complained about for months. Why was he so upset now?

Wooster read the younger man's mind. "A peace treaty, damn it! On precisely the same terms we suggested a year ago! The damn fools are even going to send down Macomb to negotiate with the heathens." MacDuff was surprised. Alexander Macomb was the highest-ranking officer in the army, a man who rarely left his desk in Washington. For the War Department to dispatch the Commanding General to Florida was a sign that they were serious about these negotiations. The only explanation was that the administration had been forced into it by the opposition Whigs in Congress.

MacDuff was skeptical. "Will the Indians negotiate, sir?"

"Don't know why they shouldn't. It would seem they've gotten what they wanted." The reality gave them both reason to pause. This was the fourth campaign they had served in since the war had begun. So much had transpired in that time. They had seen battles large and small, and had lost a good many friends. Everyone they knew had been seriously ill at one time or another, and many had not survived those illnesses. They had burned Seminole villages, and they had come upon settler's homes that had been burned by the Seminoles. They had seen innocent women and children killed and abused by men on both sides. They had killed Indians, and they had shaken their hands in friendship. They had freed blacks, and they had sent some of them back into slavery. For three and a half years they had been fighting, and as far as either one could tell, it had all been a waste.

So why was Wooster so upset? Didn't they all want the war to end? The colonel soon supplied the answer: "My God, MacDuff! The damn Indians have whipped us."

June 30, 1839
Ft. Brooke

To:
Miss Maria Wooster
St. Augustine, E. Florida

Dearest Maria,

I write in haste, having just received orders to prepare the men of the company for detached duty. It seems we are to proceed in the morning, by steamer, south to the Caloosahatchee, where we are to erect and protect a trading post. This is all part of Genl. Macomb's agreement with the Seminoles. The orders come at an especially inconvenient time for the company, many of whom are on sick list. MacDuff, as you know, is on furlough, and Sgt. Bigelow is in confinement for taking liberties with the young daughter of a citizen of this town. Bigelow is a scoundrel and should be drummed out of the service, but corrupt as he is, he is a good sergeant, something that is hard to come by these days. He will join us as soon as Genl. Taylor releases him from confinement, but for the moment, he will be missed.

I know, dear love, these many months of separation have been difficult, but perhaps it is for the best. Had we been in each other's presence, our passions may have overruled our propriety. Your father means us no ill, and I respect his wisdom in this matter. Honor dictates that to have you I must maintain his trust, a task I shall not fail at. Perhaps, if this peace holds and the war truly ends, he will happily consent to our union. Pray to our Lord that such be the case.

With undying love,

Your <u>Most</u> Obdt. Serv.
Sparkes

Spring had passed and summer was settling upon the peninsula of Florida. General Macomb and staff arrived from Washington, intent on fulfilling their duty and concluding a treaty with the Seminoles. Taking up residence at Fort King, Macomb spent the first few weeks trying to entice the reluctant natives into coming in for talks. After their experiences with General Jesup, the Seminoles were understandably wary of the white flag. Macomb persisted, however, and finally arranged a meeting with Chitto Fixico, a representative of Abee-Aka and the Mikasukis. Kachi-Hadjo gave his blessing to the meeting but declined to attend. He'd already traveled that path and doubted if he could escape from prison a second time. As for Holata Bolek, Halek Tustenuggee, and the Alachua chiefs, they simply refused to discuss the matter.

Talks didn't commence until mid-May, but once started, they went surprisingly smooth. The government's offer was simple, and Chitto found little to argue with. Macomb told him if the Seminoles remained peaceable, they would be allowed to live southwest of Lake Okeechobee. There was no talk of how long the Indians could remain there and no mention of surveyors coming in to mark boundaries. In truth, neither side saw much use for such limitations. The land was so inhospitable that no one could imagine anyone but a Seminole surviving there. To many whites, even that was doubtful.

In private conversations with his officers, Macomb was optimistic but somewhat disingenuous toward the Indians. When asked if he were concerned by the fact that all negotiations were going through a lesser chief of but one of the major bands, the general confidently pointed out that Chitto spoke for Abee-Aka and that all the Seminoles would follow Abee-Aka's lead. When asked how long the Seminoles would be allowed to remain in their new reservation, Macomb said that when they became a problem they would simply be rounded up and shipped west. When asked why he wasn't going to get a written treaty, he offered that the Indians had no faith in treaties, so why bother with one?

Whatever reservations Chitto had about the negotiations, he them kept to himself. Although he was speaking on behalf of Abee-Aka, Chitto knew there was no guarantee the mercurial old man would accept the deal that had been worked out. Getting the Alachuas and some of the smaller bands to go along was even more problematic. Chitto also worried about what would happen in a few years, when white settlers inevitably moved south. Would the Great Father in Washington protect the Seminole reservation? It also bothered him that Macomb had never asked him to place his mark upon a written treaty. He knew how much faith the white men put in their papers with the strange marks. Did this treaty mean so little to Big Chief Macomb that it was not worth the paper?

To help entice the Indians to move south, Macomb promised to set up a trading post on the Caloosahatchee River, near the north end of the reservation but far from any white settlement. Throughout the negotiations, the general never mentioned why it had all come to this point. Neither he nor anyone in Washington was willing to admit that the Seminoles had forced the government to sue for peace. For his part, Chitto had seen the wisdom of not bringing the matter up. It was as good a deal as his people were likely to get, and he saw no reason to jeopardize it.

Much to everyone's relief and surprise, the fighting actually stopped. The few Seminoles who remained in the northern part of the peninsula gradually drifted south. White settlers cautiously went back to their homesteads and planted their crops, while the army began to reassign troops to healthier, more northern locations. It was like a pleasant dream, and no one wanted it to end. Even Colonel Wooster lost his usual cynicism.

Then suddenly, in late June, the colonel's mood turned to one of deep anger. It wasn't the normal, cathartic rage that was brought on by the everyday frustrations of a grossly mismanaged war. That sort of anger passed quickly, a form of therapy that did its work then subsided. This time the rage lasted. The insult had been personal and had come from someone he thought of as a friend. General Taylor had ordered Sparkes and the men of Company "B" to the Caloosahatchee for the purpose of establishing the trading post called for in Macomb's treaty. Taylor hadn't picked Company "B" because it was the best qualified or without other duties. He had done it to hurt Wooster.

It wasn't the order itself that angered Wooster; he had never tried to protect Sparkes from the dangers of military life. Instead, it was the situation. As far as Wooster was concerned, the mission to the Caloosahatchee was unnecessarily dangerous, especially in light of the restrictions Taylor had placed on it. Only one company would be going, nowhere near enough men to quickly erect a post in the heart of enemy territory. On top of that, Sparkes's company was unusually shorthanded. Until a large blockhouse was completed, the soldiers and the men who ran the trading post would be extremely vulnerable. As far as Wooster was concerned, Taylor was sending Sparkes on a suicide mission.

Wooster also knew there was nothing he could do about it. Taylor had been specific in the details and had left no room for argument. If Wooster questioned the order, Taylor would charge him with favoritism toward Sparkes. The romance between Sparkes and Maria was no secret. Taylor was attempting to hurt Wooster in his most vulnerable place: through his daughter.

The colonel was well aware of the reason for Taylor's animosity. Word had somehow gotten out that Wooster had been critical of Taylor's handling of the Battle of Okeechobee and of his lack of initiative in the past winter's offensive. Wooster had never made public comments concerning the matters, but had, perhaps, been a bit indiscreet in private conversations. Taylor's star was rising, and he didn't want anyone dimming the light.

Two years earlier, when both men had been of equal rank, Wooster might have confronted Taylor over the matter. Now that it was "General" Taylor, the two men had ceased to regard each other with equal respect. The pair had once been good friends; now they were drifting towards enmity. Their relationship was, if nothing else, another casualty of war.

~~~

It was a pleasant morning, at least for mid-July in south Florida. There was a good breeze, some cloud cover, and fewer-than-normal numbers of mosquitoes and sand fleas. Sparkes tossed a pack over his shoulder and headed for the canoe. Corporal Yates, his only non-commissioned officer, followed close behind. "Is the lieutenant sure he doesn't want to take someone with him?"

Sparkes looked at the small clearing on the wide point of land where the trading post was being erected. There were less than two dozen tents of varying sizes, a large pile of logs, and not much else. There was too much work to be done, and none of the twenty-seven soldiers could be spared. "No thank you, Corporal. It seems to be a nice enough day for a quiet trip downriver to the supply ship. I'll just drop off these dispatches so that Captain Sands can get underway, then I'll paddle back. I should return before dark."

"Aye, sir, as you wish."

"Try to raise the blockhouse walls a few logs high today. I'll feel more secure when there is someplace to take cover in."

"Aye, sir, should be no problem. We could've had it all done a week ago, had General Taylor given us sufficient force."

Sparkes was in agreement. "Our commander holds little hope for General Macomb's peace treaty, Corporal. We shall have to make do with what he has given us."

Yates nodded. "Aye, sir, so it seems. Still, if he has such low faith in the treaty, why do we have so few men? There's not another soldier within a hundred miles of this place."

Sparkes understood the man's anxiety. Until the blockhouse was complete, the whole company was dangerously exposed. "Hopefully we'll not have need of more men. The Indians have seemed peaceable enough."

"They do seem pleased with the war being ended, sir."

Whatever the mood of the Indians, Sparkes was wary. "Pleased or not, Mr. Yates, we need to keep our guard up. I have fought the Indians too long to place much faith in their protestations of friendship."

"I take your meaning, sir."

Sparkes cast an eye toward the sky. "Perhaps the rains will hold off this afternoon. Just in case I need to stop at one of the islands and take refuge from the lightning, I've taken my bedroll and the India Rubber cloth. Don't be concerned for me until morning."

Sparkes stepped into the canoe as Yates prepared to push him off. "Very well, sir. Have a good day." The corporal watched as Sparkes paddled down river. He then turned and went back to the camp. As the soldiers gathered, Yates took one last look at the departing canoe. "There's work to be done today, lads! But first, I think we need a spot of rum to get us in the mood. C'mon, gather round!"

~~~

The canoe moved effortlessly, pushed along by a strong easterly breeze. Sparkes hoped the wind eased by the time he headed back up-river. The Caloosahatchee was wide and normally docile this close to the Gulf of Mexico, but in a strong wind the waves could get high enough to make travel in a small canoe very difficult.

The easy pace allowed the young man time to reflect on his present situation. It had been over four years since he'd graduated from West Point. They had been difficult years. He had survived serious wounds and yellow fever, along with numerous other minor injuries and lesser diseases. He had broken the "thou shall not kill" Commandment more than once and had seriously considered breaking one or two others. He had waded through frozen swamps and had suffered from intolerable heat. He had gone without food or had eaten things that no sane man would have touched. All of these things had taken a toll on him. He was tired.

Yet he could not complain. Other men had suffered worse. Many had died. He had been promoted twice in that period of time, first to brevet first lieutenant, then to fully commissioned first lieutenant. Perhaps, if this mission were a success, he would receive a brevet captaincy. He had experienced the thrill of battle and the close friendship of comrades-in-arms. Most of all, he had found love.

Now that the war appeared to be ending, the future seemed boundless. He could remain in the army, or he could return to civilian life. Emily's husband had made him a very good offer. In truth, much of it depended upon Maria's father. Having the colonel's blessing was important to Sparkes, and he would never do anything that might drive a wedge between Wooster and his daughter. He knew the value of a close family relationship. He had felt the love of his grandparents, his sister, and his many aunts, uncles, and cousins. He also knew what happened when families lost that love. His own mother had disappeared because of it.

It had been four months since Sparkes had been in St. Augustine and seen Maria. He and the colonel had gone to the old city to greet General Macomb, and their arrival had forced Maria into an awkward situation: As both men entered the house, she had to decide who she would embrace first. Wooster had settled the problem by stepping back slightly and gently pushing Sparkes forward. Without saying a word, the colonel had given his blessing to the couple's relationship. Nothing more needed to be said, and nothing was.

Sparkes smiled as he remembered Maria's face. She was eighteen now, certainly of marriageable age. Only the war stood between them, a circumstance as real as the impenetrable forests and swamps that made travel between north and south Florida a near impossibility. It was clearly understood that Sparkes and Maria intended to wed, but the colonel had insinuated that no marriage would take place until they were all safely away from the seat of war. Leaving the army was unthinkable for the time being. There was, after all, a peace to be secured, and neither man would abandon his mission. The best Sparkes could hope for was that the Fourth Infantry would be transferred to another part of the country. Despite the present truce, it didn't seem likely.

The separation from Maria was difficult, made worse by the aggravation of a stalemated war. Both he and the colonel had been anxious to go on the offensive but were forced to suffer through General Taylor's defensive war. To be confined to the area around Tampa Bay had been like torture. They had reasonably good intelligence as to where several Seminole bands were located, but never received the authority to go after them. On the other hand, Macomb's peace treaty seemed a cruel hoax: Sparkes trusted neither the intentions of the Indians nor the promises of the government. Sooner or later one party or the other would break faith and the war would be renewed.

Sparkes sighed and dug the paddle into the water. He would grow old in this war; either that, or the war would kill him. Whichever way it went, Maria seemed, for the moment, a distant, unattainable aspiration.

~~~

Sparkes's return to camp commenced later than he had expected. The regular afternoon thunderstorm had been unusually violent, and he had been forced to take refuge on the supply ship for several hours. A strong east wind and an outgoing tide made the trip upriver all the more difficult. By the time the sun set, he was exhausted and at least an hour from camp.

Finding a small island in mid-river, Sparkes decided to rest for awhile before going on. As he stepped ashore, he swatted one mosquito, then another. He looked out at the moonlit river. Out on the water, the stiff breeze would keep the insects at bay. Stepping back into the canoe, he shoved off and paddled out into the river. Throwing out a stone anchor, he lay down in the bottom of the vessel and pulled his bedroll over him. Florida, he thought, was the most useless place humanity had ever fought over. Even after the Seminoles were removed, the mosquitoes would still be there.

~~~

Private Robert Priestly watched as the other sentry walked toward the small group of tents that were lined up near the banks of the Caloosahatchee River. It was near midnight, time for the changing of the watch, and his companion was going about the business of waking up their replacements. As was his habit since childhood, Priestly closed his eyes and turned his thoughts toward heaven. *Almighty Father, grant us a peaceful night and a quiet morning. Protect our small company and guide us through our perils so that we may return safely to our loved ones. Watch over Ma and Pa and Betsy and let them know I miss them. In the name of . . .*

"Jesus Christ!" the other sentry yelled as he saw the muzzle flashes erupt from the surrounding woods. He saw Priestly twisting on the ground screaming "God, no!   Please God, no!" then, almost instinctively, he swung his musket up and took aim at the first moving object he saw. He pulled the trigger, but before he could tell if he had hit anything, he felt a bullet slam into his chest. Before he could scream, another bullet tore through his jaw. Before he hit the ground, he was dead.

In a matter of moments there were shouts coming from every direction. Some were the war whoops of a hundred warriors charging into the camp, while others came from soldiers that were coming to the realization that they were under attack. Although the soldiers slept with their loaded muskets by their sides, it did them little good. By the time they were able to get on their feet and out of the tents, the Indians were upon them. Some of the soldiers never made it out of their bedrolls and were stabbed where they lay. Others were shot as they emerged from their tents. Those that managed to break free were pursued. Some were caught and slain with the tomahawk. Others were shot.

Less than half the soldiers made it to the river, hoping they could swim to safety. One, unable to swim, drowned. On the shore, the Indians fired into the water, hoping to hit some of the fleeing men. Finally, a tall, muscular warrior stepped forward and ordered them to cease fire. Halek Tustenuggee had heard there was a ship at the mouth of the river earlier in the day. If it were still there, troops might soon be coming. It was best to take the time to go through all the supplies and trade goods the white men had brought, destroying what they didn't want and carrying off the rest.   There would always be another opportunity to kill more soldiers.

~~~

Sparkes, some distance away from the camp and sleeping soundly in the canoe, did not awaken until the attack was almost complete. At first he paddled furiously toward the camp, then after a few minutes he assumed a more measured pace. He knew that he was already too late to save any of his men, and there was little use in showing up while the attackers were still there. Indeed, there was no good reason even to return to the camp, other than to provide details for an official report. If he lived to make one.

It took over an hour to make the trip, and by the time he arrived all was quiet and the moon was near setting. Not knowing if any Indians had remained behind, he beached the canoe a short distance below the camp at the edge of the clearing. Moving with as little noise as possible, he skirted the edge of the woods, his eyes constantly looking for stragglers, either white or Seminole. For several minutes he stood behind a tree and peered into the camp. Nothing moved. Taking a deep breath, Sparkes stepped out into the open.

The first body he came to was that of the sentry, Private Priestly. Even in the fading moonlight it was easy to see the slice across Priestly's throat and the bloody top of his head. As the lieutenant moved through the camp he found more dead, mutilated bodies. All had been stripped of any weapons or valuables. Included among the dead were the sutler and his two assistants. A quick body count told Sparkes that some of the men were missing. Three possibilities came to mind as to where they might be: They could have been taken as prisoners, which only meant their deaths were painfully postponed. They might have swum to the other side of the river, but he certainly wasn't going to risk calling out to them. The other possibility was that they had taken to the woods. If so, there was little chance he would find any of them until daylight, and then only by good fortune. It also occurred to him that all three possibilities might apply. There was no real reason to believe all the missing men were in the same place.

Sparkes walked over to the large tent where the sutler had stored his trade goods. If any provisions were to be found, this would be the most likely place. As he began to rummage through the debris, he found little that was useful. Whoever had done this had been thorough. He was about to look into an upturned crate of hardtack when he heard distant voices. They were not speaking English. Picking up his rifle, Sparkes moved cautiously to the opening of the tent, which faced east. It seemed the approaching Indians were coming from that direction. Taking quick stock of the situation, he noticed that the Indians had sliced a large opening in the opposite side of the tent, probably to let in more light from the setting moon. Wasting no time, Sparkes slipped through the opening and made for the cover of the woods.

After taking refuge behind a palmetto bush, Sparkes watched as a pair of warriors strolled nonchalantly into the ruined camp. For the most part, they ignored the bodies and went straight for the tents, looking for what few valuables might have been left behind. They didn't find much, but began to accumulate a small pile of odds and ends in the middle of the camp. Then one of the warriors took a walk down by the shoreline to check that no one was approaching from the opposite shore. Satisfied that they were alone, he began to turn around. Suddenly he let out with a low yelp. He had spotted Sparkes's canoe.

The pair stepped over to the vessel and began to converse excitedly as they looked through what they had found. They were pleased by the bedroll, very happy with the cartridge box, and bewildered by the piece of India Rubber cloth. Pushing the canoe into the river, one of the warriors got in and paddled closer to the center of camp. After bringing the vessel ashore, the pair continued their rummaging for about half an hour, then loaded their loot aboard the canoe and commenced to paddle upriver.

After they were well out of sight, Sparkes stepped from his hiding place and cautiously entered the clearing. He went to the few tents that were still standing and looked for some food. There was none to be found. There was also no ammunition or any sort of weaponry. In a way, it was an indication of how the war was affecting the Indians. In times past, they would have ignored hardtack and been less picky about what weapons they took. Whoever had attacked the camp had been hungry and poorly supplied.

Unfortunately, Sparkes was no better off. His cartridge box and even his canteen had been in the canoe. Looking about, he found one of the soldier's canteens, but it was empty. All the others he found appeared to have been smashed by a tomahawk. Hanging the empty canteen from his shoulder, Sparkes walked over to a stump and took a seat. Filling it up in the river was useless; the water was too salty this close to the Gulf. Looking at his rifle, he realized it was almost as useless as the canteen. He had loaded it earlier in the day and doubted it would fire. Fortunately it was one of the new percussion cap models, so at least there was a chance. But what good would that do? The last thing he needed was to bring attention to his presence. In the end, the weapon might prove most useful in signaling a passing boat.

He looked about the ruined camp and contemplated his options. His best chance of reaching aid would have been to take the canoe and paddle over to Charlotte Harbor, where there was some expectation of finding a navy patrol. If need be, he could have paddled all the way to Tampa Bay. Now, with the canoe gone, that option was removed. Staying in place and waiting for someone to come by was also out of the question. That someone might be an Indian. In truth, there was but one option: Walk to Charlotte Harbor and hope to be spotted by a navy patrol. If he were lucky enough to find food, he could walk all the way to Tampa Bay if he had to.

Charlotte Harbor was, at best, a day's march. Getting to his feet, he shouldered his rifle, adjusted the empty canteen, and walked over to the remnants of his tent. The attackers had slashed it and torn it down after searching through it. Moving the torn canvas aside, he sifted through the debris. The first thing he picked up was a hat. It was the middle of summer and the head covering would come in handy. The small portable desk he had brought was smashed, but within the remains he found a letter from Maria. He stuffed the letter into his coat pocket, kicked aside a few other pieces of wreckage, and then shook his head. Other than the letter, there was little else he cared to carry along. Walking away from the tent, he suddenly stopped, lowered himself to one knee, and said a prayer for his fallen comrades. He then rose, gave a last, sad look at the camp, and marched off into the woods.

~~~

As the two Indians who had taken the canoe paddled up the Caloosahatchee, they spoke freely to each other, not the least bit worried about attracting anyone's attention. One subject they discussed was the finding of the canoe. At first they had assumed the attackers had missed it because it had not been readily visible from the center of camp. The more they thought about it, however, the more they came to believe that someone might have arrived after the attack. If so, that person was still around. It was something they would have to mention to their chief.

~~~

Sparkes was getting lost. He had assumed the Caloosahatchee ran east to west, but in fact, from where he had started it flowed very much southwest. Guided by his incorrect mental map, he believed the quickest way to reach Charlotte Harbor was to walk northwest. In truth, he was headed more north than anything. Keeping a sense of direction was proving impossible. The moon had set and between the trees and an intermittent cloud cover, Polaris and most of the other stars were often out of sight. Streams, thickets, and bogs forced him to frequently alter his course. If nothing else, it was confusing to be walking about in a monotonous pine forest in the dark of night.

When the sun rose and he could get his bearings he turned west, assuming the harbor couldn't be far off. Unfortunately, he was much farther inland than he thought and spent hours trudging through the woods before there was any significant change in scenery. By the time he reached the vicinity of the harbor, it was late in the day. As he tried to approach the shore line, he faced another problem. Dense mangrove forests and innumerable small islands surrounded the land, making it impossible to reach open water. Moving back inland, he found a comfortable spot and tried to get some sleep.

It was a horrid night. Insects droned in his ears incessantly. Every odd noise made him jump, his imagination converting any unfamiliar sound into an approaching Seminole, a stalking panther, or a hungry bear. And like that imaginary bear, he too was hungry. He had filled his canteen at one of the small streams he had crossed, but he had found nothing worth eating. He had seen countless Coontie plants, the staple food of the Seminoles, but it did him little good. It was well known that the starchy roots were toxic unless processed properly, and that knowledge was not in Sparkes's possession. He'd seen numerous birds and squirrels, but wasn't yet willing to risk using the rifle to kill one. He also realized that his percussion cap rifle put him at a disadvantage: There was no flint lock, and therefore no flint to use in making a fire.

As he lay in the darkness, a myriad of thoughts went through the lieutenant's mind. Even if he did manage to survive, his military career was effectively over. The fact that he had lost an entire command would hang over him like a dark cloud for the rest of his time in the army, and it didn't really matter that he had been sent into a dangerous situation with insufficient force. The only way he could emerge from this situation as a hero would be to get killed. He also wondered how much it would affect his intentions to marry Maria. The colonel might feel that Sparkes, with little chance of promotion, was not a fitting husband for his daughter. Sparkes could always take his brother-in-law's offer to join him in the business in Cincinnati, but would the colonel consent to having his daughter live so far away? On the other hand, Sparkes was confident that Maria wouldn't let such considerations stand in their way, yet the worries would not leave his mind.

His thoughts also drifted to the men of his command. Many of them had served in Company "B" since before the commencement of the war. There were a few that he was truly fond of. None, he had to admit, did he strongly dislike. It brought a tear to his eye to think of them being stabbed and hacked to death, for the most part utterly defenseless. He thought of Private Priestly. There was probably no more devout a Christian in the entire army. He and Sparkes had spent many an hour discussing the Bible, and on more than one occasion the lieutenant had heard the private praying for the company's safety. Sparkes looked skyward and wondered, *If God would not answer the prayers or protect someone like Priestly, one of His most faithful followers, would He answer anyone's prayers?* Sparkes began to sob softly. The simple, quiet faith that had been part of his life since childhood began to crumble. He would never pray again.

Sparkes then began to question the matter of his own survival. At first he had assumed that God had spared him for a reason. As he lay in the darkened wilderness, his own humility put an end to such thoughts. Was he truly more deserving than any of those soldiers? Indeed, was he more deserving than any of the other countless good people, Seminole, black, or white, who had perished in this unholy war? He doubted it. In the end, he had to admit that he had been spared a horrible death by mere luck. He also came to the realization that his continued survival was not in God's hands, but in his own. As he tried to comprehend his future, both for the next day and the rest of his life, he drifted off to sleep.

Sparkes awoke the next morning still very hungry and little refreshed from the intermittent sleep he'd had. He headed northwest again, determined to find his way to Charlotte Harbor. With luck he would locate a stream and follow it down to the harbor, and perhaps the mangroves would be thinner at that point. There was also the hope that in the shallow waters of the harbor he would come across one of the oyster beds he'd seen or find some clams. He might even fashion a spear using his pocket knife and, with luck, spear a fish within the tangled mangrove roots.

He was tired, walking almost aimlessly through one of the more open patches of pine woods, when he saw the Indians. He should have seen them much earlier. They were two of them on horseback, standing not more than a hundred feet in front of him, waiting calmly for the weakened white man to notice them. For a long moment, Sparkes just stared at them. There wasn't much else he could think to do. He was certainly in no condition to run away. He also had the presence of mind to realize that if they had meant to kill him, they would have done it by now. Finally, as he and the Indians stared at each other, he knew there was but one thing to do: He raised his rifle, but instead of pointing it at the warriors, he held it out flat, as a sign of surrender.

~~~

News of the massacre on the Caloosahatchee traveled swiftly throughout the Territory. Two days after the attack a cutter from the Revenue Service happened to be in the area and sent a launch up river. Upon finding the destruction, the crew conducted a swift search for survivors, found a few who had been hiding along the banks of the river, then immediately sailed for Tampa Bay. From there, express riders fanned out, carrying the news to every post in Florida. Word also spread among the Indians. Whatever the reason for the attack, both sides took it as a sign that the war had recommenced. Throughout

Florida raids took place and troops were on the move. The hoped-for peace had evaporated.

When news reached St. Augustine, Maria flew into a panic. The note from her father that Sparkes was not among the dead was of little comfort. She could only imagine that he had been captured by the Seminoles and was suffering some unspeakable, savage torture.

Her first impulse was to pack her bags and catch the first ship to Tampa Bay. Nero shook his head. "Massa colonel not gonna be happy wi' dat."

Maria bristled. "Curse my father! Mister Sparkes is in danger, and I need to go to him."

Nettie was as sympathetic as she could be but could not ignore the logic of the situation. "An' what you gonna do once you get to Fort Brooke, chile? Ain't nobody knows where he be. You gonna go find him when the whole army can't?" She wrapped Maria in her arms, as she had done so many times before. "Ain't nothin' you can do, chile."

Maria began to sob. Nettie was right, and the feeling of helplessness hurt even more. Then Nero repeated the fact he considered most important: "Massa colonel won't like it."

Maria suddenly understood a contradiction that was inescapable: She was old enough to make her own decisions and didn't need her father's permission. She also realized that now, more than ever, she needed to be with him. She stood tall, breaking free of Nettie's embrace. "Nero, go to the barracks and find out when the next large force departs for Tampa Bay or the next steamer leaves for there."

The old man shook his head more emphatically than before. "Massa colonel ain't gonna like it."

~~~

It was dark by the time Sparkes and his captors reached the Seminole camp. The two escorts, who Sparkes recognized as the men who had taken his canoe, motioned him toward a small, open-sided hut. Seated under the low roof was a lone figure. It was Kachi-Hadjo. The lieutenant took a seat on the ground across from the chief. Kachi-Hadjo said nothing. Sparkes had but one question: "Why?"

The calmness in the chief's voice hid the anxiety he was feeling. "You must carry a talk to Wooster."

Sparkes shook his head. It wasn't the right answer. "Why did you attack us?"

A girl approached carrying a bowl. It was Ki-tee. She handed the bowl to Sparkes. Answers could wait. Using his fingers, he spooned the porridge-like Sofkee into his mouth. It was bland, but it was the most wonderful thing he had ever tasted.

Momentarily satisfied, Sparkes set the bowl down. Once again, he asked why they had been attacked. Kachi-Hadjo shook his head. He needed to make Sparkes understand. "We did not attack you. It was Halek Tustenuggee and the Spanish Indians."

Sparkes did not understand the distinction. He'd never heard of these Spanish Indians. "Who?"

Kachi-Hadjo wasn't surprised at the white man's ignorance. Until the war had forced the Seminoles into the Everglades, the group known as the Spanish Indians had kept quietly to themselves, existing deep in the swamps and living off the land and whatever they could salvage from the numerous vessels that wrecked upon the Florida coast. "Even in peace, there are thieves and there are murderers. The Spanish Indians are outlaws even to the Seminoles. They are men who have been banished from our tribe, they are the sons and daughters of the Cuban fisherman who used to fish these coasts, and they count among their numbers the last of the old Calusas and a few runaway slaves. A true Seminole will have nothing to do with them." He gave Sparkes a moment to digest the information. "They wished nothing more than plunder. Tustenuggee and his band joined with them because you were so few in number and could be easily defeated. You were fools to have so weak a guard."

Sparkes almost pleaded for a plausible explanation. "But we had a treaty."

After all these years, the whites still didn't understand the different groups that made up the Seminole Nation. More correctly, they didn't *want* to understand. "Your Big Chief Macomb made his peace with some of the Seminoles, not with all of us. He made his treaty with Abee-

Aka and the Mikasukis, and we did not attack you. Tustenuggee does not want peace. He makes war because he enjoys the kill. Tustenuggee is an Alachua; he did not meet with Macomb. The Spanish Indians make peace with no one, not even Seminoles. They live as they please, and make war on who they please. Macomb did not meet with them." A slight hint of desperation was evident in Kachi-Hadjo's tone. Everything he had fought for was being lost. "You must go to Wooster and tell him that the Mikasukis did not do this, that we want peace. Maybe he can talk to Big Chief Macomb."

Sparkes shook his head. "Macomb has gone back to Washington." He also knew that no matter who Wooster spoke to, it would make no difference. It may not have been what Kachi-Hadjo wanted to hear, but it was the truth. "It will do no good. The chiefs in Washington do not know Alachuas, Mikasukis, or Spanish Indians. They will say that we extended our hand in friendship, and the Seminoles put a tomahawk in our backs. There will cry out that the war must continue until every last Seminole is dead or in the west. No longer will the white man feel he can trust the word of the Seminole."

Kachi-Hadjo stared back with dignified calm in his eyes. He knew Sparkes was right. The peace that Kachi-Hadjo had longed for had been destroyed by his own people. Still, the blame could not be placed all on one side. "And can the Seminole trust the word of the white man? Even Tustenuggee would have buried his tomahawk had he felt the Great Father in Washington would keep his word. Was it the Seminole who broke the treaty that we marked at Moultrie Creek? Where were the annuities you promised us, the blankets for our women and the tools with which to cultivate the land? Where was the protection from the evil whites who abused our women and children and stole our cattle? When did the white man drive off the slave catchers who took our black brothers? How many of our chiefs and warriors have you taken prisoner under the white flag? Do not speak to the Seminole of trust. It is a word the white man has never taught us the meaning of."

They both sat in silence. Sparkes ate a bit more and drank from a wooden cup Ki-tee brought to him. He watched the girl as she tended to the food and utensils. She was perhaps ten or eleven, still with the look of a child. As with most of the Seminole children he had seen, she was quiet and shy, at least in the presence of whites. He had noted that boisterous play was rarely seen among the Indian children. He could understand why: Remaining free meant going unnoticed by the whites. The Indian that made loud noises in the countryside might alert a white patrol to the presence of a hidden village. All in all, it was best to remain unobtrusive.

Sparkes sighed and looked at Kachi-Hadjo. "Please give up. You cannot win this war."

Kachi-Hadjo shrugged. "Can the white man? Do you have so much gold that you can spend it all in fighting we few Seminoles? Do you have so many soldiers that you can lose them all to the sickness that lives in this land? We all grow tired of this war. Maybe the big chiefs in Washington will tire of it before there are no more Seminoles to make war upon."

"And if you hold out until there are too few Seminoles to live in this place, what will you have won? Is it not better to take your people and go to the west?"

Kachi-Hadjo shook his head. It was hard to explain his love for the land, the animals, the vegetation that surrounded him, and the spirits that permeated all of it. "This I cannot do. The bones of my loved ones rest in these sands. I cannot yet leave them."

Sparkes looked at Ki-tee. "And how long will it be before you bury her bones in these sands?"

22

August 2, 1839
Ft. Brooke

To:
Mrs. David Kilgour
Cincinnati, Ohio

My Dear Sister,

I am very happy to inform you that contrary to reports you have no doubt read, I am not a casualty of the Caloosahatchee Massacre. By the best of good fortune, I was away from camp at the time of the attack and therefore escaped with my life. I wandered about the forest for two days afterwards, somewhat lost and near starved, before being rescued by warriors from the band of the great chief Kachee-Hadjo, who you may have heard referred to as Mad Panther. Kachee-Hadjo was not party to the attack and wishes only peace. After I had regained my strength, his warriors led me to a place where the Navy patrols often come ashore. I was thus rescued and brought to this place, where I have been questioned much, but little listened to.

Precisely how this unprovoked attack will affect the conduct of the war remains to be seen, but it can be said with certainty that Genl. Macomb's peace is dead. I suppose we can assume that our illustrious leaders in Washington will now be forced by public clamor to pursue the war with increased vigor. It is a foul, unnecessary war, for most of the Seminoles wish only to be left alone in their watery fastnesses. As always, it is the work of a few outlaws that cause untold pain and suffering to the innocent.

The emotions I feel are difficult to express and at times contradictory. Foremost, I feel pain at the loss of my good men, and regret that I was not there in their hour of need. There is, of course, the lingering question as to whether anything would have been different had I been there. Would I have set a better guard? Would I have been able to lead any sort of defense? The most likely result is that there would have been one more name on the casualty list. Perhaps, like the hapless Major Dade, they would have named a county after me. Obviously, I feel the utmost relief that I was spared and that those others who escaped have been rescued, but there is also great concern as to what the loss of a command will do to my career. I of course feel the appropriate anger toward those who committed this most vile act, but also a deep indignation that Genl. Macomb negotiated such a weak treaty and that Genl. Taylor did not provide us with sufficient men to protect the camp. In truth, I place more blame for the attack on the Generals than on those who committed it. More than anything, I feel profound sadness that this miserable war must surely continue for many painful years to come, and that countless more innocents will needlessly suffer.

What the coming weeks hold for me I do not know. My dear Company "B" is no more. Sickness had already thinned our numbers, and our sergeant is in confinement. Those few who survived the massacre were rescued by the Navy and taken to Key West. Colonel Wooster is on an inspection tour and MacDuff is on furlough, though I expect that news of the attack has already turned his path in this direction.

Other than the loss of my men, what pains me most is the knowledge that those who hold me dear have suffered anguish over my presumed loss. I have already sent word to my beloved Maria in St. Augustine, and I hope this letter reaches you without undo delay. Do give my love to David, Lizzy, Kenneth, and dear little Jacob. For some short time, I thought I might never have the good fortune to see any of you again.

Your very much alive and affectionate brother,
Jacob

It was a long, burning kiss, the kind that leaves a memory. Sparkes was enfolded in Maria's arms, knowing he shouldn't be, knowing he didn't want it to end. Her smell was all about the air, her taste all over his lips. He had dreamt of this, but the dream was pale by comparison. She relaxed, released her embrace, and parted her mouth from his.

Sparkes took a deep breath. He had recovered from his ordeal at the Caloosahatchee and his strength had returned, but he was afraid that his resolve remained weak. As much as he wanted her there with him, he knew it was not wise. "You should not have come."

For Maria there had been no alternative. "Could I remain in St. Augustine knowing that you were missing?"

"Could you have done any good here?"

A devilish smile came to her face. "I can do good service now!" Once again she came close, pressing her lips to his. She had waited so long for this moment. Since his departure from St. Augustine in October, the pair had shared many letters, each one drawing them closer together. She had expressed no reservations about her love for him, and he had freely admitted his love for her. The only things that stood between them were the war, the Florida peninsula, and her father. For the moment, two of the three had been removed. The third was yet to be dealt with.

Sparkes was torn. He wanted Maria, but he wanted her on the proper terms. He would not risk a split with the colonel. With great reluctance and willpower, he withdrew from her embrace. "Your father will not be pleased. You were safer in St. Augustine."

She shook her head. "Was I? The week before I left, Tustenuggee and his band attacked a troupe of actors not ten miles from the city. They killed three of the poor players and took all their fine costumes. St. Augustine is so poorly defended that I was forced to sleep with a pistol by my bedside." Sparkes saw the face of a determined woman. Maria was ready to commence her adult life, and Sparkes knew that he was the focus of that future. More than anything he wanted it to be happy future, and without the consent of the colonel it simply would not be.

It was also very dangerous to be out and about in Florida, even with a military escort. Several months earlier, the young wife of Lieutenant Montgomery had been traveling between Fort Wooster and Fort Brooke with an escort of a dozen soldiers. Sparkes could still see the utter anguish in the eyes of Montgomery when news was received that the party had been attacked midway between the two forts, a little over ten miles from where he and Maria now stood. Montgomery had gathered what men were available and had immediately ridden to his wife's aid, but they were too late. He found his wife stabbed, shot, scalped, and mutilated in an unspeakable manner. Beside her was a dying soldier who, with his last breath, apologized for not being able to protect the lady. Maria had accompanied a force of two hundred men, but even that was no guarantee against one lone warrior intent on making a name.

~~~

The four chiefs sat around the fire, each one oblivious to the smoke that rose toward the noon-day sun and to the scores of warriors surrounding them. It was a traditional type fire, with four logs of roughly equal lengths radiating out from the center, each one pointing in one of the cardinal directions. In each quadrant sat one of the chiefs, each man an equal distance from the man to his right and left. In the northeast quadrant sat Abee-Aka, the old medicine man. Directly opposite sat Halek Tustenuggee. The two men peered angrily at each other through the smoke. Between them to the southeast sat Kachi-Hadjo, chief of the Mikasukis, and opposite him sat Holata Bolek, chief of the Alachua Seminoles. The latter two men rarely looked at each other. They were too busy keeping their eyes on Abee-Aka and Tustenuggee.

It was the third day of the annual Green Corn Ceremony, the most important event of the Seminole year. Every Indian that could possibly reach the secluded hammock was there. It was a time of feasting and fasting, of purging and purification. It was a time when old bonds were restored and new relationships begun. It was also the time when punishments were handed down.

The first day of the Green Corn Ceremony had been spent primarily in preparation, gathering wood for the fires, building the Big House, and setting up the ball court. In the afternoon the first ball game was played, allowing the young men and women a chance to socialize and flirt. In the evening, the stomp dancing had gone on until almost midnight. The second day had been the feast day, accompanied by more ball games and dancing. The third day was the most solemn. It was a fast day, which began with the taking of the Black Drink, which would induce a purifying vomit. Then, near mid-day, the court was held. Foremost among the things to be reckoned with on this occasion was the matter of Tustenuggee's raid on the white camp at the Caloosahatchee.

As Abee-Aka stared at Tustenuggee, he chanted in a low voice and rattled some small bones held in his hands. Tustenuggee spit into the fire. "Your curses and spells do not frighten me, old man. Tustenuggee fears no one!"

Kachi-Hadjo and Bolek glanced knowingly at each other. It was all bravado: *Everyone* feared Abee-Aka. Tustenuggee sneered at the medicine man. "You look into a future that the most simple-minded woman could predict, old liar. If you know so much, tell us how to defeat the white man."

Abee-Aka shook his head slowly. He then spoke in a weak voice that somehow commanded everyone's attention. "We had already defeated the white man. We had won the right to stay in our homeland. Now, because of Tustenuggee and the Spanish Indians, the white soldiers pursue us again." The dark, deep-set eyes burned into Tustenuggee. "Did you gain so much in those things that you stole that it will pay for the lands we will lose? Did you gain so much joy from lifting the scalps of the soldiers that it will make up for the sorrow of our women and children?"

The angry warrior pointed his finger across the smoke. "*You* made peace with the white man, not I! Is there a warrior fool enough to trust the soldier's white flag? Is there a chief so weak-minded as to believe the promises of the Great Father in Washington?"

Bolek sensed a danger if the conversation continued to heat up. Already the surrounding warriors had divided into two groups, Alachuas and Mikasukis. Should Tustenuggee lose his temper and physically attack Abee-Aka, a civil war among the Seminoles might result. Something needed to be done to prevent it. As a young chief, however, Bolek was unsure of the strength of his authority. Did he have the power to challenge either Tustenuggee or Abee-Aka and the Mikasukis? He looked across the fire at Kachi-Hadjo. The other man nodded slightly, turned his eyes toward Tustenuggee, them rolled them skywards.

Tustenuggee continued to carry on about the evil whites and cowardice of Abee-Aka. The medicine man closed his eyes and continued to chant, his voice growing more strident. In the background, warriors began to talk loudly, voicing their support for one or the other. Suddenly Bolek yelled, "Silence!"

For a moment, everyone obeyed the command, more out of surprise than respect for Bolek's leadership. Then Tustenuggee informed Bolek that, "I will be silent when I wish to be silent."

Every warrior in the clearing stood motionless as the two men eyed each other. It was as direct a challenge to Bolek's authority as Tustenuggee could display without drawing a weapon. Then a firm voice came from the opposite side of the fire. "Tustenuggee will be silent when *our* chief commands it." Kachi-Hadjo had made certain that everyone understood that Bolek was head chief of all the Seminoles and that the Mikasukis were placing themselves under his authority.

Tustenuggee backed down. He wasn't afraid of Bolek, but he knew better than to cross Kachi-Hadjo. Still, he wondered why the Mikasuki chief was supporting someone who ought to be a rival. "A chief remains strong only so long as he has followers. His followers remain loyal only so long as it benefits them. What benefit does Kachi-Hadjo derive from supporting Bolek?"

It was a question that had to be answered. Kachi-Hadjo was the older, more experienced chief. He was as closely related to the line of Cowkeeper as Bolek was and therefore just as eligible to be head chief of all the Seminoles. The only difference was that the title had traditionally gone to an Alachua, not a Mikasuki. The war had disrupted many traditions. Why not that one? If he had wanted to, Kachi-Hadjo could have called a council and taken over as head chief. Why should he relinquish that authority to someone else? The surrounding warriors would want to know. "What do I benefit? I am concerned more with what I may lose than what I may gain. I do not wish to lose the peace that exists amongst our peoples, and I do not wish to lose the small hope we have of remaining in our homeland. That is enough for Kachi-Hadjo."

Tustenuggee laughed. "The white man will never give you peace. He will hunt you like the wolf that has attacked his cattle. Kachi-Hadjo hides in these swamps like a frightened rabbit. Tustenuggee does not hide. He takes the war to the white man. There shall be no peace with the white man so long as Tustenuggee is a Seminole war leader."

Bolek now understood the price of Kachi-Hadjo's support: He raised his voice so all could hear. "If the Seminole are to contend with the white men, we must speak with one voice. If Tustenuggee cannot speak the talk of his chief, then Tustenuggee must be a Seminole no more."

Tustenuggee jumped to his feet. "So Bolek is now the plaything of the Mikasukis? Does he think he can so easily banish Tustenuggee? Does he think that my followers will not travel behind me?"

Kachi-Hadjo already knew the answer to the question. It had to do with the fact that Seminole clan life centered on the female side of the family. "Does Tustenuggee think that his warriors will give up their loved ones to join the Spanish Indians? Our homes may be simple, but they are better than those of the outlaws. The white man will someday make peace with the Seminoles; he will never make peace with the Spanish Indians."

Bolek stood up and addressed the assembled warriors. "Tustenuggee is to be banished, for it was he who attacked the soldiers' camp and lost the peace we had won at so great a cost. Those of his warriors who wish to join him in exile with the Spanish Indians are free to join him. Leave your mothers and your wives behind, for there is no good home among the outlaws. Better that your women should be captured by the whites and sent to the land in the west than to live among the Spanish Indians."

Kachi-Hadjo came to his feet. "Let those who wish to follow Tustenuggee into exile gather behind him. Those who wish to remain with the Seminole will gather behind Bolek and Kachi-Hadjo." Both he and Bolek then stepped around the fire and took a place by Abee-Aka's side.

A handful of Alachua warriors stepped to the area behind Tustenuggee. The majority, however, moved to a position alongside the Mikasukis. Tustenuggee kicked dirt into the fire and turned away. "You may have your peace with the white man, if you can get it, but there will never be peace with Tustenuggee!"

~~~

A group of soldiers were busy cleaning and making minor repairs to the east blockhouse of Fort King when Colonel Wooster and his accompanying squad of soldiers arrived. Unlike previous years, the post had remained occupied for the summer but with a minimal garrison. Today, however, it was unusually crowded. A meeting was to take place between Colonel Wooster and General Taylor, the two highest officers serving in Florida. It was now mid-September and four months had passed since the two men had seen each other. Taylor had been managing the war from St. Augustine, while Wooster had been fighting it from Fort Brooke.

The debacle on the Caloosahatchee had brought certain matters to a head. Word had reached Washington about a possible feud between Taylor and Wooster. Both men had friends in Congress and in the press. No one at the War Department wanted the bitterness to escalate. Secretary Poinsett was frustrated at the war's lack of progress, and Commanding General Macomb was unhappy that his peace deal had fallen through. Both men were inclined to blame Taylor, but neither one wanted to make a lot of noise about it in the press. They already had enough trouble with Congress.

In the end, the matter was handled through a pair of letters. The first directed Taylor to focus more attention on the southern portion of the Territory. The second was a carefully worded personal note to both men that strongly suggested the two officers settle their differences. Taylor, knowing he had sent Sparkes to the Caloosahatchee with insufficient force, saw the letter as a rebuke. Wooster saw it as a vindication.

As the colonel walked into the blockhouse, he was surprised at how little it had changed over the years. Taylor was seated at the same table where General Clinch had sat before the war started. In his mind, Wooster could see Lieutenant Smith and Agent Thompson standing off to the side. Four years had gone by since they had met in this room, all hoping to somehow avert an Indian war. Despite their best efforts, they had failed, and Wooster was still angry, both at himself and at those who had let it happen. Smith and Thompson were now long dead, murdered by Asi-Yoholo, and Clinch had resigned in disgust. At times, Wooster wished that he had done the same.

A trio of junior officers mumbled a greeting and left the blockhouse, leaving Taylor and Wooster alone. There was an awkward moment of silence as the pair eyed each other. For just a second, a devious thought ran through Wooster's mind: *If Taylor doesn't come around, I'd be within my rights to request a transfer. I could get out of this miserable war.* Taylor stood up and offered his hand. "Good morning, Will." Wooster savored the small victory: They were back on a first name basis. The War Department's displeasure must have been clear.

Wooster took the hand and shook it. "Morning, Zach."

"Glad to hear Lieutenant Sparkes came through it all right. Pity about the other men."

It was as much of an apology as Wooster could expect. Zachary Taylor was not the sort of man to admit he was wrong. Wooster also knew that he'd better not rub salt in the wound. "The fortunes of war, Zach. Only nations win wars. People always lose."

Both men relaxed a bit. The delicate moments had been gotten through. Taylor quickly moved on to other business. "We're going to need to move some men around. Fortunately, the War Department has sent down a batch on new recruits. Major Pierce has already left St. Augustine with them. They should be at Fort Brooke when you return."

Wooster listened as Taylor laid out his plans for the winter campaign. It shifted the war south, but it was still not as aggressive as Wooster would have liked. It was, in truth, more or less what he had expected. Taylor fought battles. He didn't know how to fight wars.

~~~

Three days later Wooster was back at Fort Brooke. It was a much larger, busier place than it had been four years ago, before it had become the center of a major war. A small town had grown up around the post, a collection of modest homes, crude shacks, and various businesses. Some of the residents were there as refugees, afraid to return to their homes as long as the war continued. Others were there to cater to the needs of the army or those who had some other business with the war.

Destroying the lives of the Seminoles required enormous amounts of supplies and the services of countless individuals, which meant every sort of profiteer and opportunist had found his way to Tampa Bay.

As he approached the fortification Wooster saw the clean white tents belonging to the new recruits. Parading about were the fresh young soldiers, their uniforms neat, their eyes full of hope, and their minds filled with thoughts of adventure. *Give them a year in Florida,* Wooster thought, *and they'll look a damn sight different.* From past experience, he knew that about half of them were fresh off the boat from Europe and about half of those couldn't speak English. Within a week he'd know which of those men were most likely to be a deserter. Recruiters were supposed to weed out the misfits, but with the officer receiving a bounty of two dollars a head, there was an incentive to sign up whoever wandered through the door.

As he turned his mount toward the gate Wooster caught the eye of Major Pierce, the officer who had brought the recruits from St. Augustine. As their horses came alongside, the two men saluted. "Major Pierce, good to see you again. I hope your journey was a pleasant one."

The major looked a little nervous. "Made all the more delightful by the presence of your lovely daughter, sir."

The news didn't come as a complete surprise to Wooster. He smiled and put a hand on the other officer's shoulder. "Wouldn't let you say 'no,' would she?"

Pierce smiled back. "I did, sir, but it did no good. She had her own horse and a mule for her baggage. If I hadn't prevailed upon her to ride in one of the wagons, she'd have simply followed us. My apologies, sir, but she is, to say the least, a determined young lady."

The colonel laughed. "No apologies necessary, Major. She did the same thing to General Scott, so you stand in good company. And thank you for seeing to her safety." He looked out at the recruits. "Are the men ready for their assignments?"

"Yes, sir. I have practiced them in the manual of arms and drilled them on the tactics of Indian warfare as much as possible since their arrival in Florida. They will serve well in any company you may assign them to."

Wooster nodded his approval. "I shall issue their assignments within the day." He turned his horse and headed for the fort. "Have a good day, Major."

Before entering the fort, Wooster brought his horse to a halt and took a moment to think. Maria's presence created a problem. After four years of keeping Sparkes close by, Wooster was about to send the young officer to a distant, dangerous posting. It had been a difficult decision to make, especially after the Caloosahatchee affair. In the end, it had come down to military necessity. Experienced officers were needed elsewhere. Without the presence of Maria, everyone would have seen the assignment in a strictly military manner. Now, with her here, the rumors would fly. He also knew that the person who would question his motives the most would be his own daughter. She would not see the military necessity. She would only see it as a move to keep her from Sparkes. He shrugged. The orders were already written.

The thoughts of what he would say to Maria kept circulating through his mind as he left the stable and walked toward his quarters, where he suspected Sparkes and Maria would be. He hoped not to find them in some sort of compromising situation, though he knew better. There would be embraces and kisses, but nothing more. As he neared the building he searched for some way to warn them of his approach. At the far end of the parade ground he saw Sergeant Bigelow and called out to the man in a voice that could be heard well outside the walls of the fort. "Sergeant!" Bigelow came running up, a submissive look on his face. Wooster's voice was anything but welcoming. "Well, Sergeant, I see the Captain of the Guard has seen fit to release you from confinement, as I requested. Do not consider this a sign of leniency on my part. I simply have use of you elsewhere. Should you engage is such lecherous conduct again, I shall spare neither the lash, your rank, and if the offense be serious enough, your life. There are whores enough around this post. Use them and keep clear of the innocents. Do you understand, Sergeant?"

Bigelow looked to the ground. "Yes, sir."

"Good. Now report to Major Pierce. Tell him I want you to start working with the new recruits."

"Aye, sir. Thank you, sir."

Wooster watched as the sergeant walked away. Good soldier; sad excuse for a man. Shaking his head, he continued on toward the small house that served as his quarters. With luck, Maria and Sparkes had heard his voice. He strode up the steps and walked through the door. He did not knock. It was, after all, *his* house.

As he entered the room, both Sparkes and Maria rose from their seats at the table. They had been holding hands. Maria rushed toward him; Sparkes looked nervous. Father and daughter embraced, though each held something back. Maria started to speak, but Wooster held up a finger, signaling her to be silent. "I understand your concern for Lieutenant Sparkes, but it is not so much the reason for your coming here that displeases me, it is the manner in which you did it. Your safety was not an assignment Major Pierce had been ordered to accept. I should have thought better of you."

He was right, of course, and she knew better than to try and convince him otherwise. "Yes, father."

"And were it not for other matters of greater concern, I would send you back by the first available steamer."

"Yes, father." She didn't know how to take the statement. He was allowing her to stay, but she got the feeling she wasn't going to be happy about it.

Wooster turned to Sparkes. "How are you feeling, Lieutenant?"

Like Maria, he wasn't sure what to read into the colonel's words. He had long ago recovered from the ordeal at the Caloosahatchee and had been performing his normal duties for some time. "Quite well, sir."

"Good. We have work to do. I have just returned from a meeting with General Taylor, who has received orders from Secretary Poinsett as to the distribution of troops for the coming winter campaign. We're taking the war south, into the Everglades. Fort Lauderdale is to be re-occupied, and I'm sending you and MacDuff there." Maria started to interrupt, but Wooster gave her a look that served to keep her silent. "We need good officers at the front, and you and MacDuff are the best I've got."

He then reached into his coat, pulled forth a folded piece of paper, and handed it to Sparkes. During the meeting with Taylor, Wooster had bent over backwards to avoid any sort of confrontation. He had, however, insisted on one thing. Sparkes read the letter. "10 September 1839. To all concerned personnel: Pending approval by the authorities in Washington City, First Lieutenant Jacob Sparkes, Fourth Infantry, is to be considered as having the brevet rank of Captain, United States Army. Signed, Zachary Taylor, General Commanding, Army of the South."

Wooster smiled and reached out to shake Sparkes's hand. "You are, *Captain*, the first officer I've met who has received a promotion upon the loss of a command. Congratulations."

Sparkes smiled broadly. All his fears as to how the loss at the Caloosahatchee would affect his future disappeared. Maria gave him a quick embrace and a discreet kiss on the cheek. She wasn't sure whether she should thank her father or curse him. She knew that he had taken a personal risk in securing the promotion for Sparkes. She also knew that he was sending the man she loved to a distant and dangerous place.

Sparkes understood the same reality, but was limited to only one response. "Thank you, sir."

"You deserve it, Mr. Sparkes. Now go see Major Pierce, find Bigelow, and select two companies from among the recruits. Leave both companies about ten men short. We'll make up the difference with those of your company who have gotten out of the hospital or are at Key West. One of those companies will be under your command; the other will be under MacDuff's. I will assign you your lieutenants after I have reviewed the list of available officers. As soon as MacDuff returns from patrol, both companies will board the first available ship and embark for Fort Lauderdale."

Sparkes knew it was his cue to leave. After again shaking the colonel's hand, he picked up his hat. "Thank you for the confidence, sir."

There was an awkward silence between father and daughter until Sparkes was sufficiently clear of the building. Maria was stunned. She had come all the way from St. Augustine to be with Sparkes and now her father was sending him away. She looked at the colonel, tears in her eyes. There was a battle raging within, one between hurt and anger. For the moment, anger won out. "How could you!"

Wooster looked at her with sympathy. "The decision was already made. Your presence only made it more difficult."

"Hasn't he been through enough? He was almost killed a few weeks ago!"

"He's as healthy as any other officer and as subject to the dangers. It's what he signed on for."

A solution to the problem came quickly to her mind. "I'll tell him to resign his commission."

Wooster shook his head. He'd actually thought of telling Sparkes the same thing. "You and I both know he won't do it. He's like his father and his grandfather: The job isn't done yet."

"Why does it have to be *his* job? What does he owe Florida? Let someone else chase the damn Seminoles!"

A picture suddenly came into Wooster's mind. It was the last time Erastus Sparkes had looked into his eyes. Although no words had been spoken, the message was clear: *Do it!* Neither of them had asked to be there, neither of them wanted it to end that way. Neither of them had had a choice.

She wanted an answer. "Are you just going to order Jacob to his death!"

Wooster's eyes closed and his head lowered. The words were almost inaudible. "If the duty calls for it."

The look of anger in Maria's eyes changed to one of deep sadness. There was no use blaming her father. It was the damn war and what her father called the "miserable pride of a soldier," the need to do one's duty, no matter what the personal cost. She also had to admit that she knew the feeling as well as anyone. No one made her visit the sick and wounded in the hospital. No one had forced her to make the dangerous trip across the peninsula with Major Pierce. She was as duty-bound as either of the men she loved.

Maria began to weep softly, giving in to the inevitability of the situation. Wooster folded her in his arms, just as he had done countless other times when duty or destiny had brought her to tears. "There now, child, it will all work out for the best."

"Oh, father, I love him so."

He stroked her hair. "I know, dear child, I know."

23

Cincinnati
September 3, 1839

To:
Lt. Jacob Sparkes
Ft. Brooke, Tampa Bay, East Florida

Dear Jacob,

Tears of both sorrow and joy may stain this paper as I write. We are, of course, most thankful to hear that you have survived the horrible events on the Caloosahatchee. It was nearly three weeks between the time we heard of the brutal attack and the day we received your letter telling us of your miraculous escape. Thank God you were preserved, for we have suffered tragedy enough in our home.

I know not how to tell you this, so I shall come to it straight-away. Little Jacob has died. He was taken with fever near a fortnight past. The doctor attended often and no effort was spared to aid in his recovery, but all was to no avail.

For the first week of his illness I was quite beside myself, fearing the loss of my son and believing I had also lost my dear brother. David was the rock upon which I rested, his every waking hour spent in tending to dear Jacob or reassuring me that you would yet be found alive. Perhaps we prayed too much, for God could not answer all that we asked of Him. On the day that we received your letter, Jacob appeared to be getting the better of the fever. His color had returned, he ate a bit of bread, and he smiled for the first time in days. We did believe that it was a sign that God was watching over you both.

Sadly, the fever returned, and the poor child suffered much from fits of vomiting, constant sweats, and loose movements. I cannot tell you how painful it is to watch as someone so helpless and innocent is slowly destroyed before your eyes, and there is nothing you can do to prevent it. Lizzy and Kenneth are of course most distraught, but as is the habit of youth, will soon recover their former happiness. For myself, I cannot say.

    I am sorry, dear brother, to have had to tell you this most distressing news. I know how much little Jacob meant to you. I pray that when you and Maria become man and wife, you will be blessed with such a sweet child. From the love you have shown my children, I know you will be the most devoted father to your own.

Your most loving sister,
Emily

    Sparkes stood on the beach in front of Fort Lauderdale and looked at a bloodhound that lay curled up on the sand. He would have shot the creature had his pistol had been loaded, but as it was, killing the animal wasn't worth the effort of loading the weapon. It wasn't that the dog had done anything wrong or was especially annoying. The animal was simply a symbol of all that was wrong with the Florida War.

    Sparkes shook his head as he looked upon the dog. Someone in Tallahassee had heard of the time when the British had employed bloodhounds during a seemingly endless slave revolt in Jamaica. Within months of the dogs' arrival the mountain hideouts of the runaway slaves had been located, bringing an end to the war. To the Florida Territorial Legislature, bloodhounds sounded like the perfect way to end the interminable Seminole conflict. A commission was sent to Cuba and returned with a large pack of the animals. Floridians were confident that the Indian hideouts would soon be discovered and the natives rounded up.

    At first the dogs looked as if they might indeed be a Godsend. A few slaves were sent off into hiding, and several hours later the dogs were sent in search of them. In almost every experiment the dogs found their quarry. Handlers and hounds were dispatched throughout the peninsula and began to accompany army patrols. It was then that the realities became evident. The land in southern Florida was often under water, and the nose of a bloodhound was useless when wet. It was also discovered that the hounds had little inclination to follow the trail of an

Indian. The dogs had been bred and trained to track runaway blacks. The scent of an Indian held little interest for them.

Then there were the political problems. Abolitionists were convinced the dogs had been imported strictly for the purpose of tracking runaway slaves. At the same time, softhearted do-gooders had visions of the dogs tearing into the flesh of defenseless Indian women and children. Even Sparkes knew better. The dogs had been trained to intimidate runaway slaves, not harm them. Petitions had flooded Congress, calling for the dogs to be withdrawn. In the end, the Secretary of War had been forced to issue strict guidelines concerning the use of the dogs, which included keeping them muzzled when on the prowl. For Sparkes and the rest of the army, it had all been much ado about nothing. Like the war itself, the bloodhounds seemed a colossal waste of time and money.

Sparkes looked at the dog and snarled. The hound took it as a friendly gesture, rose, and approached the man, his tail wagging. The officer remembered an article from a Tallahassee newspaper that had told how ferocious the animals were. Humbug. A child could play with them.

The early December air was pleasantly warm and moist, and other than the crude fortification and a few outbuildings, there were no other structures in sight. The sound of footsteps on sand caused Sparkes to look around. MacDuff stepped wordlessly to his side as both men looked out toward the ocean. It was at times like these that MacDuff felt the most inadequate. He was good at making light of things, but there was simply nothing in this situation to make light of. The best he could say was, "Sorry to hear about the boy. I know he was dear to you."

Sparkes nodded slightly. "Thank you." He reached down and picked up a piece of driftwood and threw it half-heartedly at the dog. The animal yelped slightly when the stick hit it, but did not run off. Sparkes sat down on the sand and shook his head. "I just feel so damn useless. Had I been anywhere else in the country I would have gone straight to Cincinnati to be with them. Instead I find myself at the most god-forsaken end of the earth, unable to even send a letter until the next damn boat arrives."

MacDuff took a seat next to his friend and offered the only advice he could think of. "Take a furlough. You've got the time coming. Go spend a week or two with Maria. Hell, go to Cincinnati if you must. We're certainly not accomplishing anything here."

Sparkes shook his head. "I doubt that I could face Emily now, it's been so many weeks. Anyway, Maria and the colonel are bound for the Court of Inquiry at Fredericksburg." He gazed north along the beach, looking at nothing in particular. "For the moment, this may be the best place for me."

MacDuff felt the need to say something that would lift his friend's spirits and get his mind off the loss of his nephew, but nothing came to mind. Even The Bard failed him. Shakespeare was, after all, the master of tragedy, and the last thing Sparkes needed was more tragedy. MacDuff nodded towards the dog, which had returned for more abuse. "Do you think he could sniff me out a good woman?" It was lame, but it was something.

Sparkes forced a weak smile. He knew that MacDuff was trying to brighten his spirits and appreciated the effort. "The only thing I've seen him sniff is another dog's ass."

Off in the distance they could see Sergeant Bigelow and a company of soldiers working at their daily drills. Sparkes shook his head in disbelief, sinking back into his foul mood. Their orders from General Taylor had been to "patrol the environs around Fort Lauderdale and pursue the enemy wherever he may be found." Taylor had given them men, ammunition, and enough supplies to complete the task, but he hadn't given them any boats. All they had was one deep-keeled launch from the navy. Fort Lauderdale was surrounded by swamp land. The only way to "patrol and pursue" was by canoe or some other shallow draft vessel. They were no closer to defeating the Seminoles in Fort Lauderdale than they had been at Fort Brooke. Sparkes motioned toward the soldiers. If he and MacDuff were going to sit on the beach and commiserate on their troubles, it was best to start with the obvious. "Do you suppose Taylor will ever send us some boats so that we can actually go forth and fight some Indians?"

MacDuff scoffed at the idea. "Methinks he's more likely to tell us to take the men and build a causeway across the whole damned Everglades."

Sparkes snickered. "And build a blockhouse every twenty miles." If it weren't for the friendship of MacDuff, the war would have driven him mad years ago.

"Aye, then he can say we've civilized the whole of Florida, and when the Indians hear the news they'll just pack up and leave." He reached out and began to scratch the top of the dog's head. "What in the name of Andrew Jackson did I do to deserve the worst posting in the army?"

Sparkes shrugged. "Probably the same thing I did."

MacDuff put his hand on his friend's shoulder. "You, my friend, are here to keep you away from Colonel Wooster's lovely daughter. I, on the other hand, am completely innocent, yet I am exiled with you. Where's the justice in that, I ask?" He laughed and recited an ironic line from *The Merchant of Venice*. "Be assured thou shall have justice, more than thou desirest."

Sparkes thoughts turned to Maria. The few days they had spent together at Fort Brooke had been wonderful. Now, wrapped in grief over the death of his nephew, he needed her. MacDuff was right. Fort Lauderdale was, as much as anything, a place of exile.

~~~

Colonel Wooster smiled at Maria and shrugged. The clerk had informed the colonel that he was to be the next witness. Exactly why he had been ordered to Fredericksburg, Maryland, was still a mystery. All he knew was that he was to be a witness at the Court of Inquiry into why Winfield Scott's campaign of 1836 had been such a colossal failure.

As far as Wooster was concerned, the whole affair had gotten entirely out of hand. Indeed, the inquiry had little to do with Scott's campaign. Instead it was nothing more than a venue where powerful personalities could air their differences. The seeds of the dispute had been planted the moment General Gaines set foot in Florida during the first months of the war. Both men had failed to end the conflict, and both had immediately taken to blaming each other. The long-standing hatred between the two men had boiled over into the public press, forcing the president to call for an inquiry into the whole affair.

In the meantime the dispute had widened to encompass other notable figures. General Jesup had written a letter to President Jackson voicing concerns about Scott's handling of the Creek War, and the letter had found its way into the papers. Soon after that, General Clinch and former Secretary of War Cass began to blame one another for being unprepared for the war in Florida. Clinch was also engaged in a particularly venomous public exchange with Governor Call concerning the conduct of the Florida Volunteers at the Battle of the Withlacoochee. Wooster could only hope that the coolness between himself and General Taylor didn't deepen to the point where he found himself in a similar situation. All in all, the whole matter was disgusting. The army seemed to spend more time fighting itself than the Indians.

Maria looked around the packed gallery. There were a large number of newspaper people in attendance along with a few ladies. There were also quite a few onlookers gathered at the windows, braving the cold December wind. Much of the audience was made up of army officers. A few had attempted to flirt with her, but she brushed them off. The man she loved was risking his life daily in the most horrid conditions imaginable, while these men were enjoying the pleasures of the city. It was especially irksome that at a time when her father was begging the War Department for officers, many had found a way to totally escape duty in the war zone.

The lack of officers had been a problem since the first year of the war. Those with political connections had been able to secure favorable postings in other parts of the nation, while others had taken extended sick leaves. Indeed, on their first night in Fredericksburg, the colonel had found one of his supposedly-ill lieutenants coming out of a tavern. Maria had wanted to slap the man. The colonel had handled the matter more discreetly, saying, "I assume you will be returning to your company in the morning, Lieutenant." Instead, the man resigned his commission.

The first day of the inquiry was something of a circus. Politicians from the capital, sensing an audience, came to make self-serving speeches. Maria began to realize why the war had gone on for so long: No one in the capital knew what was going on in Florida, and by the tone of the conversations, they really didn't care to. All they wanted to do was complain about the cost of the war and how it was affecting their own political ambitions. None of them had offered any sort of solution.

The first speaker was a Whig Senator from Connecticut. He carried on at length about the mistreatment of the poor Indians but thoroughly neglected to mention the sufferings of the settlers or the men in uniform. Maria had seen enough death and destruction in the past four years to make her realize that everyone in Florida was suffering, and as far as she could tell, it was for no good reason at all. Her father pointed out the real reason for the senator's opposition to the war: Because his state no longer had any significant number of Indians, his constituents saw little reason to pay for an Indian war.

A member of the same Whig Party spoke next, this time in favor of the war. The Congressman from Tennessee elaborated endlessly about the "heathen savages," peppering his speech with numerous references to "the tomahawk and the scalping knife." Maria wanted to ask him about the tomahawks and scalping knives carried by the militiamen and volunteers and to what use they had been put when attacking Indian villages. Once again her father pointed out the political realities: The Cherokees of Tennessee were also resisting removal, but instead of going on the warpath, they had gone to court. Like the Seminoles, they were fighting a losing battle.

As it turned out, the Democrats were no more unified than the Whigs. A Representative from South Carolina also spoke in favor of the war, pointing out how many hundreds of his state's slaves had fled to the safety of the Seminole villages and how they were now armed and threatening to lead a slave uprising throughout the South. Maria knew how many millions of slaves there were in the South and how very few had somehow managed to find freedom in Florida. She also knew that what few still remained in the Territory were on the run and in hiding.

The final Congressman to speak was a Democrat from Ohio. He began his performance with an indignant speech about the astronomical costs of the war. It seemed to be the only subject upon which everyone could agree. Then he waded into the real purpose for his being there. The House had imposed a "gag rule" that forbid any debate concerning the subject of slavery. As the Congressman was quick to point out, the gag rule did not apply to a military Court of Inquiry. He then launched into a lengthy harangue on the evils of slavery, especially as it applied to the Florida War. By the time he finished, Maria had almost forgotten that it was an *Indian* War.

On the second day of the inquiry the court read a letter from General Gaines, who had chosen not to attend. It was a lengthy piece, outlining Scott's deficiencies as a general and what Gaines considered to be the obvious reasons for the failure of Scott's campaign. Gaines concluded by naming the men he considered to be the nation's two greatest traitors: Benedict Arnold and Winfield Scott. Following that, the court recessed for a longer than usual lunch, giving the audience time to digest their food and the contents of Gaines's explosive letter.

In the afternoon, Generals Clinch and Jesup took the witness stand. Clinch gave a long, and ultimately confusing, account of the disasters that took place in the early months of the war and why none of it was his fault. Both Wooster and Maria fell asleep during Clinch's testimony. General Jesup spent most of his time justifying his capture of Asi-Yoholo and the other Seminole chiefs under a flag of truce. His criticisms of Scott's conduct, the real reason for Jesup's being there, were more or less forgotten. All in all, it made for a long afternoon.

On the third day, the court began to call other witnesses. Some of the civilians who testified were critical of Scott, but none of the military men would say a word against him. When Alexander Macomb retired or passed on, Winfield Scott would most likely be the Commanding General of the Army. To cross Scott would mean the end of an officer's career. The only man in the army who could safely take on Scott was General Gaines. At the end of the day, most people felt that Scott had been naïve, but not negligent.

The following day was reserved for General Scott to make his defense. If nothing else, it promised to be an entertaining event. Scott arrived in his most resplendent uniform, adorned with medals, gold epaulettes, sashes, cords, collars, and oversized buttons. Maria looked at the gleaming accessories and whispered to her father, "You cannot afford to be a general." Scott did not take the witness stand, but paraded in front of the bench, his six and a quarter foot frame towering over the court. He may have been speaking in his own defense, but he was not on the defensive.

His voice booming like a cannon, Scott fired his first round. "When the Doge of Genoa was brought to Versailles to debase himself before Louis XIV for some imagined offence, he was asked what, in that most opulent palace, amazed him the most. 'To find myself here!' was the reply." And so it went, for the entire day. He readily admitted that the campaign had been a disappointment, but proceeded to place the blame on everyone else, including God, who had committed the offense of creating such an abominable land as Florida in the first place. He even implicated Andrew Jackson, who most Americans revered *more* than God. His most scathing words, however, were reserved for General Gaines. In his eyes, Gaines was *worse* than Benedict Arnold. By the time he was finished, everyone in the courtroom was exhausted, but no one had fallen asleep.

Scott commenced to call his defense witnesses in the afternoon. Among them was Colonel Wooster, who had barely finished taking the oath when Scott approached and leveled his first question. "Colonel Wooster, you and I have known each other since those days on the Niagara frontier, when we both nearly died at the hands of the damned Redcoats. Do you consider me the equal of Benedict Arnold?"

Wooster was not going to allow himself to become a pawn in the battle between Scott and Gaines. He attempted to deflect the question with a bit of humor. "I would say, sir, that Benedict Arnold stands in a class of his own."

Scott wasn't going to let him off that easy. "More to the point, Colonel: Do you consider me a traitor?"

Wooster would not play favorites. "I would have to say, sir, that both you and General Gaines are the finest, most loyal officers I have ever had the pleasure to serve under."

"And General Jesup?"

"His loyalty, sir, has never come into question."

Mildly rebuffed, Scott went immediately to the heart of the matter. "And what, Colonel, do you feel are the causes for the disappointing outcome of our campaign of March and April of 1836?"

Wooster had thought long and hard about the answer. "We failed, sir, because you are a pompous ass who has no idea how to fight an Indian war. Did you honestly expect the damn savages to form a line and exchange volleys? Did you not think that the sound of a marching band and cannons fired at noon every day might alert the enemy to our presence, giving them time to make good their escape? Did you really think that you could precisely time the marches of three large columns through unmapped territory? Blame the climate and the topography if you must, but remember that a good commander should take all such things into account.

"Do not, however, think you are the only one to blame. There is certainly guilt enough to spread around. Shall we start with our beloved Andrew Jackson? Has he ever made a treaty with the Indians that could be considered anything close to fair? Has he ever attempted to enforce the provisions of those treaties that were in favor of the red men? And what of our good friends in Congress? Have they ever seen the Indians as anything more than an issue to be used when electioneering?

"But let us not stop there: We can, indeed, blame General Gaines for being more concerned about making you look bad than with winning the war. We can blame General Jesup, in his position as Quartermaster General, for failing to keep you well supplied. We can blame General Clinch for not acting sooner and Secretary Cass for failing to provide the necessary means to prevent the war. If we care to, General, we can even blame the damn redskins for not seeing the futility of trying to protect their homes and families, or the American public for not understanding that even Indians need a place to live. Blame whoever you like, sir, but in the end, you were in charge and the responsibility must rest on your shoulders."

Those words, of course, were never uttered. Like every other officer present, Wooster had his own career to protect. Once again it was God, the maker of climate and topography, who shouldered the blame for the continued failure of the Florida War.

~~~

Halek Tustenuggee raised his hands as a signal for the canoes to stop. By the fading March moonlight he could see Indian Key just ahead. If they were successful, it would be a great coup, and his people would tell the tale for years to come. Bolek and Kachi-Hadjo be damned: He would fight the war without them.

Tustenuggee had led fourteen canoes for three days, traveling by moonlight through the open waters of Florida Bay and spending each day hidden on a deserted key. The white man's ships had never seen them. Indian Key was the isolated island where Captain Houseman had his home, and where Perrine, the man who grew strange plants, lived. Several other families had settled there, feeling they were safe, so far from the mainland. The settlers would soon learn that there was no place in Florida that was safe from the wrath of Halek Tustenuggee.

There was also much booty to be had on the island. Houseman was a rich man, his fortune made from the business of salvaging cargoes from the many vessels that wrecked along the Florida coast. Perrine was also rumored to be a rich man, having nothing better to do with his life than raise strange plants. Perrine also had a woman and children with him. There may or may not be gold, but there were trophies to be had. He especially liked to lift the scalps from the women while they were still alive and to burn them in their most sensitive places. The more terrified the screams, the more he reveled in the act.

As the other canoes drew alongside, Tustenuggee gave instructions to his warriors. It was less than an hour before dawn. Their landing would be a complete surprise. With luck, not a white man would escape. The canoes separated, each making for a different landing place.

Each warrior paddled silently; Tustenuggee had promised death to anyone who gave them away.

One by one the canoes came ashore. The Indians formed into several groups, each headed for a specific target. Suddenly one of the Indian rifles accidentally discharged. The warriors froze. Tustenuggee could see a figure appear in the window of the nearest house. The chief raised his rifle and fired. There was a scream and the sound of shattering glass.

With the element of surprise gone, the warriors began to shout and run toward the houses. Within the largest house, Dr. Henry Perrine quickly roused his family. The noted botanist swiftly led his wife, their teenage daughter Anna, and young son Joshua to the rear of the house. He lifted a carpet and placed his finger in a knothole in one of the floorboards. Lifting the hatch, he ushered his wife and children down into the crawlspace beneath the house. He was about to step down when he heard the front door crash open. To linger where he was would expose the hiding place of his family. He quickly lowered the hatch and replaced the carpet. He then ran up the stairway, past the second floor, and through another hatch onto a small landing on the roof. Once there, he stood atop the hatch, hoping to prevent the pursuing Indians from coming through.

Beneath the house, Mrs. Perrine and the children cowered in a corner, as far from the hatch as they could get. She held her children close, her hands over their mouths. Sobbing lightly she prayed, both for the three of them and for her husband. She could hear the Indians ransacking the home and could hear gunfire, both in the house and elsewhere on the island. Instinctively, she knew her husband had gone to the roof. She also knew it was a vulnerable place, a small platform barely large enough for three people to stand abreast. She and Henry had gone there often to gaze at the stars and share intimate moments away from the children and the other island inhabitants.

As the trio huddled in their dark corner, they heard a shot just outside the house followed by a war whoop. Mrs. Perrine shuddered and closed her eyes. Henry was dead. She knew it. Suddenly she heard crackling noises from above, and fear gripped her as she realized the house was being set afire. Smoke began to seep through the floorboards, and the daughter panicked. Covering the girl's mouth to prevent the scream, Mrs. Perrine whispered, "Anna! No! They'll hear you!" Joshua began clawing at the dirt that secured the palmetto logs that made up the building's foundation. His mother and sister quickly joined in. It was their only hope. Before long, the flaming house would collapse on top of them.

They dug furiously as the fire grew above them. A flaming floor timber crashed down and smoke began to fill the crawl space. An ember fell on Anna's nightgown, setting it afire. Without a thought, she tore the gown from her body. Naked, she continued to claw at the dirt. Grabbing onto the end of the log, Joshua pulled with all his strength. The mother also took hold and the log moved. All three pulled in unison and the log came free.

It was a small opening, but the boy exited easily. Anna, with the sand scraping against her skin, also struggled through. Mrs. Perrine looked at the opening. She was simply too large to pass through. As mother and children looked at each other, the building settled. The opening closed to a width of no more than three inches. "Run!" she screamed. "Run to the skiff! Row to the schooner!"

"Mother!" The boy tore at the logs, but they would not move. The daughter sobbed and tried to help, then remembered about the Indians. Taking her brother's hand, she pulled him away. He resisted, his eyes fixed on his mother's. "Go!" were the last words he heard her say.

Nearby was a small dock with a rowboat tied to it. Undetected by the Indians, the children ran to the boat, untied the lines, and began to row toward a small schooner anchored offshore. In the predawn light they could see sailors on deck, muskets in hand. As they approached, a shot rang out and a musket ball splashed in front of them. Both screamed and began yelling at the crew, identifying themselves as children and not Indians. The sailors put down their weapons and urged the pair on. They could also see three canoes approaching from the island.

Although the children had a head start on the Indians, the gap was closing swiftly. With Joshua on one oar and Anna on the other, their uncoordinated rowing caused the canoe to move erratically. The Indians, intent on capturing their prey, dug their paddles into the water with a determined effort.

On board the schooner, the captain ordered the anchor raised and the sails set. Perhaps he could inch a bit closer to the fleeing youths. As the first canoe came within range, the sailors began to fire on it, but with little effect. It still looked doubtful as to whether the children would reach the schooner in time.

Sensing the danger, Anna pushed her brother from his seat and took hold of both oars. With all her strength she pulled, heading directly for the schooner. Although the pursuing Indians were still closing in, it looked as if they might at least get close enough for the sailor's fire to drive the attackers off.

As the sails began to fill with the light breeze, the captain ordered the helm hard over. The ship began to move slowly toward the fleeing boat. Four sailors armed with muskets moved to the bow of the vessel and began to take aim at the approaching canoes. Two of them fired, and one of the shots struck the side of the lead canoe. The warriors in the two vessels following it stopped, realizing they could not reach their goal in time. The lead canoe, however, kept up its pursuit. The warrior in front had seen the naked girl. She was a prize he would not willingly give up.

Setting his paddle aside, the warrior picked up his rifle. If he could kill the boy, the boat might falter long enough for him to reach it and drag the girl into the canoe. As he took aim, one of the sailors on the schooner did the same. Both weapons fired at once. Anna screamed as a rifle ball cut her leg. The warrior dropped his rifle, raised his hand to his face, and slumped to the floor of the vessel. The warrior at the rear of the canoe, realizing the goal was now unattainable, broke off the chase. As the schooner drew close, Anna let go of the oars and began to cry uncontrollably.

3 May 1840
Department of War
Washington City

To:

Brvt. Brig. Genl. Zachary Taylor
Commanding, Army of the South

General:

    The Secretary of War is pleased to inform you that he has considered your request to be relieved of command of the Army of the South and will acquiesce to your wishes. While the President does not wish to lose a man of your ability and character at a time when your experience is most needed, he is cognizant that after two years in a most trying position, you are more than deserving of a change of station.

    The Secretary is most grateful for your efforts to bring this painful and protracted conflict to a close. The very fact that a man of your obvious talents has been unable to end this war only shows how entrenched and intransigent the enemy is. We are sure that with the commendable groundwork you have provided, your successor will be able to terminate this war in a short amount of time.

    You will turn command of the Army of the South over to Col. Wm. A. Wooster, 4th Infty., as soon as practical arrangements can be made. Unless advised otherwise, you will report to Jefferson Barracks, Missouri, at the end of your requested furlough.

Your Most Obdt. Serv.
Alexander Macomb,
General Commanding
U. States Army

* * *

3 May 1840
Department of War
Washington City

To:
Col. Wm. A. Wooster
Commanding, 4th Infty.

Colonel:
   The Secretary of War is pleased to inform you that effective upon the departure of Genl. Taylor from the theatre of war, you will assume command of the Army of the South. Both President Van Buren and the Secretary have full faith that you will bring this most disastrous conflict to a speedy and honorable conclusion. To assist in this endeavor, the Secretary gives you full discretion over the deployment of the forces at your command. The President has also ordered the Department of the Navy to extend its full cooperation to you and has placed the Florida Squadron at your disposal.
   Due to budgetary constraints imposed by Congress, we have found it necessary to dispense with the use of Militia and Volunteer forces, and will rely totally on U. States Regulars. In the spirit of greater economy, you will also dismiss all civilian employees of the Army of the South that you do not deem indispensable to the prosecution of the war. We realize these measures will be unpopular with the population of the Territory, and should any officials question your decisions in this matter, please refer them to this office.
   Both the Secretary and I congratulate you on this appointment and have full confidence in your abilities.

Your Most Obdt. Serv.
Alexander Macomb,
General Commanding
U. States Army

It was early June, 1840, and Colonel Wooster sat at the head of a long table, the officers of Fort Lauderdale gathered before him. In all their eyes he saw doubt, fatigue, and indifference. As their new commanding officer it would be his duty to change those attitudes. Most of the faces were familiar: Belmont, his faithful second in command, had taken over the Fourth Infantry upon Wooster's elevation. Also present were his two most trusted officers, Captains

Sparkes and MacDuff. Wooster was well aware that all of the men present were fine officers. He also knew that they were all disgusted with the war.

When Wooster was certain he had secured the group's undivided attention, he set his coffee cup down and stood up. "Gentlemen, as you are no doubt well aware, the War Department has decided to place me in command of this interminable war. Let it be known that I have every intention of being the last commander of the Florida War. For nearly five years we have been fighting the Seminoles, and they have stymied us at every turn. Under General Jesup we sent over nine thousand men against the Indians and still they eluded us. During its course the war has cost the government almost as much as the entire federal budget of 1836. Our most illustrious generals have all come to this theatre of war and all have left with their reputations tarnished. Gentlemen, this situation cannot endure."

Major Childs, the commander of Fort Lauderdale, felt the need to defend his position. He was, after all, the senior officer closest to the actual fighting. "It has not been for lack of effort, sir."

Wooster took a deep breath. It was imperative that the status quo be changed, and the process had to begin with the men in charge. He would be firm with his officers, but he would not blame them for the incompetence of their superiors and the politicians in Washington. "In truth, Major, I consider our efforts to have been somewhat half-hearted. General Taylor, fine soldier that he is, saw fit to protect the settlements, rather than carry the war to the savages." He paused, letting the men grumble their agreement. Taylor had ordered these men to this remote location but had failed to give them any clear mission beyond keeping the area secure. The result had been a serious breakdown in morale. The colonel knew the war couldn't be won if his officers didn't want to win it.

Not only did low morale sap a man's will to fight, it also deadened his thought processes. These were all skilled officers. Nearly all had attended West Point, yet they had forgotten one of the most basic maxims of war: "Gentlemen, no war can truly end if both sides are fighting a defensive conflict. We must carry this war to the Seminoles. We must give them a reason to emigrate."

MacDuff was skeptical and his frustration was beginning to show. As far as he knew, every stratagem had been tried. In the final months of his command, General Taylor had been reduced to the policy of "If you can't beat them, buy them." The officers at Fort Lauderdale had long ago concluded that if that was the way the commander wanted the war to be fought, that was how they would fight it. "What more inducements can we offer, sir? That damn fool agent they sent down from Washington was offering Kachi-Hadjo and Bolek $10,000 apiece just to pack up and go west. I've been in the army near ten years and haven't seen that much money. It's damn insulting, sir. What more can we do?"

It was precisely the question Wooster wanted, and he jumped on it. "We can do what we are supposed to do, Captain! We go to war. We burn their homes, uproot their crops, and destroy their hideouts. In short, we make life impossible for them. Then they'll give up."

Wooster had been watching Sparkes. The tone of his letters had been depressive, causing Maria to be concerned about his mental well-being. In the nine months since Sparkes had been sent to Fort Lauderdale, the couple had been together but once. Sparkes had gone to Fort Brooke to pick up a batch of new recruits and had spent four wonderful days in her company, but the time had been entirely too short. The death of his nephew, the separation from her, and the difficult conditions at Fort Lauderdale seemed to be taking an excessive toll on the young man. Of all the men at the table Sparkes seemed the most distant; the man most ready to give up. His response to Wooster's announcement of a new offensive against the Seminoles backed up that impression: "Haven't they suffered enough, sir?"

Wooster wanted to be firm, but he did not want to seem callous. He lowered his voice and slowly shook his head. "No, Mr. Sparkes, they have not. If such were the case they would have given up and gone west by now." Sparkes's concern for the enemy was dangerous for the war effort, but perfectly understandable. They all wanted the war to end. They all blamed the war on the government, and they all knew that the government could end the war whenever it cared to. At times the Seminoles seemed totally irrelevant to the discussion. They were out there, being hammered at, and no one seemed to know why. Wooster looked at each man in turn. All had the same look on their faces as Sparkes. "I understand your feelings on this matter, gentlemen, and I share them. I do not hate the Indians. Indeed, I respect them. They are simply defending their homes as best they can."

MacDuff pressed the matter, knowing they had been fighting an endless war against an enemy that had withstood more than anyone should have had to. "Then why, sir, do we continue to pursue them? This place will be a wasteland for centuries to come. My God, sir, why can't we just let the damn savages have it?"

Everyone in the room, including MacDuff, knew the answer. They just needed to hear it from their commander. "That is not our decision to make, Captain. We are soldiers, and it is our duty to carry out the orders of the nation's elected leaders. If there is anyone in this room who feels otherwise, he should not be wearing this uniform." He let the men grumble a bit. They were all dedicated officers, and none of them appeared ready to resign his commission. "We are not here to argue about the imbecilic dictates of the politicians in Washington. Our mission is to bring peace to Florida. If that means driving every last Seminole from the peninsula, then that is what we will do, whether we like the task or not." It was a point he needed to make clear. "Gentlemen, I share your frustrations. I have seen hundreds of good men die in the past five years, nearly all of them squandered for no gain whatsoever. I have seen this Territory laid waste and her citizens savagely murdered. We have all seen our fellow soldiers take their own lives rather than face another day of service in Florida. I want it to end."

Lieutenant Jennings, Sparkes's second in command, had a more practical question. "We all do, sir, but what good is it to chase the damn savages into the swamp? We burn their villages this year and when we come back next year, there they are again."

"And that, Lieutenant, is precisely what we have been doing wrong. We have not taken the war to the enemy in the summer months. For fully half of every year the Seminoles can recover from their wounds, plant their crops, re-supply their munitions, and live in relative peace. By the time the season for active campaigning resumes, they are as well prepared for war as we are. We cannot win this war if we continue to retreat every summer."

Even Belmont was surprised by the comment. "What are you proposing, sir?"

"Gentlemen, we shall take to the field year-round. Scour the Everglades until every last Seminole haunt is discovered and destroyed. When their families are reduced to starvation, the chiefs will bring their people in for emigration. If we capture any women and children, we will immediately send them west. Believe me, when the warriors grow lonely, they will turn themselves in. Sooner or later, there will be no Seminoles left in Florida."

Childs voiced a concern that was on everyone's mind. "What of our own men, sir? Campaigning in the sickly season will devastate our ranks. Moving about in this flooded landscape is almost impossible. The heat, the insects, and the disease will wipe out half our men. Look at our losses for the previous summers, sir. A summer campaign will double our losses."

"No, Major, it will not. Disease breeds in the crowded posts we retreat to each summer. Men become lazy and fall prey to the purveyors of cheap whiskey. Taking to the field will remove them from the evils of a sedentary camp life and decrease the incidence of disease. The exercise alone will make them healthier. Yes, we will lose men, but no more than if we sit rotting at these damned forts. We can only hope that whatever loss we sustain will hasten the end of this disastrous war. I worry about casualties as much as anyone, but the only way to end the dying is to end the war."

MacDuff was still skeptical, but ready to discuss the particulars. "Will the rules of engagement change, sir?"

Wooster smiled. He knew what MacDuff was alluding to. "If you are referring to the prohibition against dressing in Indian clothing, Captain, all I can say is that it is still against army regulations. Just see to it that I never hear of it." His mood turned serious again as he came to the most distasteful part of his orders. "The most significant change in the way we fight the Indians will be in our treatment of warriors. Any warrior that continues to resist will be shot or hung on site. Those that surrender will be taken prisoner.   As always, all prisoners, especially women and children, will be treated kindly." It was a point he needed to stress. If the government didn't have the courage to end the war peaceably, then Wooster would have to do it by the only means available to him: He would have to defeat the Seminoles militarily. He didn't particularly like it, but that was his duty.   It did not mean, however, that he had to turn into a ruthless butcher. "We are *not* here to exterminate the Indians. Whether or not we, or they, believe it, it is in the Indians' best interests that this war end and that they be removed to their new homes in the west. We are officers and we are gentlemen. We *will* fight this war with as much honor as we possibly can."

Woodruff, a young officer serving under MacDuff, wanted specifics. "By what means, sir? The whole damn southern half of the peninsula is going to be underwater for the next six months. We are soldiers, sir, not alligators."

Wooster motioned to an officer who had been sitting off to the side, not taking part in the conversation. "A valid question, Mr. Woodruff. I believe most of you know Commander McLaughlin of the navy. He has had some experience in the southwest portion of the Territory and will explain the methods we will use. Commander?"

McLaughlin stood up and approached the table. "Gentlemen, your soldiers are about to become sailors, and my sailors are about to become soldiers. The talents and experience of each will enable us to wage an entirely new kind of warfare. Let me explain . . ."

~~~

It was late afternoon when the meeting broke up. As the officers left the building Wooster called out to Sparkes. "Captain Sparkes!"

"Yes, sir?"

"Fancy a stroll toward the ocean?"

It was more an order than a request. "My pleasure, Colonel."

As they departed the fort and walked down the sandy banks of the New River, Wooster reached into his coat and produced a letter.

Handing it to Sparkes, he said, "From my daughter. I also have a parcel for you. You will understand that no matter how much she implored me, I could not let her accompany me on this trip."

Sparkes understood the colonel's reasoning. The other officers and men at the post were just as lonely and bored as he was. It would be unfair for Sparkes to enjoy some female companionship when his comrades were denied such simple pleasures. "Yes, sir, I cannot disagree. Still, sir, there is little that I wouldn't give to see her right now."

Wooster put a hand on Sparkes's shoulder. "I would have been very unhappy had you felt any different." A nostalgic smile came over his face. "I felt much the same when we fought the Seminoles with Jackson over twenty years ago. I had met Maria's mother in New Orleans perhaps a month before the regiment was ordered to the Apalachicola. If there had been any honorable way to escape going to Florida, I would certainly have taken it. For the better part of a year I think I received but three letters from her due to changes in postings and unreliable mails. There was not a day went by that I did not worry that she had forgotten me. Yet when I finally did return to New Orleans the first thing she said to me was, 'Has Major Wooster come to propose marriage?' Unlike me, you should have no doubt that your love anxiously awaits your return."

"I do not doubt your daughter's love, sir, but I do have doubts that I shall live to see the end of this infernal war."

"How long this war lasts will be determined by you and me and those who fight alongside us. We can fall into fits of melancholy, or we can drive the Seminoles out. I, for one, will not rest until this war is over and you and Maria can raise a family in peace."

Sparkes took a deep breath. The colonel seemed more approachable than ever. Perhaps it was safe to broach a delicate subject. "I have, sir, been offered a fine position in Cincinnati."

Wooster was not surprised or offended. Maria had also made mention of the offer from Sparkes's brother-in-law. The first thought that came to his mind was, *Take my daughter and get as far away from this death trap as you can.* He never said it. Instead, the mind of the soldier won out. "That will have to be your decision, Mr. Sparkes. I would not stand in your way. I would only ask that you consider your duty."

"I have been in Florida for five years, sir. I do believe my duty has been fulfilled."

Wooster could not disagree. "To the nation, yes." He then turned and motioned toward the fort. "But what about them? I will tell you a secret, Mr. Sparkes: A soldier doesn't fight for his country or for some lofty ideals set down on paper, although the politicians and the preachers would have you believe otherwise. A soldier fights for the man beside him. You can resign your commission and walk away from this war; there would be no dishonor in it. But you will also be walking away from your men and from loyal friends like MacDuff and Jennings. They have stood beside you, Mr. Sparkes. Will you continue to stand by them?"

Sparkes nodded. Wooster was right. "It is, sir, the only reason I have remained in the army."

"No, son, it is not." Sparkes looked at the colonel with mild surprise. It was the first time he had called him "son." "No, Mr. Sparkes, you remain here because the job is not yet finished. A sense of duty is a strange thing, Captain. Your grandfather was famous for it, and rightly so. I saw it in your father, and I see it in you. It is irrational and inexplicable, but it is the way we are. It is one of the reasons I hold you in high regard and one of the reasons Maria loves you so."

Sparkes had no response. He had never thought of it in that way. Was he there only because of some strange characteristic handed down from his grandfather? Why was he so driven to complete the mission? "I've always seen duty as some great and heavy debt, sir, but I don't know who I owe it to."

Wooster didn't have that problem. He knew all too well where his sense of duty came from and to whom he owed his personal debt. It was time that Sparkes knew, too. "Let me tell you about duty, Mr. Sparkes." He took a deep breath; the story would be painful for both of them. "During the Battle of Fort Erie, your father and I were sent by General Gaines to protect a section of the wall that was considered weak. It was in a storeroom, and there were only about twenty men left in our company. I was the captain, and your father was my lieutenant. He was like a brother to me by then, much like you and MacDuff. We took up position and were able to keep up an effective fire from the small windows in the wall until the British brought a cannon to bear. Each shot they fired made the timbers in that wall crack and shudder. The best we could do was take hurried shots between cannon rounds, but we knew the British would eventually break through. In that eventuality, out best hope would be to confine the redcoats to the storeroom after they breached the wall, so I sent some of the men to bring a cannon of our own, loaded with grapeshot.

"Just as they returned, one of the British cannon balls succeeded in breaking through the wall. Wood went flying everywhere. A foot-long piece of timber was impaled in my thigh. Your father immediately ran to my aid. As he lifted me off the floor I saw a horde of redcoats making for the breach. It was then that I issued the most painful order of my career. I ordered your father to hold that breach at all costs. Both of us knew he would not survive; there were simply too many of the enemy. Yet hold it he did. I never saw a saber wielded with such fury. Not a redcoat could stand against him. For those few minutes, Erastus Sparkes had found his meaning in life."

Wooster looked out to sea, not wanting to remember what happened next. "Then, just as I thought he might possible hold on, a British bayonet caught your father in the back. He was the last American standing, the only one left to keep the redcoats out. If they were going to be stopped, I had to use the cannon, but I couldn't fire because your father was still there. I couldn't run to him and he couldn't crawl away, so he did the one thing he could to hopefully save me and the other Americans in that fort. He looked at me, a defiant smile on his lips, and nodded ever so slightly. All I could do was cry out to him and put the match to the powder."

Both men stood in silence, watching the eternal waves break onto the shore. "That is the meaning of duty, son. Duty makes you order your best friend to his death, and duty makes him carry out that order, no matter what the consequences. And it was duty that forced me to fire that cannon, ending the life of someone that was as dear to my heart as any man could ever be."

~~~

Kachi-Hadjo watched as the five riders approached the secluded clearing. At the head of the group was Colonel Wooster, his tall frame and graying hair easily recognized. Three of the men appeared to be common soldiers, while the fourth was the Indian guide that Kachi-Hadjo had sent to bring the colonel to the meeting place. Wooster had posted a white flag at a frequently used boat landing near Ft. Lauderdale and had let it be known that he wished for a parley. Despite the warnings of Abee-Aka, Kachi-Hadjo had agreed. He did not trust the white men, but he trusted this white man.

Wooster slid off his horse and instructed the others to remain behind. Standing before him was the largest oak tree he had ever seen. It had to be at least fifteen feet in circumference, and covered an area over one hundred feet in diameter. Situated in the middle of a large clearing, it was the perfect place for a parley.

Kachi-Hadjo was sitting under the tree on the branch of a massive fallen limb. The Indian smiled as he rose. "Wooster does not bring a white flag."

"I have heard the Seminole no longer trusts the white flag."

"It depends on who carries it, my friend." He motioned for Wooster to have a seat on an opposite branch of the same fallen limb. The colonel noticed that both branches were worn smooth from having been sat on frequently. It was as if the limb had fallen strictly for the purpose of providing a convenient place to sit down and have a discussion. No one had to tell him that this was what the Indians called a "council oak." Kachi-Hadjo offered Wooster a cigar. "I did not bring a pipe. I think I like these better." Wooster lit the cigar from a small burning twig. It was a fine cigar, probably Cuban. Evidently the navy's patrols weren't stopping all the smugglers. The chief sat back, stretching out his legs. "You have come to talk of peace?"

Wooster shrugged. "Or war. It is in your hands."

Kachi-Hadjo was wary. "It is the white man who brings war to the Seminole. If the white man stays north of the Okee-Chobee, there will be no war."

Wooster nodded, but he also knew the reality of the situation. "Even the Great Father in Washington cannot make that happen. My people will not stop moving into new lands until there is no land left to conquer. It is the way of the American people. Our god has told us to subdue the earth and we shall, whether or not it is right, or wise, or neither. For those that would conquer the land, the Seminole is but an annoyance, something bothersome that must be removed, like dust in the eye."

Kachi-Hadjo smiled. "So now we are no better than dust?"

"And in the great passing of events from the beginning of time, the white man is no better than the fly that lands upon the dung heap. But for that one fly, and for that one moment, that dung heap is everything. My people will have this dung heap, no matter how foul it is. It is a matter of pride, nothing more."

The word "pride" resonated with the chief. "Pride may also belong to the maggot that makes its home in the dung heap." He looked up, motioning to the great tree that spread above them. "You say your god has told you to conquer the earth. This is a strange god. Look upon this tree. The Great Spirit made it to be greater than all the other oaks in the forest. He set it apart from the others and gave it strong medicine. It is a tree that the Great Spirit looks down upon and smiles when he sees it. To him it is a favorite child. The Seminole knows this and reveres this tree. We protect it and hold our most sacred ceremonies under its branches. The white man's god would have you cut this tree down and use its sacred wood to build great ships so that you may conquer lands across the sea. This I cannot understand."

The colonel knew Kachi-Hadjo was right. His own first thoughts when he had seen the tree centered on how all that wood would be used. Slightly embarrassed, he felt the need to defend his nation. "The United States does not seek to build an empire like the British. We do not conquer our neighbors." The moment the words left his mouth, he knew how false they sounded.

Kachi-Hadjo laughed. "The Seminole are not your neighbors? The Creek and Cherokee are not your neighbors?" He shook his head. "I know of what you speak: These are already your lands; you have purchased them from the Spanish. The Agent Thompson told us this. But is that true? Did not your Great Father Jackson conquer these lands when the Spanish still claimed them? And did you then not force them to enter into a treaty? Your talks with the Spaniards were like your talks with the red men. You conquer first; then you talk. There is no honor in such talks." Kachi-Hadjo sighed. "You have come once again, like the other big chiefs before you, to ask the Seminole to leave his home. We are a proud people. We will not leave."

Wooster nodded. Right or wrong, he needed to make Kachi-Hadjo understand something important: "I come not to ask you to leave, but to tell you that you must go west. This war must end, my friend, and I will end it."

Kachi-Hadjo saw the determination in Wooster's eyes, and it worried him. The best he could do was bluff. "You will fare no better than the others who have said the same."

"No, my friend, it shall be different now. I will come after you, your villages, your crops, your women, and your children. You will find no rest, and you will find no food. My people have told me to end this war. I shall not fail them."

Kachi-Hadjo felt a chill run through his body. Wooster would do as he said he would. It would be the end of the Seminole people living in Florida. Yet, like his adversary, the chief also knew the meaning of duty to his people. "You are a man of your word, Wooster. I believe you will come after us and that the Seminole will suffer much. But this will be a small suffering compared to that which we will feel if we lose our pride and our homeland. You say it is your duty to drive the Seminole from this land. I say that it is my duty to fight to stay in our homes. It is past the point of making sense, my friend." He took a long draw on his cigar. "You are right: It is pride; nothing more. But what is a man without pride? What are a people without a home? I thank you for offering us this chance to make peace. If we could keep our pride and our homes, I would surely take it. But that is not what your people offer." The chief stood up. "Today my heart weeps, for peace shall come to the Seminole only when he lies in his grave."

25

Hesaketa-Mese, Giver of Breath! Hear the words of Kachi-Hadjo!

These are dark days for my people. For five winters we have fought to drive the white man from our homeland, yet he does not go away. Many of my people say you have abandoned us and left us to the false mercies of the white men. I do not believe this is true, but I long for a sign that will tell us what we must do to once again win your favor.

Many have been our sorrows. My father, Micco Phillip, has died on the way to the new land and is buried far from his kinsman, where his spirit must forever be lonely. Many of our women and children have been taken captive by the army and have been sent to the new lands in the west. The warriors who are left behind long for their wives and their little ones and talk of giving up the fight and going to the west to be with their loved ones. I cannot tell them this is wrong, for even if we were to win this war, the white men would not return our loved ones to us.

It is our women and children who suffer most in this war. We must live in damp swamps and unhealthy places where the crops do not grow well. We must keep our villages and fields hidden from the white soldiers, or they will destroy them. Already we have lost many fields and much corn. Our women have only torn dresses to wear and often are clothed in little more than the large cloth bags the white men discard. It shames them to wear the white man's cast-offs, but there is no choice. Our babies must go naked and often have little to eat, even those that feed at their mother's breast, for their mothers are often weak and without milk. Why must the innocent suffer the most?

My mother and my wife are buried in these sands; I do not wish to leave them. I do not wish to take Ki-tee from them. Yet I believe the fight will now be harder. The white man's big chief Taylor has left; he could not conquer us. But now the white men are led by the one called Wooster. He is a man I know, a true warrior.

He says it is his duty to his people to drive the Seminole from this land, and I think he will do it. Tell me, Hesaketa-Mese, is it time to give up the fight?

Gator John peered into the cypress swamp, looking for any sign of where an Indian might be hiding. He knew they were there; he had seen signs on the trail leading up to the swamp. John had hoped he would be out west by now, far away from this bitter war. He didn't like what he was doing, but he had no choice. He was a black man, and it was unwise for any black man, free or slave, to make a white man unhappy. When Colonel Wooster had asked if he would remain behind as a guide and interpreter, John had known it was a request he could not refuse.

It was also to his advantage. As a free black man, the army was obligated to pay him for his services. He was also making friends among the officers who were serving in Florida. Someday he would be living in the new Indian Territory, surrounded by hostile Creeks who would be more than willing to sell him into slavery. Having a friend in the military could be a great advantage. A man like Wooster could provide protection and might also help secure the goods or monies that the government had promised.

Gaining the favor and the trust of officers had its price. Although a free man, he often had to act like a slave. It was degrading, but necessary. He also had to do his job well. That meant being a guide that actually led the army to Seminole villages or camps. If John did not deliver now, these officers would not deliver later. On occasion, it also meant killing the same men he had recently fought alongside.

It was a difficult thing to do, and it bothered him. In light of that, he often let the Indians get off the first shot. He then reasoned that if they were trying to kill him, he was justified in trying to kill them. He often wondered what would happen when the war ended and he and the men he was helping to capture were finally gathered together in the new Indian Territory. Would they let the past die or would they want revenge? The war in Florida might end, but it very well continue in the west.

As he pondered all of this, a slight movement caught his eye. At first he thought it was a squirrel's tail, but then he dismissed the idea. The movement hadn't been right, and there had been no barking. He lifted his rifle slightly, cocked the hammer, and checked the powder in the pan. Bringing the sight to his eye, he squeezed the trigger. The gun fired and a ball buried itself in the tree where he had seen the motion.

Suddenly, the swamp erupted in smoke and flame. John immediately fell to the ground and began to reload the gun. He heard a soldier scream and saw others run for cover before returning fire. Tearing open a paper cartridge, he poured a bit of powder into the pan and emptied the rest into the barrel. Next he wrapped the lead shot in the paper, placed it in the barrel, and used the ramrod to tamp it into place. Getting up, John hurried toward a tree. Several shots flew by as he ran.

He heard the officer, a young fellow named Sparkes, call out for his men to advance. The soldiers formed a crude line and quickly rushed into the swamp. Both sides fired, but no one seemed to have been hit. John ran forward to be with the troops, and another ball passed close by his breast. It was a surprise; he had expected the Indians to have retreated after the soldiers charged. As he came alongside Sparkes, John pulled a small metal flask from his trousers. Taking a long draught, John wiped his mouth and shouted, "Lordy, Massa, I feels mighty queer, the Injen fight so strong." He then ran forward, slipped behind a tree and took a quick look out into the swamp.

He saw an Indian turn to run, and thought he recognized the warrior. Raising his rifle, he took aim, fired, and saw the Indian fall. Moving back behind the tree, he reloaded, cocked the gun, and once again looked into the swamp. This time, his eyes met those of Kachi-Hadjo. Both men quickly aimed, both fired, and both narrowly missed. Ducking behind the tree again, John reloaded. When he next looked into the swamp, he saw no one. The firing had stopped. The Seminoles had fled. John let out his breath. He rarely missed, and neither did Kachi-Hadjo. Had both of them intentionally erred? He really didn't know.

~~~

Kachi-Hadjo didn't like the white trader. He was the sort of person who told you he was your greatest friend, but would be the first to spit at you when your back was turned. He was dirty and had eyes that shifted about, always looking for someone who wasn't there. If it had been another place and time, Kachi-Hadjo would have cut the man's throat just to keep him from speaking another lie. He would not have even lifted his scalp, for from such a man it would be no trophy.

The trader had spoken many lies, all of them with the look of complete sincerity on his face. He had told how the white men were tiring of the war, how they were fighting ten other Indian nations and the British, and that if the Seminoles could hold out for another year or two, the Americans would give up and allow all the Indians who had been sent west to return to Florida. Kachi-Hadjo had not bothered to argue; it would have been no use. He knew it all to be false, and that the only thing the trader wanted was for the Seminoles to keep buying powder. What worried Kachi-Hadjo most was that some of his warriors were willing to believe the white man's lies.

Kachi-Hadjo suffered the white man's presence only because he needed him. The trader had brought a keg of powder and also a keg of whiskey. The negotiations had been bitter. The trader had argued that because he was breaking the white man's laws the price was much higher. Kachi-Hadjo had argued that the trader always broke the law, so why should the price be higher today? In the end, the number of skins Kachi-Hadjo could offer were only enough to buy one of the kegs. For Kachi-Hadjo, the choice was simple: They must have the powder. A few of his warriors disagreed. They too were giving up on the war.

It was becoming increasingly difficult for Kachi-Hadjo and his people to buy powder, whiskey, or anything else they needed. Since Wooster and his men had come to south Florida, their small boats and ships seemed to be everywhere, making it hard for the Indians to contact the smugglers they relied upon. To make matters worse, the Seminoles now had fewer goods to offer the traders. Kachi-Hadjo knew the reasons, but couldn't do much about it. With the increased military patrols, his people had less time to devote to hunting and the preparation of hides. Even the act of hunting was problematical.

Powder and lead were scarce, and the noise from a rifle discharge might alert a nearby military patrol. They could still hunt with bow and arrow, but they had been using rifles for so long that the knowledge of how to select the proper wood for a bow and how to fashion the arrows had diminished. Most of the elders who had possessed that skill had either died from the harshness of the war or had gone out west. It annoyed Kachi-Hadjo that they had been forced to live like outlaws, scavenging what they could from the wrecks that came ashore on Florida's coast, but without that, they would have had almost nothing to offer in trade.

Kachi-Hadjo and the smuggler continued to haggle over the price of the keg of powder. At one point the trader threw up his hands and shook his head. "Look here, Mr. Mad Panther, There just ain't the market for these damn skins like there used to be. The northerners and the English just ain't buying like they used to." For some reason, it was the only thing the white man said that Kachi-Hadjo believed.

~~~

Sparkes reached over the side of the canoe and scooped up a handful of water and splashed it on his face. He had been wishing that it was cool water, but he knew better. It was mid-September in south Florida, and the men joked that the water was hot enough to cook potatoes in. He looked behind him and saw a soldier in the following vessel quickly unbutton his trousers. The other men in the canoe shifted their weight to allow the soldier to sit on the side of the boat with most of his posterior suspended over the shallow water. Yet another case of diarrhea. It was an eventuality of service in Florida.

It was an odd looking crew. About a quarter of the men were sailors, some of them black. There was also a pair of Marines. At first glance it was difficult to tell which branch of the service a man might belong to. Sparkes's soldiers had traded their blue woolen winter uniforms for the white cotton and linen garments allowed them in summer, which weren't that different from what the sailors wore. For the most part the men worked well together, though some of the soldiers found it difficult to serve alongside the black sailors. At the first sign of trouble, Sparkes had made it clear that all personal animosities were to be dispensed with for the duration of the mission. The men would be depending on each other for many weeks; they didn't need to be fighting amongst themselves.

The weather was hot, well into the higher nineties. The air was thick, and Sparkes often felt as if he were traveling through an unseen cloud of steam. The small fleet of eleven canoes moved in near silence through the tall grass, gliding over a terrain covered by about a foot or two of water. In this flat, flooded landscape every foot of change in elevation had a dramatic effect on the vegetation. Where the land was lowest, sawgrass prairies prevailed. Where the land was less often submerged, massive cypress swamps would grow. In areas that were dry most of the time, dense hardwood hammocks would appear. In those places that were normally dry, thin pine forests would be the norm. The amount of water covering the ground depended on the time of year. During the dry winter, even the sawgrass prairies could dry up. During an especially wet summer, the pinewoods might be under an inch or so of water. The whole southern portion of the peninsula was like this, with little islands of pine or hammock land dotting the landscape, offering innumerable hiding places for the wary Seminoles. Sparkes doubted if the army could ever find them all. If the weather had been cooler, the mosquitoes absent, the food tolerable, and if they were not in danger of being shot at, Sparkes and his men might have actually enjoyed the trip. At least the first week of it. After six weeks, the entire endeavor was wearing thin.

Rarely was a word spoken between the men, and unless they were completely in the open, all communication was by hand signal. Their mission was to capture Indians, and if the Seminoles had any idea that white soldiers were in the area, they would quickly disappear. That had happened several times early in the mission, but Sparkes and his men had gotten better at moving in silence and keeping their locations concealed. They had also learned to navigate in the Everglades, which could often be as featureless as a wheat field.

Sparkes had been assisted in his navigation by two very different men. The first was Midshipman Dillard of the navy. With his sextant, notebooks, compass, and pocket watch, Dillard acted as if he were navigating from the deck of forty-four gun frigate rather than a tipsy canoe. Some of the men laughed at the efforts, but not Sparkes. By the time the expedition returned to Fort Lauderdale, he would have an accurate map of everywhere they had been. Sooner or later they would have maps marking every possible Seminole hideout. And sooner could not arrive soon enough.

The other person who was most helpful in Sparkes's quest to find his way in the trackless Everglades was their guide and interpreter, Gator John. Having been raised among the Indians, John knew his way around the peninsula as well as any Seminole. Both men seemed to have the same goal in mind: Locate as many villages as they possibly could so that the war might end.

As the canoe glided through a channel in the sawgrass, Sparkes heard a light tapping come from the back of the vessel. Looking around, he saw John point to a small knot of cypress trees. Sparkes nodded and held his hand aloft, signaling the other boats to follow his lead. They continued along for about a quarter mile before turning into another channel. At first it seemed to lead them away from the cypress head, but then it changed course and went directly toward it.

Upon reaching the edge of the cypress head, the men quietly exited their canoes and began to wade silently through the water. The movement was slow and laborious, through water that varied from three inches to three feet deep. Holding their weapons and their cartridge boxes above their heads, the men took each step with deliberate care. The sound of splashing could alert any villagers of their approach. Sparkes saw one of the men wince silently as his foot struck an unseen cypress root.

Sparkes and John, both in the lead, saw the clearing simultaneously. It was a small field, planted mostly in pumpkins and beans. At the opposite end of the field were three thatch-covered platforms. No Indian was in sight. Sparkes ordered the men to fan out. When they were in position, he motioned them forward.

With guns at the ready, he and the men moved from the water out onto dry land. No one tried to stop them. They cautiously crossed the field and approached the huts. A small fire was burning with a pot of sofkee cooking. Someone had been there, but had left in a hurry. John looked at the ground. He could see footprints leading off into the sawgrass, toward another cypress head. The Seminoles had made a timely escape. Turning to Sparkes, John broke the silence. "A few squaws and chillen, maybe an ol' man. Done gone now."

Sparkes shook his head. What could have given them away? He spit on the ground. It didn't matter. Another day wasted. It had been over a year since he had come to Fort Lauderdale and four months since Colonel Wooster had taken command of the war. In some ways he was thankful to be out in the field and on the trail of the enemy, but as far as he could tell, it was still a waste. It was a waste of time, for they could never hope to capture every last Seminole, no matter how many years it took. It was certainly a waste of money, yet for all the money the government was spending in Florida, little of it found its way to the common soldier, who was paid as little as eight dollars a month and carried a musket that had been made a quarter century earlier. It was also a waste of good men's lives. All this waste to capture a band of savages that would harm no one if simply left alone. His temper began to seethe. He missed a good bed, good food, clean clothes, and most of all, he missed Maria.

While Sparkes stood fuming, an old Indian stepped from behind a cluster of trees, leveled his ancient rifle, and pulled the trigger. The powder in the pan flashed, but the gun failed to fire. As the old man fumbled with the mechanism, Sparkes lunged forward, seized the weapon by the barrel, and tore it from the old man's grip. Then, with all his might, Sparkes swung the rifle, smashing the butt into the Indian's skull. The old man fell to the ground, blood seeping from a gash in his head. Swinging the rifle like an axe, Sparkes repeatedly pummeled the man's chest until Midshipman Dillard ran up and took the weapon from his hands.

Exhausted, Sparkes sat on the ground and lowered his head into his hands. He was trembling. As the men gathered around, Dillard knelt beside Sparkes and put a hand on his shoulder. "It's alright, Sparkes, I think we all could have done it at one time or another."

Sparkes took a deep breath and looked at Sergeant Bigelow. "Post a guard. We'll spend the night here. Have the men bring the canoes up, and then destroy whatever crops we don't need. We'll tear down the huts when we leave in the morning."

"Aye, sir." Catching the eye of a passing soldier, Bigelow shook his head and spoke in a low tone. "I sure would like to catch a few Indians now and then." He winked and gave a wicked smile. "Preferably a nice young squaw."

Sparkes looked down at the dead Indian, trying to fathom his own feelings. He should have felt remorse, even guilt for having beaten the old man so mercilessly. He should have felt anger for having found himself in such a situation. As near as he could tell, however, he felt nothing. A pair of soldiers stood nearby, not sure what to do. He looked up at them with tired eyes. "Bury the son-of-a-bitch, damn it."

As Bigelow walked across the clearing, he abruptly came to a halt. The soldier by his side began to say something but was stopped by an upraised hand. The sergeant was listening intently. After a minute, he shook his head, a puzzled look on his face. Bigelow narrowed his eyes, as if it would help him hear better. "Thought I heard a baby cry. Just for a second." Both men moved toward the edge of the swamp, not making a sound. They peered into the cypress forest, straining to hear any human sound. All they heard were birds.

After a few minutes Bigelow relaxed and turned around. "Damn birds." He looked at the soldier. "Take five men and bring the boats up."

Not twenty feet away, a Seminole woman let her breath slowly escape. Only her head was above water, the rest of her body being hidden behind the large base of a huge cypress. Tears filled her eyes, but she did not sob. Under the water, held tightly in her arms, was a lifeless infant. The child had begun to cry, and the only way to keep him from being heard was to hold him under water. She could not let herself be taken prisoner. Her husband was away with Kachi-Hadjo, and her other children were safe at another village. Besides, she'd heard what the soldiers did to captured women. She shuddered and stroked the unresponsive body. Thankfully, the child hadn't struggled long.

26

To:
Mrs. David Kilgour
Cincinnati, Ohio

My Dearest Emily,

Once again I find myself in the **unhappy** position of having to wish you a Merry Christmas and a Joyous New Year from this most distressing of places. Four days ago we marked the <u>sixth</u> anniversary of the commencement of this unfortunate war, and unless I be taken from this earth, I fear that I shall probably be sending you the <u>same</u> sad tidings from this <u>same</u> miserable place a year from now. Never could I have imagined the war lasting this long. When it occurs to me that I arrived in Florida as a youth of but twenty and will leave it closer to the age of thirty, it astounds me. Should I suddenly appear at your door, you would not recognize me. My robust former self has been replaced by a gaunt, bearded, filthy man who looks as if he has been lost in the desert for the better part of a year. Fear not for my health, however. There is naught wrong with me that a good bath, clean clothes, and a week or two of decent food would not cure (should I ever have the joy of experiencing those luxuries again). That, and an end to this accursed war.

The tedium of this place renders even the most agreeable things disagreeable. The weather yesterday was perfectly delightful, especially when compared to what you might have experienced in Cincinnati, yet all we could do was complain of the slight frost in the morning and the fact that we were sweating by late afternoon. Although surrounded by my good companions and laugh as we often do, there remains an emptiness in my soul that only the society of those most dear to me could relieve. Could I be in the company of you or my beloved Maria but one day a month, I could endure this place with ease. But wishes are not granted for those *who live in Florida.*

As for the war, it moves inexorably on, with progress measured in terms of squaws captured or villages burnt, or, most sadly, in the number of soldiers lost to disease or homesteads destroyed by Indian raids. As for soldiers or warriors actually killed in battle, it is indeed a rare occurrence. Each side chips away at the most defenseless of their enemy, and neither gains any real victories. Only the knowledge of our greater resources gives us any confidence of eventual triumph.

Perhaps now that Genl. Harrison is to assume the Presidency and the Whigs are ascendant in Congress, the politics of this miserable war may change. Indeed, it is only the politicians who keep us at war. The Indians have been so reduced as to make them an enemy in name only. They are more akin to outlaws, being but a few belligerent bands that commit crimes against civilians, never against the army. It was Jackson, his toady Van Buren, and the southern slavers who urged this war upon us and who would not let it end. Perhaps wiser heads will now prevail in Washington City.

We leave once more on patrol within the week. Because we are now into the dry season, most of our travel will be on foot. Our greatest difficulty at such times is in the procurement of water. It is not unusual to be forced to dig for it, finding it a foot or so below the surface. Rarely is this water fit to drink, being the color and consistency of ink, but drink it we must, for there is naught else to be had.

The news that you are again with child fills me with mixed feelings. I am, of course, happy for you and David, knowing as I do how much you love children. Yet I am also apprehensive, remembering the loss of dear little Jacob and the difficulty you experienced whilst bringing him into this world. I would say that "my prayers are with you," but the Lord seems to have long since quit listening to my supplications. I know not how I shall feel when at last Maria and I are man and wife and she is in a similar condition.

But such times shall for the moment remain far in the future. For now, I can do little but wish you, David, Kenneth and Lizzy a bountiful New Year. Write often, as the occasional letter is one of the few joys we have here.

Your Most Affectionate Brother,
Jacob

Seven years had passed since John Bemrose, then a lad of sixteen years and fresh off the boat from England, arrived in St. Augustine as a newly-recruited hospital orderly. Both Colonel Wooster and Dr. Weightman had immediately taken a liking to the lad. Perhaps it was the Englishman's diminutive size. Perhaps it was his ready smile or his eagerness to be helpful. Whatever it was, both men had wanted to take him under their wing. In less than a week, Wooster had made a bargain with the doctor that allowed the young man to serve as the colonel's clerk in the afternoon and evenings, after his duties at the hospital were finished. For almost eight months, until the arrival of Sparkes, Bemrose had eaten and slept at the colonel's residence. For Maria, the relationship had been similar to what she might have had with a close cousin. Even after he had returned to full-time duties as an orderly, the pair remained close. Both had grown to adulthood during the Florida War. Now, in the late spring of 1841, Bemrose was headed home.

The young steward was much revered within the regiment for the aid he had given to the sick and the wounded. Yet he too had become a casualty of war. More than once the fevers that surrounded him had laid him low. During those times, Dr. Weightman had rarely left the young man's side. The care that Bemrose had given to others was remembered, and soldiers often looked in on him. Thanks to their constant care and attention he had always been nursed back to health. The last bout, however, had been the worst. The fever had left him dangerously weak and thin. As much as Weightman hated to lose him, he also knew that it was time for the young man to leave Florida. The next attack of fever might well be fatal.

The doctor had made one last attempt to keep the young man from returning to England. In an act of affection and generosity, he had once again offered to sponsor the lad to the College of Surgeons at Philadelphia. Bemrose had been gracious in his refusal to accept the offer, doubting that he had the strength to complete the courses. More than that, his illness had brought with it a severe case of homesickness. As he had told the doctor, he wanted to "once more breathe me native air." He had never talked about why he had left England in the first place. For whatever reasons, it was time to return to his homeland.

A small group of people gathered on the pier in front of Fort Brooke to wish their friend farewell. Doctor Weightman rested his hand on Bemrose's shoulder. In a way, he felt as if he were losing a son. "Should you regain your health and wish to once again venture across the ocean, the offer will forever stand, you know." The pair embraced for a moment, then stepped apart. They both wiped away a tear.

"And ever shall I 'old you dear to me 'eart for making the offer, Doctor, sir. You 'ave done me great 'onor, you 'ave, an' I shall never forget it, you can be sure."

Wooster stepped forward and took the departing man's thin hand. "It has been my pleasure, Mr. Bemrose, to see you grow into a fine young man." He then handed him an envelope. "Should anyone not immediately recognize your obvious qualities, feel free to present them this letter of reference. I have done my meager best to convey my deep respect."

Bemrose wiped another tear from his eye. The war had destroyed so many lives, but in a way, it had enriched his beyond measure. The memories of these people would remain strong forever. "I can do little but thank you, sir. I cannot think what I did to deserve such fine treatment."

As Wooster stepped back, Maria moved forward and embraced her friend warmly. When they had first met, he had stood a head taller than her. Now she towered over him. She slowly released her embrace. She actually felt she might crush his weakened frame. "I shall miss you, Johnny. You were such a good companion."

He smiled and held her hand tightly. "I trust Captain Sparkes will fill the void, ma'am."

"In my future, yes, but when I think upon the past, it will always be your memory that will make me smile. Do find a good wife back in your home country. You will make a good father and husband."

She bent forward and kissed him on the cheek. He knew the sort of woman he would look for when he returned at last to his home.

~~~

Halek Tustenuggee peered from behind the woodpile, surveying the small town. There was no guard, no sign of the army or the militia. It was as he had suspected: The whites were totally unprepared for an attack. It had been several years since Seminole warriors had come this far north. The inhabitants would think they were safe, that all the hostile Indians were far south in the Everglades. Tustenuggee was about to show them how wrong they were. Now that summer had come, there was little use to stay in the south. The soldiers and their boats were traveling throughout the southern wetlands, making it hard to find any place to make a permanent camp.

It was a few hours before dawn, and the moon, just a few days past full, was beginning to set. It was the perfect time to strike. Tustenuggee smiled. He would see the look of terror in the women and children's eyes as they begged to be spared. He would spare no one.

There had, in truth, been little to revel in lately. The army's patrols had finally caught up with the outlaw Spanish Indians that he had been associated with for the past few years. Fortunately, Tustenuggee had been gone at the time of their capture, but his band had been reduced to little more than a dozen warriors. The army, with captured Seminoles and blacks as their guides, had located nearly every refuge in the peninsula. White towns and villages in the central and southern part of the Territory posted guards and were always on the lookout for any sign of Indians. Whites who took to the trails traveled in armed groups, and homesteaders always seemed to have a rifle at hand. Tustenuggee could hurt the white men, but he had come to the realization that he could never drive them away. He knew the war was lost, and that his people were doomed. Yet he was never going to surrender. He would rather die a warrior. For him, the war provided nothing more than an opportunity to kill the hated white man.

The chief raised his hand, motioning to his warriors. One by one, a dozen men came out from the foliage and began to move down the narrow dirt street. They passed two small houses and headed toward what appeared to be a storefront. He stopped to look in the front window and smiled. Before attacking the inhabitants, they needed to secure whatever plunder they could find. There would not be time to gather it later.

Moving around to the back of the building, Tustenuggee came to a door. He pushed, but it did not move. It was no doubt barred from the inside. Making his way to the side of the store, he tried a window. It swung open. He motioned for one of the smaller warriors to come forward, and then helped him climb into the building. As the warrior silently moved to unlock the back door, Tustenuggee and the others went to meet him.

It was then that the dog attacked. First there was barking, then the sound of an Indian screaming. A candle lit in an upstairs window. Tustenuggee immediately returned to the open window and vaulted in. A man came running down the stairs, rifle in hand. Catching sight of the Indian being attacked by the dog, the man fired, killing the warrior. Tomahawk in hand, Tustenuggee charged at the store owner. The man turned his rifle around and began to swing wildly, sending goods from the shelves in all directions. Tustenuggee ducked then lunged. He swung his tomahawk, but the man managed to deflect it. Tustenuggee swung again and hit the merchant a glancing blow on the side of the head. The white man fell to the floor.

Tustenuggee could hear sounds from the rooms above. There were no women's screams, only heavy footsteps and the shouting of men. When he had looked in the store's front window he had seen barrels of food and shelves filled with trade goods. He had not been able to read the sign that said, "Rooms to rent—upstairs." Suddenly the dog was before him, growling and snapping its jaws. The chief turned and ran, diving through the window and tumbling out onto the ground. As he and his warriors came out into the street, he could see candles and oil lamps being lit in several of the houses. One of the doors opened and a man stepped out, rifle in hand. Tustenuggee quickly grabbed a gun from one of the warriors and fired. The white man jumped back into the house and hastily shut the door. Tustenuggee saw the candle go out and a window open.

The chief cursed. In a matter of minutes, the entire town would be up. It was time to leave. The raid had been a failure, he had lost an irreplaceable warrior, and now the entire northern part of the territory would be on the alert. They would have to look elsewhere for scalps and plunder.

~~~

MacDuff stood with his hands on his hips and shook his head. Before him stretched the largest, most perfectly cultivated field he had seen since his arrival in Florida. The plants were arranged in neat rows with the different crops planted in well-ordered plots. There were at least a hundred acres of corn, pumpkins, potatoes, peas, melons, tobacco, rice, and sugar cane, with hardly a weed in sight. "Damn, Sparky, we should move the fort up here. We could feed the entire regiment for a year with all this."

Sparkes looked the fields over from end to end, making mental calculations. At first, the extent of the fields had been deceiving. The plots were numerous, divided by rows of sawgrass and bushes that concealed them from passersby, but connected by well-worn foot paths. The whole complex extended for a mile or more. "What do you think? A thousand bushels of potatoes?"

"At least. Maybe two thousand. A few hundred bushels of corn, too. I can't believe it." The discovery of the fields served to emphasize the problems the army faced in the war. Major Childs had received a report that Abee-Aka was hiding in the area north of Fort Lauderdale. Childs had developed an obsession about capturing Abee-Aka and had dispatched MacDuff, Sparkes, and fifty men in a small fleet of boats to find the illusive old Indian. They had traveled for a week, paddling in the lagoons behind the barrier islands or hauling the vessels overland, finding little of value and absolutely no Indians. Then, about thirty miles north of the fort, they had stumbled upon a narrow freshwater lake that extended for at least fifteen miles. Along the shore of the lake ran these fields, for the most part hidden from sight. Only the tassels on the corn plants had given them away. MacDuff continued to shake his head. "You know we scouted not more than a few miles from this lake when we camped at Fort Jupiter at the end of Jesup's campaign."

Sparkes nodded in agreement as he watched one of the soldiers cut a melon open and begin to eat. How many more hidden farms like this one were scattered throughout the peninsula? He remembered General Jesup's remark about having better maps of the interior of China than he did of the interior of Florida. "And the colonel talks about starving the damn savages into submission."

MacDuff laughed; then his eye caught sight of a soldier bending over, his bayonet in hand, reaching for an especially fine melon. "Touch that melon, Kirchoffen, and it will cost you fifty lashes!" The soldier stood up and slowly backed away. "I've discovered that 'lashes' is the only word of English that damn Hessian knows." MacDuff looked back toward the boats. He yelled, "George!" and the slave came running up. The skinny boy that MacDuff had acquired in 1836 had grown into a strong young man. "Fetch me that melon."

Sergeant Bigelow approached and rendered a casual salute. "Any orders, sir?"

Sparkes nodded. "Have the men make camp. We're going to be here a few days." A look of firm resolve then came over his face. "I want these fields totally destroyed. Not a plant will be left standing, and not a fruit or a vegetable will be left that could possibly be eaten. Harvest whatever we can use or take with us, and destroy the rest. If the plants are mature enough to bear seeds, I want them smashed and thrown into the lake. I want this land to be as worthless as that patch of sawgrass."

Bigelow smiled and turned to leave. "It'll be a pleasure, sir." The sergeant had noticed a change in Sparkes over the past few years. Early in the war the young lieutenant would have shown some remorse over destroying something that another person had obviously put so much effort into. Now, like the rest of the soldiers, Captain Sparkes seemed to revel in the destruction. MacDuff, on the other hand, seemed to have been affected by the war in an opposite manner. At the beginning of the war he would have handed out lashes for almost any infraction. Now he merely threatened the punishment. For good or bad, the war was changing everybody.

MacDuff then gave Bigelow an additional command. "Make sure you post an alert guard. Whoever's been tending these fields can't be far off." He then turned and looked at the heavy foliage on the other side of the lake. "Somebody put a lot of care into this place. I'll bet the tears are flowing now."

~~~

Chia-chee wept. In his entire adult life, he had never cried. When his wife had been taken prisoner and when his son had been slain in battle, he had forced back the tears. Now, as he watched the soldiers joyously uproot his plants and gleefully smash pumpkins and melons, he could not suppress the sobs. Too old to fight the white man and too young to fade into death, he had devoted all the efforts of his mind and body into those fields. Abee-Aka had known of his skill with plants and had placed these fields in his care. Kachi-Hadjo had assigned old men, women, and children to assist him. Both leaders had praised his work. These crops, they had said, would save their people and allow the Seminoles to remain in their homeland. Now, just like his people, his precious fruits and vegetables were being destroyed.

The soldiers could not have come at a worse time. Many of the crops were beginning to ripen, and a small amount had already been harvested. Within a month, nearly all of it would have been gathered and stored away. His people would have eaten well this winter. Now they would eat nothing.

He watched as the soldiers tore up a row of squash plants, throwing them high up into the air and laughing as the dirt flew. It would have been easy to hate the white man, were it not for a memory that played across his mind. Early in the war he had joined a war party that was sent to destroy a deserted plantation near St. Augustine. Like the other warriors, he had danced around the large plantation house as it burned to the ground. Was that home any less important to the plantation owner than these fields were to him? Were the soldiers that were tearing up his crops any more evil than he was? He knew better. Evil was in the hearts of all men, no matter what the color of their skin. The man who could carefully build a house or lovingly tend a garden was just as capable of happily destroying the hard work of somebody else. He began to weep again, but this time it wasn't for his crops. It was for all mankind.

~~~

It was a late afternoon in early November, 1841, and a wonderful day was coming to a close. Commander McLaughlin of the navy had been at Tampa Bay and had invited the officers of Fort Brooke and their wives out for a cruise on his flagship. The *Flirt* was a sleek schooner built expressly for service in the Florida War and had more of the look of a fine sailing yacht than a warship. Mild temperatures, a calm sea, fresh breezes, and good company had made the day delightful. For a few precious hours, as the ship glided across Tampa Bay and out into the Gulf of Mexico, the war was forgotten and no one uttered the word "Seminole."

Now, as the colonel and Maria strolled back toward the small two-story home they had built outside Fort Brooke, they noticed Dr. Weightman standing on the front porch, a worried look on his face. The pair stepped up their pace, knowing that whatever news the doctor was there to deliver, it wasn't good. Both of them immediately assumed the news concerned either Sparkes or MacDuff, but dismissed the idea, knowing that no ship from Fort Lauderdale had arrived in Tampa Bay that day.

As they stepped onto the porch, the doctor took Maria by the hand. "It's Nero. He's very ill." The young woman quickly let go of Weightman's hand and ran into the house. The doctor then turned to the colonel. "It's his heart. I don't suspect he'll last the night."

"Is there anything we can do?"

"Make him comfortable and watch over Nettie. I'll stop back by before retiring, just to see how he's doing."

"Thank you, Richard"

As the two shook hands, the doctor said, "I know how much he means to you and Maria. I wish there was more I could do."

Wooster nodded slightly. "I wish there was more I could have done for them both over the years." As the doctor stepped off the porch, Wooster entered the house. Both Maria and Nettie would be inconsolable.

It was a comfortable house and no bigger than they needed. There was a center hallway with a parlor on one side and a dining room on the other. The servants' quarters were at the end of the hallway. Upstairs were two bedrooms, one for Maria and one for the colonel. The kitchen was out back, detached from the house for fire safety. The colonel entered the servants' quarters and turned toward Nero's bed. The old man lay quietly, his eyes closed, his breathing slow and shallow. Maria and Nettie stood by the bedside, close by each other's side, their hands clasped together. The colonel put a hand on Nettie's shoulder and gave a slight squeeze. He really didn't need to say anything; she understood how he felt. Wooster looked at Maria and nodded toward the parlor. She took the hint and turned, leading Nettie out of the room.

The colonel took a chair and sat by Nero's bed. "Hello, old friend."

A faint smile came across the kind black face and the eyes opened slightly. "Ain't it s'post to be goodbye?"

"I don't think I can say that."

"Tain't so hard. I done said it a dozen times to Nettie this afer'noon."

Wooster nodded. The man's simple humor would not be subdued. "Is there anything I can do for you?"

"You know Massa Colonel, I sho would like to die a free man. Do you think you could sign them papers we talked about so long ago?"

"Of course. And Nettie's too."

The old man smiled. "You ain't gonna turn her out now, are you?"

"No more than I would turn out my own mother."

"Well, bein's I never met your Momma, I don't rightly know what that means."

They both laughed a little, and the colonel said, "I should have done this long ago."

"Ain't no never mind, Massa. I never felt I was anymore a slave to you than you be a slave to the army. We both done made the choice of what kind o' life we was gonna live a long time ago, an' we's stuck with it. You know, I could o' been a free man once. It was just after the war with them Brits, and my massa's boat done stopped in Pens'cola for a few days. I got to talking to some of them boys there, and they said, 'Ya wanna run away? We can help ya. We'll take you on a boat across the bay and get you to this Negro Fort over on the Apalach' River. Sho' was tempting."

The old man's eye's closed for a moment, and he took a deep breath. "But you know, Massa, there was Nettie at home an' all, and I says, 'No, she done trusted me to come back, and the massa done trusted me off the boat, so I'll jus' stays where I at.' Now if I'd been some plantation slave or had some hateful massa, I'd a gone, but right then, it jus' wasn't worth it. Ain't none of us knows what's comin', good or bad. If I'd a' run, I could o' been a free man all my life, or you might o' killed me when you blowed up that Negro Fort way back then. Then again, by stayin' with my massa I could o' been sold down the river, or I could o' been sold to you good folks. I guess the Lord done looked out for me the best a black man can expec' around here. I got no complaints. There's a lot a people got a bunch more to complain about than I do. That's for sho."

Nero smiled, closed his eyes, and rested. Wooster looked down at the man and felt a deep sense of pity. He'd always known Nero to be much more intelligent than he acted. It was more than unfortunate that they lived in a society where a man of promise and talent was forced to act and live the life of a fool. It was deeply immoral.

Nero coughed slightly and reopened his eyes. "You know, Massa, there's some folks got the fire in 'em, and them that don't. You now, you got the fire. Oh yeah, you gonna be the best damn colonel in the army." Wooster smiled. Nero knew him well. "Now you look at mos' your soldiers, and they ain't got much fire. They jus' happy to be in the army where they don' have t' think 'bout much. It da' same way with the black man, cause you know we is as much a man as any white man. Some of us got the fire and ain't never gonna be no man's slave. Others, likes me, ain't got much fire. We figure the Lord done put us here in the land o' slaves an' we's got to make do as bes' we can. I suppose me an' Nettie done alright." He closed his eyes again and took several breaths, each more labored than the last. He opened his eyes and smiled at the colonel. "An' I guess what little fire I has is 'bout to go out."

~~~

It was now late autumn and the ceaseless patrols into the Everglades continued. For close to eighteen months Colonel Wooster's offensive had taken the war to the Seminoles, but still the conflict wore on. A few isolated raids by outlaw bands in north Florida had everyone seeing Indian sign and clamoring for the militia to be called out. The sudden death of President Harrison along with the bitter distrust between his successor, John Tyler, and Congress seemed to result in a paralyzed administration that couldn't decide what it wanted to do in Florida. For the soldiers and the Seminoles, the suffering was unrelenting.

Sparkes sat on a log in front of a smoldering fire, brushed aside the mosquitoes, and watched the glowing embers float up to the stars. He should have been satisfied with the day's work, but he wasn't. It was nothing more than another island in the Everglades, another ten or twelve Seminole women and children taken prisoner, along with a pair of old men. As always, the warriors had been away. There had been one Indian casualty, an old woman who had been mistaken for a warrior. At least that was what the soldier had told him.

MacDuff walked up and sat down beside him. "No luck. Gator John says neither one of those old men is Abee-Aka. I'm actually beginning to believe those stories that say old Sam can disappear whenever he wants to."

Sparkes kept staring at the fire. "For all we know, he could have died two years ago." He looked at the captives. "How many more of these damn redskins can there be? Seven or eight-hundred?"

MacDuff shrugged. "At the most." Pulling a knife from under his belt, he began to throw it at a log near his feet, sticking it every time. "How long have we been out here now? Four weeks? Or is it five?"

Sparkes didn't comment. MacDuff became equally silent and kept looking at the log in front of him, sticking the knife into it. Neither one wanted to think of how long they had been out on patrol or how much longer they might yet be. For several minutes, the only sound was that of the knife hitting the wood. Then MacDuff exclaimed, "Damn!" and threw the blade with exceptional force. "My God, Sparkes! What the hell's the purpose of it all? How many men have we lost since this damn war started? A thousand? What is that? One man for every three of the filthy savages we've shipped west? Why do we keep at it? Why don't we resign our commissions and take up an honorable profession? I could run a whorehouse in Charleston and feel I was a more upstanding member of the community than I am now."

Sparkes didn't answer. In truth, he couldn't imagine any profession in which he would feel useful. If he had not joined the army, he might have become a minister. Considering the things he'd done, he doubted that God would have him now, and, in truth, Sparkes no longer had much use for God. He wasn't even sure Maria would still have him.

MacDuff continued his musings. "This war has become habit, Sparkes, a damned purgatory we feel comfortable in. Hell can't be a whole lot worse, but at least we know what to expect here. I swear there are times when I long for some Seminole warrior to just jump out of the bushes and put a bullet through my skull. It seems to be the only way I'll ever leave this place."

Sparkes knew the feeling well. Just two days earlier he had watched a Seminole hut being put to the torch. For a few terrifying moments he had felt the strongest urge to walk into the flaming structure and be consumed by the fire. He reached forward and pulled MacDuff's knife from the log and stared at it. He wondered if he could slit his own throat.

MacDuff reached over and gently took the knife from Sparkes. "You feeling all right, Sparky?"

Sparkes turned his eyes away. "Just tired. Haven't been sleeping well."

"Aye, and you haven't been eating much lately, not that there's much worth eating out here."

"Haven't been hungry."

There probably wasn't an officer in Florida who hadn't gone through these periods of deep melancholy. Most everyone pulled out of it. A few, however, had taken their own lives. A line from *Hamlet* ran through MacDuff's mind. *Though this be madness, yet there is method in it.* No, there was no method to this self-destructive madness; it was just the war. "Shut me up before I do something stupid, Sparkes! I actually find myself enjoying this occasionally." He stood up. It was time to go to bed. "George! You worthless black ass! Where's my bedroll?" He looked back down at Sparkes. "Did Bigelow set the guard?"

"Can't say that I told him to, but he always does."

For a moment, the insects and the frogs ceased their incessant chatter, and a still silence pervaded the camp. In the quiet, Sparkes and MacDuff could hear the muffled cries of a Seminole woman. Instinctively, the pair looked away from one another, reminded of something they didn't care to acknowledge. Bigelow had set a special guard on the women, and before the night was through, most of the soldiers would have taken part in what had become known as "making sure the women didn't escape." Sparkes remembered how Colonel Wooster, much earlier in the war, had punished Bigelow for nothing worse than lifting the skirt of a female prisoner. What would the colonel think of his future son-in-law turning a blind eye to unrestrained rape? Could Sparkes somehow justify such actions to Maria? He shrugged. At the moment, he really didn't care.

~~~

Kachi-Hadjo could hear the soft breathing of Ki-tee and the slight snore of Playful Otter, but he could not hear the voice of his mother. For some months the voice had been getting weaker, the words less intelligible, and the tone more melancholy. It had always been the most soothing of sounds, but lately it had become the most saddening. He had finally come to a realization that he had been avoiding for so long: The spirit of his mother was leaving.

She had never actually said it, and he hadn't expected her to. When he heard his mother's voice, it was not as if they were holding a conversation. When she spoke, images formed in his mind, images that usually filled him with warmth. The images had become less comforting of late and slower to form. She was fading from his presence, and he was unsure of where she was going. Was she going to his father, Micco Phillip? Was she going to the new lands in the west to join the other spirits of her clan? Perhaps she was going to the final resting place of all spirits. What Kachi-Hadjo feared most was that she was fading entirely, that her spirit would be no more. He had always believed that it was the thoughts of the living that kept the spirits of the departed alive. When all the Seminoles were driven from Florida, would the spirits disappear with them?

27th November, 1841
Ft. Brooke

To:
Capt. Jacob Sparkes
Fort Lauderdale

My Dearest Jacob,

As if the loss of dear old Nero were not enough, the painful passing of time is once again brought to my attention. Father this morning mentioned that today is the anniversary of the day Chalo Emathla was slain. It is truly impossible to believe that the war is soon to enter its seventh year. Although I cannot imagine that we have been at war for so long, but one look in the mirror tells me it is so. I was but a child when it began, all curls and giggles. I am now in my twentieth year, a woman who is ready to become your wife. Only this unending war keeps us apart.

How much we have changed since those days! Your uniform was new and spotless, your manner gallant yet apprehensive. I have grown a head taller at least and have taken on the proportions of a lady. You have grown a beard and show a slight thinning of your hair. You were then a young man filled with the dreams of glory to be won on the battlefield. You are now a mature man who understands the reality of war. I was then a silly girl filled with the dreams of a child. I now await the day when I shall have a child of my own.

Oh! How I do long to see you! If I concentrate with all my mind, I can still feel your lips upon mine. Although we are not yet wed, I find my life is little different from the other women here at the post whose husbands serve throughout the Territory. We gather for our needlework and baking, and chat endlessly about how life will be so much better when we leave this place. Most of all, we all patiently await the return of our loved ones and gather excitedly whenever a ship arrives from the area in which our beloveds serve.

I will close for now, for there is much to attend to. Although I cannot recall Nero ever doing a day's worth of woman's work, his presence, as well has his dear person, is sorely missed. Nettie is doing as well as can be expected, though the house is much less lively without her and Nero's constant good-natured bickering. What we need is another man in this house. I have been looking, but all the good ones seem to be in Fort Lauderdale.

Please, my dear, keep yourself safe, and extend our best wishes to Capt. MacDuff. And pray, my love, that this war will soon be over. Only then will our love be complete.

With undying love and affection,
Yours eternally,
Maria.

Maria pulled her dressing gown tight, trying to block out the cold February night air as she came down the steps, heading for the faint glow from the fireplace in the dining room. As she entered the room she stopped short, a little surprised at what she saw. "Father?" The colonel looked up from his chair at the table, but said nothing. "I'm sorry, Father, I thought it was Nettie. Ever since Nero died she's been getting up at night. I'm starting to worry about her."

Wooster nodded. "I sent her back to bed about an hour ago."

Maria tried to make out the face of the parlor clock, but couldn't discern the hands in the darkness. "What time is it? How long have you been up?"

"Sometime after two, I imagine. I've rather lost track." He yawned and rubbed his face.

As Maria took a seat at the table she noticed that it was covered with papers. Most of them were familiar to her eyes. For the better part of the past two years she had taken on the duties of Regimental Clerk, filling in after Sparkes had been dispatched to Fort Lauderdale. The task had made her feel useful and, by sharing in her father's work, had brought the pair closer. She gave him a concerned look. "Why are you looking at these now? I'll tend to them in the morning."

The colonel stared at the various dispatches, petitions, and letters that littered the table. "I'm beginning to think the only command I'm fit for is Postmaster General." He took off his reading glasses and set them on the table. "I have two months to end this war, and I don't know how I'll do it." Maria looked over the papers scattered before her, trying to imagine which one contained the ultimatum. Wooster shook his head. "Oh, no one's said it, but I know it's coming. At the beginning of May I will have had command of this war for two years. That is when the War Department's patience will run out." Putting his spectacles back on, he picked up a letter, held it below a small candelabrum, and read from it. "We find it increasingly difficult to believe that only one small band of savages is causing this much trouble." He set that letter down and picked up another. "Surely it must be in your power to bring this protracted conflict to a close."

As part of her duties Maria had opened most of the letters that lay in front of her father but had rarely read them. She now began to understand the pressure he was under. She reached out and put her hand on her father's. "It cannot go on much longer."

"If they replace me, my career will be over. I'll never make general."

"And I will still love you, and your troops will still hold you in the highest regard." She shuffled through the papers on the table. "Surely these are not all complaints from the War Department."

"They may as well be." He picked a letter up and gently waved it at her. "This is Dr. Weightman's monthly medical report. Hundreds on sick list and another twenty-three dead of disease. Can you imagine how that looks when the Secretary of War reads it?" Searching through another stack, he found an especially irritating petition. "And this one, signed by the good citizens of Alachua County, complaining about the closing of Fort Micanopy, saying that 'Indian signs' are reported almost daily. No one bothers to mention that the Indian signs are planted and reported by militiamen who want nothing more than to be called out so that they can collect twenty dollars while riding about the countryside rustling cattle." He set the petition down and sighed. "I should have transferred out of Florida the moment this war started."

"What more can they ask you to do without more men and supplies, which no one up in Washington seems willing to spend the money on? The campaign is going as well as can be expected. We've sent hundreds of the Seminoles west and except for Halek's band, the savages are rarely seen north of the Withlacoochee."

"They don't really care what I do. They just want to be able to say the war is over. And they can't do that until Kachi-Hadjo, Halek Tustenuggee, and old Medicine Man Sam are either on their way west or dead." He tapped his fingers on the table, coming to a decision he didn't like. "I already have a 'shoot on sight' order out on Halek. The other two I can deal with, but if I can't convince Kachi-Hadjo or Sam to come in soon, I'll have to extend the order to them, too."

~~~

Major Childs watched as Kachi-Hadjo approached Fort Lauderdale, a white cloth tied to the barrel of his rifle. Shaking his head, he turned to MacDuff. "Does this damned game ever end?"

The captain smiled. "Not until someone in Washington says it does."

"We could just shoot him."

Both men knew better. "I don't think the colonel would look kindly upon such an act. Kachi-Hadjo is the one chief who can end this war. Like it or not, the game must be played."

Over the years every post commander in Florida had faced the same dilemma. A chief or headman would come in to parley, making promises to emigrate, but there was always the same problem: The members of his band had been scattered into innumerable small camps because of the army's incessant patrols, and it would take time to gather them all. It would also take provisions, because the army had ruined all the Indians' crops. In addition, the chief's people would be afraid to travel while the soldiers were about. If at all possible, he would ask, could the patrols be withdrawn for a short time?

Hoping that for once the Indians were sincere, the post commanders would hand over provisions and order a short cessation of offensive operations. They would wait, knowing it had all been a ruse.

Rarely did a chief return, and then only to ask for more time and provisions. Wooster had largely put a stop to the practice, but had let it stand for Kachi-Hadjo and a few other leaders that he felt were worth dealing with.

For Kachi-Hadjo the war had turned into a very serious game of hide and seek that he was slowly losing. His warriors could attack white homesteads, but they could not stop the army from destroying Seminole villages. He could kill a thousand settlers, but he could never force the Americans to return one person from the new homeland in the west. The cause was lost.

Childs and MacDuff strode out of the fort to greet the chief, following a routine that everyone knew. Kachi-Hadjo placed his rifle on the ground while MacDuff drew his medieval sword and drove the tip of the blade into the sand. The major then asked the obvious question. "For what purpose does Mad Panther come to Fort Lauderdale? Does he wish to speak of peace between our peoples?"

As Kachi-Hadjo began to recite his lines, he realized that this time he truly wanted the soldiers to believe him. He actually wanted the war to end. "Long have our two peoples fought. Much blood has soaked into these sands. My people have suffered much, as have the white men. Many trophies have we taken, but many of our women and little ones have been sent to far-away lands. As each day passes another of my brothers or sisters is taken away. The time has come to talk of peace."

Childs had heard the talk before. "Mad Panther has spoken these words to us in the past, but never does the war end. If the Seminole wants peace, he must surrender. Where are your warriors? Where are your women and children?"

"They are scattered like the egrets after the first shot is fired into their flock. Your soldiers have forced us from our hiding places and have destroyed our fields. Our women are hungry, as are the babies at their breasts. Our warriors hunt for food, not for whites to kill." And it was all very true.

Childs was unusually impatient this day. "Have you come to surrender or to simply ask for provisions and waste our time?"

Kachi-Hadjo became wary. The major did not seem as cooperative as he normally was. "I will bring my people in, but it will take time. Your soldiers forced them to flee before I could locate them all. I will need time. I will need food. My people cannot travel on empty stomachs." He said it as sincerely as he possibly could.

Was it all just another lie? Childs wasn't so sure this time. There had been much more feeling in Kachi-Hadjo's voice. It was so difficult to tell where the truth ended and the deceit began. He could not argue with the fact that the patrols had been effective in scattering the Seminoles and destroying their means of subsistence. It was now late winter and the Indians' stores must be running low. Kachi-Hadjo was correct in saying that his people were hungry and could not travel without provisions. The only question was where they might be traveling to. Were they going to come in for emigration or were they going to go deeper into the Everglades? There was no way to know.

MacDuff leaned over towards Childs. "May we have a word, sir?"

The two men stepped away from the chief, turned their backs toward him, and spoke in hushed voices. MacDuff offered a suggestion. "Something's different this time, sir. He sounds like he really means it. I think we should demand a hostage, sir. It is the only way we can be sure of his sincerity. And not some sick old woman who they can afford to give up."

Childs nodded. The pair turned back to Kachi-Hadjo. "You must bring us a hostage to show your good faith. When you do this, we will withdraw our patrols for two weeks and give you food. You must bring us a hostage that you would not wish to live without."

MacDuff knew who they needed. "You must bring us your daughter."

Kachi-Hadjo showed no outward emotion. "This will take time. She is with Medicine Man Sam, and I do not know where they are." It was the truth, but he had no way to convince the officers of that fact. In reality, he did not mind leaving Ki-tee as a hostage. She would be safe and well fed. If, on the other hand, she were captured by one of the patrols, the soldiers might use her cruelly and slit her throat. Were she in the fort, she would be treated well. Kachi-Hadjo knew the war was ending and that sooner or later he would have to give up. Perhaps the time was right, before something terrible happened to his daughter. "If I bring Ki-tee, you must promise that she will not be sent west without me."

Childs nodded. "She will remain at this post."

Kachi-Hadjo bent over and picked up his rifle. "I shall return with Ki-tee."

~~~

While the parley was taking place at Fort Lauderdale, the war continued in the Everglades. Far to the southwest of the fort a village was being destroyed. Sparkes surveyed the scene. There were a few open-air huts being put to the torch, less than an acre of corn and squash being uprooted, and only one Indian prisoner to be interrogated. It was, however, a very important Indian. It was Ki-tee, Kachi-Hadjo's daughter.

If it had not been for Gator John, even she would have made an escape into the hammocks. She had been gathering the Coontie root when she saw her father's old friend come from around a stand of cypress trees. Not realizing he was in the employ of the army, she had rushed toward him, eager for his friendly embrace. By the time she saw the soldiers it was too late to get away.

Sparkes should have been overjoyed, but at the moment he was far too distracted. Holding his head, he sat down on a log. His second in command, Lieutenant Jennings, walked up, a concerned look on his face. "Are you going to be all right, sir? You seem to be getting worse by the day."

Sparkes did not look up. He felt as if his life were running out. "I honestly don't know, Jennings. All strength seems to have left me. We'll rest here for the remainder of today and take up the march tomorrow. I'm not the only one who is sick. God knows we could all do with a rest."

"I'll not argue with that, sir." Jennings was worried. Yes, there were other men who were sick, but none as seriously as Sparkes.

Sparkes took a deep breath and tried to stand up. Jennings reached over and put a hand under his commander's arm. Sparkes steadied himself and took a step. Suddenly he stopped, bent over, and began to retch. The lieutenant put both hands on the captain's shoulders to keep the man from falling. "Sir, you're vomiting blood. We need to get you to a doctor."

Sparkes wiped the blood from his mouth. "Other than old Medicine Man Sam, I doubt that you'll find one here abouts."

Jennings bit his lip. He needed to make a painful decision. It was imperative that they pursue the Indians, but he could not let his commander's condition worsen without making some sort of effort to get him medical help. "We have to get you to Fort Lauderdale, sir."

Sparkes gave his lieutenant a stern look. "We'll not end the mission on my account, Mr. Jennings. We're getting too close to catching Kachi-Hadjo or old Sam. John says that if Ki-tee wasn't with her father, she would have been with Sam. We can't stop now."

Jennings shook his head and walked off, trying to think of a way to continue the hunt for the Indians and save Sparkes at the same time. As he watched Gator John chat with Ki-tee, a plan began to form. Looking about, he caught sight of Sergeant Bigelow limping along on an improvised crutch. "Bigelow! Come here!"

The sergeant slowly hobbled over. "Aye, sir?"

"How's the foot?" The sergeant had dropped a heavy cypress canoe on his foot several days earlier, tearing the skin and breaking several bones. The result was an extremely swollen, badly bruised appendage that he could put very little weight on.

"About the same, sir."

"Does it bother you to paddle a canoe?"

Bigelow smiled, showing a semi-toothless grin. "It's a damn sight easier than walking, sir."

"Good. Captain Sparkes needs to see a doctor, and, for that matter, so do you. Do you think you can find your way back to Fort Lauderdale?"

Bigelow took a moment to think. "Aye, sir, with a compass."

"You can use the captain's. I want you to take that Indian canoe over there and carry Captain Sparkes back to Fort Lauderdale. Are you up to it?"

Bigelow was hesitant. It was a long way and the Indians could be anywhere. "Just the two of us, sir?"

Jennings looked in the direction of John and Ki-tee. "No, you're going to have a passenger."

Within a few minutes, Jennings, accompanied by Bigelow and Gator John, approached Sparkes. As he listened, the captain shook his head. "There is no need for this, Lieutenant. I can die in the field, just like any other soldier."

Jennings smiled. "Yes, sir, I suppose you could, but that might not happen for days. In the meantime, both you and Bigelow are slowing us down."

Sparkes wasn't convinced. "What's to keep the girl from escaping or calling out for help?"

Gator John supplied the answer. "I been talking to her, Massa Cap'n, telling her how good it is that we caught her, how the war's gonna be over, and how her and her pappy gonna be together again. If I tell her how 'portant it be to get you to the fort, she'll paddle the boat herself."

Jennings pressed his case. "With all due respect, sir, you're a dead man if you don't get into that canoe. And the way Bigelow's foot is, so is he. You both need a doctor. As for the girl, sir, I think she'll do whatever Gator John advises her to do. We'll bind her well enough to where it shouldn't be a problem anyway. The simple fact is, sir, the sooner we get her to Fort Lauderdale, the sooner we can get Mad Panther to turn himself in. That's the first place he'll go looking for her." He turned back to Bigelow. "One canoe traveling quietly and at night has a reasonable chance of getting through. We're not more than twenty miles from the interior depot, and after you reach there you'll have an escort and not more than a day's trip to Fort Lauderdale. Do you think you can do it?"

Bigelow looked at Sparkes, the canoe, then off in the direction of Fort Lauderdale. Jennings was right. Sparkes was dying and someone might soon have to amputate his own foot. There really wasn't much choice. He shrugged. "God willing, sir, and with some luck."

"Good." Jennings turned to a soldier standing nearby. "Willis, help the sergeant gather what he needs." He then looked to Bigelow. "Take two of Mr. Colt's test rifles. I know you don't like them, but they may give you an edge if you're spotted by the redskins. Take whatever provisions you think you'll need."

"Aye, sir."

~~~

The trio paddled steadily for the rest of the day and most of the night, attempting to put as many miles between themselves and any pursuing Seminoles as possible. Ki-tee's ankles were bound securely but not painfully, with about a foot of line between each leg, allowing her some freedom of movement. John had told her not to try and escape and that above all else, she needed to see that Sparkes made it to Fort Lauderdale. She remembered that Sparkes and her father had been friendly when he was at their camp after the Caloosahatchee Massacre. If Gator John and her father thought he was a good man, than so did she.

It had been a clear night and the stream was sufficiently well defined to allow them to find their way without much difficulty. As the sun rose, they decided to stop and rest for an hour or two. Finding a small embankment that was well hidden from view, they came ashore clumsily, Ki-tee with her ankles tied, Bigelow on his bad foot, and Sparkes in his weakened state. Bigelow tied the girl's wrists lightly and fastened the rope to a tree. John had told her to expect this, that it was just the white man's way and that they meant her no harm. He'd said no white man would ever fully trust an Indian but that she could trust Captain Sparkes.

Sparkes and Bigelow sat down at the opposite side of the mound and leaned against a pair of small trees. The Captain smiled at the girl, closed his eyes, and immediately fell asleep. Before long, Ki-tee was also asleep. The sergeant looked down at the sleeping officer. As near as he could tell, Sparkes was so weak that the sound of a gunshot wouldn't wake him. Dragging his injured foot behind him, Bigelow slowly inched toward the girl. When he was next to her he ran his hand along her leg. "Pretty little thing."

Ki-tee's eyes flew open. She attempted to scream, but found a hand placed firmly over her mouth, gripping her jaw tightly. The sergeant smiled menacingly and whispered, "Now you be a good girl and take it easy, and we both gonna have us some fun." To test her, he relaxed the pressure over her mouth ever so slightly. As the hand eased its grip she pushed her face forward and bit down as hard as she could. Bigelow seethed, "You little bitch!" and struck out at the girl. This time her screams were heard.

Sparkes shook himself awake and sat up. "Bigelow! Leave her be! My God, man, she's just a child."

Bigelow didn't turn around. "Looks old enough to be made a woman, I'd say." Reaching down, he began to untie Ki-tee's ankle bindings.

"Bigelow! Stop this immediately!" The voice was weak and not very commanding, but it was the best Sparkes could do.

The sergeant turned around, a look of contempt in his eyes. "What's the problem, Cap? Ain't like you ain't let us have our way with 'em plenty of times a-fore. Too good to watch?"

Sparkes struggled to his feet and stumbled toward the sergeant's back. This girl and her father had saved his life. They had been merciful to him when he had been the most vulnerable. Putting both his hands on Bigelow's shoulders, he attempted to pull the man away from the struggling girl.

Spinning around, Bigelow pushed Sparkes away. The officer staggered against a tree but maintained his footing. The sergeant stood up, hobbled on his sore foot, and advanced, rage in his eyes. Muttering, "You son-of-a-bitch," he drove his fist into Sparkes's stomach. The officer doubled over and retched, blood flowing from his mouth, then fell to the ground while clutching his stomach. Bigelow smiled, knelt down, and punched the injured man in the ribs. Sparkes let out a feeble scream and curled up in pain. The sergeant then took the two rifles and

Sparkes's sword, put them in the canoe, and pushed it to the other side of the small stream.

Bigelow turned back to Ki-tee, who was struggling to get up. Taking hold of the girl's ankles, he pulled her back to the ground. Reaching behind him, he brought forth a large knife and brandished it in front of her. Terrified, she held perfectly still. Laughing, the sergeant took a quick look back at Sparkes. "Hope you enjoy the show, Captain."

Bigelow knelt before the girl and brought the blade of his knife up to her throat. He then drew it lightly across her neck, cutting the skin just enough to draw a few drops of blood. He held the blade in front of her so that she could see the blood, and then drove the knife hard into the ground next to her shoulder. She shuddered and went limp. Bigelow licked his lips, enjoying the look of terror on Ki-tee's face. "I think I'm gonna have so much fun we may just camp out here a few days."

Kneeling in front of the girl, he tilted his head back and let out a sadistic laugh. Suddenly he saw the blur of a rope passing in front of his face, and then felt it tighten around his neck. Behind him, Sparkes pulled tightly on the rope, using all his strength to choke the soldier. Bigelow frantically clawed at the rope, trying to loosen its grip. Sparkes closed his eyes and pulled harder on the rope. One thought kept going through his mind, accompanied by a mental picture of the father he had never known. *This is my breach in the wall.* The pain in his stomach was growing greater, and he began to scream. His vision began to blur and the earth seemed to be spinning slowly. He knew that in a moment he would faint.

Ki-tee sobbed as she watched the two men struggle. Her eyes widened when she saw her rescuer's head droop and the two men fall to the ground. Neither one moved.

28

To:
Col. Wooster,
Ft. Brooke

Colonel,

I write in haste, with tidings both welcome and troubling. First, I must beg that both you and your daughter proceed to this place with all dispatch. I have instructed the captain of the <u>American</u> to refuel upon arrival at Tampa Bay and await your embarkation. He is in protest, saying his ship must proceed to Pensacola for refit, but I would respectfully suggest you prevail upon him to follow my instructions.

The reasons for this unusual request are two-fold. The most immediate reason concerns Capt. Sparkes. Yesterday morning a canoe approached the interior depot paddled by an Indian girl. Lying within the vessel was Capt. Sparkes, unconscious and gravely ill. He is now under doctor's care, and remains unconscious. His fate, I fear, is in the hands of God. Both Doctor Motte and I feel it would aid in his recovery were your daughter to be present.

The second reason for requesting your presence at this post has to do with the girl who was paddling the canoe. She is Kittee, the daughter of Kachee-Harjo. Just two days prior, Maj. Childs and I met with him, and he indicated that he wanted peace and was intending to locate his daughter and leave her here as a good-faith hostage. As all the interpreters are out with the patrols, we have not been able to determine from the girl what transpired. The oddest thing is that she brought with her a white man's scalp and keeps indicating that it somehow belongs to Sparkes. The scalp appears as if it might be Sergeant Bigelow's.

Precisely how all this came about is an utter mystery. Capt. Sparkes has been on patrol for several weeks and was not expected back for some time. The whereabouts of Lt. Jennings and the remainder of the command are at present unknown. Major Childs has dispatched several patrols and personally leads one of them. I am at present in command of this post with a minimal garrison.

Major Childs and I feel strongly that when Kachee-Harjo finds that his daughter is at this post, he will immediately come for a parley, perhaps to surrender. It is an opportunity we must not let slip through our fingers.

Please excuse the forward tone of this letter. I speak my mind out of a deep affection for Capt. Sparkes and a fervent wish that we may have an opportunity to end this ghastly war.

Your Most Obt. Svt.
Horatio MacDuff
Capt., U.S.A.

There had been no question that Colonel Wooster and Maria would comply with MacDuff's request. Both of them were concerned about Sparkes and both would have taken any chance offered that would lead to the end of the war. Now, however, as the *American* fought against the gale, they were beginning to wish they had taken another route to Fort Lauderdale.

Captain Sands cast a nervous eye at the compass, trying to determine an approximate heading as the compass card pivoted and rocked in response to the violent rolling and pitching of the vessel. Putting a hand on the helmsman's shoulder, he attempted to shout above the howling of the wind in the rigging. "Try to hold her to due north as best you can, lad!" Sands shook his head; he hoped he was somewhere close to where he thought he was.

The *American* was a solid vessel, but not the most seaworthy ship Sands had ever sailed, if, indeed, "sailed" was the proper word. In the center of the ship was a massive steam engine that drove a pair of large paddlewheels mounted on either side of the vessel. Sands still wasn't won over to the idea of steam power, and neither had been the ship's designers. Just in case the engine failed, they had mounted a pair of masts, one fore and one aft, to which a modest amount of sail could be set. Sands was glad they had fitted the ship with masts; he had been forced to use them more than once.

Suddenly there was a loud crack from the forward end of the ship. The captain peered through the thick sheets of rain and saw the foremast lean toward the bow of the boat. "Clear the deck! The foremast's going! Bring in the lookout!"

Halfway up the teetering mast a lookout clung to a line, desperately trying to keep from falling to the deck as the mast swung violently in the storm. There was another snap, this one even louder, as the mast completely broke free and came crashing down, falling across the port bow of the boat. As the mast hit the deck, the lookout was jolted loose from his perch and ejected into the churning sea. "Man overboard!" was shouted numerous times, and another sailor ran to the aft rail with a life ring in his hand, ready to throw it to the drifting seaman. Several men, including the captain, strained to catch sight of the lost man, calling out his name, desperately trying to save him. Then someone saw blood in the wake of the paddlewheel.

Sands turned away from the rail. There was no time to mourn the lost man, not if the ship was to be saved. The mast was still attached to the vessel by the numerous lines that had held it in place. The drag of the wood, the canvas, and the cordage was pulling the ship hard to port and was threatening to get caught up in the port paddlewheel. "Get the axes! Cut that damn thing loose!" Sailors ran forward and began to cut the lines. It was desperate and dangerous work. The lines were under extreme strain, and when cut, could whip back with enough force to kill a man. As the last lines were cut, the mast fell free, hitting the wooden guard surrounding the paddlewheel. Pieces of lumber went flying, but the paddle remained intact and turning. Sands let out his breath as the mast drifted astern. It could have been much worse.

Wooster fought the wind and rain as he worked his way along the railing toward the ship's stern. As he came alongside the captain he cupped his hands around his mouth and shouted, "Can we make Fort Dallas?"

Sands shook his head and wiped the salt spray and rain from his eyes. "Not unless this storm totally abates. The entrance to Biscayne Bay is too treacherous, and the approaches to the Miami River are too difficult in weather like this. We must, Colonel, hold course for Fort

Lauderdale. Besides, for all I know, we may have already passed Fort Dallas." Wooster gave a quizzical glance. Sands explained, "The northward current is swift in these straits and hard to gauge. Until the sky clears, I have no way of knowing precisely where we are."

The ship shuddered as the port paddlewheel came out of the water. Sands looked worried. "I only hope she holds up. The axles on both those wheels are worn more than I'd like to see." Shaking his head, he called out to the ship's Bosun. "Mr. Bailey! Hoist a shortened sail on the mizzen and prepare a sea anchor!"

Wooster went below, leaving the care of the ship to its master. Entering his cabin, he found Maria sitting on the edge of a bunk, bent over, a large pitcher in her hands. He sat down next to her and put his arm around her. She moaned. Looking up, her weary eyes gazed into his. "Why aren't you sick?" He couldn't tell if she were curious or jealous.

He shrugged. "I have no idea. I ought to be." He stood up and patted her on the back. "But I will be if I stay in here with you. I think I shall go back on deck." At that moment there was a loud crack and the sound of shouting from the engine room. The ship suddenly lurched to port, then back to starboard. Wooster could hear the loud hissing of steam and the sound of footsteps racing across the deck above him.

For some minutes, the ship lurched back and forth, sending both Wooster and Maria against opposite walls of the stateroom. Wooster staggered for the door. Before he could reach it, a sailor threw the door open from the outside. Both men nearly lost their balance as the ship began a turn to the left. Regaining his footing, the sailor shouted, "The captain wishes you on deck, sir!"

Both men ran up the ladder and onto the pitching deck. Looking out over the side, Wooster saw the paddlewheels were no longer turning. He looked to Sands, who was shouting orders to the crew. The captain remained calm, and when all his orders were being carried out he turned to the colonel. "The axle has snapped and we've lost our engine." He looked up at the small bit of sail that billowed from the mizzenmast. "With such a small amount of canvas I can't control her very well. She's in the devil's hands now. You and your people had best be prepared to abandon ship."

Wooster moved swiftly back below decks. Going from cabin to cabin, he ordered Maria, Dr. Weightman, and the half dozen soldiers who had accompanied them to begin throwing supplies and weapons into their bags. When all was ready, they proceeded onto the deck. A sailor approached and led them toward one of the ship's boats. Fastening a line around one of the vessel's oarlocks, the sailor attempted to steady the boat as Wooster and his companions threw their bags aboard.

Their luggage stowed, Wooster and the others moved toward the bow of the ship and huddled against one of the railings, trying to stay out of the driving rain and out of the way of the ship's crew. For more than two hours the vessel tossed, waves breaking over the bow and soaking everyone on deck. Wooster held Maria close, sheltering her as best he could. He watched intently as two lookouts stationed at the forward-most point of the deck peered out into the storm, looking for any sight of land.

The rain slackened slightly and one of the lookouts shouted, "Land ho! Off the port bow! Less than a mile!" Wooster thought he saw it, but then it disappeared as the rain increased again. Sands ordered a hard turn to starboard, but the ship was slow to respond. If he was that close to shore, the sandbar had to be very near by. Suddenly there was a grinding noise and the ship swung violently onto its port side before partially righting itself.

Sands wasted no time. He knew the situation and the likely outcome. The *American* was hard aground on the sandbar and would be smashed to pieces by the incoming waves. It was no use trying to save her. They had better save themselves. "Abandon ship! Take to the boats and make for shore! Once we get over the bar, the beach won't be far beyond. Move smartly lads! Try to stay together, now."

The boat that hung on the port side was protected from the waves by the ship's hull and was launched with little trouble. The boat on the starboard side was proving more difficult. Each crashing wave threatened to destroy it while still in the davits. After several attempts it was safely put over the side, but not before most of the weapons and provisions stored inside were swept away.

Wooster, Maria, and the soldiers had loaded into the portside boat along with a number of sailors. The oars were quickly put to work, and the boat steered toward shore. The men rowed strongly; with the ocean as violent as it was, it was imperative to reach the beach as quickly as possible. As they entered calmer water on the other side of the bar, they saw the other lifeboat come around the *American*'s stern, smash into it, then bounce off. Then a breaking wave slammed into the lifeboat, capsizing it and sending men into the churning water. Wooster ordered the sailors to turn around in an attempt to pick up the survivors. Fighting wind and waves, the lifeboat fought its way back to the *American*. One by one the soaked and exhausted survivors were helped aboard. Not every one was found.

~~~

The castaways crawled out from under the overturned boat as the rain began to stop. Wooster and Captain Sands surveyed what they had managed to bring ashore: twenty-three men, one woman, seven muskets, the colonel's pistol, and his sword. A few of the sailors had knives. Seventeen men had been lost. The soldiers looked over the ammunition they had managed to salvage. There was little of it, and all of it was questionable. The muskets were loaded and distributed among the soldiers and Dr. Weightman. The pistol was given to Captain Sands, and Wooster kept his sword. The remaining men broke the boat's oars in half or picked up stout pieces of driftwood to use as clubs. It was the best they could do. There was a small amount of biscuit and a little rain water that had been collected in a cup. Hopefully, Fort Lauderdale was not far off.

Precisely where the fort might be located turned out to be the main topic of discussion. For all anyone knew, they could be either north or south of it. In the end, they had to go with Captain Sands's instincts. Shouldering their weapons and a few small bags, the group headed south along the beach.

It was a wide beach, with low dunes above the tide line, covered with thin vegetation. Behind the dune line was a thin mangrove forest, sometimes giving way to pines where the ground was higher. No one knew the time of day. Wooster's pocket watch had been lost and Sands's had failed after filling with water. With the sun having been obscured by clouds all day, the best they could guess was that it was mid-afternoon. There was some discussion as to whether they should stop at dark or continue on. In the end, the gentlemen gallantly decided that when Maria became fatigued, the group would stop. Wooster smiled to himself. As long as there was any doubt as to Sparkes's condition, Maria would never stop.

Aware of the possibility of being attacked, Wooster posted a flanker on their right side. For protection, he placed Maria at the middle of the party, with Dr. Weightman and himself slightly ahead of and behind her. Captain Sands led the way. Still, Wooster was not overly concerned. Halek Tustenuggee was the only remaining chief who was outwardly aggressive, and there was no reason to believe he was anywhere near Fort Lauderdale. Still, there was always the chance of running into outlaws, both Indian and white. Wreckers made their living along this coast, and many of the practitioners of the trade could be considered little more than pirates. It was best to keep alert.

~~~

From a place of concealment among the mangroves, Halek Tustenuggee observed the comings and goings of the soldiers at Fort Lauderdale. As he had suspected, they were relaxed, confident that no one would attack them in the vicinity of their post. After all, who did they have to fear? Kachi-Hadjo, Abee-Aka, and Holato Bolek were all in hiding or on the run. Those chiefs were doing their best to avoid the whites, hoping the war would end when the army tired of chasing them.

Tustenuggee was of a different mind. He wanted the war to continue. It didn't matter that the cause was lost. He knew as well as anyone that it had been lost from the very beginning. No matter how well the Seminoles fought or how many whites they killed, the army and the settlers would never stop coming. Men like Kachi-Hadjo and

Abbe-Aka talked about going to war to protect their homes and their people. They were lying to themselves. Everyone had known that the war could only lead to the destruction of those very same things.

From the very outset, Tustenuggee had known the real reasons for going to war: pride, hatred, and the need for revenge. The white man's insults had simply become impossible to endure. Tustenuggee had long ago realized that the only way to escape the white man's abuse was to die. If such was the case, then he would go down fighting, taking as many of the hated whites with him as possible.

Yet he was certainly in no hurry to die. There were too many whites left to kill. He would not willingly sacrifice himself to the army or allow himself to be captured. He would strike where he was least expected and when his enemy was the most vulnerable. He knew the soldiers were searching for him and his band, so he kept on the move. He and his warriors had given up their homes and their families, knowing that for outlaws like themselves, peace would never come.

Thus it happened that he was now in south Florida, observing life at Fort Lauderdale. For the moment, conditions were not safe in the north. His men needed a rest. He had friends nearby, other outlaws who could provide him and his warriors with a temporary place of refuge. Their camp was about ten miles north of the fort, and Tustenuggee had come to see if the camp was in any danger of being discovered. What he had seen had been encouraging. The white patrols were concentrating their efforts to the west, not to the north. For the time being, their camp would be safe.

His thoughts were interrupted by the sound of a familiar bird call. It was, at best, a poor imitation of a bird, but it served the purpose. Leaving his observation post, he went in search of the sound's source. Following the call, he came upon one of his warriors sitting comfortably in the tall grass. "Why do you come for Tustenuggee?"

"There has been a shipwreck not far from our camp. The survivors walk this way. There are some soldiers, one with a long knife, and a woman."

Tustenuggee took a moment to think. He had wanted to avoid the whites for several weeks, to give his men time to rest and to gather supplies. Attacking this group of survivors would bring pursuit from the army and force his band to find a new refuge. Yet the opportunity to kill soldiers and to take a woman captive was certainly tempting. "How many are there?"

"No more than thirty."

It was not good odds. He only had ten warriors. Still, if they were castaways, they would likely be poorly armed. He would have to have a look at the group, and then decide. "How far are they from the narrows? Can you gather our warriors there before the whites reach the place?" The warrior nodded his head in the affirmative. Tustenuggee smiled. "Good. I will meet you there. Then we will decide if they live or die."

~~~

It was hot on the beach, and the sun reflecting off the sand and water was blinding. The castaways were all thirsty, but only one of the soldiers had thought to bring a canteen, so water was being tightly rationed. Captain Sands was hopeful nonetheless. He had passed this beach many times during the war and parts of it looked familiar. He was confident that Fort Lauderdale would be reached before the end of day.

On they walked, keeping their path on the firmest part of the sand, close to where the waves died. As the castaways passed a particularly large dune, the flanker turned and walked toward it, dutifully checking to make sure no one was behind it. As he approached the top of the dune he stopped and craned his neck, expecting to see nothing but sand. Instead, he saw a group of warriors and the muzzle of a rifle pointed directly at his chest. The last thing he saw was the flash of exploding gunpowder.

The warriors rose swiftly and fired a hurried volley at the exposed whites. Wooster pushed Maria to the sand and covered her body with his. Beside them, Dr. Weightman knelt in the sand, bent over, gasping as blood seeped from a wound in his chest. He then lowered himself slowly to the sand, his eyes facing the ocean.

Wooster rolled off Maria and shouted to everyone, "Roll around! Spread out!" He took a quick look at the other men. Besides the doctor, one other had been slightly wounded, another was dead.

Taking hold of Maria, he pushed her behind Weightman's dying body. She looked into the doctor's eyes in disbelief. He smiled faintly. "Take cover behind me, dear. A few more bullets won't make any difference." She had known the doctor for well over ten years and had considered him one of her closest friends. She sobbed and shuddered as she held his hand, pleading with him not to die. He smiled again, closed his eyes, and took his last breath.

By now the Indians had reloaded. Coming to their feet, they shouted and fired. A sailor screamed and rolled toward the water. The soldiers attempted to return fire, but most of the guns misfired. Wooster picked up the musket he had given Dr. Weightman, but had little faith that it would fire. There was a moment of silence as the Indians reloaded, hidden by the dune. Wooster counted the seconds and judged the distance to the sand dune where the enemy was taking cover. Once again, the Indians rose to fire. This time, two of the soldier's muskets fired, as did Wooster's. One Indian fell.

Wooster reloaded the musket then handed it to one of the sailors. There were no more than twelve Seminoles. It would take close to thirty seconds to reach the dune, which was about how long it would take the warriors to reload. It would be close, but if they could make it over the crest of the dune, they stood a good chance of overwhelming the enemy. He called out to the men on either side of him. "Charge after the next volley, on my word. Pass it down." He turned to Maria. "Stay here!" She began to protest, but he shook his head. "Sparkes will need you."

The Indians fired a ragged volley, but did not rise up to take aim. Wooster rose to his feet and raised his sword. "Charge!" The rest of the men jumped up and followed the colonel, shouting at the top of their lungs. An Indian rose and fired, killing one of the sailors. The other warriors rushed to reload their rifles before the white men could reach them. Only two managed to get off a shot before Wooster and his men came over the dune, but no one was hit.

Tomahawks and scalping knives faced rifle butts and wooden clubs. At the center of the Indian force was a tall warrior that Wooster immediately recognized as Halek Tustenuggee. When Tustenuggee had seen who the castaways were, he had raised his hands to the sky and thanked the Breath Giver for delivering Wooster into his hands. The colonel's sword and his daughter's scalp would be his greatest trophies.

The two men ran at each other, the Indian with his tomahawk raised, Wooster with his sword at the ready. Tustenuggee swung first, but Wooster dodged the blow. The Indian immediately swung again, hoping to catch the officer off guard, but Wooster was ready and caught the handle of the tomahawk with his blade and jerked it out of his adversary's hand. Tustenuggee's weapon went flying off toward the ocean.

Before Wooster could bring his sword back into a defensive position, Tustenuggee lunged at him. Both men tumbled to the sand, each one gripping the other's wrist. They struggled for several minutes, neither one able to gain an advantage, until the chief shook Wooster's hand and the sword fell free. He then rolled away from the weapon, taking the colonel with him. Freeing one hand, he reached behind him and grabbed his hunting knife. With a swift motion, he attempted to drive it into Wooster's chest. Wooster brought his knee up in hopes of deflecting his opponent's arm. Both men were partially successful. The colonel gasped as he felt the blade enter his side. Yet it was neither a deep nor a fatal wound.

Tustenuggee was now off balance. Wooster pushed him away and instinctively reached out for the sword. Tustenuggee lashed out and drove the knife into Wooster's leg. The colonel screamed but did not stop reaching for the sword. Tustenuggee came to his knees and held his knife aloft. This time he would find the white man's heart. Wooster looked up. The sword was out of reach, and the Indian was above him, ready to strike.

Suddenly Tustenuggee's eyes widened, his back arched, and he screamed in pain. He turned, and his eyes fell upon the face of an enraged woman.   In her hands was Tustenuggee's own bloody tomahawk, poised to strike again. It was the last thing he saw.

Realizing the battle was lost, the other Indians tried to flee, but only two managed to escape. As Maria came to his side, Wooster reached for her hand. She was, if nothing else, truly a soldier's daughter. The colonel tried to take a deep breath, but could not. Tustenuggee's knife had punctured his lung. He relaxed and breathed easy as Maria sat down in the sand and cradled his head in her lap.

As the group sat on the sand, collecting their thoughts and tending to the wounded, Maria looked down the length of the beach. In the distance she could see galloping horses splashing through the surf, soldiers in the saddles. She gripped her father's hand tightly and began to cry. Soon her father would receive medical attention, and she would be by Sparkes's side. Everything would be all right.

As the riders came into view, Wooster smiled. It was MacDuff with a squad of soldiers, men of Wooster's own Fourth Infantry. More important, by MacDuff's side was Kachi-Hadjo. The war would soon be over.

29

To:
Chester & Emma MacDuff
Spartanburg County, S. Carolina

Dear Mother and Father,

My deepest regrets for not having written to you more often, but I feel the news contained herein shall more than make up for my lack of correspondence. Indeed, this is the letter that I have long been waiting to pen. This very morning, standing before the walls of the fortification which guards St. Augustine, Col. Wooster declared this miserable, interminable war to be over. For nearly seven years we have fought the Seminoles, but at last it is finished.

You might imagine that some great "Huzzah!" arose from the assembled troops, but such was not the case. We have all suffered entirely too much in this war to feel any jubilation. The most we feel is profound relief. The Colonel's statement was simply a formality, something that we all wanted and needed to hear. Since the slaying of Halek Tustenuggee and with the departure of Mad Panther for the west, there is no one left to fight. There are but a few hundred Indians who remain hidden in the Everglades, and the only chiefs of any consequence are old Medicine Man Sam and Holata Bolek, neither of which poses any threat to the population.

It was, indeed, a most solemn ceremony. The bodies of our fallen comrades have been gathered from throughout the Territory and have been brought to this place to be interred in a common grave in the military cemetery adjacent to the St. Francis Barracks. An obelisk will be erected and the graves will be covered with three small pyramids. A procession with full military honors was held, proceeding from the fort to the burial ground. I nearly wept to think of all the good lives wasted in the pursuit of this disgraceful conflict. It was a price too dear.

The most touching moment of the day was the departure of Mad Panther, whom we all know as Kachee-Harjo. Before the funeral procession took place, the great chief and his daughter boarded a boat that would take them out to the ship lying at anchor just past the bar. As he stood on the pier, he clasped hands with the Colonel and made a most eloquent speech. It is a pity indeed that such a brave and honorable man could not be permitted to remain in the land of his birth, a land that he fought so gallantly to defend. Such a man is not a savage; he is a patriot.

Perhaps the man I pity most is Col. Wooster. He has suffered much from this war and will receive little recompense for his efforts. Of all the officers who commanded in Florida, he was the only true soldier. When I think upon the man I knew at the beginning of the war, I hardly believe the same man now stands before me. Way back in '36, when I first came under his command, he was a force unto himself, tall, firmly built, energetic, and a man of supreme confidence. Today he is shrunken, weakened, and lacking in that self-assurance that so utterly defined him. His hair, once nearly black, is now mostly gray. The wound he received at the hands of Halek has not healed well, and he often coughs blood. More than that, he has become a melancholy soul. The prosecution of this evil war has made him question his own sense of duty to the nation. He sees no nobility in what has been done here, and only feels disgrace at having been party to the machinations of land speculators and scheming politicians. Should he receive his general's star, which he most richly deserves, I doubt that he will take any great satisfaction in it.

And so, with the end of this dreaded war comes the end of my inglorious military career. Like the Colonel, I have seen too much of war. I am no longer the "Warlike Harry" of my youth. The time has come for me to find a home, settle down, and become a productive citizen. The family blade shall be hung by the mantle, a remembrance of the evil I have seen. I did, this day, hand my letter of resignation to the Colonel.

Yet I have kept the most important news to the last. I am soon to be married. The bride- to-be is Maria, the daughter of Colonel Wooster. Since the tragic passing of our dear friend Sparkes, Maria and I have grown very close. Indeed, we both wept together as we stood by his deathbed at Ft. Lauderdale, the one supporting the other. Most sorely do I miss dear Sparkes. Never did I know a more honorable soul. He had been my closest companion throughout the worst of this war, and was the one man who could lift my spirits when they had sunken to their lowest depths. In the months that have passed since we lost him, my admiration and affection for Maria has grown immensely. She has lost her first love and is watching her dear father decline before her eyes, yet her quiet dignity remains and serves to inspire me. I wish with all my heart that she and Sparkes could have been together, but fate has prevailed and we are left with what we have.

As I have painfully learned over the past seven years, little in life is as I would have expected it to be. I had always thought that marriage would be far off in my future and when it did occur, it would be an event filled with giddiness and celebration. For Maria and me, things are different. We are like an old couple who have survived the worst of times and whose appreciation for each other has grown stronger because of the experience. This war has not only taken our friends and our dreams, it has taken the happiness of our youthful years. I will advise you of the date of the ceremony.

As to what our future holds, I cannot say with any certainty. For the foreseeable future, we will remain in Florida. The Colonel has homes both here in St. Augustine and at Tampa Bay, and I have purchased several good holdings within the Territory. Now that the war is over, Florida will surely become a member of the Union and will no doubt prosper. There is a future here, and we mean to be a part of it. The only thing we know without a doubt is that our first-born son will bear the name of "Jacob" in honor of dear Sparkes.

One other small bit of news: George, my boy, ran off on the day we abandoned Ft. Lauderdale. He took one of the canoes we were going to leave behind and simply paddled off into the Everglades. I suppose that after all those times he was out on patrol with us, he reckoned he knew how to live in the swamps as well as any Seminole. Oddly enough, I was not upset with his leaving. Just another casualty of war. I actually wish him well.

And now I must close. I suppose this should have been a more joyous letter, what with the end of the war and the announcement of my coming nuptials, but such is not the stuff of life. "Oft expectation fails, and most oft there where most it promises; and oft it hits where hope is coldest, and despair most fits." The dreams of youth have been fulfilled: I have done the soldier's duty and I have found love. Had these things not come at such a painful cost, I should consider myself the luckiest man alive. As it is, I am content, nothing more.

Your most loving son,
Horatio

The small boat bobbed atop the waves as it remained tied to the pier. From his seat inside the boat, Gator John looked up at the dock. Standing closest to the boat were Kachi-Hadjo and Ki-tee. Across from them were Colonel Wooster, Maria, and MacDuff. All had a solemn look on their face. Kachi-Hadjo nodded. It was time to go. He held out his hand to the colonel, who took it and clasped his other hand over it.

Kachi-Hadjo did likewise and the pair gave a slight shake. They both knew that the one man Kachi-Hadjo truly wanted to say "good-bye" to was not present. It was the man who had given his life to save an Indian child.

As Wooster looked into his former adversary's eyes he tried to find words to fit his emotions. *Enemy?* The word did not apply. Kachi-Hadjo was no more his enemy than anyone else gathered there that day. Both men had simply been doing what they had to. The real enemies were much harder to spot. They were far away, sitting in offices, buying and selling the Earth and its people, and telling more lies. It was not an Indian enemy that had caused Sparkes's death, but one of his own men, yet another casualty in a war that should never have been waged.

Duty. The word had such a hollow ring to it. Throughout his life he had done the soldier's duty, feeling he was helping to build a nation where honor and justice were held in high regard. Now he felt as if that devotion to duty had been betrayed. Neither honor nor justice had played a part in the Florida War. There were so many people who had disappointed him. Many of them he knew by name. Some of them were good friends. The person who had disappointed him the most, however, was William A. Wooster.

At every turn in this miserable war, Wooster had seen the folly and the injustice. Yet beyond a small circle of confidential friends, he had said nothing. He had let Clinch cross the Withlacoochee in that old canoe. He had agreed with Scott's plan, even though he knew it was worse than a waste of time. He had watched Moniac wade into the stream at the Wahoo Swamp and had not followed. He had obeyed Jesup's order to take Kachi-Hadjo and Asi-Yoholo prisoner while standing next to a white flag. He had allowed Zachary Taylor to send the Missouri Volunteers and his friends in the Sixth Infantry into the killing fields at Okeechobee. Worst of all, he had ordered the son of his dearest friend and the love of his only daughter to a place where he would suffer, sicken, and die. *Honor.* He had deceived himself into thinking he knew the meaning of the word.

In the end, there was but one word that described how he felt. He gripped Kachi-Hadjo's hands firmly. "I am truly sorry, my friend."

Maria untied a thin leather thong that was knotted behind her neck. Attached to the thong was an exquisite shell, perfectly formed and lustrous in its color. Sparkes had found it while walking the beach at Fort Lauderdale and had given it to Maria as a present. She approached Ki-tee and handed the shell to the Indian girl. She then turned to Kachi-Hadjo, knowing that Ki-tee did not speak English. "Tell her that it was a gift from Mr. Sparkes and that she should keep it as a remembrance of both her homeland and of the man who saved her." Her lips quivered, and a tear fell from her eye. She reached out and took MacDuff's hand, holding it tightly. "Tell her that when the world appears to be darkest, there will always be someone to help her see it through."

Kachi-Hadjo took her other hand with both of his. "Our hearts feel the same pain. This war has taken something from both of us that we loved very deeply. I have lost my home; you have lost the soldier Sparkes. They cannot be replaced, and they cannot be forgotten. But the pain of such loss does not mean we cannot be happy again. I have Ki-tee, I have my good friend Gator John, and I have my people who have gone west before me. Someday they will help me to smile again. You have your father and this man who now loves you. You will someday have many children. They will all help you smile again."

The terms of peace that had been worked out between Wooster and Kachi-Hadjo had been simple: As long as the Seminoles kept to the southwest corner of the peninsula they would remain unmolested. They both knew that even though the land was worthless, someday the white men would want even that, and a new treaty would have to be negotiated or another war fought to decide the remaining Seminoles' fate. For Kachi-Hadjo, it was irrelevant. Wooster's primary demand had been that Kachi-Hadjo and his band must emigrate to the west. As long as the much-feared Mad Panther was on the loose, settlers and politicians would be hesitant to accept the peace.

In the end, two of the chief's closest friends had made the thought of leaving Florida easier to accept: Holata Bolek had said, "You have fought bravely so that the Seminole might remain in his homeland, and in this you have been victorious. Because you fought the good fight, our people have not been totally driven from this land. You have given your life for this cause, just as surely as the warrior whose dying blood has soaked these sands. We shall all die some day, my friend; some of us here, some of us there, but the Seminole people shall always walk upon this land. Long shall our people remember your sacrifice and long shall we honor the name of Kachi-Hadjo."

Gator John had been more direct: "They gonna need us out there, ol' frien'."

There were two companies of soldiers and numerous townspeople gathered at the foot of the pier. Kachi-Hadjo felt he needed to speak to them. "When I was but a child I saw the white man from afar and wondered what he might be. My father told me the white people were like the good bear, whose skin could clothe us and whose meat could nourish us, but like an angry bear, they could turn on us and with their great claws destroy us. When the Spanish left this land the American white man came to us like the good bear, offering us food and clothing and saying he was our friend. Then, like the angry bear, the white man came upon us. Horses, cattle, and fields he took from us. He abused our women and children and told us to go from the land of our fathers. As men of honor, we could not do this, and we fought to stay in the land where the spirits of our ancestors dwell."

He then took a quick look into Wooster's eyes. "For seven winters my people fought to remain in the land of their birth. From the start, the men we fought against had no honor. They took our chiefs and warriors while we stood under the sacred white flag. Then they tried to buy us and when that did not work, they sent dogs after us. They came to us with lies and expected us to listen. They were fools." He stopped as a murmur of agreement swept through the crowd. "Then the new Great Father in Washington sent this man against us. He fought like a true warrior, with his heart and with honor. His friend Sparkes saved my daughter. After seven winters of blood, the time for peace has come. The spirits of those who have fallen call out to me. They have told me that it is time for Kachi-Hadjo to find a new home. I feel the weight of their sadness in my heart."

He stood erect, a proud look on his face. "The Great Spirit gave this land to the Seminole, but, as he does with all things in their time, he has now taken it away. He has given it to the white man, but what will the white man do with it? Will he cut the skin of the land with many roads? Will he fell the most beautiful trees to make bigger and bigger towns? Will he clear the forest to plant fields so that slaves may toil in the burning sun? Will he make the swamps dry and the rivers run foul? If he does, then the Great Spirit will look down upon it all and say 'Let the white man keep this land. There is nothing here worth having.'"

Kachi-Hadjo turned and stepped down into the boat. He then reached up and lifted Ki-tee from the pier and into the vessel. He looked east, past the sandbar, toward the waiting transport that would take him and his people to the new land in the west. He put a hand on Gator John's shoulder. "Let us begin the journey, old friend. Our people will need us."

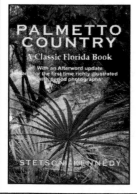